FANTASY ADVENTURE

STARLESS NIGHT

R. A. Salvatore

TSR Inc.

STARLESS NIGHT

Random House and its affiliate companies have worldwide distribution rights in the book trade for English language products of TSR, Inc.

Distributed to the book and hobby trade in the United Kingdom by TSR Ltd.

Distributed to the toy and hobby trade by regional distributors.

Cover art by Robh Ruppel.

First Printing: August 1993
Printed in the United States of America
Library of Congress Number: 92-61100

9 8 7 6 5 4 3 2 1

ISBN: 1-56076-653-0

TSR, Inc.
P.O. Box 756
Lake Geneva, WI 53147
U.S.A.

TSR Ltd.
120 Church End, Cherry Hinton
Cambridge CB1 3LB
United Kingdom

Books by
R. A. Salvatore

The Icewind Dale Trilogy
The Crystal Shard
Streams of Silver
The Halfling's Gem

The Dark Elf Trilogy
Homeland
Exile
Sojourn

The Cleric Quintet
Canticle
In Sylvan Shadows
Night Masks
The Fallen Fortress
The Chaos Curse
(July 1994)

The Legacy
Starless Night

And on the first day, Ed created the
FORGOTTEN REALMS® world and gave my
imagination a place to live.

To Ed Greenwood, with all my thanks and admiration.

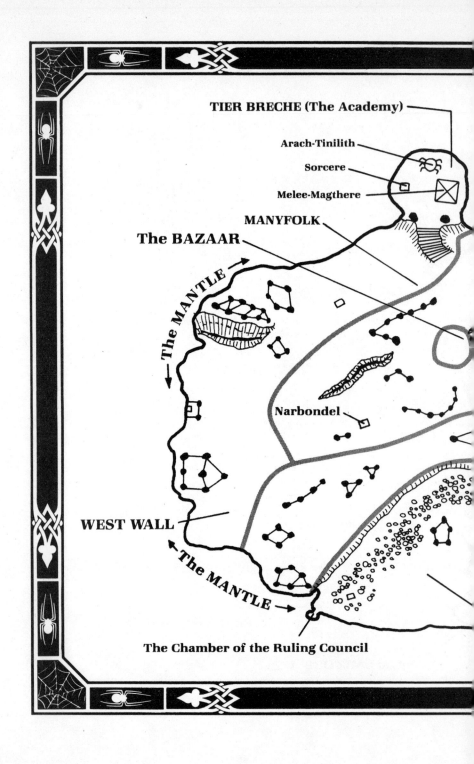

TIER BRECHE (The Academy)

Arach-Tinilith

Sorcere

Melee-Magthere

MANYFOLK

The BAZAAR

The MANTLE

Narbondel

WEST WALL

The MANTLE →

The Chamber of the Ruling Council

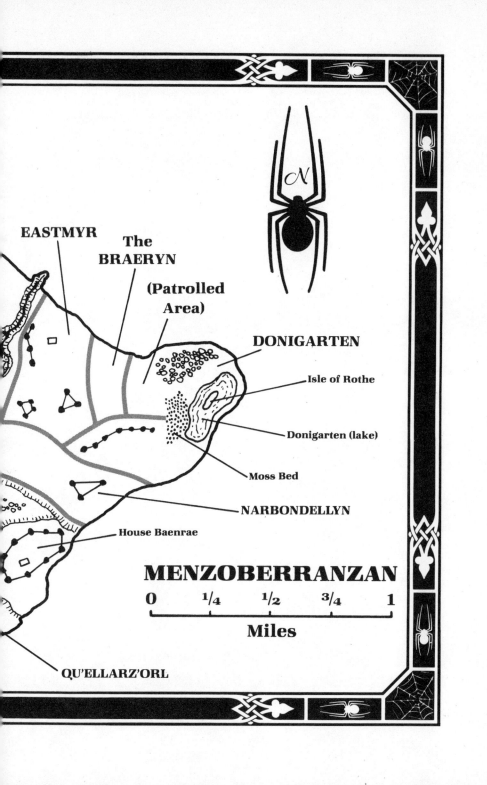

EASTMYR

The
BRAERYN

(Patrolled
Area)

DONIGARTEN

Isle of Rothe

Donigarten (lake)

Moss Bed

NARBONDELLYN

House Baenrae

MENZOBERRANZAN

0   1/4   1/2   3/4   1

Miles

QU'ELLARZ'ORL

PROLOGUE

rizzt ran his fingers over the intricate carvings of the panther statuette, its black onyx perfectly smooth and unmarred even in the ridged areas of the muscled neck. So much like Guenhwyvar, it looked, a perfect representation. How could Drizzt bear to part with it now, fully convinced that he would never see the great panther again?

"Farewell, Guenhwyvar," the drow ranger whispered, his expression sorrowful, almost pitiful, as he stared at the figurine. "I cannot in good conscience take you with me on this journey, for I would fear your fate more than my own." His sigh was one of sincere resignation. He and his friends had fought long and hard, and at great sacrifice, to get to this point of peace, yet Drizzt had come to know that it was a false victory. He wanted to deny it, to put Guenhwyvar back in his pouch and go blindly on, hoping for the best.

Drizzt sighed away the momentary weakness and handed the figurine over to Regis, the halfling.

Regis stared up at Drizzt in disbelief for a long, silent while, shocked by what the drow had told him and had demanded of him.

"Five weeks," Drizzt reminded him.

The halfling's cherubic, boyish features crinkled. If Drizzt did not return in five weeks, Regis was to give Guenhwyvar to Catti-brie and tell both her and King Bruenor the truth of Drizzt's departure. From the drow's dark and somber tones, Regis understood that Drizzt did not expect to return.

On sudden inspiration, the halfling dropped the figurine to his bed and fumbled with a chain about his neck, its clasp caught in the long, curly locks of his brown hair. He finally got the thing undone and produced a pendant, dangling a large and magical ruby.

Now Drizzt was shocked. He knew the value of Regis's gemstone and the halfling's craven love of the thing. To say that Regis was acting out of character would be an incredible understatement.

"I cannot," Drizzt argued, pushing the stone away. "I may not return, and it would be lost. . . ."

"Take it!" Regis demanded sharply. "For all that you have done for me, for all of us, you surely deserve it. It's one thing to leave Guenhwyvar behind—it would be a tragedy indeed if the panther fell into the hands of your evil kin—but this is merely a magical token, no living being, and it may aid you on your journey. Take it as you take your scimitars." The halfling paused, his soft gaze locking with Drizzt's violet orbs. "My friend."

Regis snapped his fingers suddenly, stealing the quiet moment. He rambled across the floor, his bare feet slapping on the cold stone and his nightshirt swishing about him. From a drawer he produced yet another item, a rather unremarkable mask.

"I recovered it," he said, not wanting to reveal the whole story of how he had acquired the familiar item. In truth, Regis had gone from Mithril Hall and found Artemis Entreri hanging helplessly from a jutting stone far up the side of a ravine. Regis promptly had looted the assassin, then cut the seam of Entreri's cloak. The halfling had listened with some measure of satisfaction as the cloak, the only thing holding the battered, barely conscious man aloft, began to rip.

Drizzt eyed the magical mask for a long time. He had taken it from the lair of a banshee more than a year before. With it, its user could change his entire appearance, could hide his identity.

"This should help you get in and out," Regis said hopefully. Still Drizzt made no move.

"I want you to have it," Regis insisted, misunderstanding the drow's hesitation and jerking it out toward Drizzt. Regis did not realize the significance the mask held for Drizzt Do'Urden. Drizzt had once worn it to hide his identity, because a dark elf walking the surface world was at a great disadvantage. Drizzt had come to see the mask as a lie, however useful it might be, and he simply could not bring himself to don it again, whatever the potential gain.

Or could he? Drizzt wondered then if he could refuse the gift. If the mask could aid his cause—a cause that would likely affect those he was leaving behind—then could he in good conscience refuse to wear it?

No, he decided at length, the mask was not that valuable to his cause. Three decades out of the city was a long time, and he was not so remarkable in appearance, not so notorious, certainly, that he would be recognized. He held out his upraised hand, denying the gift, and Regis, after one more unsuccessful try, shrugged his little shoulders, and put the mask away.

Drizzt left without another word. Many hours remained before dawn; torches burned low in the upper levels of Mithril Hall, and few dwarves stirred. It seemed perfectly quiet, perfectly peaceful.

The dark elf's slender fingers, lightly touching, making not a sound, traced the grain of a wooden door. He had no desire to disturb the person within, though he doubted that her sleep was very restful. Every night, Drizzt wanted to go to her and comfort her, and yet he had not, for he knew that his words would do little to soothe Catti-brie's grief. Like so many other nights when he had stood by this door, a watchful, helpless guardian, the ranger ended up padding down the stone corridor, filtering through the shadows of low-dancing torches, his toe-heel step making not a whisper of sound.

With only a short pause at another door, the door of his dearest dwarven friend, Drizzt soon crossed out of the living areas. He came into the formal gathering places, where the king of Mithril Hall entertained visiting emissaries. A couple of dwarves—Dagna's troops probably—were about in here, but they heard and saw nothing of the drow's silent passing.

Drizzt paused again as he came to the entrance of the Hall of Dumathoin, wherein the dwarves of Clan Battlehammer kept their most precious items. He knew that he should continue, get out of the place before the clan began to stir, but he could not ignore the emotions pulling at his heartstrings. He hadn't come to this hallowed hall in the two weeks since his drow kin had been driven away, but he knew that he would never forgive himself if he didn't take at least one look.

The mighty warhammer, Aegis-fang, rested on a pillar at the center of the adorned hall, the place of highest honor. It seemed fitting, for to Drizzt's violet eyes, Aegis-fang far outshone all the other artifacts: the shining suits of mail, the great axes and helms of heroes long dead, the anvil of a legendary smith. Drizzt smiled at the notion that this warhammer hadn't even been wielded by a dwarf. It had been the weapon of Wulfgar, Drizzt's friend, who had willingly given his life so that the others of the tight band might survive.

Drizzt stared long and hard at the mighty weapon, at the gleaming mithril head, unscratched despite the many vicious battles the hammer had seen and showing the perfectly etched sigils of the dwarven god Dumathoin. The drow's gaze drifted down the item, settling on the dried blood on its dark adamantite handle. Bruenor, so stubborn, hadn't allowed that blood to be cleaned away.

Memories of Wulfgar, of fighting beside the tall and strong, golden-haired and golden-skinned man flooded through the drow, weakening his knees and his resolve. In his mind, Drizzt looked again into Wulfgar's clear eyes, the icy blue of the northern sky and always filled with an excited sparkle. Wulfgar had been just a boy, his spirit undaunted by the harsh realities of a brutal world.

Just a boy, but one who had willingly sacrificed everything, a song on his lips, for those he called his friends.

"Farewell," Drizzt whispered, and he was gone, running this time, though no more loudly than he had walked before. In a few seconds, he crossed onto a balcony and down a flight of stairs, into a wide and high chamber. He crossed under the watchful eyes of Mithril Hall's eight kings, their likenesses cut into the stone wall. The last of the busts, that of King Bruenor Battlehammer, was the most striking. Bruenor's visage was stern, a grim look intensified by a deep scar running from his forehead to his jawbone, and with his right eye gone.

More than Bruenor's eye had been wounded, Drizzt knew. More than that dwarvish body, rock tough and resilient, had been scarred. Bruenor's soul was the part most pained, slashed by the loss of a boy he had called his son. Was the dwarf as resilient in spirit as in body? Drizzt knew not the answer. At that moment, staring at Bruenor's scarred face, Drizzt felt that he should stay, should sit beside his friend and help heal the wounds.

It was a passing thought. What wounds might still come to the dwarf? Drizzt reminded himself. To the dwarf and to all his remaining friends?

* * * * *

Catti-brie tossed and squirmed, reliving that fateful moment, as she did every night—at least, every night that exhaustion allowed her to find sleep. She heard Wulfgar's song to Tempus, his god of battle, saw the serene look in the mighty barbarian's eye, the look that denied the obvious agony, the look that allowed him to chop up at the loose stone ceiling, though blocks of heavy granite had begun to tumble all about him.

Catti-brie saw Wulfgar's garish wounds, the white of bone, his skin ripped away from his ribs by the sharklike teeth of the yochlol, an evil, extradimensional beast, an ugly lump of waxy flesh that resembled a half-melted candle.

The roar as the ceiling dropped over her love brought Catti-brie up in her bed, sitting in the darkness, her thick auburn hair matted to her face by cold sweat. She took a long moment to control her breathing, told herself repeatedly that it was a dream, a terrible memory, but ultimately, an event that had passed. The torchlight outlining her door comforted and calmed her.

She wore only a light slip, and her thrashing had knocked her blankets away. Goose bumps rose on her arms, and she shivered, cold and damp and miserable. She roughly retrieved the thickest of her covers and pulled them tightly to her neck, then lay flat on her back, staring up into the darkness.

Something was wrong. She sensed that something was out of place.

Rationally, the young woman told herself that she was imagining things, that her dreams had unnerved her. The world was not right for Catti-brie, far from right, but she told herself forcefully that she was in Mithril Hall, surrounded by an army of friends.

She told herself that she was imagining things.

* * * * *

Drizzt was a long way from Mithril Hall when the sun came up. He didn't sit and enjoy the dawn this day, as was his custom. He hardly looked at the rising sun, for it seemed to him now a false hope of things that could not be. When the initial glare had diminished, the drow looked out to the south and east, far across the mountains, and remembered.

His hand went to his neck, to the hypnotic ruby pendant Regis had given him. He knew how much Regis relied on this gem, loved it, and considered again the halfling's sacrifice, the sacrifice of a true friend. Drizzt had known true friendship; his life had been rich since he had walked into a forlorn land called Icewind Dale and met Bruenor Battlehammer and his adopted daughter, Catti-brie. It pained Drizzt to think that he might never again see any of them.

The drow was glad to have the magical pendant, though, an item that might allow him to get answers and return to his friends, but he held more than a little guilt for his decision to tell Regis of his departure. That choice seemed a weakness to Drizzt, a need to rely on friends who, at this dark time, had little to give. He could rationalize it, though, as a necessary safeguard for the friends he would leave behind. He had instructed Regis to tell Bruenor the truth in five weeks, so that, in case Drizzt's journey proved unsuccessful, Clan Battlehammer would at least have time to prepare for the darkness that might yet come.

It was a logical act, but Drizzt had to admit that he had told

Regis because of his own need, because he had to tell someone.

And what of the magical mask? he wondered. Had he been weak in refusing that, too? The powerful item might have aided Drizzt and, thus, aided his friends, but he had not the strength to wear it, to even touch it.

Doubts floated all about the drow, hovered in the air before his eyes, mocking him. Drizzt sighed and rubbed the ruby between his slender black hands. For all his prowess with the blade, for all his dedication to principles, for all his ranger stoicism, Drizzt Do'Urden needed his friends. He glanced back toward Mithril Hall and wondered, for his own sake, if he had chosen rightly in undertaking this quest privately and secretly.

More weakness, stubborn Drizzt decided. He let go of the ruby, mentally slapped away the lingering doubts, and slid his hand inside his forest-green traveling cloak. From one of its pockets he produced a parchment, a map of the lands between the Spine of the World Mountains and the Great Desert of Anauroch. In the lower right-hand corner Drizzt had marked a spot, the location of a cave from which he had once emerged, a cave that would take him home.

Part 1

DUTY BOUND

o race in all the Realms better understands the word vengeance than the drow. Vengeance is their dessert at their daily table, the sweetness they taste upon their smirking lips as though it was the ultimate delicious pleasure. And so hungering did the drow come for me.

I cannot escape the anger and the guilt I feel for the loss of Wulfgar, for the pains the enemies of my dark past have brought to the friends I hold so dear. Whenever I look into Catti-brie's fair face, I see a profound and everlasting sadness that should not be there, a burden that has no place in the sparkling eyes of a child.

Similarly wounded, I have no words to comfort her and doubt that there are any words that might bring solace. It is my course, then, that I must continue to protect my friends. I have come to realize that I must look beyond my own sense of loss for Wulfgar, beyond the immediate sadness that has taken hold of the dwarves of Mithril Hall and the hardy men of Settlestone.

By Catti-brie's account of that fateful fight, the creature Wulfgar battled was a yochlol, a handmaiden of Lloth. With that grim information, I must look beyond the immediate sorrow and consider that the sadness I fear is still to come.

I do not understand all the chaotic games of the Spider Queen—I doubt that even the evil high priestesses know the foul creature's true designs—but there lies in a yochlol's presence a significance that even I, the worst of the drow religious students, cannot miss. The handmaiden's appearance revealed that the hunt was sanctified by the Spider Queen. And the fact that the yochlol intervened in the fighting does not bode well for the future of Mithril Hall.

It is all supposition, of course. I know not that my sister Vierna acted in concert with any of Menzoberranzan's other dark powers, or that, with Vierna's death, the death of my last relative, my link to the city of drow would ever again be explored.

When I look into Catti-brie's eyes, when I look upon Bruenor's horrid scars, I am reminded that hopeful supposition is a feeble and dangerous thing. My evil kin have taken one friend from me.

They will take no more.

I can find no answers in Mithril Hall, will never know for certain if the dark elves hunger still for vengeance, unless another force from Menzoberranzan comes to the surface to claim the bounty on my head. With this truth bending low my shoulders, how could I ever travel to Silverymoon, or to any other nearby town, resuming my normal lifestyle? How could I sleep in peace while holding within my heart the very real fear that the dark elves might soon return and once more imperil my friends?

The apparent serenity of Mithril Hall, the brooding quiet, will show me nothing of the future designs of the drow. Yet, for the sake of my friends, I must know those dark intentions. I fear that there remains only one place for me to look.

Wulfgar gave his life so that his friends might live. In good conscience, could my own sacrifice be any less?

—Drizzt Do'Urden

Chapter 1

THE AMBITIOUS ONE

he mercenary leaned against the pillar anchoring the wide stairway of Tier Breche, on the northern side of the great cavern that housed Menzoberranzan, the city of drow. Jarlaxle removed his wide-brimmed hat and ran a hand over the smooth skin of his bald head as he muttered a few curses under his breath.

Many lights were on in the city. Torches flickered in the high windows of houses carved from natural stalagmite formations. Lights in the drow city! Many of the elaborate structures had long been decorated by the soft glow of faerie fire, mostly purple and blue hues, but this was different.

Jarlaxle shifted to the side and winced as his weight came upon his recently wounded leg. Triel Baenre herself, the matron mistress of Arach-Tinilith, among the highest-ranking priestesses in the city, had tended the wound, but Jarlaxle suspected that the wicked priestess had purposely left the job unfinished, had left a bit of the pain to remind the mercenary of his failure in recapturing the renegade Drizzt Do'Urden.

"The glow wounds my eyes," came a sarcastic remark from behind. Jarlaxle turned to see Matron Baenre's oldest daughter, that same Triel. She was shorter than most drow, nearly a foot shorter than Jarlaxle, but she carried herself with undeniable dignity and poise. Jarlaxle understood her powers (and her volatile temperament) better than most, and he certainly treated the diminutive female with the greatest caution.

Staring, glaring, out over the city with squinting eyes, she moved beside him. "Curse the glow," she muttered.

"It is by your matron's command," Jarlaxle reminded her. His one good eye avoided her gaze; the other lay beneath a patch of shadow, which was tied behind his head. He replaced his great hat, pulling it low in front as he tried to hide his smirk at her resulting grimace.

Triel was not happy with her mother. Jarlaxle had known that since the moment Matron Baenre had begun to hint at her plans. Triel was possibly the most fanatic of the Spider Queen's priestesses and would not go against Matron Baenre, the first matron mother of the city—not unless Lloth instructed her to.

"Come along," the priestess growled. She turned and made her way across Tier Breche to the largest and most ornate of the drow Academy's three buildings, a huge structure shaped to resemble a gigantic spider.

Jarlaxle pointedly groaned as he moved, and lost ground with every limping step. His attempt to solicit a bit more healing magic was not successful, though, for Triel merely paused at the doorway to the great structure and waited for him with a patience that was more than a bit out of character, Jarlaxle knew, for Triel never waited for anything.

As soon as he entered the temple, the mercenary was assaulted by myriad aromas, everything from incense to the drying blood of the latest sacrifices, and chants rolled out of every side portal. Triel took note of none of it; she shrugged past the few disciples who bowed to her as they saw her walking the corridors.

The single-minded Baenre daughter moved into the higher levels, to the private quarters of the school's mistresses, and walked down one small hallway, its floor alive with crawling spiders (including a few that stood as tall as Jarlaxle's knee).

Triel stopped between two equally decorated doors and motioned for Jarlaxle to enter the one on the right. The mercenary paused, did well to hide his confusion, but Triel was expecting it.

She grabbed Jarlaxle by the shoulder and roughly spun him about. "You have been here before!" she accused.

"Only upon my graduation from the school of fighters," Jarlaxle said, shrugging away from the female, "as are all of Melee-Magthere's graduates."

"You have been in the upper levels," Triel snarled, eyeing Jarlaxle squarely. The mercenary chuckled.

"You hesitated when I motioned for you to enter the chamber," Triel went on, "because you know that the one to the left is my private room. That is where you expected to go."

"I did not expect to be summoned here at all," Jarlaxle retorted, trying to shift the subject. He was indeed a bit off guard that Triel had watched him so closely. Had he underestimated her trepidation at her mother's latest plans?

Triel stared at him long and hard, her eyes unblinking and jaw firm.

"I have my sources," Jarlaxle admitted at length.

Another long moment passed, and still Triel did not blink.

"You asked that I come," Jarlaxle reminded her.

"I demanded," Triel corrected.

Jarlaxle swept into a low, exaggerated bow, snatching off his hat and brushing it out at arm's length. The Baenre daughter's eyes flashed with anger.

"Enough!" she shouted.

"And enough of your games!" Jarlaxle spat back. "You asked that I come to the Academy, a place where I am not comfortable, and so I have come. You have questions, and I, perhaps, have answers."

His qualification of that last sentence made Triel narrow her eyes. Jarlaxle was ever a cagey opponent, she knew as well as anyone in the drow city. She had dealt with the cunning mercenary many times and still wasn't quite sure if she had broken even against him or not. She turned and motioned for him to enter the left-hand door instead, and, with another graceful bow, he did so, stepping into a thickly carpeted and decorated room lit in a soft magical glow.

"Remove your boots," Triel instructed, and she slipped out of her own shoes before she stepped onto the plush rug.

Jarlaxle stood against the tapestry-adorned wall just inside the door, looking doubtfully at his boots. Everyone who knew the mercenary knew that these were magical.

"Very well," Triel conceded, closing the door and sweeping past him to take a seat on a huge, overstuffed chair. A rolltop desk stood behind her, in front of one of many tapestries, this one depicting the sacrifice of a gigantic surface elf by a horde of dancing drow. Above the surface elf loomed the nearly translucent specter of a half-drow, half-spider creature, its face beautiful and serene.

"You do not like your mother's lights?" Jarlaxle asked. "You keep your own room aglow."

Triel bit her lower lip and narrowed her eyes once more. Most priestesses kept their private chambers dimly lit, that they might read their tomes. Heat-sensing infravision was of little use in seeing the runes on a page. There were some inks that would hold distinctive heat for many years, but these were expensive and hard to come by, even for one as powerful as Triel.

Jarlaxle stared back at the Baenre daughter's grim expression. Triel was always mad about something, the mercenary mused. "The lights seem appropriate for what your mother has planned," he went on.

"Indeed," Triel remarked, her tone biting. "And are you so arrogant as to believe that you understand my mother's motives?"

"She will go back to Mithril Hall," Jarlaxle said openly, knowing that Triel had long ago drawn the same conclusion.

"Will she?" Triel asked coyly.

The cryptic response set the mercenary back on his heels. He took a step toward a second, less-cushiony chair in the room, and his heel clicked hard, even though he was walking across the incredibly thick and soft carpet.

Triel smirked, not impressed by the magical boots. It was common knowledge that Jarlaxle could walk as quietly or as loudly as he desired on any type of surface. His abundant jewelry, bracelets and trinkets seemed equally enchanted, for they would ring and tinkle or remain perfectly silent, as the mercenary desired.

"If you have left a hole in my carpet, I will fill it with your heart," Triel promised as Jarlaxle slumped back comfortably in the covered stone chair, smoothing a fold in the armrest so that the fabric showed a clear image of a black and yellow *gee'antu* spider, the Underdark's version of the surface tarantula.

"Why do you suspect that your mother will not go?" Jarlaxle asked, pointedly ignoring the threat, though in knowing Triel Baenre, he honestly wondered how many other hearts were now entwined in the carpet's fibers.

"Do I?" Triel asked.

Jarlaxle let out a long sigh. He had suspected that this would be a moot meeting, a discussion where Triel tried to pry out what bits of information the mercenary already had attained, while offering little of her own. Still, when Triel had insisted that Jarlaxle come to her, instead of their usual arrangement, in which she went out from Tier Breche to meet the mercenary, Jarlaxle had hoped for something substantive. It was quickly becoming obvious to Jarlaxle that the only reason Triel wanted to meet in Arach-Tinilith was that, in this secure place, even her mother's prying ears would not hear.

And now, for all those painstaking arrangements, this all-important meeting had become a useless bantering session.

Triel seemed equally perturbed. She came forward in her chair suddenly, her expression fierce. "She desires a legacy!" the female declared.

Jarlaxle's bracelets tinkled as he tapped his fingers together, thinking that now they were finally getting somewhere.

"The rulership of Menzoberranzan is no longer sufficient for the likes of Matron Baenre," Triel continued, more calmly, and she moved back in her seat. "She must expand her sphere."

"I had thought your mother's visions Lloth-given," Jarlaxle remarked, and he was sincerely confused by Triel's obvious disdain.

"Perhaps," Triel admitted. "The Spider Queen will welcome the conquest of Mithril Hall, particularly if it, in turn, leads to the capture of that renegade Do'Urden. But there are other considerations."

"Blingdenstone?" Jarlaxle asked, referring to the city of the svirfnebli, the deep gnomes, traditional enemies of the drow.

"That is one," Triel replied. "Blingdenstone is not far off the path to the tunnels connecting Mithril Hall."

"Your mother has mentioned that the svirfnebli might be dealt with properly on the return trip," Jarlaxle offered, figuring that he had to throw some tidbit out if he wanted Triel to continue so openly with him. It seemed to the mercenary that Triel must be deeply upset to be permitting him such an honest view of her most private emotions and fears.

Triel nodded, accepting the news stoically and without surprise. "There are other considerations," she repeated. "The task Matron Baenre is undertaking is enormous and will require allies along the way, perhaps even illithid allies."

The Baenre daughter's reasoning struck Jarlaxle as sound. Matron Baenre had long kept an illithid consort, an ugly and dangerous beast if Jarlaxle had ever seen one. He was never comfortable around the octopus-headed humanoids. Jarlaxle survived by understanding and outguessing his enemies, but his skills were sorely lacking where illithids were concerned. The mind flayers, as members of the evil race were called, simply didn't think the same way as other races and acted in accord with principles and rules that no one other than an illithid seemed to know.

Still, the dark elves had often dealt successfully with the illithid community. Menzoberranzan housed twenty thousand skilled warriors, while the illithids in the region numbered barely a hundred. Triel's fears seemed a bit overblown.

Jarlaxle didn't tell her that, though. Given her dark and volatile mood, the mercenary preferred to do more listening than speaking.

Triel continued to shake her head, her expression typically sour. She leaped up from the chair, her black-and-purple, spider-adorned robes swishing as she paced a tight circle.

"It will not be House Baenre alone," Jarlaxle reminded her, hoping to comfort Triel. "Many houses show lights in their windows."

"Mother has done well in bringing the city together," Triel

admitted, and the pace of her nervous stroll slowed.

"But still you fear," the mercenary reasoned. "And you need information so that you might be ready for any consequence." Jarlaxle couldn't help a small, ironic chuckle. He and Triel had been enemies for a long time, neither trusting the other—and with good reason! Now she needed him. She was a priestess in a secluded school, away from much of the city's whispered rumors. Normally her prayers to the Spider Queen would have provided her all the information she needed, but now, if Lloth sanctioned Matron Baenre's actions (and that fact seemed obvious), Triel would be left, literally, in the dark. She needed a spy, and in Menzoberranzan, Jarlaxle and his spying network, Bregan D'aerthe, had no equal.

"We need each other," Triel pointedly replied, turning to eye the mercenary squarely. "Mother treads on dangerous ground, that much is obvious. If she falters, consider who will assume the seat of the ruling house."

True enough, Jarlaxle silently conceded. Triel, as the eldest daughter of the house, was indisputably next in line behind Matron Baenre and, as the matron mistress of Arach-Tinilith, held the most powerful position in the city behind the matron mothers of the eight ruling houses. Triel already had established an impressive base of power. But in Menzoberranzan, where pretense of law was no more than a facade against an underlying chaos, power bases tended to shift as readily as lava pools.

"I will learn what I may," Jarlaxle answered, and he rose to leave. "And will tell you what I learn."

Triel understood the half-truth in the sly mercenary's words, but she had to accept his offer.

Jarlaxle was walking freely down the wide, curving avenues of Menzoberranzan a short while later, passing by the watchful eyes and readied weapons of house guards posted on nearly every stalagmite mound—and on the ringed balconies of many low-hanging stalactites as well. The mercenary was not afraid, for his wide-brimmed hat identified him clearly to all in the city, and no house desired conflict with Bregan D'aerthe. It was the most secretive of bands—few in the city could even guess at the numbers in the group—and its bases were tucked away in the many nooks and crannies of the wide cavern. The company's reputation was widespread, though, tolerated by the ruling houses, and most in the city would name Jarlaxle among the most powerful of Menzoberranzan's males.

So comfortable was he that Jarlaxle hardly noticed the lingering stares of the dangerous guards. His thoughts were inward, trying to decipher the subtle messages of his meeting with Triel. The assumed plan to conquer Mithril Hall seemed very promising. Jarlaxle had been to the dwarven stronghold, had witnessed its defenses. Although formidable, they seemed meager against the strength of a drow army. When Menzoberranzan conquered Mithril Hall, with Matron Baenre at the head of the force, Lloth would be supremely pleased, and House Baenre would know its pinnacle of glory.

As Triel had put it, Matron Baenre would have her legacy.

The pinnacle of power? The thought hung in Jarlaxle's mind. He paused beside Narbondel, the great pillar time clock of Menzoberranzan, a smile widening across his ebon-skinned face.

"Pinnacle of power?" he whispered aloud.

Suddenly Jarlaxle understood Triel's trepidations. She feared that her mother might overstep her bounds, might be gambling an already impressive empire for the sake of yet another acquisition. Even as he considered the notion, Jarlaxle understood a deeper significance to it all. Suppose that Matron Baenre was successful, that Mithril Hall was conquered and Blingdenstone after that? he mused. What enemies would then be left to threaten the drow city, to hold together the tentative hierarchy in Menzoberranzan?

For that matter, why had Blingdenstone, a place of enemies so near Menzoberranzan, been allowed to survive for all these centuries? Jarlaxle knew the answer. He knew that the gnomes unintentionally served as the glue that kept Menzoberranzan's houses in line. With a common enemy so near, the drow's constant infighting had to be kept under control.

But now Matron Baenre hinted at ungluing, expanding her empire to include not only Mithril Hall, but the troublesome gnomes as well. Triel did not fear that the drow would be beaten; neither did she fear any alliance with the small colony of illithids. She was afraid that her mother would succeed, would gain her legacy. Matron Baenre was old, ancient even by drow standards, and Triel was next in line for the house seat. At present, that would

21

be a comfortable place indeed, but it would become far more tentative and dangerous if Mithril Hall and Blingdenstone were taken. The binding common enemy that kept the houses in line would be no more, and Triel would have to worry about a tie to the surface world a long way from Menzoberranzan, where reprisals by the allies of Mithril Hall would be inevitable.

Jarlaxle understood what Matron Baenre wanted, but now he wondered what Lloth, backing the withered female's plans, had in mind.

"Chaos," he decided. Menzoberranzan had been quiet for a long, long time. Some houses fought—that was inevitable. House Do'Urden and House DeVir, both ruling houses, had been obliterated, but the general structure of the city had remained solid and unthreatened.

"Ah, but you are delightful," Jarlaxle said, speaking his thoughts of Lloth aloud. He suddenly suspected that Lloth desired a new order, a refreshing housecleaning of a city grown boring. No wonder that Triel, in line to inherit her mother's legacy, was not amused.

The bald mercenary, himself a lover of intrigue and chaos, laughed heartily and looked to Narbondel. The clock's heat was greatly diminished, showing it to be late in the Underdark night. Jarlaxle clicked his heels against the stone and set out for the Qu'ellarz'orl, the high plateau on Menzoberranzan's eastern wall, the region housing the city's most powerful house. He didn't want to be late for his meeting with Matron Baenre, to whom he would report on in his "secret" meeting with her eldest daughter.

Jarlaxle pondered how much he would tell the withered matron mother, and how he might twist his words to his best advantage.

How he loved the intrigue.

Chapter 2

FAREWELL RIDDLES

leary-eyed after yet another long, restless night, Cattibrie pulled on a robe and crossed her small room, hoping to find comfort in the daylight. Her thick auburn hair had been flattened on one side of her head, forcing an angled cowlick on the other side, but she didn't care. Busy rubbing the sleep from her eyes, she nearly stumbled over the threshold and paused there, struck suddenly by something she did not understand.

She ran her fingers over the wood of the door and stood confused, nearly overwhelmed by the same feeling she had felt the night before, that something was out of place, that something was wrong. She had intended to go straight to breakfast, but felt compelled to get Drizzt instead.

The young woman shuffled swiftly down the corridor to Drizzt's room and knocked on the door. After a few moments, she called, "Drizzt?" When the drow didn't answer, she gingerly turned the handle and pushed the door open. Catti-brie noticed immediately that Drizzt's scimitars and traveling cloak were gone, but before she could begin to think about that, her eyes focused on the bed. It was made, covers tucked neatly, though that was not unusual for the dark elf.

Catti-brie slipped over to the bed and inspected the folds. They were neat, but not tight, and she understood that this bed had been made a long while ago, that this bed had not been slept in the previous night.

"What's all this?" the young woman asked. She took a quick look around the small room, then made her way back out into the hall. Drizzt had gone out from Mithril Hall without warning before, and often he left at night. He usually journeyed to Silverymoon, the fabulous city a week's march to the east.

Why, this time, did Catti-brie feel that something was amiss? Why did this not-so-unusual scene strike Catti-brie as very out of place? The young woman tried to shrug it away, to overrule her heartfelt fears. She was just worried, she told herself. She had lost Wulfgar and now felt overprotective of her other friends.

Catti-brie walked as she thought it over, and soon paused at another door. She tapped lightly, then, with no response forthcoming (though she was certain that this one was not yet up and about), she banged harder. A groan came from within the room.

Catti-brie pushed the door open and crossed the room, sliding to kneel beside the tiny bed and roughly pulling the bedcovers down from sleeping Regis, tickling his armpits as he began to squirm.

"Hey!" the plump halfling, recovered from his trials at the hands of the assassin Artemis Entreri, cried out. He came awake immediately and grabbed at the covers desperately.

"Where's Drizzt?" Catti-brie asked, tugging the covers away more forcefully.

"How would I know?" Regis protested. "I have not been out of my room yet this morning!"

"Get up." Catti-brie was surprised by the sharpness of her own voice, by the intensity of her command. The uncomfortable feelings tugged at her again, more forcefully. She looked around the room, trying to discern what had triggered her sudden anxiety.

She saw the panther figurine.

Catti-brie's unblinking stare locked on the object, Drizzt's dearest possession. What was it doing in Regis's room? she wondered. Why had Drizzt left without it? Now the young woman's logic began to fall into agreement with her emotions. She skipped across the bed, buried Regis in a jumble of covers (which he promptly pulled tight around his shoulders), and retrieved the panther. She then hopped back and tugged again at the stubborn halfling's blanket shell.

"No!" Regis argued, yanking back. He dove facedown to his mattress, pulling the ends of the pillow up around his dimpled face.

Catti-brie grabbed him by the scruff of the neck, yanked him from the bed, and dragged him across the room to seat him in one of the two wooden chairs resting at opposite sides of a small table. Pillow still in hand, still tight against his face, Regis plopped his head straight down on the table.

Catti-brie took a firm and silent hold on the end of the pillow, quietly stood, then yanked it suddenly, tearing it from the surprised halfling's grasp so that his head knocked hard against the bare wood.

Groaning and grumbling, Regis sat straight in the chair and ran stubby fingers through his fluffy and curly brown locks, their bounce undiminished by a long night's sleep.

"What?" he demanded.

Catti-brie slammed the panther figurine atop the table, leaving it before the seated halfling. "Where is Drizzt?" she asked again, evenly.

"Probably in the Undercity," Regis grumbled, running his tongue all about his cottony-feeling teeth. "Why don't you go ask Bruenor?"

The mention of the dwarvish king set Catti-brie back on her heels. Go ask Bruenor? she silently scoffed. Bruenor would hardly speak to anyone, and was so immersed in despair that he probably wouldn't know it if his entire clan up and left in the middle of the night!

"So Drizzt left Guenhwyvar," Regis remarked, thinking to downplay the whole thing. His words fell awkwardly on the perceptive woman's ears, though, and Catti-brie's deep blue eyes narrowed as she studied the halfling more closely.

"What?" Regis asked innocently again, feeling the heat of that unrelenting scrutiny.

"Where is Drizzt?" Catti-brie asked, her tone dangerously calm. "And why do ye have the cat?"

Regis shook his head and wailed helplessly, dramatically dropping his forehead again against the table.

Catti-brie saw the act for what it was. She knew Regis too well to be taken in by his wily charms. She grabbed a handful of curly brown hair and tugged his head upright, then grabbed the front of his nightshirt with her other hand. Her roughness startled the halfling; she could see that clearly by his expression, but she did not relent. Regis flew from his seat. Catti-brie carried him three quick steps, then slammed his back against the wall.

Catti-brie's scowling visage softened for just a moment, and her free hand fumbled with the halfling's nightshirt long enough that she could determine that Regis was not wearing his magical ruby pendant, an item she knew he never removed. Another curious, and certainly out-of-place, fact that assailed her sensibilities, fed her growing belief that something indeed was terribly wrong.

"Suren there's something going on here that's not what it's supposed to be," Catti-brie said, her scowl returning tenfold.

"Catti-brie!" Regis replied, looking down to his furry-topped feet, dangling twenty inches from the floor.

"And ye know something about it," Catti-brie went on.

"Catti-brie!" Regis wailed again, trying to bring the fiery young woman to her senses.

Catti-brie took up the halfling's nightshirt in both her hands, pulled him away from the wall, and slammed him back again, hard. "I've lost Wulfgar," she said grimly, pointedly reminding Regis that he might not be dealing with someone rational.

Regis didn't know what to think. Bruenor Battlehammer's

daughter had always been the levelheaded one of the troupe, the calm influence that kept the others in line. Even cool Drizzt had often used Catti-brie as a guidepost to his conscience. But now . . .

Regis saw the promise of pain set within the depths of Catti-brie's deep blue, angry eyes.

She pulled him from the wall once more and slammed him back. "Ye're going to tell me what ye know," she said evenly.

The back of Regis's head throbbed from the banging. He was scared, very scared, as much for Catti-brie as for himself. Had her grief brought her to this point of desperation? And why was he suddenly caught in the middle of all this? All that Regis wanted out of life was a warm bed and a warmer meal.

"We should go and sit down with Brue—" he began, but he was summarily interrupted as Catti-brie slapped him across the face.

He brought his hand up to the stinging cheek, felt the angry welt rising there. He never blinked, eyeing the young woman with disbelief.

Catti-brie's violent reaction had apparently surprised her as much as Regis. The halfling saw tears welling in her gentle eyes. She trembled, and Regis honestly didn't know what she might do.

The halfling considered his situation for a long moment, coming to wonder what difference a few days or weeks could make. "Drizzt went home," the halfling said softly, always willing to do as the situation demanded. Worrying about consequences could come later.

Catti-brie relaxed somewhat. "This is his home," she reasoned. "Suren ye don't mean Icewind Dale."

"Menzoberranzan," Regis corrected.

If Catti-brie had taken a crossbow quarrel in her back, it would not have hit her harder than that single word. She let Regis down to the floor and tumbled backward, falling into a sitting position on the edge of the halfling's bed.

"He really left Guenhwyvar for you," Regis explained. "He cares for both you and the cat so very much."

His soothing words did not shake the horrified expression from Catti-brie's face. Regis wished he had his ruby pendant, so that he might use its undeniable charms to calm the young woman.

"You can't tell Bruenor," Regis added. "Besides, Drizzt might not even go that far." The halfling thought an embellishment of the truth might go a long way. "He said he was off to see Alustriel, to try to decide where his course should lead." It wasn't exactly true—Drizzt had only mentioned that he might stop by Silverymoon to see if he might confirm his fears—but Regis decided that Catti-brie needed to be given some hope.

"You can't tell Bruenor," the halfling said again, more forcefully. Catti-brie looked up at him; her expression was truly one of the most pitiful sights Regis had ever seen.

"He'll be back," Regis said to her, rushing over to sit beside her. "You know Drizzt. He'll be back."

It was too much for Catti-brie to digest. She gently pulled Regis's hand off her arm and rose. She looked to the panther figurine once more, sitting upon the small table, but she had not the strength to retrieve it.

Catti-brie padded silently out of the room, back to her own chambers, where she fell listlessly upon her bed.

* * * * *

Drizzt spent midday sleeping in the cool shadows of a cave, many miles from Mithril Hall's eastern door. The early summer air was warm, the breeze off the cold glaciers of the mountains carrying little weight against the powerful rays of the sun in a cloudless summer sky.

The drow did not sleep long or well. His rest was filled with thoughts of Wulfgar, of all his friends, and of distant images, memories of that awful place, Menzoberranzan.

Awful and beautiful, like the dark elves who had sculpted it.

Drizzt moved to his shallow cave's entrance to take his meal. He basked in the warmth of the bright afternoon, in the sounds of the many animals. How different was this from his Underdark home! How wonderful!

Drizzt threw his dried biscuit into the dirt and punched the floor beside him.

How wonderful indeed was this false hope that had been dangled before his desperate eyes. All that he had wanted in life was to escape the ways of his kin, to live in peace. Then he had come to the surface, and soon after, had decided that this place—this place of buzzing bees and chirping birds, of warm sunlight and alluring moonlight—should be his home, not the eternal darkness of those tunnels far below.

Drizzt Do'Urden had chosen the surface, but what did that choice mean? It meant that he would come to know new, dear friends, and by his mere presence, trap them into his dark legacy. It meant that Wulfgar would die by the summons of Drizzt's own sister, and that all of Mithril Hall might soon be in peril.

It meant that his choice was a false one, that he could not stay.

The disciplined drow calmed quickly and took out some more food, forcing it past the angry lump in his throat. He considered his course as he ate. The road before him would lead out of the mountains and past a village called Pengallen. Drizzt had been there recently, and he did not wish to return.

He would not follow the road at all, he decided at length. What purpose would going to Silverymoon serve? Drizzt doubted that Lady Alustriel would be there, with the trading season open in full. Even if she was, what could she tell him that he did not already know?

No, Drizzt had already determined his ultimate course and he did not need Alustriel to confirm it. He gathered his belongings and sighed as he considered again how empty the road seemed without his dear panther companion. He walked out into the bright day, straight toward the east, off the southeastern road.

* * * * *

Her stomach did not complain that breakfast—and lunch—had passed and still she lay motionless on her bed, caught in a web of despair. She had lost Wulfgar, barely days before their planned wedding, and now Drizzt, whom she loved as much as she had the barbarian, was gone as well. It seemed as though her entire world had crumbled around her. A foundation that had been built of stone shifted like sand on the blowing wind.

Catti-brie had been a fighter all of her young life. She didn't remember her mother, and barely recalled her father, who had been killed in a goblin raid in Ten-Towns when she was very young. Bruenor Battlehammer had taken her in and raised her as his own daughter, and Catti-brie had found a fine life among the dwarves of Bruenor's clan. Except for Bruenor, though, the dwarves had been friends, not family. Catti-brie had forged a new family one at a time—first Bruenor, then Drizzt, then Regis, and, finally, Wulfgar.

Now Wulfgar was dead and Drizzt gone, back to his wicked homeland with, by Catti-brie's estimation, little chance of returning.

Catti-brie felt so very helpless about it all! She had watched Wulfgar die, watched him chop a ceiling down onto his own head so that she might escape the clutches of the monstrous yochlol. She had tried to help, but had failed and, in the end, all that remained was a pile of rubble and Aegis-fang.

In the weeks since, Catti-brie had teetered on the edge of control, trying futilely to deny the paralyzing grief. She had cried often, but always had managed to check it after the first few sobs with a deep breath and sheer willpower. The only one she could talk to had been Drizzt.

Now Drizzt was gone, and now, too, Catti-brie did cry, a flood of tears, sobs wracking her deceptively delicate frame. She wanted Wulfgar back! She protested to whatever gods might be listening that he was too young to be taken from her, with too many great deeds ahead of him.

Her sobs became intense growls, fierce denial. Pillows flew across the room, and Catti-brie grabbed the blankets into a pile and heaved them as well. Then she overturned her bed just for the pleasure of hearing its wooden frame crack against the hard floor.

"No!" The word came from deep inside, from the young fighter's belly. The loss of Wulfgar wasn't fair, but there was nothing Catti-brie could do about that.

Drizzt's leaving wasn't fair, not in Catti-brie's wounded mind, but there was nothing . . .

The thought hung in Catti-brie's mind. Still trembling, but now under control, she stood beside the overturned bed. She understood why the drow had left secretly, why Drizzt had, as was typical, taken the whole burden on himself.

"No," the young woman said again. She stripped off her night-clothes, grabbed a blanket to towel the sweat from her, then donned breeches and chemise. Catti-brie did not hesitate to consider her actions, fearful that if she thought about things rationally, she might change her mind. She quickly slipped on a chain-link coat of supple and thin mithril armor, so finely crafted by the dwarves that it was barely detectable after she had donned her sleeveless tunic.

Still moving frantically, Catti-brie pulled on her boots, grabbed her cloak and leather gloves, and rushed across the room to her closet. There she found her sword belt, quiver, and Taulmaril the Heartseeker, her enchanted bow. She ran, didn't walk, from her room to the halfling's and banged on the door only once before bursting in.

Regis was in bed again—big surprise—his belly full from a breakfast that had continued uninterrupted right into lunch. He was awake, though, and none too happy to see Catti-brie charging at him once more.

She pulled him up to a sitting position, and he regarded her curiously. Lines from tears streaked her cheeks, and her splendid blue eyes were edged by angry red veins. Regis had lived most of his life as a thief, had survived by understanding people, and it wasn't hard for him to figure out the reasons behind the young woman's sudden fire.

"Where did ye put the panther?" Catti-brie demanded.

Regis stared at her for a long moment. Catti-brie gave him a rough shake.

"Tell me quick," she demanded. "I've lost too much time already."

"For what?" Regis asked, though he knew the answer.

"Just give me the cat," Catti-brie said. Regis unconsciously glanced toward his bureau, and Catti-brie rushed to it, then tore it open and laid waste to the drawers, one by one.

"Drizzt won't like this," Regis said calmly.

"To the Nine Hells with him, then!" Catti-brie shot back. She found the figurine and held it before her eyes, marveling at its beautiful form.

"You think Guenhwyvar will lead you to him," Regis stated more than asked.

Catti-brie dropped the figurine into a belt pouch and did not bother to reply.

"Suppose you do catch up with him," Regis went on as the young woman headed for the door. "How much will you aid Drizzt in a city of drow? A human woman might stand out a bit down there, don't you think?"

The halfling's sarcasm stopped Catti-brie, made her consider for the first time what she meant to do. How true was Regis's reasoning! How could she get into Menzoberranzan? And even if she did, how could she even see the floor ahead of her?

"No!" Catti-brie shouted at length, her logic blown away by that welling, helpless feeling. "I'm going to him anyway. I'll not stand by and wait to learn that another of me friends has been killed!"

"Trust him," Regis pleaded, and, for the first time, the halfling began to think that maybe he would not be able to stop the impetuous Catti-brie.

Catti-brie shook her head and started for the door again.

"Wait!" Regis called, begged, and the young woman pivoted about to regard him. Regis hung in a precarious position. It seemed to him that he should run out shouting for Bruenor, or for General Dagna, or for any of the dwarves, enlisting allies to hold back Catti-brie, physically if need be. She was crazy; her decision to run off after Drizzt made no sense at all.

But Regis understood her desire, and he sympathized with her with all his heart.

"If it was meself who left," Catti-brie began, "and Drizzt who wanted to follow . . ."

Regis nodded in agreement. If Catti-brie, or any of them, had gone into apparent peril, Drizzt Do'Urden would have taken up the chase, and taken up the fight, no matter the odds. Drizzt, Wulfgar, Catti-brie, and Bruenor had gone more than halfway across the continent in search of Regis when Entreri had abducted him. Regis had known Catti-brie since she was just a child, and had always held her in the highest regard, but never had he been more proud of her than at this very moment.

"A human will be a detriment to Drizzt in Menzoberranzan," he said again.

"I care not," Catti-brie said under her breath. She did not understand where Regis's words were leading.

Regis hopped off his bed and rushed across the room. Catti-brie braced, thinking he meant to tackle her, but he ran past, to his desk, and pulled open one of its lower drawers. "So don't be a human," the halfling proclaimed, and he tossed the magical mask to Catti-brie.

Catti-brie caught it and stood staring at it in surprise as Regis ran back past her, to his bed.

Entreri had used the mask to get into Mithril Hall, had, through its magic, so perfectly disguised himself as Regis that the halfling's friends, even Drizzt, had been taken in.

"Drizzt really is making for Silverymoon," Regis told her.

Catti-brie was surprised, thinking that the drow would have simply gone into the Underdark through the lower chambers of Mithril Hall. When she thought about it, though, she realized that Bruenor had placed many guards at those chambers, with orders to keep the doors closed and locked.

"One more thing," Regis said. Catti-brie looped the mask on her belt and turned to the bed, to see Regis standing on the shifted mattress, holding a brilliantly jeweled dagger in his hands.

"I won't need this," Regis explained, "not here, with Bruenor and his thousands beside me." He held the weapon out, but Catti-brie did not immediately take it.

She had seen that dagger, Artemis Entreri's dagger, before. The assassin had once pressed it against her neck, stealing her courage, making her feel more helpless, more a little girl, than at any other time in her life. Catti-brie wasn't sure that she could take it from Regis, wasn't sure that she could bear to carry the thing with her.

"Entreri is dead," Regis assured her, not quite understanding her hesitation.

Catti-brie nodded absently, though her thoughts remained filled with memories of being Entreri's captive. She remembered the man's earthy smell and equated that smell now with the aroma of pure evil. She had been so powerless . . . like the moment when the ceiling fell in on Wulfgar. Powerless now, she wondered, when Drizzt might need her?

Catti-brie firmed her jaw and took the dagger. She clutched it tightly, then slid it into her belt.

"Ye mustn't tell Bruenor," she said.

"He'll know," Regis argued. "I might have been able to turn aside his curiosity about Drizzt's departure—Drizzt is always leaving—but Bruenor will soon realize that you are gone."

Catti-brie had no argument for that, but, again, she didn't care. She had to get to Drizzt. This was her quest, her way of taking back control of a life that had quickly been turned upside down.

She rushed to the bed, wrapped Regis in a big hug, and kissed him hard on the cheek. "Farewell, me friend!" she cried, dropping him to the mattress. "Farewell!"

Then she was gone, and Regis sat there, his chin in his plump hands. So many things had changed in the last day. First Drizzt, and now Catti-brie. With Wulfgar gone, that left only Regis and Bruenor of the five friends remaining in Mithril Hall.

Bruenor! Regis rolled to his side and groaned. He buried his face in his hands at the thought of the mighty dwarf. If Bruenor ever learned that Regis had aided Catti-brie on her dangerous way, he would rip the halfling apart.

Regis couldn't begin to think of how he might tell the dwarven king. Suddenly he regretted his decision, felt stupid for letting his emotions, his sympathies, get in the way of good judgment. He understood Catti-brie's need and felt that it was right for her to go after Drizzt, if that was what she truly desired to do—she was a grown woman, after all, and a fine warrior—but Bruenor wouldn't understand.

Neither would Drizzt, the halfling realized, and he groaned again. He had broken his word to the drow, had told the secret on the very first day! And his mistake had sent Catti-brie running into danger.

"Drizzt will kill me!" he wailed.

Catti-brie's head came back around the doorjamb, her smile wider, more full of life, than Regis had seen it in a long, long time. Suddenly she seemed the spirited lass that he and the others had come to love, the spirited young woman who had been lost to the world when the ceiling had fallen on Wulfgar. Even the redness had flown from her eyes, replaced by a joyful inner sparkle. "Just ye hope that Drizzt comes back to kill ye!" Catti-brie chirped, and she blew the halfling a kiss and rushed away.

"Wait!" Regis called halfheartedly. Regis was just as glad that Catti-brie didn't stop. He still thought himself irrational, even stupid, and still knew that he would have to answer to both Bruenor and Drizzt for his actions, but that last smile of Catti-brie's, her spark of life so obviously returned, had settled the argument.

Chapter 3

BAENRE'S BLUFF

he mercenary silently approached the western end of the Baenre compound, creeping from shadow to shadow to get near the silvery spiderweb fence that surrounded the place. Like any who came near House Baenre, which encompassed twenty huge and hollowed stalagmites and thirty adorned stalactites, Jarlaxle found himself impressed once more. By Underdark standards, where space was at a premium, the place was huge, nearly half a mile long and half that wide.

Everything about the structures of House Baenre was marvelous. Not a detail had been overlooked in the craftsmanship;

slaves worked continually to carve new designs into those few areas that had not yet been detailed. The magical touches, supplied mostly by Gromph, Matron Baenre's elderboy and the archmage of Menzoberranzan, were no less spectacular, right down to the predominant purple and blue faerie fire hues highlighting just the right areas of the mounds for the most awe-inspiring effect.

The compound's twenty-foot-high fence, which seemed so tiny anchoring the gigantic stalagmite mounds, was among the most wonderful creations in all of Menzoberranzan. Some said that it was a gift from Lloth, though none in the city, except perhaps ancient Matron Baenre, had been around long enough to witness its construction. The barrier was formed of iron-strong strands, thick as a drow's arm and enchanted to grasp and stubbornly cling stronger than any spider's web. Even the sharpest of drow weapons, arguably the finest edged weapons in all of Toril, could not nick the strands of Baenre's fence, and, once caught, no monster of any strength, not a giant or even a dragon, could hope to break free.

Normally, visitors to House Baenre would have sought one of the symmetrical gates spaced about the compound. There a watchman could have spoken the day's command and the strands of the fence would have spiraled outward, opening a hole.

Jarlaxle was no normal visitor, though, and Matron Baenre had instructed him to keep his comings and goings private. He waited in the shadows, perfectly hidden as several foot soldiers ambled by on their patrol. They were not overly alert, Jarlaxle noted, and why should they be, with the forces of Baenre behind them? House Baenre held at least twenty-five hundred capable and fabulously armed soldiers and boasted sixteen high priestesses. No other house in the city—no five houses combined—could muster such a force.

The mercenary glanced over to the pillar of Narbondel to discern how much longer he had to wait. He had barely turned back to the Baenre compound when a horn blew, clear and strong, and then another.

A chant, a low singing, arose from inside the compound. Foot soldiers rushed to their posts and came to rigid attention, their weapons presented ceremoniously before them. This was the spectacle that showed the honor of Menzoberranzan, the disciplined, precision drilling that mocked any potential enemy's claims that dark elves were too chaotic to come together in common cause or common defense. Non-drow mercenaries, particularly the gray dwarves, often paid handsome sums of gold and gems simply to view the spectacle of the changing of the Baenre house guard.

Streaks of orange, red, green, blue, and purple light rushed up the stalagmite mounds, to meet similar streaks coming down from above, from the jagged teeth of the Baenre compound's stalactites. Enchanted house emblems, worn by the Baenre guards, created this effect as male dark elves rode subterranean lizards that could walk equally well on floors, walls, or ceilings.

The music continued. The glowing streaks formed myriad designs in brilliant formations up and down the compound, many of them taking on the image of an arachnid. This event occurred twice a day, every day, and any drow within watching distance paused and took note each and every time. The changing of the Baenre house guard was a symbol in Menzoberranzan of both House Baenre's incredible power, and the city's undying fealty to Lloth, the Spider Queen.

Jarlaxle, as he had been instructed by Matron Baenre, used the spectacle as a distraction. He crept up to the fence, dropped his wide-brimmed hat to hang at his back, and slipped a mask of black velvet cloth, with eight joint-wired legs protruding from its sides, over his head. With a quick glance, the mercenary started up, hand over hand, climbing the thick strands as though they were ordinary iron. No magical spells could have duplicated this effect; no spells of levitation and teleportation, or any other kind of magical travel, could have brought someone beyond the barrier. Only the rare and treasured spider mask, loaned to Jarlaxle by Gromph Baenre, could get someone so easily into the well-guarded compound.

Jarlaxle swung a leg over the top of the fence and slipped down the other side. He froze in place at the sight of an orange flash to his left. Curse his luck if he had been caught. The guard would likely pose no danger—all in the Baenre compound knew the mercenary well—but if Matron Baenre learned that he had been discovered, she would likely flail the skin from his bones.

The flaring light died away almost immediately, and as Jarlaxle's eyes adjusted to the changing hues, he saw a handsome young drow with neatly cropped hair sitting astride a large lizard, perpendicular to the floor and holding a ten-foot-long mottled lance. A death lance, Jarlaxle knew. It was coldly enchanted, its hungry and razor-edged tip revealing its deadly chill to the mercenary's heat-sensing eyes.

Well met, Berg'inyon Baenre, the mercenary flashed in the intricate and silent hand code of the drow. Berg'inyon was Matron Baenre's youngest son, the leader of the Baenre lizard riders, and no enemy of, or stranger to, the mercenary leader.

And you, Jarlaxle, Berg'inyon flashed back. *Prompt, as always.*

As your mother demands, Jarlaxle signaled back. Berg'inyon flashed a smile and motioned for the mercenary to be on his way, then kicked his mount and scampered up the side of the stalagmite to his ceiling patrol.

Jarlaxle liked the youngest Baenre male. He had spent many days with Berg'inyon lately, learning from the young fighter, for Berg'inyon had once been a classmate of Drizzt Do'Urden's at Melee-Magthere and had often sparred against the scimitar-wielding drow. Berg'inyon's battle moves were fluid and near-perfect, and knowledge of how Drizzt had defeated the young Baenre heightened Jarlaxle's respect for the renegade.

Jarlaxle almost mourned that Drizzt Do'Urden would soon be no more.

Once past the fence, the mercenary replaced the spider mask in a pouch and walked nonchalantly through the Baenre compound, keeping his telltale hat low on his back and his cloak tight about his shoulder, hiding the fact that he wore a sleeveless tunic. He couldn't hide his bald head, though, an unusual trait, and he knew that more than one of the Baenre guards recognized him as he made his way casually to the house's great mound, the huge and ornate stalagmite wherein resided the Baenre nobles.

Those guards didn't notice, though, or pretended not to, as they had likely been instructed. Jarlaxle nearly laughed aloud; so many troubles could have been avoided just by his going through a more conspicuous gate to the compound. Everyone, Triel included, knew full well that he would be there. It was all a game of pretense and intrigue, with Matron Baenre as the controlling player.

"*Z'ress!*" the mercenary cried, the drow word for strength and the password for this mound, and he pushed on the stone door, which retracted immediately into the top of its jamb.

Jarlaxle tipped his hat to the unseen guards (probably huge minotaur slaves, Matron Baenre's favorites) as he passed along the narrow entry corridor, between several slits, no doubt lined with readied death lances.

The inside of the mound was lighted, forcing Jarlaxle to pause and allow his eyes to shift back to the visible light spectrum. Dozens of female dark elves moved about, their silver-and-black Baenre uniforms tightly fitting their firm and alluring bodies. All eyes turned toward the newcomer—the leader of Bregan D'aerthe was considered a fine catch in Menzoberranzan—and the lewd way the females scrutinized him, hardly looking at his face at all, made Jarlaxle bite back a laugh. Some male dark elves resented such leers, but to Jarlaxle's thinking, these females' obvious hunger afforded him even more power.

The mercenary moved to the large black pillar in the heart of the central circular chamber. He felt along the smooth marble and located the pressure plate that opened a section of the curving wall.

Jarlaxle found Dantrag Baenre, the house weapon master, leaning casually against the wall inside. Jarlaxle quickly discerned that the fighter had been waiting for him. Like his younger brother, Dantrag was handsome, tall (closer to six feet than to five), and lean, his muscles finely tuned. His eyes were unusually amber, though they shifted toward red when he grew excited. He wore his white hair pulled back tightly into a ponytail.

As weapon master of House Baenre, Dantrag was better outfitted for battle than any other drow in the city. Dantrag's shimmering black coat of mesh mail glistened as he turned, conforming to the angles of his body so perfectly that it seemed a second skin. He wore two swords on his jeweled belt. Curiously, only one of these was of drow make, as fine a sword as Jarlaxle had ever seen. The other, reportedly taken from a surface dweller, was said to possess a hunger of its own and could shave the edges off hard stone without dulling in the least.

The cocky fighter lifted one arm to salute the mercenary. As he did so, he prominently displayed one of his magical bracers, tight straps of black material lined with gleaming mithril rings. Dantrag had never told what purpose those bracers served. Some thought that they offered magical protection. Jarlaxle had seen Dantrag in battle and didn't disagree, for such defensive bracers were not uncommon. What amazed the mercenary even more was the fact that, in combat, Dantrag struck at his opponent first more often than not.

Jarlaxle couldn't be sure of his suspicions, for even without the bracers and any other magic, Dantrag Baenre was one of the finest fighters in Menzoberranzan. His principal rival had been Zak'nafein Do'Urden, father and mentor of Drizzt, but Zak'nafein was dead now, sacrificed for blasphemous acts against the Spider Queen. That left only Uthegental, the huge and strong weapon master of House Barrison Del'Armgo, the city's second house, as a suitable rival for dangerous Dantrag. Knowing both fighters' pride, Jarlaxle suspected that one day the two would secretly meet in a battle to the death, just to see who was the better.

The thought of such a spectacle intrigued Jarlaxle, though he never understood such destructive pride. Many who had seen the mercenary leader in battle would argue that he was a match for either of the two, but Jarlaxle would never play into such intrigue. To Jarlaxle it seemed that pride was a silly thing to fight for, especially when such fine weapons and skill could be used to bring more substantive treasures. Like those bracers, perhaps? Jarlaxle mused. Or would those fabulous bracers aid Dantrag in looting Uthegental's corpse?

With magic, anything was possible. Jarlaxle smiled as he continued to study Dantrag; the mercenary loved exotic magic, and nowhere in all the Underdark was there a finer collection of magical items than in House Baenre.

Like this cylinder he had entered. It seemed unremarkable, a plain circular chamber with a hole in the ceiling to Jarlaxle's left and a hole in the floor to his right.

He nodded to Dantrag, who waved his hand out to the left, and Jarlaxle walked under the hole. A tingling magic grabbed him and gradually lifted him into the air, levitating him to the great mound's second level. Inside the cylinder, this area appeared identical to the first, and Jarlaxle moved directly across the way, to the ceiling hole that would lead him to the third level.

Dantrag was up into the second level as Jarlaxle silently floated up to the third, and the weapon master came up quickly, catching Jarlaxle's arm as he reached for the opening mechanism to this level's door. Dantrag nodded to the next ceiling hole, which led to the fourth level and Matron Baenre's private throne room.

The fourth level? Jarlaxle pondered as he followed Dantrag into place and slowly began to levitate once more. Matron Baenre's private throne room? Normally, the first matron mother held audience in the mound's third level.

Matron Baenre already has a guest, Dantrag explained in the hand code as Jarlaxle's head came above the floor.

Jarlaxle nodded and stepped away from the hole, allowing Dantrag to lead the way. Dantrag did not reach for the door, however, but rather reached into a pouch and produced some silvery-glowing dust. With a wink to the mercenary, he flung the dust against the back wall. It sparkled and moved of its own accord, formed a silvery spider's web, which then spiraled outward, much like the Baenre gates, leaving a clear opening.

After you, Dantrag's hands politely suggested.

Jarlaxle studied the devious fighter, trying to discern if treachery was afoot. Might he climb through the obvious extradimensional gate only to find himself stranded on some hellish plane of existence?

Dantrag was a cool opponent, his beautiful, chiseled features, cheekbones set high and resolute, revealing nothing to Jarlaxle's usually effective, probing gaze. Jarlaxle did go through the opening, though, finally deciding that Dantrag was too proud to trick him into oblivion. If Dantrag had wanted Jarlaxle out of the way, he would have used weapons, not wizard's mischief.

The Baenre son stepped right behind Jarlaxle, into a small, extradimensional pocket sharing space with Matron Baenre's throne room. Dantrag led Jarlaxle along a thin silver thread to the far side of the small chamber, to an opening that looked out into the room.

There, on a large sapphire throne, sat the withered Matron Baenre, her face crisscrossed by thousands of spidery lines. Jarlaxle spent a long moment eyeing the throne before considering the matron mother, and he unconsciously licked his thin lips. Dantrag chuckled at his side, for the wary Baenre could understand the mercenary's desire. At the end of each of the throne's arms was set a

41

huge diamond of no fewer than thirty carats.

The throne itself was carved of the purest black sapphire, a shining well that offered an invitation into its depths. Writhing forms moved about inside that pool of blackness; rumor said that the tormented souls of all those who had been unfaithful to Lloth, and had, in turn, been transformed into hideous driders, resided in an inky black dimension within the confines of Matron Baenre's fabulous throne.

That sobering thought brought the mercenary from his casing; he might consider the act, but he would never be so foolish as to try to take one of those diamonds! He looked to Matron Baenre then, her two unremarkable scribes huddled behind her, busily taking notes. The first matron mother was flanked on her left by Bladen'Kerst, the oldest daughter in the house proper, the third oldest of the siblings behind Triel and Gromph. Jarlaxle liked Bladen'Kerst even less than he liked Triel, for she was sadistic in the extreme. On several occasions, the mercenary had thought he might have to kill her in self-defense. That would have been a difficult situation, though Jarlaxle suspected that Matron Baenre, privately, would be glad to have the wicked Bladen'Kerst dead. Even the powerful matron mother couldn't fully control that one.

On Matron Baenre's right stood another of Jarlaxle's least favorite beings, the illithid, Methil El-Viddenvelp, the octopus-headed advisor to Matron Baenre. He wore, as always, his unremarkable, rich crimson robe, its sleeves long so that the creature could keep its scrawny, three-clawed hands tucked from sight. Jarlaxle wished that the ugly creature would wear a mask and hood as well. Its bulbous, purplish head, sporting four tentacles where its mouth should have been, and milky-white pupilless eyes, was among the most repulsive things Jarlaxle had ever seen. Normally, if gains could be made, the mercenary would have looked past a being's appearance, but Jarlaxle preferred to have little contact with the ugly, mysterious, and ultimately deadly illithids.

Most drow held similar feelings toward illithids, and it momentarily struck Jarlaxle as odd that Matron Baenre would have El-Viddenvelp so obviously positioned. When he scrutinized the female drow facing Matron Baenre, though, the mercenary understood.

She was scrawny and small, shorter than even Triel and appearing much weaker. Her black robes were unremarkable, and she wore no other visible equipment—certainly not the attire befitting a matron mother. But this drow, K'yorl Odran, was indeed a matron mother, leader of Oblodra, the third house of Menzoberranzan.

K'yorl? Jarlaxle's fingers motioned to Dantrag, the mercenary's facial expression incredulous. K'yorl was among the most despised of Menzoberranzan's rulers. Personally, Matron Baenre hated K'yorl, and had many times openly expressed her belief that Menzoberranzan would be better off without the troublesome Odran. The only thing that had stopped House Baenre from obliterating Oblodra was the fact that the females of the third house possessed mysterious powers of the mind. If anyone could understand the motivations and private thoughts of mysterious and dangerous K'yorl, it would be the illithid, El-Viddenvelp.

"Three hundred," K'yorl was saying.

Matron Baenre slumped back in her chair, a sour expression on her face. "A pittance," she replied.

"Half of my slave force," K'yorl responded, flashing her customary grin, a well-known signal that not-so-sly K'yorl was lying.

Matron Baenre cackled, then stopped abruptly. She came forward in her seat, her slender hands resting atop the fabulous diamonds, and her scowl unrelenting. Her ruby-red eyes narrowed to slits. She uttered something under her breath and removed one of her hands from atop the diamond. The magnificent gem flared to inner life and loosed a concentrated beam of purple light, striking K'yorl's attendant, an unremarkable male, and engulfing him in a series of cascading, crackling arcs of purple-glowing energy. He cried out, threw his hands up in the air, and fought back against the consuming waves.

Matron Baenre, lifted her other hand and a second beam joined the first. Now the male drow seemed like no more than a purple silhouette.

Jarlaxle watched closely as K'yorl closed her eyes and furrowed her brow. Her eyes came back open almost immediately, and she stared with disbelief at El-Viddenvelp. The mercenary was worldly enough to realize that, in that split second, a battle of wills had just occurred, and he was not surprised that the mind flayer had apparently won out.

The unfortunate Oblodran male was no more than a shadow by then, and a moment later, he wasn't even that. He was simply no more.

K'yorl Odran scowled fiercely, seemed on the verge of an explosion, but Matron Baenre, as deadly as any drow alive, did not back down.

Unexpectedly, K'yorl grinned widely again and announced lightheartedly, "He was just a male."

"K'yorl!" Baenre snarled. "This duty is sanctified by Lloth, and you shall cooperate!"

"Threats?" spoke K'yorl.

Matron Baenre rose from her throne and walked right in front of the unflinching K'yorl. She raised her left hand to the Oblodran female's cheek, and calm K'yorl couldn't help but wince. On that hand Matron Baenre wore a huge golden ring, its four uncompleted bands shifting as though they were the eight legs of a living spider. Its huge blue-black sapphire shimmered. That ring, K'yorl knew, contained a living *velsharess orbb*, a queen spider, a far more deadly cousin of the surface world's black widow.

"You must understand the importance," Matron Baenre cooed.

To Jarlaxle's amazement (and he noted that Dantrag's hand immediately went to his sword hilt, as though the weapon master would leap out of the extradimensional spying pocket and slay the impudent Oblodran), K'yorl slapped Matron Baenre's hand away.

"Barrison Del'Armgo has agreed," Matron Baenre said calmly, shifting her hand upright to keep her dangerous daughter and illithid advisor from taking any action.

K'yorl grinned, an obvious bluff, for the matron mother of the third house could not be thrilled to hear that the first two houses had allied on an issue that she wanted to avoid.

"As has Faen Tlabbar," Matron Baenre added slyly, referring to the city's fourth house and Oblodra's most hated rival. Baenre's words were an obvious threat, for with both House Baenre and House Barrison Del'Armgo on its side, Faen Tlabbar would move quickly to crush Oblodra and assume the city's third rank.

Matron Baenre slid back into her sapphire throne, never taking her gaze from K'yorl.

"I do not have many house drow," K'yorl said, and it was the first time Jarlaxle had ever heard the upstart Oblodran sound humbled.

"No, but you have kobold fodder!" Matron Baenre snapped. "And do not dare to admit to six hundred. The tunnels of the Clawrift beneath House Oblodra are vast."

"I will give to you three thousand," K'yorl answered, apparently thinking the better of some hard bargaining.

"Ten times that!" Baenre growled.

K'yorl said nothing, merely cocked her head back and looked down her slender, ebon-skinned nose at the first matron mother.

"I'll settle for nothing less than twenty thousand," Matron Baenre said then, carrying both sides of the bargaining. "The defenses of the dwarven stronghold will be cunning, and we'll need ample fodder to sort our way through."

"The cost is great," K'yorl said.

"Twenty thousand kobolds do not equal the cost of one drow life," Baenre reminded her, then added, just for effect, "in Lloth's eyes."

K'yorl started to respond sharply, but Matron Baenre stopped her at once.

"Spare me your threats!" Baenre screamed, her thin neck seeming even scrawnier with her jaw so tightened and jutting forward. "In Lloth's eyes, this event goes beyond the fighting of drow houses, and I promise you, K'yorl, that the disobedience of House Oblodra will aid the ascension of Faen Tlabbar!"

Jarlaxle's eyes widened with surprise and he looked at Dantrag, who had no explanation. Never before had the mercenary heard, or heard of, such a blatant threat, one house against another. No grin, no witty response, came from K'yorl this time. Studying the female, silent and obviously fighting to keep her features calm, Jarlaxle could see the seeds of anarchy. K'yorl and House Oblodra would not soon forget Matron Baenre's threat, and given Matron Baenre's arrogance, other houses would undoubtedly foster similar resentments. The mercenary nodded as he thought of his own meeting with fearful Triel, who would likely inherit this dangerous situation.

"Twenty thousand," K'yorl quietly agreed, "if that many of the troublesome little rats can be herded."

The matron mother of House Oblodra was then dismissed. As

45

she entered the marble cylinder, Dantrag dropped out of the end of the spider filament and climbed from the extradimensional pocket, into the throne room.

Jarlaxle went behind, stepping lightly to stand before the throne. He swept into a low bow, the *diatryma* feather sticking from the brim of his great hat brushing the floor. "A most magnificent performance," he greeted Matron Baenre. "It was my pleasure that I was allowed to witness—"

"Shut up," Matron Baenre, leaning back in her throne and full of venom, said to him.

Still grinning, the mercenary came to quiet attention.

"K'yorl is a dangerous nuisance," Matron Baenre said. "I will ask little from her house drow, though their strange mind powers would prove useful in breaking the will of resilient dwarves. All that we need from them is kobold fodder, and since the vermin breed like muck rats, their sacrifice will not be great."

"What about after the victory?" Jarlaxle dared to ask.

"That is for K'yorl to decide," Matron Baenre replied immediately. She motioned then for the others, even her scribes, to leave the room, and all knew that she meant to appoint Jarlaxle's band to a scouting mission—at the very least—on House Oblodra.

They all went without complaint, except for wicked Bladen' Kerst, who paused to flash the mercenary a dangerous glare. Bladen'Kerst hated Jarlaxle as she hated all drow males, considering them nothing more than practice dummies on which she could hone her torturing techniques.

The mercenary shifted his eye patch to the other eye and gave her a lewd wink in response.

Bladen'Kerst immediately looked to her mother, as if asking permission to beat the impertinent male senseless, but Matron Baenre continued to wave her away.

"You want Bregan D'aerthe to keep close watch on House Oblodra," Jarlaxle reasoned as soon as he was alone with Baenre. "Not an easy task—"

"No," Matron Baenre interrupted. "Even Bregan D'aerthe could not readily spy on that mysterious house."

The mercenary was glad that Matron Baenre, not he, had been the one to point that out. He considered the unexpected conclusion, then grinned widely, and even dipped into a bow of salute as he came to understand. Matron Baenre wanted the others, particularly El-Viddenvelp, merely to think that she would set Bregan D'aerthe to spy on House Oblodra. That way, she could keep K'yorl somewhat off guard, looking for ghosts that did not exist.

"I care not for K'yorl, beyond my need of her slaves," Matron Baenre went on. "If she does not do as she is instructed in this matter, then House Oblodra will be dropped into the Clawrift and forgotten."

The matter-of-fact tones, showing supreme confidence, impressed the mercenary. "With the first and second houses aligned, what choice does K'yorl have?" he asked.

Matron Baenre pondered that point, as though Jarlaxle had reminded her of something. She shook the notion away and quickly went on. "We do not have time to discuss your meeting with Triel," she said, and Jarlaxle was more than a little curious, for he had thought that the primary reason for his visit to House Baenre. "I want you to begin planning our procession toward the dwarvish home. I will need maps of the intended routes, as well as detailed descriptions of the possible final approaches to Mithril Hall, so that Dantrag and his generals might best plan the attack."

Jarlaxle nodded. He certainly wasn't about to argue with the foul-tempered matron mother. "We could send spies deeper into the dwarven complex," he began, but again, the impatient Baenre cut him short.

"We need none," she said simply.

Jarlaxle eyed her curiously. "Our last expedition did not actually get into Mithril Hall," he reminded.

Matron Baenre's lips curled up in a perfectly evil smile, an infectious grin that made Jarlaxle eager to learn what revelation might be coming. Slowly, the matron mother reached inside the front of her fabulous robes, producing a chain on which hung a ring, bone white and fashioned, so it appeared, out of a large tooth. "Do you know of this?" she asked, holding the item up in plain view.

"It is said to be the tooth of a dwarf king, and that his trapped and tormented soul is contained within the ring," the mercenary replied.

"A dwarf king," Matron Baenre echoed. "And there are not so

many dwarvish kingdoms, you see."

Jarlaxle's brow furrowed, then his face brightened. "Mithril Hall?" he asked.

Matron Baenre nodded. "Fate has played me a marvelous coincidence," she explained. "Within this ring is the soul of Gandalug Battlehammer, First King of Mithril Hall, Patron of Clan Battlehammer."

Jarlaxle's mind whirled with the possibilities. No wonder, then, that Lloth had instructed Vierna to go after her renegade brother! Drizzt was just a tie to the surface, a pawn in a larger game of conquest.

"Gandalug talks to me," Matron Baenre explained, her voice as content as a cat's purr. "He remembers the ways of Mithril Hall."

Sos'Umptu Baenre entered then, ignoring Jarlaxle and walking right by him to stand before her mother. The matron mother did not rebuke her, as the mercenary would have expected for the unannounced intrusion, but rather, turned a curious gaze her way and allowed her to explain.

"Matron Mez'Barris Armgo grows impatient," Sos'Umptu said.

In the chapel, Jarlaxle realized, for Sos'Umptu was caretaker of the wondrous Baenre chapel and rarely left the place. The mercenary paused for just a moment to consider the revelation. Mez'Barris was the matron mother of House Barrison Del'Armgo, the city's second-ranking house. But why would she be at the Baenre compound if, as Matron Baenre had declared, Barrison Del'Armgo had already agreed to the expedition?

Why indeed.

"Perhaps you should have seen to Matron Mez'Barris first," the mercenary said slyly to Matron Baenre. The withered old matron accepted his remark in good cheer; it showed her that her favorite spy was thinking clearly.

"K'yorl was the more difficult," Baenre replied. "To keep that one waiting would have put her in a fouler mood than usual. Mez'Barris is calmer by far, more understanding of the gains. She will agree to the war with the dwarves."

Matron Baenre walked by the mercenary to the marble cylinder; Sos'Umptu was already inside, waiting. "Besides," the first matron mother added with a wicked grin, "now that House Oblodra has come into the alliance, what choice does Mez'Barris have?"

She was too beautiful, this old one, Jarlaxle agreed. Too beautiful. He cast one final, plaintive look at the marvelous diamonds on the arms of Baenre's throne, then sighed deeply and followed the two females out of House Baenre's great stronghold.

Chapter 4

THE FIRE IN HER EYES

atti-brie pulled her gray cloak about her to hide the dagger and mask she had taken from Regis. Mixed feelings assaulted her as she neared Bruenor's private chambers; she hoped both that the dwarf would be there, and that he would not.

How could she leave without seeing Bruenor, her father, one more time? And yet, the dwarf now seemed to Catti-brie a shell of his former self, a wallowing old dwarf waiting to die. She didn't want to see him like that, didn't want to take that image of Bruenor with her into the Underdark.

She lifted her hand to knock on the door to Bruenor's sitting room, then gently cracked the door open instead and peeked in. She saw a dwarf standing off to the side of the burning hearth, but it wasn't Bruenor. Thibbledorf Pwent, the battlerager, hopped about in circles, apparently trying to catch a pesky fly. He wore his sharp-ridged armor (as always), complete with glove nails and knee and elbow spikes, and other deadly points protruding from every plausible angle. The armor squealed as the dwarf spun and jumped, an irritating sound if Catti-brie had ever heard one. Pwent's open-faced gray helm rested in the chair beside him, its top spike half as tall as the dwarf. Without it, Catti-brie could see, the battlerager was almost bald, his remaining thin black strands of hair matted greasily to the sides of his head, then giving way to an enormous, bushy black beard.

Catti-brie pushed the door a little farther and saw Bruenor sitting before the low-burning fire, absently trying to flip a log so that its embers would flare to life again. His halfhearted poke against the glowing log made Catti-brie wince. She remembered the days not so long ago, when the boisterous king would have simply reached into the hearth and smacked the stubborn log with his bare hand.

With a look to Pwent (who was eating something that Catti-brie sincerely hoped was not a fly), the young woman entered the room, checking her cloak as she came in to see that the items were properly concealed.

"Hey, there!" Pwent howled between crunchy bites. Even more than her disgust at the thought that he was eating a fly, Catti-brie was amazed that he could be getting so much chewing out of it!

"Ye should get a beard!" the battlerager called, his customary greeting. From their first meeting, the dirty dwarf had told Catti-brie that she'd be a handsome woman indeed if she could only grow a beard.

"I'm working at it," Catti-brie replied, honestly glad for the levity. "Ye've got me promise that I haven't shaved me face since the day we met." She patted the battlerager atop the head, then regretted it when she felt the greasy film on her hand.

"There's a good girl," Pwent replied. He spotted another flitting insect and hopped away in pursuit.

"Where ye going?" Bruenor demanded sharply before Catti-brie

51

could even say hello.

Catti-brie sighed in the face of her father's scowl. How she longed to see Bruenor smile again! Catti-brie noted the bruise on Bruenor's forehead, the scraped portion finally scabbing over. He had reportedly gone into a tirade a few nights before, and had actually smashed down a heavy wooden door with his head while two frantic younger dwarves tried to hold him back. The bruise combined with Bruenor's garish scar, which ran from his forehead to the side of his jaw, across one socket where his eye had once been, made the old dwarf seem battered indeed!

"Where ye going?" Bruenor asked again, angrily.

"Settlestone," the young woman lied, referring to the town of barbarians, Wulfgar's people, down the mountain from Mithril Hall's eastern exit. "The tribe's building a cairn to honor Wulfgar's memory." Catti-brie was somewhat surprised at how easily the lie came to her; she had always been able to charm Bruenor, often using half-truths and semantic games to get around the blunt truth, but she had never so boldly lied to him.

Reminding herself of the importance behind it all, she looked the red-bearded dwarf in the eye as she continued. "I'm wanting to be there before they start building. If they're to do it, then they're to do it right. Wulfgar deserves no less."

Bruenor's one working eye seemed to mist over, taking on an even duller appearance, and the scarred dwarf turned away from Catti-brie, went back to his pointless fire poking, though he did manage one slight nod of halfhearted agreement. It was no secret in Mithril Hall that Bruenor didn't like talking of Wulfgar—he had even punched out one priest who insisted that Aegis-fang could not, by dwarvish tradition, be given a place of honor in the Hall of Dumathoin, since a human, and no dwarf, had wielded it.

Catti-brie noticed then that Pwent's armor had ceased its squealing, and she turned about to regard the battlerager. He stood by the opened door, looking forlornly at her and at Bruenor's back. With a nod to the young woman, he quietly (for a rusty-armored battlerager) left the room.

Apparently, Catti-brie was not the only one pained by the pitiful wretch Bruenor Battlehammer had become.

"Ye've got their sympathy," she remarked to Bruenor, who

seemed not to hear. "All in Mithril Hall speak kindly of their wounded king."

"Shut yer face," Bruenor said out of the side of his mouth. He still sat squarely facing the low fire.

Catti-brie knew that the implied threat was lame, another reminder of Bruenor's fall. In days past, when Bruenor Battlehammer suggested that someone shut his face, he did, or Bruenor did it for him. But, since the fights with the priest and with the door, Bruenor's fire, like the one in the hearth, had played itself to its end.

"Do ye mean to poke that fire the rest o' yer days?" Catti-brie asked, trying to incite a fight, to blow on the embers of Bruenor's pride.

"If it pleases me," the dwarf retaliated too calmly.

Catti-brie sighed again and pointedly hitched her cloak over the side of her hip, revealing the magical mask and Entreri's jeweled dagger. Even though the young woman was determined to undertake her adventure alone, and did not want to explain any of it to Bruenor, she prayed that Bruenor would have life enough within him to notice.

Long minutes passed, quiet minutes, except for the occasional crackle of the embers and the hiss of the unseasoned wood.

"I'll return when I return!" the flustered woman barked, and she headed for the door. Bruenor absently waved her away over one shoulder, never bothering to look at her.

Catti-brie paused by the door, then opened it and quietly closed it, never leaving the room. She waited a few moments, not believing that Bruenor remained in front of the fire, poking it absently. Then she slipped across the room and through another doorway, to the dwarf's bedroom.

Catti-brie moved to Bruenor's large oaken desk—a gift from Wulfgar's people, its polished wood gleaming and designs of Aegis-fang, the mighty warhammer that Bruenor had crafted, carved into its sides. Catti-brie paused a long while, despite her need to be out before Bruenor realized what she was doing, and looked at those designs, remembering Wulfgar. She would never get over that loss. She understood that, but she knew, too, that her time of grieving neared its end, that she had to get on with the business of living. Especially now, Catti-brie reminded herself, with another of her friends apparently walking into peril.

In a stone coffer atop the desk Catti-brie found what she was looking for: a small locket on a silver chain, a gift to Bruenor from Alustriel, the Lady of Silverymoon. Bruenor had been thought dead, lost in Mithril Hall on the friends' first passage through the place. He had escaped from the halls sometime later, avoiding the evil gray dwarves who had claimed Mithril Hall as their own, and with Alustriel's help, he found Catti-brie in Longsaddle, a village to the southwest. Drizzt and Wulfgar had left long before that, on their way south in pursuit of Regis, who had been captured by the assassin Entreri.

Alustriel had then given Bruenor the magical locket. Inside was a tiny portrait of Drizzt, and with this device the dwarf could generally track the drow. Proper direction and distance from Drizzt could be determined by the degrees of magical warmth emanating from the locket.

The metal bauble was cool now, colder than the air of the room, and it seemed to Catti-brie that Drizzt was already a long way from her.

Catti-brie opened the locket and regarded the perfect image of her dear drow friend. She wondered if she should take it. With Guenhwyvar she could likely follow Drizzt anyway, if she could get on his trail, and she had kept it in the back of her mind that, when Bruenor learned the truth from Regis, the fire would come into his eyes, and he would rush off in pursuit.

Catti-brie liked that image of fiery Bruenor, wanted her father to come charging in to her aid, and to Drizzt's rescue, but that was a child's hope, she realized, unrealistic and ultimately dangerous.

Catti-brie shut the locket and snapped it up into her hand. She slipped out of Bruenor's bedroom and through his sitting room (with the red-bearded dwarf still seated before the fire, his thoughts a million miles away), then rushed through the halls of the upper levels, knowing that if she didn't get on her way soon, she might lose her nerve.

Outside, she regarded the locket again and knew that in taking it, she had cut off any chances that Bruenor would follow. She was on her own.

That was how it had to be, Catti-brie decided, and she slipped the chain over her head and started down the mountain, hoping to get to Silverymoon not so long after Drizzt.

* * * * *

He slipped as quietly and unobtrusively as he could along the dark streets of Menzoberranzan, his heat-seeing eyes glowing ruby red. All that he wanted was to get back to Jarlaxle's base, back with the drow who recognized his worth.

"*Waela rivvil!*" came a shrill cry from the side.

He stopped in his tracks, leaned wearily against the pile of broken stone near an unoccupied stalagmite mound. He had heard those words often before—always those two words, said with obvious derision.

"*Waela rivvil!*" the drow female said again, moving toward him, a russet tentacle rod in one hand, its three eight-foot-long arms writhing of their own accord, eagerly, as though they wanted to lash out with their own maliciousness and slap at him. At least the female wasn't carrying one of those whips of fangs, he mused, thinking of the multi-snake-headed weapons many of the higher-ranking drow priestesses used.

He offered no resistance as she moved to stand right in front of him, respectfully lowered his eyes as Jarlaxle had taught him. He suspected that she, too, was moving through the streets inconspicuously—why else would a drow female, powerful enough to be carrying one of those wicked rods, be crawling about the alleys of this, the lesser section of Menzoberranzan?

She issued a string of drow words in her melodic voice, too quickly for this newcomer to understand. He caught the words *quarth*, which meant command, and *harl'il'cik*, or kneel, and expected them anyway, for he was always being commanded to kneel.

Down he went, obediently and immediately, though the drop to the hard stone pained his knees.

The drow female paced slowly about him, giving him a long look at her shapely legs, even pulling his head back so that he could stare up into her undeniably beautiful face, while she purred her name, "Jerlys."

She moved as if to kiss him, then slapped him instead, a stinging smack on his cheek. Immediately, his hands went to his sword and dirk, but he calmed and reminded himself of the consequences.

Still the drow paced about him, speaking to herself as much as to him. "*Iblith*," she said many times, the drow word for excrement, and finally he replied with the single word "*abban*," which meant ally, again as Jarlaxle had coached him.

"*Abban del darthiir!*" she cried back, smacking him again on the back of his head, nearly knocking him flat to his face.

He didn't understand completely, but thought that *darthiir* had something to do with the faeries, the surface elves. He was beginning to figure out then that he was in serious trouble this time, and would not so easily get away from this one.

"*Abban del darthiir!*" Jerlys cried again, and this time her tentacle rod, and not her hand, snapped at him from behind, all three tentacles pounding painfully into his right shoulder. He grabbed at the wound and fell flat to the stone, his right arm useless and the waves of pain rolling through him.

Jerlys struck again, at his back, but his sudden movement had saved him from a hit by all three of the tentacles.

His mind raced. He knew that he had to act fast. The female kept taunting him, smacking her rod against the alley walls, and every so often against his bleeding back. He knew for certain then that he had caught this female by surprise, that she was on a mission as secret as his own, and that he would not likely walk away from this encounter.

One of the tentacles slapped off the back of his head, dazing him. Still his right arm remained dead, weakened by the magic of a simultaneous three-strike.

But he had to act. He moved his left hand to his right hip, to his dirk, then changed his mind and brought it around the other side.

"*Abban del darthiir!*" Jerlys cried again, and her arm came forward.

He spun about and up to meet it, his sword, not of drow make, flaring angrily as it connected with the tentacles. There came a green flash, and one tentacle fell free, but one of the others snaked its way through the parry and hit him in the face.

"*Jivvin!*" the amused drow cried the word for play, and she elaborated most graciously, thanking him for his foolish retaliation, for making it all such fun.

"Play with this," he said back at her, and he came forward, straight ahead with the sword.

A globe of conjured darkness fell over him.

"*Jivvin!*" Jerlys laughed again and came forward to smack with her rod. But this one was no novice in fighting dark elves, and, to the female's surprise, she did not find him within her globe.

Around the side of the darkness he came, one arm hanging limp, but the other flashing this way and that in a marvelous display of swordsmanship. This was a drow female, though, highly trained in the fighting arts and armed with a tentacle rod. She parried and countered, scoring another hit, laughing all the while.

She did not understand her opponent.

He came in a straightforward lunge again, spun about to the left as if to continue with a spinning overhand chop, then reversed his grip on the weapon, pivoted back to the right, and heaved the sword as though it were a spear.

The weapon's tip dove hungrily between the surprised female's breasts, sparking as it sliced through the fine drow armor.

He followed the throw with a leaping somersault and kicked both feet forward so that they connected on the quivering sword hilt, plunging the weapon deeper into the malevolent female's chest.

The drow fell back against the rock pile, stumbling over it until the uneven wall of the stalagmite supported her at a half-standing angle, her red eyes locked in a wide stare.

"A pity, Jerlys," he whispered into her ear, and he softly kissed her cheek as he grasped the sword hilt and pointedly stepped on the writhing tentacles to pin them down on the floor. "What pleasures we might have known."

He pulled the sword free and grimaced as he considered the implications of this drow female's death. He couldn't deny the satisfaction, however, at taking back some of the control in his life. He hadn't gone through all his battles just to wind up a slave!

He left the alley a short while later, with Jerlys and her rod buried under the stones, and with a bounce returned to his step.

Chapter 5

OVER THE YEARS

rizzt felt the gazes on him. They were elven eyes, he knew, likely staring down the length of readied arrows. The ranger casually continued his trek through the Moonwood, his weapons tucked away and the hood of his forest-green cloak back off his head, revealing his long mane of white hair and his ebon-skinned elven features.

The sun made its lazy way through the leafy green trees, splotching the forest with dots of pale yellow. Drizzt did not avoid these, as much to show the surface elves that he was no ordinary drow as for his honest love of the warmth of sunlight. The trail was wide and smooth, unexpected in a supposedly wild and thick forest.

As the minutes turned into an hour and the forest deepened around him, Drizzt began to wonder if he might pass through the Moonwood without incident. He wanted no trouble, certainly, wanted only to be on with, and be done with, his quest.

He came into a small clearing some time later. Several logs had been arranged into a square around a stone-blocked fire pit. This was no ordinary campsite, Drizzt knew, but a designated meeting place, a shared campground for those who would respect the sovereignty of the forest and the creatures living within its sheltered boughs.

Drizzt walked the camp's perimeter, searching the trees. Looking to the moss bed at the base of one huge oak, the drow saw several markings. Though time had blurred their lines, one appeared to be a rearing bear, another a wild pig. These were the marks of rangers, and with an approving nod, the drow searched the lower boughs of the tree, finally discovering a well-concealed hollow. He reached in gingerly and pulled out a pack of dried food, a hatchet, and a skin filled with fine wine. Drizzt took only a small cup of the wine, but regretted that he could not add anything to the cache, since he would need all the provisions he could carry, and more, in his long trek through the dangerous Underdark.

He replaced the stores after using the hatchet to split some nearby deadwood, then gently carved his own ranger mark, the unicorn, in the moss at the base of the trunk and returned to the nearest log to start a fire for his meal.

"You are no ordinary drow," came a melodic voice from behind him before his meal was even cooked. The language was Elvish, as was the pitch of the voice, more melodic than that of a human.

Drizzt turned slowly, understanding that several bows were probably again trained on him from many different angles. A single elf stood before him. She was a young maiden, younger than even Drizzt, though Drizzt had lived only a tenth of his expected life. She wore forest colors, a green cloak, much like Drizzt's, and a brown tunic and leggings, with a longbow resting easily over one shoulder and a slender sword belted on one hip. Her black hair shone so as to be bluish and her skin was so pale that it reflected that blue hue. Her eyes, too, bright and shining, were blue flecked with gold. She was a silver elf—a moon elf, Drizzt knew.

In his years of living on the surface, Drizzt Do'Urden had encountered few surface elves, and those had been gold elves. He had encountered moon elves only once in his life, on his first trip to the surface in a dark elf raid in which his kin had slaughtered an small elf clan. That horrible memory rushed up at Drizzt as he faced this beautiful and delicate creature. Only one moon elf had survived that encounter, a young child that Drizzt had secretly buried beneath her mother's mutilated body. That act of treachery against the evil drow had brought severe repercussions, costing Drizzt's family the favor of Lloth, and, in the end, costing Zak'nafein, Drizzt's father, his life.

Drizzt faced a moon elf once more, a maiden perhaps thirty years of age, with sparkling eyes. The ranger felt the blood draining from his face. Was this the region to which he and the drow raiders had come?

"You are no ordinary drow," the elf said again, still using the Elvish tongue, her eyes flashing dangerously and her tone grim.

Drizzt held his hands out to the side. He realized that he should say something, but simply couldn't think of any words—or couldn't get them past the lump in his throat.

The elf maiden's eyes narrowed; her lower jaw trembled, and her hand instinctively dropped to the hilt of her sword.

"I am no enemy," Drizzt managed to say, realizing that he must either speak or, likely, fight.

The maiden was on him in the blink of a lavender eye, sword flashing.

Drizzt never even drew his weapons, just stood with his hands out wide, and his expression calm. The elf slid up short of him, her sword raised. Her expression changed suddenly, as though she had noticed something in Drizzt's eyes.

She screamed wildly and started to swing, but Drizzt, too quick for her, leaped forward, caught her weapon arm in one hand, and wrapped his other arm about her, pulling her close and hugging her so tightly that she could not continue the fight. He expected her to claw him, or even bite him, but, to his surprise, she fell limply into his arms and slumped low, her face buried in his chest and her shoulders bobbing with sobs.

Before he could begin to speak words to comfort, Drizzt felt the keen tip of an elven sword against the back of his neck. He let go of the female immediately, his hands out wide once more, and another elf, older and more stern, but with similarly beautiful features, came from the trees to collect the young maiden and help her away.

"I am no enemy," Drizzt said again.

"Why do you cross the Moonwood?" the unseen elf behind him asked in the Common tongue.

"Your words are correct," Drizzt replied absently, for his thoughts were still focused on the curious maiden. "I mean only to cross the Moonwood, from the west to the east, and will bring no harm to you or the wood."

"The unicorn," Drizzt heard another elf say from behind, from near the huge oak tree. He figured that the elf had found his ranger mark in the moss. To his relief, the sword was taken away from his neck.

Drizzt paused a long moment, figuring that it was the elves' turn to speak. Finally, he mustered the nerve to turn about—only to find that the moon elves were gone, disappeared into the brush.

He thought of tracking them, was haunted by the image of that young elven maiden, but realized that it was not his place to disturb them in this, their forest home. He finished his meal quickly, made sure that the area was cleaned and as he had found it, then gathered up his gear and went on his way.

Less than a mile down the trail, he came upon another curious sight. A black-and-white horse, fully saddled, its bridle lined with tinkling bells, stood quietly and calmly. The animal pawed the ground when it saw the drow coming.

Drizzt spoke softly and made quiet sounds as he eased over to it. The horse visibly calmed, even nuzzled Drizzt when he got near. The animal was fine, the ranger could tell, well muscled and well groomed, though it was not a tall beast. Its coat held black and white splotches, even on its face, with one eye surrounded by white, the other appearing as though it was under a black mask.

Drizzt searched around, but found no other prints in the ground. He suspected that the horse had been provided by the elves, for him, but he couldn't be sure, and he certainly didn't want to steal someone's mount.

He patted the horse on the neck and started to walk past. He had gone only a few steps when the horse snorted and wheeled about. It galloped around the drow and stood again before him on the path.

Curious, Drizzt repeated the movement, going by the beast, and the horse followed suit to stand before him.

"Did they tell you to do this?" Drizzt asked plainly, stroking the animal's muzzle.

"Did you instruct him so?" Drizzt called loudly to the woods around him. "I ask the elves of Moonwood, was this horse provided for me?"

All that came in response was the protesting chatter of some birds disturbed by Drizzt's shout.

The drow shrugged and figured that he would take the horse to the end of the wood; it wasn't so far anyway. He mounted up and galloped off, making great progress along the wide and flat trail.

He came to the eastern end of Moonwood late that afternoon, long shadows rolling out from the tall trees. Figuring that the elves had given him the mount only so that he could be gone of their realm more quickly, he brought the horse to a halt, still under the shadows, meaning to dismount and send it running back into the forest.

A movement across the wide field beyond the forest caught the drow ranger's eye. He spotted an elf atop a tall black stallion, just outside the brush line, looking his way. The elf put his hands to his lips and gave a shrill whistle, and Drizzt's horse leaped out from the shadows and ran across the thick grass.

The elf disappeared immediately into the brush, but Drizzt did not bring his horse up short. He understood then that the elves had chosen to help him, in their distant way, and he accepted their gift and rode on.

Before he set camp that night, Drizzt noticed that the elven rider was paralleling him, some distance to the south. It seemed that there was a limit to their trust.

* * * * *

Catti-brie had little experience with cities. She had been through Luskan, had flown in an enchanted chariot over the splendor of mighty Waterdeep, and had traveled through the great southern city of Calimport. Nothing, though, had ever come close to the sights that awaited her as she walked the wide and curving avenues of Silverymoon. She had been here once before, but at the time, she had been a prisoner of Artemis Entreri and had hardly noticed the graceful spires and free-flowing designs of the marvelous city.

Silverymoon was a place for philosophers, for artists, a city known for tolerance. Here an architect could let his imagination soar along with a hundred-foot spire. Here a poet could stand on the street corner, spouting his art and earning a fair and honest living on the trinkets that passersby happened to toss his way.

Despite the seriousness of her quest, and the knowledge that she soon might walk into darkness, a wide smile grew on Catti-brie's face. She understood why Drizzt had often gone from Mithril Hall to visit this place; she never guessed that the world could be so varied and wonderful.

On impulse, the young woman moved to the side of one building, a few steps down a dark, though clean, alleyway. She took out the panther figurine and set it on the cobblestones before her.

"Come, Guenhwyvar," Catti-brie called softly. She didn't know if Drizzt had brought the panther into this city before or not, didn't know whether she was breaking any rules, but she believed that Guenhwyvar should experience this place, and believed, too, for some reason, that, in Silverymoon, she was free to follow her heart.

A gray mist surrounded the figurine, swirled, and gradually took shape. The great panther, six-hundred pounds of inky black, muscled cat, its shoulders higher than Catti-brie's waist, stood before her. Its head turned from side to side as it tried to fathom their location.

"We're in Silverymoon, Guen," Catti-brie whispered.

The panther tossed its head, as though it had just awakened, and gave a low, calm growl.

"Keep yerself close," Catti-brie instructed, "right by me side. I'm not for knowing if ye should be here or not, but I wanted ye to see the place, at least."

They came out of the alley side by side. "Have ye seen the place before, Guen?" Catti-brie asked. "I'm looking for Lady Alustriel. Might ye know where that'd be?"

R. A. Salvatore

The panther bumped close to Catti-brie's leg and moved off, apparently with purpose, and Catti-brie went right behind. Many heads turned to regard the curious couple, the road-dirty woman and her unusual companion, but the gazes were innocuous enough, and not one person screamed or hurried away in fright.

Coming around one sweeping avenue, Guenhwyvar almost ran headfirst into a pair of talking elves. They jumped back instinctively and looked from the panther to the young woman.

"Most marvelous!" one of them said in a singsong voice.

"Incredible," the other agreed. He reached toward the panther slowly, testing the reaction. "May I?" he asked Catti-brie.

She didn't see the harm and nodded.

The elf's face beamed as he ran his slender fingers along Guenhwyvar's muscled neck. He looked to his more hesitant companion, his smile seeming wide enough to take in his ears.

"Oh, buy the cat!" the other agreed excitedly.

Catti-brie winced; Guenhwyvar's ears flattened, and the panther let out a roar that echoed about the buildings throughout the city.

Catti-brie knew that elves were fast afoot, but these two were out of sight before she could even explain to them their mistake. "Guenhwyvar!" she whispered harshly into the panther's flattened ear.

The cat's ears came up, and the panther turned and rose on its haunches, putting a thick paw atop each of Catti-brie's shoulders. It bumped its head into Catti-brie's face and twisted to rub against her smooth cheek. Catti-brie had to struggle just to keep her balance and it took her a long while to explain to the panther that the apology was accepted.

As they went on, pointing fingers accompanied the stares, and more than one person slipped across the avenues ahead to get on the opposite side of the street and let the woman and cat pass. Catti-brie knew that they had attracted too much attention; she began to feel foolish for bringing Guenhwyvar here in the first place. She wanted to dismiss the cat back to the Astral Plane, but she suspected that she couldn't do so without attracting even more attention.

She wasn't surprised a few moments later, when a host of armed soldiers wearing the new silver-and-light-blue uniforms of the city guard, surrounded her at a comfortable distance.

"The panther is with you," one of them reasoned.

"Guenhwyvar," Catti-brie replied. "I am Catti-brie, daughter of Bruenor Battlehammer, Eighth King of Mithril Hall."

The man nodded and smiled, and Catti-brie relaxed with a deep sigh.

"It is indeed the drow's cat!" another of the guardsmen blurted. He blushed at his uncalled-for outburst, looked to the leader, and promptly lowered his eyes.

"Aye, Guen's the friend of Drizzt Do'Urden," Catti-brie replied. "Is he about in the city?" she couldn't help asking, though, logically, she would have preferred to ask the question of Alustriel, who might give her a more complete answer.

"Not that I have heard," replied the guard leader, "but Silverymoon is honored by your presence, Princess of Mithril Hall." He dipped a low bow, and Catti-brie blushed, not used to—or comfortable with—such treatment.

She did well to hide her disappointment about the news, reminding herself that finding Drizzt was not likely to be easy. Even if Drizzt had come into Silverymoon, he had probably done so secretly.

"I have come to speak with Lady Alustriel," Catti-brie explained.

"You should have been escorted from the gate," the guard leader groused, angered by the lack of proper protocol.

Catti-brie understood the man's frustration and realized that she had probably just gotten the unwitting soldiers at the Moonbridge, the invisible structure spanning the great River Rauvin, in trouble. "They did not know me name," she added quickly, "or me quest. I thought it best to come through on me own and see what I might."

"They did not question the presence of such a—" He wisely caught himself before saying "pet." "A panther?" he went on.

"Guen was not beside me," Catti-brie replied without thinking, then her face crinkled up, realizing the million questions she had probably just inspired.

Fortunately, the guards did not belabor the point. They had heard enough descriptions of the impassioned young woman to be satisfied that this was indeed the daughter of Bruenor Battle-hammer. They escorted Catti-brie and Guenhwyvar (at a respectful distance) through the city, to the western wall and the graceful and enchanting palace of Lady Alustriel.

Left alone in a waiting chamber, Catti-brie decided to keep Guenhwyvar by her side. The panther's presence would give her tale credibility, she decided, and if Drizzt had been about, or still was, Guenhwyvar would sense it.

The minutes slipped by uneventfully, and restless Catti-brie grew bored. She moved to a side door and gently pushed it open, revealing a decorated powder room, with a wash basin and a small, gold-trimmed table, complete with a large mirror. Atop it was an assortment of combs and brushes, a selection of small vials, and an opened coffer containing many different colored packets of dye.

Curious, the young woman looked over her shoulder to make sure that all was quiet, then moved in and sat down. She took up a brush and roughly ran it through her tangled and thick auburn hair, thinking she should try to appear her best when standing before the Lady of Silverymoon. She scowled when she noticed dirt on her cheek, and quickly dipped her hand in the water basin and rubbed it roughly over the spot, managing a smile when it was gone.

She peeked out of the anteroom again, to make sure that no one had come. Guenhwyvar, lying comfortably on the floor, looked up and growled.

"Oh, shut yer mouth," Catti-brie said, and she slipped back into the powder room and inspected the vials. She removed the tight top of one and sniffed, and her blue eyes opened wide in surprise at the powerful aroma. From outside the door, Guenhwyvar growled again and sneezed, and Catti-brie laughed. "I know what ye mean," she said to the cat.

Catti-brie went through several of the vials, crinkling her nose at some, sneezing at more than one, and finally finding one whose aroma she enjoyed. It reminded her of a field of wildflowers, not overpowering, but subtly beautiful, the background music to a spring day.

She nearly jumped out of her boots, nearly stuffed the vial up her nose, when a hand grasped her shoulder.

Catti-brie spun about, and her breath was stolen away. There stood Alustriel—it had to be!—her hair shining silver and hanging halfway down her back and her eyes sparkling more clearly than any Catti-brie had ever seen—more clearly than any eyes except Wulfgar's sky-blue orbs. The memory pained her.

Alustriel was fully half a foot above Catti-brie's five and a half, and gracefully slender. She wore a purple gown of the finest silk, with many layers that seemed to hug her womanly curves and hide them alluringly all at once. A high crown of gold and gems sat atop her head.

Guenhwyvar and the lady apparently were not strangers, for the panther lay quietly on its side, eyes closed contentedly.

For some reason that she did not understand, that bothered Catti-brie.

"I have wondered when we would at last meet," Alustriel said quietly.

Catti-brie fumbled to replace the cap on the vial and replace it on the table, but Alustriel put her long, slender hands over the young woman's (and Catti-brie felt like a young and foolish girl at that moment!) and eased the vial into her belt pouch instead.

"Drizzt has spoken often of you," Alustriel went on, "and fondly."

That thought, too, bothered Catti-brie. It might have been unintentional, she realized, but it seemed to her that Alustriel was being just a bit condescending. And Catti-brie, standing in road-dusty traveling clothes, with her hair hardly brushed, certainly was not comfortable beside the fabulous woman.

"Come to my private chambers," the lady invited. "There we might speak more comfortably." She started out, stepping over the sleeping panther. "Do come along, Guen!" she said, and the cat perked up immediately, shaking away its laziness.

"Guen?" Catti-brie mouthed silently. She had never heard anyone besides herself, and very rarely Drizzt, call the panther so familiarly. She gave a look to the cat, her expression hurt, as she obediently followed Alustriel out of the room.

What had at first seemed to Catti-brie an enchanted palace now made her feel terribly out of place as Alustriel led her along the sweeping corridors and through the fabulous rooms. Catti-brie kept looking to her own trail, wondering fearfully if she might be leaving muddy tracks across the polished floors.

Attendants and other guests—true nobility, the young woman realized—stared as the unlikely caravan passed, and Catti-brie could not return the gazes. She felt small, so very small, as she walked behind the tall and beautiful Alustriel.

Catti-brie was glad when they entered Alustriel's private sitting room and the lady closed the door behind them.

Guenhwyvar padded over and hopped up on a thickly upholstered divan, and Catti-brie's eyes widened in shock.

"Get off there!" she whispered harshly at the panther, but Alustriel only chuckled as she walked past, dropping a hand absently on the comfortable cat's head and motioning for Catti-brie to take a seat.

Again Catti-brie turned an angry gaze on Guenhwyvar, feeling somewhat betrayed. How many times had Guenhwyvar plopped down on that very same couch? she wondered.

"What brings the daughter of King Bruenor to my humble city?" Alustriel asked. "I wish I had known that you would be coming. I could have better prepared."

"I seek Drizzt," Catti-brie answered curtly, then winced and sat back at the sharper-than-intended tone of her reply.

Alustriel's expression immediately grew curious. "Drizzt?" she echoed. "I have not seen Drizzt in some time. I had hoped that you would tell me that he, too, was in the city, or at least on his way."

Suspicious as she was, thinking that Drizzt would try to avoid her and that Alustriel would undoubtedly go along with his wishes, Catti-brie found that she believed the woman.

"Ah, well." Alustriel sighed, sincerely and obviously disappointed. She perked up immediately. "And how is your father?" she asked politely. "And that handsome Wulfgar?"

Alustriel's expression changed suddenly, as though she had just realized that something must be terribly out of place. "Your wedding?" she asked hesitantly as Catti-brie's lips thinned in a scowl. "I was preparing to visit Mithril Hall . . ."

Alustriel paused and studied Catti-brie for a long while.

Catti-brie sniffed and braced herself. "Wulfgar is dead," she said evenly, "and me father is not as ye remember him. I've come in search of Drizzt, who has gone out from the halls."

"What has happened?" Alustriel demanded.

Catti-brie rose from her chair. "Guenhwyvar!" she called, rousing the panther. "I've not the time for tales," she said curtly to Alustriel. "If Drizzt has not come to Silverymoon, then I've taken too much of yer time already, and too much o' me own."

She headed for the door and noticed it briefly glow blue, its wood seeming to expand and tighten in the jam. Catti-brie walked up to it anyway and tugged on the handle, to no avail.

Catti-brie took a few deep breaths, counted to ten, then to twenty, and turned to face Alustriel.

"I've a friend needing me," she explained, her tone even and dangerous. "Ye'd best be opening the door." In days to come, when she looked back on that moment, Catti-brie would hardly believe that she had threatened Alustriel, the ruler of the northwest's largest and most powerful inland city! She had threatened Alustriel, reputably among the most powerful mages in all the north!

At that time, though, the fiery young woman meant every grim word.

"I can help," Alustriel, obviously worried, offered. "But first you must tell me what has transpired."

"Drizzt hasn't the time," Catti-brie growled. She tugged futilely on the wizard-locked door again, then banged a fist against it and looked over her shoulder to glare at Alustriel, who had risen and was slowly walking her way. Guenhwyvar remained on the divan, though the cat had lifted its head and was regarding the two intently.

"I have to find him," Catti-brie said.

"And where will you look?" replied Alustriel, her hands out defenselessly as she stepped before the young woman.

The simple question took the bluster out of Catti-brie's ire. Where indeed? she wondered. Where to even begin? She felt helpless, standing there, in a place she did not belong. Helpless and foolish and wanting nothing more than to be back home, beside her father and her friends, beside Wulfgar and Drizzt, with everything the way it had been . . . before the dark elves had come to Mithril Hall.

Chapter 6

DIVINE SIGN

atti-brie awoke the next morning on a pillowy soft bed in a plush chamber filled with fine lace draperies that let the filtered sunrise gently greet her sleepy gaze. She was not used to such places, wasn't even used to sleeping above ground.

She had refused a bath the night before, even though Lady Alustriel had promised her that the exotic oils and soaps would bubble around her and refresh her. To Catti-brie's dwarven-reared sensibilities, this was all nonsense and, worse, weakness. She bathed often, but in the chill waters of a mountain stream and

70

without scented oils from far-off lands. Drizzt had told her that the dark elves could track enemies by their scent for miles through the Underdark's twisting caverns, and it seemed silly to Catti-brie to bath in aromatic oils and possibly aid her enemies.

This morning, though, with the sun cascading through the gauzy curtains, and the wash basin filled again with steamy water, the young woman reconsidered. "Suren ye're a stubborn one," she quietly accused Lady Alustriel, realizing that Alustriel's magic was likely the reason that steam once again rose off the water.

Catti-brie eyed the line of bottles and considered the long and dirty road ahead, a road from which she might never return. Something welled inside her then, a need to indulge herself just once, and before her pragmatic side could argue, she had stripped off her clothes and was sitting in the hot tub, the fizzing bubbles thick about her.

At first, she kept glancing nervously to the room's door, but soon she just let herself sink lower in the tub, perfectly relaxed, her skin warm and tingling.

"I told you." The words jolted Catti-brie from her near-slumber. She sat up straight, then sank back immediately, embarrassed, as she noticed not only Lady Alustriel, but a curious dwarf, his beard and hair snowy white and his gowns silken and flowing.

"In Mithril Hall, we've the habit o' knocking before we go into someone's private room," Catti-brie, regaining a measure of her dignity, remarked.

"I did knock," Alustriel replied. "You were lost in the warmth of the bath."

Catti-brie brushed her wet hair back from her face, getting a handful of suds on her cheek. She managed to salvage her pride and ignore the froth for a moment, then angrily slapped it away.

Alustriel merely smiled.

"Ye can be leaving," she snapped at the too dignified lady.

"Drizzt is indeed making for Menzoberranzan," Alustriel announced, and Catti-brie came forward again, anxiously, her embarrassment lost in the face of more important news.

"I ventured into the spirit world last night," Alustriel explained. "There one might find many answers. Drizzt traveled north of Silverymoon, through the Moonwood, on a straight line for the

71

mountains surrounding Dead Orc Pass."

Catti-brie's expression remained quizzical.

"That is where Drizzt first walked from the Underdark," Alustriel went on, "in a cave east of the fabled pass. It is my guess that he means to return by the same route that led him from the darkness."

"Get me there," the young woman demanded, rising from the water, too intent for modesty.

"I will provide mounts," Alustriel said as she handed the younger woman a thick towel. "Enchanted horses will allow you to speed across the land. The journey should take you no more than two days."

"Ye cannot use yer magic to just send me there?" Catti-brie asked. Her tone was sharp, as though she believed that Alustriel was not doing all that she could.

"I do not know cave's location," the silver-haired lady explained.

Catti-brie stopped toweling herself, nearly dropped her clothing, which she had gathered together, and stared blankly, helplessly.

"That is why I have brought Fret," Alustriel explained, holding up a hand to calm the young woman.

"Fredegar Rockcrusher," the dwarf corrected in a strangely melodic, singsong voice, and he swept his arm out dramatically and dipped a graceful bow. Catti-brie thought he sounded somewhat like an elf trapped in a dwarf's body. She furrowed her brow as she closely regarded him for the first time; she had been around dwarves all of her life and had never seen one quite like this. His beard was neatly trimmed, his robes perfectly clean, and his skin did not show the usual hardness, rockiness. Too many baths in scented oils, the young woman decided, and she looked contemptuously at the steaming tub.

"Fret was with the party that first tracked Drizzt from the Underdark," Alustriel continued. "After Drizzt had left the area, my curious sister and her companions backtracked the drow's trail and located the cave, the entrance to the deep tunnels.

"I hesitate to point the way for you," the Lady of Silverymoon said after a long pause, her concern for the young woman's safety evident in her tone and expression.

Catti-brie's blue eyes narrowed, and she quickly pulled on her breeches. She would not be looked down upon, not even by Alustriel, and would not have others deciding her course.

"I see," remarked Alustriel with a nod of her head. Her immediate understanding set Catti-brie back.

Alustriel motioned for Fret to retrieve Catti-brie's pack. A sour expression crossed the tidy dwarf's face as he moved near the dirty thing, and he lifted it gingerly by two extended fingers. He glanced forlornly at Alustriel, and when she did not bother to look back at him, he left the room.

"I did not ask ye for any companion," Catti-brie stated bluntly.

"Fret is a guide to the entrance," Alustriel corrected, "and nothing more. Your courage is admirable, if a bit blind," she added, and before the young woman could find the words to reply, Alustriel was gone.

Catti-brie stood silently for a few moments, water from her wet hair dripping down her bare back. She fought away the feeling that she was just a little girl in a big and dangerous world, that she was small indeed beside the tall and powerful Lady Alustriel.

But the doubts lingered.

Two hours later, after a fine meal and a check on provisions, Catti-brie and Fret walked out of Silverymoon's eastern gate, the Sundabar Gate, beside Lady Alustriel, an entourage of soldiers keeping a respectful but watchful distance from their leader.

A black mare and a shaggy gray pony awaited the two travelers.

"Must I?" Fret asked for perhaps the twentieth time since they had left the castle. "Would not a detailed map suffice?"

Alustriel just smiled and otherwise ignored the tidy dwarf. Fret hated anything that might get him dirty, anything that would keep him from his duties as Alustriel's best-loved sage. Certainly the road into the wilds near Dead Orc Pass qualified on both counts.

"The horseshoes are enchanted, and your mounts will fly like the wind itself," Alustriel explained to Catti-brie. The silver-haired woman looked over her shoulder to the grumbling dwarf.

Catti-brie was not quick to respond, offered no thanks for Alustriel's effort. She had said nothing to Alustriel since their meeting earlier that morning, and had carried herself with an unmistakably cool demeanor.

"With luck, you will arrive at the cave before Drizzt," Alustriel said. "Reason with him and bring him home, I beg. He has no place in the Underdark, not anymore."

"Drizzt's 'place' is his own to decide," Catti-brie retorted, but she was really implying that her own place was hers to decide.

"Of course," Alustriel agreed, and she flashed that smile—that knowing grin that Catti-brie felt belittled her—again.

"I did not hinder you," Alustriel pointed out. "I have done my best to aid your chosen course, whether I think it a wise choice or not."

Catti-brie snickered. "Ye just had to add that last thought," she replied.

"Am I not entitled to my opinion?" Alustriel asked.

"Entitled to it and givin' it to all who'll hear," Catti-brie remarked, and Alustriel, though she understood the source of the young woman's demeanor, was plainly surprised.

Catti-brie snickered again and kicked her horse into a walk.

"You love him," Alustriel said.

Catti-brie pulled hard on the reins to stop her horse and turn it halfway about. Now she wore the expression of surprise.

"The drow," Alustriel said, more to bolster her last statement, to reveal her honest belief, than to clarify something that obviously needed no further explanation.

Catti-brie chewed on her lip, as though seeking a response, then turned her mount roughly about and kicked away.

"It's a long road," Fret whined.

"Then hurry back to me," Alustriel said, "with Catti-brie and Drizzt beside you."

"As you wish, my lady," the obedient dwarf replied, kicking his pony into a gallop. "As you wish."

Alustriel stood at the eastern gate, watching, long after Catti-brie and Fret had departed. It was one of those not-so-rare moments when the Lady of Silverymoon wished that she was not encumbered with the responsibilities of government. Truly, Alustriel would have preferred to grab a horse of her own and ride out beside Catti-brie, even to venture into the Underdark, if necessary, to find the remarkable drow that had become her friend.

But she could not. Drizzt Do'Urden, after all, was a small player in a wide world, a world that continually begged audience at the

Lady of Silverymoon's busy court.

"Good speed, daughter of Bruenor," the beautiful, silver-haired woman said under her breath. "Good speed and fare well."

* * * * *

Drizzt eased his mount along the stony trail, ascending into the mountains. The breeze was warm and the sky clear, but a storm had hit this region in the last few days, and the trail remained somewhat muddy. Finally, fearing that his horse would slip and break a leg, Drizzt dismounted and led the beast carefully, cautiously.

He had seen the shadowing elf many times that morning, for the trails were fairly open, and in the up-and-down process of climbing mountains, the two riders were not often far apart. Drizzt was not overly surprised when he went around a bend to find the elf approaching from a trail that had been paralleling his own.

The pale-skinned elf, too, walked his mount, and he nodded in approval to see Drizzt doing likewise. He paused, still twenty feet from the drow, as though he did not know how he should react.

"If you have come to watch over the horse, then you might as well ride, or walk, beside me," Drizzt called. Again the elf nodded, and he walked his shining black stallion up to the side of Drizzt's black-and-white mount.

Drizzt looked ahead, up the mountain trail. "This will be the last day I will need the horse," he explained. "I do not know that I will ride again, actually."

"You do not mean to come out of these mountains?" the elf asked.

Drizzt ran a hand through his flowing white mane, surprised by the finality of those words, and by their truth.

"I seek a grove not far from here," he said, "once the home of Montolio DeBrouchee."

"The blind ranger," the elf acknowledged.

Drizzt was surprised by the elf's recognition. He considered his pale companion's reply and studied him closely. Nothing about the moon elf indicated that he was a ranger, but he knew of Montolio. "It is fitting that the name Montolio DeBrouchee lives on in legend," the drow decided aloud.

75

"And what of the name Drizzt Do'Urden?" the moon elf, full of surprises, asked. He smiled at Drizzt's expression and added, "Yes, I know of you, dark elf."

"Then you have the advantage," Drizzt remarked.

"I am Tarathiel," the moon elf said. "It was no accident that you were met on your passage through the Moonwood. When my small clan discovered that you were afoot, we decided that it would be best for Ellifain to meet you."

"The maiden?" Drizzt reasoned.

Tarathiel nodded, his features seeming almost translucent in the sunlight. "We did not know how she would react to the sight of a drow. You have our apologies."

Drizzt nodded his acceptance. "She is not of your clan," he guessed. "Or at least, she was not, not when she was very young."

Tarathiel did not reply, but the intrigue that was splayed across his face showed Drizzt that he was on the right track.

"Her people were slaughtered by drow," Drizzt went on, fearing the expected confirmation.

"What do you know?" Tarathiel demanded, his voice taking a hard edge for the first time in the conversation.

"I was among that raiding party," Drizzt admitted. Tarathiel went for his sword, but Drizzt, lightning fast, grabbed hold of his wrist.

"I killed no elves," Drizzt explained. "The only ones I wanted to fight were those who had accompanied me to the surface."

Tarathiel's muscles relaxed, and he pulled his hand away. "Ellifain remembers little of the tragedy. She speaks of it more in dreams than in her waking hours, and then she rambles." He paused and stared Drizzt squarely in the eye. "She has mentioned purple eyes," he said. "We did not know what to make of that, and she, when questioned about it, cannot offer any answers. Purple is not a common color for drow eyes, so say our legends."

"It is not," Drizzt confirmed, and his voice was distant as he remembered again that terrible day so long ago. This was the elf maiden! The one that a younger Drizzt Do'Urden had risked all to save, the one whose eyes had shown Drizzt beyond doubt that the ways of his people were not the ways of his heart.

"And so, when we heard of Drizzt Do'Urden, drow friend—

drow friend with purple eyes—of the dwarven king that has reclaimed Mithril Hall, we thought that it would be best for Ellifain to face her past," Tarathiel explained.

Again Drizzt, his mind looking more to the past than to the mountain scenery about him, merely nodded.

Tarathiel let it go at that. Ellifain had, apparently, viewed her past, and the sight had nearly broken her.

The moon elf refused Drizzt's request for him to take the horses and leave and, later that day, the two were riding again, along a narrow trail on a high pass, a way that Drizzt remembered well. He thought of Montolio, Mooshie, his surface mentor, the blind old ranger who could shoot a bow by the guidance of a pet owl's hoots. Montolio had been the one to teach a younger Drizzt of a god figure that embodied the same emotions that stirred Drizzt's heart and the same precepts that guided the renegade drow's conscience. Mielikki was her name, goddess of the forest, and since his time with Montolio, Drizzt Do'Urden had walked under her silent guidance.

Drizzt felt a wellspring of emotions bubbling within him as the trail wound away from the ridge and climbed a steeper incline through a region of broken boulders. He was terrified of what he might find. Perhaps an orc horde—the wretched humanoids were all too common in this region—had taken over the old ranger's wondrous grove. Suppose a fire had burned it away, leaving a barren scar upon the land?

They came into a thick copse of trees, plodding along a narrow but fairly clean trail, with Drizzt in the lead. He saw the wood thinning ahead, and beyond it a small field. He stopped his black-and-white horse and glanced back at Tarathiel.

"The grove," he explained, and he slipped from his saddle, Tarathiel doing likewise. They tethered the horses under the cover of the copse and crept side by side to the wood's end.

There stood Mooshie's grove, perhaps sixty yards across, north to south, and half that wide. The pines stood tall and straight—no fire had struck this grove—and the rope bridges that the blind ranger had constructed could still be seen running from tree to tree at various heights. Even the low stone wall stood intact, not a rock out of place, and the grass was low.

"Someone is living in there," Tarathiel reasoned, for the place had obviously not grown wild. When he looked to Drizzt, he saw that the drow, features set and grim, had scimitars in his hands, one glowing a soft bluish light.

Tarathiel strung his long bow as Drizzt crawled out from the brush and skittered over to the rock wall. Then the moon elf rushed off, joining his drow companion.

"I have seen the signs of many orcs since we entered the mountains," Tarathiel whispered. He pulled back on his bowstring and nodded grimly. "For Montolio?"

Drizzt returned the nod and inched up to peek over the stone wall. He expected to see orcs, and expected to see dead orcs soon after.

The drow froze in place, his arms falling limply at his sides and his breath suddenly hard to come by.

Tarathiel nudged him, looking for an answer, but with none forthcoming, the elf took up his bow and peeked over the wall.

At first he saw nothing, but then he followed Drizzt's unblinking gaze to the south, to a small break in the trees, where a branch was bobbing as though something had just brushed against it. Tarathiel caught a flash of white from the shadows beyond. A horse, he thought.

It came from the shadows then, a powerful steed wearing a coat of gleaming white. Its unusual eyes glowed fiery pink, and an ivory horn, easily half the height of the elf's body, protruded from its forehead. The unicorn looked in the companions' general direction, pawed the ground, and snorted.

Tarathiel had the good sense to duck low, and he pulled the stunned Drizzt Do'Urden down beside him.

"Unicorn!" the elf mouthed silently to Drizzt, and the drow's hand instinctively went under the front collar of his traveling cloak, to the unicorn's-head pendant Regis had carved for him from the bone of a knucklehead trout.

Tarathiel pointed back to the thick copse of trees and signaled that he and Drizzt should be leaving, but the drow shook his head. His composure returned, Drizzt again peeked over the stone wall.

The area was clear, with no indication that the unicorn was about.

"We should be gone," Tarathiel said, as soon as he, too, discerned that the powerful steed was no longer close. "Take heart that Montolio's grove is in the best of care."

Drizzt sat up on the wall, peering intently into the tangle of pines. A unicorn! The symbol of Mielikki, the purest symbol of the natural world. To a ranger, there was no more perfect beast, and to Drizzt, there could be no more perfect guardian for the grove of Montolio DeBrouchee. He would have liked to remain in the area for some time, would have dearly liked to glimpse the elusive creature again, but he knew that time was pressing and that dark corridors awaited.

He looked to Tarathiel and smiled, then turned to leave.

But he found the way across the small field blocked by the mighty unicorn.

"How did she do that?" Tarathiel asked. There was no need to whisper anymore, for the unicorn was staring straight at them, pawing the ground nervously and rolling its powerful head.

"He," Drizzt corrected, noticing the steed's white beard, a trait of the male unicorn. A thought came over Drizzt then, and he slipped his scimitars into their sheaths and hopped up from his seat.

"How did *he* do that?" Tarathiel corrected. "I heard no hoofbeats." The elf's eyes brightened suddenly, and he looked back to the grove. "Unless there are more than one!"

"There is only one," Drizzt assured him. "There is a bit of magic within a unicorn, as this one, by slipping behind us, has proven."

"Go around to the south," Tarathiel whispered. "And I will go north. If we do not threaten the beast, . . ." The moon elf stopped, seeing that Drizzt was already moving—straight out from the wall.

"Take care," Tarathiel warned. "Beautiful indeed are the unicorns, but, by all accounts, they can be dangerous and unpredictable."

Drizzt held a hand up behind him to silence the elf and continued his slow pace from the stone wall. The unicorn neighed and tossed its great head, mane flying wildly. It slammed a hoof into the ground, digging a fair-sized hole in the soft turf.

"Drizzt Do'Urden," Tarathiel warned.

By all reasoning, Drizzt should have turned back. The unicorn could have easily run him down, squashed him into the prairie, and the great beast seemed to grow more and more agitated with each step the drow took.

But the beast did not run off, and neither did it lower its great horn and skewer Drizzt. Soon, the drow was just a few steps away, feeling small beside the magnificent steed.

Drizzt reached out a hand, fingers moving slowly, delicately. He felt the outer strands of the unicorn's thick and glistening coat, then moved in another step and stroked the magnificent beast's muscled neck.

The drow could hardly breathe; he wished that Guenhwyvar were beside him, to witness such perfection of nature. He wished that Catti-brie were here, for she would appreciate this vision as much as he.

He looked back to Tarathiel, the elf sitting on the stone wall and smiling contentedly. Tarathiel's expression turned to one of surprise, and Drizzt looked back to see his hand stroking the empty air.

The unicorn was gone.

Part 2

PRAYERS UNANSWERED

ot since the day I walked out of Menzoberranzan have I been so torn about a pending decision. I sat near the entrance of a cave, looking out at the mountains before me, with the tunnel leading to the Underdark at my back.

This was the moment in which I had believed my adventure would begin. When I had set out from Mithril Hall, I had given little thought to the part of my journey that would take me to this cave, taking for granted that the trip would be uneventful.

Then I had glimpsed Ellifain, the maiden I had saved more than three decades before, when she had been just a frightened child. I wanted to go to *her again, to speak with her and help her overcome the trauma of that ter-rible drow raid. I wanted to run out of that cave and catch up with Tarathiel, and ride beside the elf back to the Moonwood.*

But I could not ignore the issues that had brought me to this place.

I had known from the outset that visiting Montolio's grove, the place of so many fond memories, would prove an emotional, even spiritual, expe-rience. He had been my first surface friend, my mentor, the one who had guided me to Mielikki. I can never express the joy I felt in learning that Montolio's grove was under the protective eye of a unicorn.

A unicorn! I have seen a unicorn, the symbol of my goddess, the pin-nacle of natural perfection! I might well be the first of my race to have ever touched the soft mane and muscled neck of such a beast, the first to encounter a unicorn in friendship. It is a rare pleasure to glimpse the signs that a unicorn has been about, and rarer still to ever gaze at one. Few in the Realms can say that they have ever been near a unicorn; fewer still have ever touched one.

I have.

Was it a sign from my goddess? In good faith, I had to believe that it was, that Mielikki had reached out to me in a tangible and thrilling way. But what did it mean?

I rarely pray. I prefer to speak to my goddess through my daily actions, and through my honest emotions. I need not gloss over what has occurred with petty words, twisting them to show myself most favorably. If Mielikki is with me, then she knows the truth, knows how I act and how I feel.

I prayed that night in the cave entrance, though. I prayed for guidance, for something that would indicate the significance of the unicorn's appear-ance. The unicorn allowed me to touch it; it accepted me, and that is the highest honor a ranger can ask. But what was the implication of that honor?

Was Mielikki telling me that here, on the surface, I was, and would continue to be, accepted, and that I should not leave this place? Or was the unicorn's appearance to show me the goddess's approval of my choice to return to Menzoberranzan?

Or was the unicorn Mielikki's special way of saying "farewell?"

That last thought haunted me all through the night. For the first time since I had set out from Mithril Hall, I began to consider what I, Drizzt Do'Urden, had to lose. I thought of my friends, Montolio and Wulfgar, who had passed on from this world, and thought of those others I would likely never see again.

A host of questions assailed me. Would Bruenor ever get over the loss of his adopted son? And would Catti-brie overcome her own grief? Would the enchanted sparkle, the sheer love of life, ever return to her blue eyes? Would I ever again prop my weary head against Guenhwyvar's muscled flank?

More than ever, I wanted to run from the cave, home to Mithril Hall, and stand beside my friends, to see them through their grief, to guide them and listen to them and simply embrace them.

Again I could not ignore the issues that had brought me to this cave. I could go back to Mithril Hall, but so could my dark kin. I did not blame myself for Wulfgar's death—I could not have known that the dark elves would come. And now I could not deny my understanding of the awful ways and continuing hunger of Lloth. If the drow returned and extinguished that—cherished!—light in Catti-brie's eyes, then Drizzt Do'Urden would die a thousand horrible deaths.

I prayed all that night, but found no divine guidance. In the end, as always, I came to realize that I had to follow what I knew in my heart was the right course, had to trust that what was in my heart was in accord with Mielikki's will.

I left the fire blazing at the entrance of that cave. I needed to see its light, to gain courage from it, for as many steps as possible as I walked into the tunnel. As I walked into darkness.

—Drizzt Do'Urden

Chapter 7

UNFINISHED BUSINESS

erg'inyon Baenre hung upside down from the huge cavern's roof, securely strapped to the saddle of his lizard mount. It had taken the young warrior some time to get used to this position, but as commander of the Baenre lizard-riders, he spent many hours watching the city from this high vantage point.

A movement to the side, behind a cluster of stalactites, put Berg'inyon on the alert. He lowered his ten-foot-long death lance with one hand; the other held the lizard's bridle while resting on the hilt of his ready hand-crossbow.

"I am the son of House Baenre," he said aloud, figuring that to be enough of a threat to defeat any possible foul play. He glanced around, looking for support, and moved his free hand to his belt pouch and his signal speculum, a shielded metal strip heated on one side and used to communicate with creatures using infravision. Dozens of other House Baenre lizard riders were about and would come rushing to Berg'inyon's call.

"I am the son of House Baenre," he said again.

The youngest Baenre relaxed almost immediately when his older brother Dantrag, emerged from behind the stalactites, riding an even larger subterranean lizard. Curious indeed did the elder Baenre look with his ponytail hanging straight down from the top of his upside-down head.

"As am I," Dantrag replied, skittering his sticky-footed mount beside Berg'inyon's.

"What are you doing up here?" Berg'inyon asked. "And how did you appropriate the mount without my permission?"

Dantrag scoffed at the question. "Appropriate?" he replied. "I am the weapon master of House Baenre. I took the lizard, and needed no permission from Berg'inyon."

The younger Baenre stared with red-glowing eyes, but said nothing more.

"You forget who trained you, my brother," Dantrag remarked quietly.

The statement was true; Berg'inyon would never forget, could never forget, that Dantrag had been his mentor.

"Are you prepared to face the likes of Drizzt Do'Urden again?" The blunt question nearly sent Berg'inyon from his mount.

"It would seem a possibility, since we are to travel to Mithril Hall," Dantrag added coolly.

Berg'inyon blew a long and low sigh, thoroughly flustered. He and Drizzt had been classmates at Melee-Magthere, the Academy's school of fighters. Berg'inyon, trained by Dantrag, had gone there fully expecting to be the finest fighter in his class. Drizzt Do'Urden, the renegade, the traitor, had beaten him for that honor every year. Berg'inyon had done well at the Academy, by every standard except Dantrag's.

"Are you prepared for him?" Dantrag pressed, his tone growing more serious and angry.

"No!" Berg'inyon glowered at his brother, sitting astride the hanging lizard, a cocky grin on his handsome face. Dantrag had forced the answer for a reason, Berg'inyon knew. Dantrag wanted to make certain that Berg'inyon knew his place as a spectator if they should happen to encounter the rogue Do'Urden together.

And Berg'inyon knew, too, why his brother wanted the first try at Drizzt. Drizzt had been trained by Zak'nafein, Dantrag's principal rival, the one weapon master in Menzoberranzan whose fighting skills were more highly regarded than those of Dantrag. By all accounts, Drizzt had become at least Zak'nafein's equal, and if Dantrag could defeat Drizzt, then he might at last come out from under Zak'nafein's considerable shadow.

"You have fought us both," Dantrag said slyly. "Do tell me, dear brother, who is the better?"

Berg'inyon couldn't possibly answer that question. He hadn't fought against, or even beside, Drizzt Do'Urden for more than thirty years. "Drizzt would cut you down," he said anyway, just to peeve his upstart sibling.

Dantrag's hand flashed faster than Berg'inyon could follow. The weapon master sent his wickedly sharp sword across the top strap of Berg'inyon's saddle, easily cutting the binding, though it was enchanted for strength. Dantrag's second hand came across equally fast, slipping the bridle from the lizard's mouthpiece as Berg'inyon plummeted from his seat.

The younger brother turned upright as he fell. He looked into that area of innate magic common to all drow, and stronger in drow nobles. Soon the descent had ceased, countered by a levitation spell that had Berg'inyon, death lance still in hand, slowly rising back up to meet his laughing brother.

Matron Baenre would kill you if she knew that you had embarrassed me so in front of the common soldiers, Berg'inyon's hand flashed in the silent code.

Better to have your pride cut than your throat, Dantrag's hands flashed in reply, and the older Baenre walked his mount away, back around the stalactites.

Beside the lizard again, Berg'inyon worked to retie the top strap and fasten together the bridle. He had claimed Drizzt to be the better fighter, but, in considering what Dantrag had just done to him, a perfectly aimed two-hit attack before he could even begin to retaliate, the younger Baenre doubted his claim. Drizzt Do'Urden, he decided, would be the one to pity if and when the two fighters faced off.

The thought pleased young Berg'inyon. Since his days in the Academy, he had lived in Drizzt's shadow, much as Dantrag had lived in Zak'nafein's. If Dantrag defeated Drizzt, then the Brothers Baenre would be proven the stronger fighters, and Berg'inyon's reputation would rise simply because of his standing as Dantrag's protegee. Berg'inyon liked the thought, liked that he stood to gain without having to stand toe-to-toe against that devilish purple-eyed Do'Urden again.

Perhaps the fight would come to an even more promising conclusion, Berg'inyon dared to hope. Perhaps Dantrag would kill Drizzt, and then, weary and probably wounded, Dantrag would fall easy prey to Berg'inyon's sword. Berg'inyon's reputation, as well as his position, would rise further, for he would be the logical choice to replace his dead brother in the coveted position as weapon master.

The young Baenre rolled over in midair to find his place on the repaired saddle, smiling evilly at the possibilities afforded him in this upcoming journey to Mithril Hall.

* * * * *

"Jerlys," the drow whispered grimly.

"Jerlys Horlbar?" Jarlaxle asked, and the mercenary leaned against the rough wall of the stalagmite pillar to consider the startling news. Jerlys Horlbar was a matron mother, one of the two high priestesses presiding over House Horlbar, the twelfth house of Menzoberranzan. Here she lay, dead, under a pile of rubble, her tentacle rod ruined and buried beside her.

It is good we followed him, the soldier's flicking fingers remarked, more to placate the mercenary leader than to make any pertinent revelations. Of course it was good that Jarlaxle had ordered that one followed. He was dangerous, incredibly dangerous, but, seeing a matron mother, a high priestess of the Spider Queen, lying dead, sliced by a wicked sword, the mercenary had to wonder if he, too, had underestimated.

We can report it and absolve ourselves of responsibility, another of Bregan D'aerthe's dark band signaled.

At first, that notion struck Jarlaxle as sound advice. The matron mother's body would be found, and there would be a serious inquiry, by House Horlbar if by no one else. Guilt by association was a very real thing in Menzoberranzan, especially for such a serious crime, and Jarlaxle wanted no part of a covert war with the twelfth house, not now, with so many other important events brewing.

Then Jarlaxle let the circumstances lead him down another avenue of possibility. As unfortunate as this event seemed, the mercenary might still turn it to profit. There was at least one wild card in this game that Matron Baenre played, an unknown factor that could take the impending chaos to new levels of glory.

Bury her once more, the mercenary signaled, *deeper under the pile this time, but not completely. I want the body found, but not for a while.*

His hard boots making not a sound, his ample jewelry quiet, the mercenary leader started from the alley.

Are we to rendezvous? one soldier flashed to him.

Jarlaxle shook his head and continued on, out of the remote alley. He knew where to find the one who had killed Jerlys Horlbar, and knew, too, that he could use this information against him, perhaps to heighten his slavish loyalty to Bregan D'aerthe, or perhaps for other reasons. Jarlaxle had to play the whole thing very carefully, he knew. He had to walk a narrow line between intrigue and warfare.

None in the city could do that better.

* * * * *

Uthegental will be prominent in the days to come.

Dantrag Baenre cringed when the thought drifted into his mind. He understood its source, and its subtle meaning. He and the weapon master of House Barrison Del'Armgo, House Baenre's chief rival, were considered the two greatest fighters in the city.

Matron Baenre will use his skills, the next telepathic message warned. Dantrag drew out his surface-stolen sword and looked at it.

It flared a thin red line of light along its impossibly sharp edge, and the two rubies set into the eyes of its demon-sculpted pommel flared with inner life.

Dantrag's hand clasped the pommel and warmed as Khazid'hea, Cutter, continued its communication. *He is strong and will fare well in the raids on Mithril Hall. He lusts for the blood of the young Do'Urden, the legacy of Zak'nafein, as greatly as you do—perhaps even more.*

Dantrag sneered at that last remark, thrown in only because Khazid'hea wanted him on the edge of anger. The sword considered Dantrag its partner, not its master, and knew that it could better manipulate Dantrag if he was angry.

After many decades wielding Khazid'hea, Dantrag, too, knew all of this, and he forced himself to keep calm.

"None desire Drizzt Do'Urden's death more than I," Dantrag assured the doubting sword. "And Matron Baenre will see to it that I, not Uthegental, have the opportunity to slay the renegade. Matron Baenre would not want the honors that would undoubtedly accompany such a feat to be granted to a warrior of the second house."

The sword's red line flared again in intensity and reflected in Dantrag's amber eyes. *Kill Uthegental, and her task will become easier*, Khazid'hea reasoned.

Dantrag laughed aloud at the notion, and Khazid'hea's fiendish eyes flared again. "Kill him?" Dantrag echoed. "Kill one that Matron Baenre has deemed important for the mission ahead? She would flay the skin from my bones!"

But you could kill him?

Dantrag laughed again, for the question was simply to mock him, to urge him on to the fight that Khazid'hea had desired for so very long. The sword was proud, at least as proud as either Dantrag or Uthegental, and it wanted desperately to be in the hands of the indisputably finest weapon master of Menzoberranzan, whichever of the two that might be.

"You must pray that I could," Dantrag replied, turning the tables on the impetuous sword. "Uthegental favors his trident, and no sword. If he proved the victor, then Khazid'hea might end up in the scabbard of a lesser fighter."

He would wield me.

Dantrag slid the sword away, thinking the preposterous claim not even worth answering. Also tired of this useless banter, Khazid'hea went silent, brooding.

The sword had opened some concerns for Dantrag. He knew the importance of this upcoming assault. If he could strike down the young Do'Urden, then all glory would be his, but if Uthegental got there first, then Dantrag would be considered second best in the city, a rank he could never shake unless he found and killed Uthegental. His mother would not be pleased by such events, Dantrag knew. Dantrag's life had been miserable when Zak'nafein Do'Urden had been alive, with Matron Baenre constantly urging him to find and slay the legendary weapon master.

This time, Matron Baenre probably wouldn't even allow him that option. With Berg'inyon coming into excellence as a fighter, Matron Baenre might simply sacrifice Dantrag and turn the coveted position of weapon master over to her younger son. If she could claim that the move was made because Berg'inyon was the better fighter, that would again spread doubt among the populace as to which house had the finest weapon master.

The solution was simple: Dantrag had to get Drizzt.

Chapter 8

OUT OF PLACE

e moved without a whisper along the lightless tunnels, his eyes glowing lavender, seeking changes in the heat patterns along the floor and walls that would indicate bends, or enemies, in the tunnel. He seemed at home, a creature of the Underdark, moving with typically quiet grace and cautious posture.

Drizzt did not feel at home, though. Already he was deeper than the lowest tunnels of Mithril Hall, and the stagnant air pressed in on him. He had spent nearly two decades on the surface, learning and living by the rules that governed the outer world. Those rules were as different to Underdark precepts as a forest wildflower was to a deep cavern fungus. A human, a goblin, even an alert surface elf, would have taken no note of Drizzt's silent passage, though he might cross just a few feet away, but Drizzt felt clumsy and loud.

The drow ranger cringed with every step, fearing that echoes were resounding along the blank stone walls hundreds of yards away. This was the Underdark, a place negotiated less by sight than by hearing and the sense of smell.

Drizzt had spent nearly two-thirds of his life in the Underdark, and a good portion of the last twenty years underground in the caverns of Clan Battlehammer. He no longer considered himself a creature of the Underdark, though. He had left his heart behind on a mountainside, watching the stars and the moon, the sunrise and the sunset.

This was the land of starless nights—no, not nights, just a single, unending starless night, Drizzt decided—of stagnant air, and leering stalactites.

The tunnel's width varied greatly, sometimes as narrow as the breadth of Drizzt's shoulders, sometimes wide enough for a dozen men to walk abreast. The floor sloped slightly, taking Drizzt even deeper, but the ceiling paralleled it well, remaining fairly consistent at about twice the height of the five-and-a-half-foot drow. For a long time, Drizzt detected no side caverns or corridors, and he was glad of that, for he didn't want to be forced into any direction decisions yet, and in this simple setup, any potential enemies would have to come at him from straight ahead.

Drizzt honestly believed that he was not prepared for any surprises, not yet. Even his infravision pained him. His head throbbed as he tried to sort out and interpret the varying heat patterns. In his younger years, Drizzt had gone for weeks, even months, with his eyes tuned exclusively to the infrared spectrum, looking for heat instead of reflected light. But now, with his eyes so used to the sun above and the torches lining the corridors of Mithril Hall, he found the infravision jarring.

Finally, he drew out Twinkle, and the enchanted scimitar glowed with a soft bluish light. Drizzt rested back against the wall and let his eyes revert to the regular spectrum, then used the sword as a guiding light. Soon after, he came to a six-way intersection, two crossing horizontal corridors intersected by a vertical shaft.

Drizzt tucked Twinkle away and looked above, up the shaft. He saw no heat sources, but was little comforted. Many of the Underdark's predators could mask their body temperatures, like a surface tiger used its stripes to crawl through thick strands of high grass. Dreaded hook horrors, for example, had developed an exoskeleton; the bony plates shielded the creature's body heat so that they appeared as unremarkable rocks to heat-sensing eyes. And many of the Underdark's monsters were reptilian, cold-blooded, and hard to see.

Drizzt sniffed the stagnant air several times, then he stood still and closed his eyes, letting his ears provide all the external input. He heard nothing, save the beating of his own heart, so he checked his gear to ensure that all was secure and started to climb down the shaft, taking care amid the dangerously loose rubble.

He nearly made it silently down the sixty feet to the lower corridor, but a single stone skidded down before him, striking the corridor's floor with a sharp crack at almost the same instant that Drizzt's soft boots quietly came down from the wall.

Drizzt froze in place, listening to the sound as it echoed from wall to wall. As a drow patrol leader, Drizzt had once been able to follow echoes perfectly, almost instinctively discerning which walls were rebounding the sound, and from which direction. Now, though, he had difficulty sorting through the echo's individual sounds. Again he felt out of place, overmatched by the brooding darkness. And again he felt vulnerable, for many denizens of the dark ways could indeed follow an echo trail, and this particular one led directly to Drizzt.

He swiftly traversed a virtual maze of crisscrossing corridors, some veering sharply and descending to pass beneath others, or climbing along natural stairs to new levels of winding ways.

Drizzt sorely missed Guenhwyvar. The panther could sort through any maze.

He thought of the cat again a short time later, when he came around a bend and stumbled upon a fresh kill. It was some type of subterranean lizard, too mutilated for Drizzt to figure out exactly what. Its tail was gone, as was its lower jaw, and its belly had been gashed open, its innards devoured. Drizzt found long tears in the skin, as though it had been raked by claws, and long and thin bruises, like those made by a whip. Beyond a pool of blood a few feet from the corpse, the drow found a single track, a paw print, in a shape and size very similar to one Guenhwyvar might make.

But Drizzt's cat was hundreds of miles away, and this kill, by the ranger's estimation, was barely an hour old. Creatures of the Underdark did not roam as did creatures of the surface; the dangerous predator was likely not far away.

* * * * *

Bruenor Battlehammer stormed along the passageway, his grief stolen, for the moment, by undeniably mounting rage. Thibbledorf Pwent bounced along beside the king, his mouth flapping one question after another and his armor squealing annoyingly with every movement.

Bruenor skidded to a stop and turned on the battlerager, put his angry scar and angry scowl in line with Pwent's bushy-bearded face. "Why don't ye get yerself a bath!" Bruenor roared.

Pwent fell back and began to choke on the command. By his estimation, a dwarf king ordering a subject to go take a bath was roughly the equivalent of a human king telling his knights to go out and kill babies. There were some lines that a ruler simply did not cross.

"Bah!" Bruenor snorted. "Good enough for ye, then. But go and grease that damned armor! How's a king to think with yer squeakin' and squealin'?"

Pwent's head bobbed his agreement with the compromise, and he bounded away, almost afraid to stay, afraid that the tyrant King Bruenor would again demand the bath.

Bruenor just wanted the battlerager away from him—he didn't really care how he accomplished that task. It had been a difficult afternoon. The dwarf had just met with Berkthgar the Bold, an emissary from Settlestone, and had learned that Catti-brie had never arrived in the barbarian settlement, even though she had been out of Mithril Hall for nearly a week.

Bruenor's mind raced over the events of his last meeting with his daughter. He recalled images of the young woman, tried to scrutinize them and remember every word she had said for some clue as to what might be happening. But Bruenor had been too absorbed on that occasion. If Catti-brie had hinted at anything other than her intentions to go to Settlestone, the dwarf had simply missed it.

His first thoughts, when talking with Berkthgar, were that his daughter had met some trouble on the mountainside. He had almost called out a dwarven contingent to scour the area, but, on an impulse, had paused long enough to ask the emissary about the cairn being erected for Wulfgar.

"What cairn?" Berkthgar had replied.

Bruenor knew then that he had been deceived, and if Catti-brie had not been alone in that deception, then Bruenor could easily guess the identity of her coconspirator.

He nearly took the wooden, iron-bound door of Buster Bracer, a highly regarded armorer, off its hinges as he burst in, catching the blue-bearded dwarf and his halfling subject by surprise. Regis stood atop a small platform, being measured so that his armor could be let out to fit his widening girth.

Bruenor bounded up beside the pedestal (and Buster was wise enough to fall back from it), grabbed the halfling by the front of his tunic, and hoisted him into the air with one arm.

"Where's me girl?" the dwarf roared.

"Settle . . ." Regis started to lie, but Bruenor began shaking him violently, whipping him back and forth through the air like some rag doll.

"Where's me girl?" the dwarf said again, more quietly, his words a threatening snarl. "And don't ye play games with me, Rumblebelly."

Regis was getting more than a little tired of being assaulted by his supposed friends. The quick-thinking halfling immediately concocted a ruse about Catti-brie having run off to Silverymoon in search of Drizzt. It wouldn't be a complete lie, after all.

Looking at Bruenor's scarred face, twisted in rage, but so obviously filled with pain, the halfling could not bring himself to fib.

"Put me down," he said quietly, and apparently Bruenor understood the halfling's empathy, for the dwarf gently lowered Regis to the ground.

Regis brushed his tunic straight, then waggled a fist before the dwarf king. "How dare you?" he roared.

Bruenor went back on his heels at the unexpected and uncharacteristic outburst, but the halfling did not relent.

"First Drizzt comes to me and forces me to hold a secret," Regis expounded, "then Catti-brie comes in and pushes me around until I tell her. Now you. . . . What fine friends I have surrounded myself with!"

The stinging words calmed the volatile dwarf, but only a little. What secret might Regis be hinting at?

Thibbledorf Pwent bounded into the room then, his armor squeaking no less, though his face, beard, and hands were certainly smeared with grease. He stopped beside Bruenor, surveying the unexpected situation for just a moment.

Pwent rubbed his hands eagerly in front of him, then ran them down the front of his cruelly ridged armor. "Should I hug him?" he asked his king hopefully.

Bruenor slapped a hand out to hold the eager battlerager at bay. "Where's me girl?" the dwarf king asked a third time, this time quietly and calmly, as though he was asking a friend.

Regis firmed his jaw, then nodded and began. He told Bruenor everything, even his role in aiding Catti-brie, in handing her the assassin's dagger and the magical mask.

Bruenor's face began to twist in rage again, but Regis stood tall (relatively speaking) and dispelled the rising ire.

"Am I to trust in Catti-brie any less than you would?" Regis asked simply, reminding the dwarf that his human daughter was no child, and no novice to the perils of the road.

Bruenor didn't know how to take it all. A small part of him wanted to throttle Regis, but he understood that he would simply be playing out his frustration, and that the halfling was really not to blame. Where else could he turn, though? Both Drizzt and Catti-brie were long gone, well on their way, and Bruenor had no idea of how he could get to them!

Neither did the scarred dwarf, at that moment, have any strength to try. He dropped his gaze to the stone floor, his anger played out and his grief returned, and, without another word, he walked from the room. He had to think, and for the sake of his dearest friend and his beloved daughter, he had to think fast.

Pwent looked to Regis and Buster for answers, but they simply shook their heads.

* * * * *

A slight shuffle, the padded footsteps of a hunting cat, perhaps, was all that Drizzt could discern. The drow ranger stood perfectly still, all his senses attuned to his surroundings. If it was the cat, Drizzt knew that it was close enough to have caught his scent, that it undoubtedly knew that something had wandered into its territory.

Drizzt spent a moment scrutinizing the area. The tunnel continued haphazardly, sometimes wide, sometimes narrow, and this entire section was broken and uneven, the floor full of bumps and holes and the walls lined by natural alcoves and deep nooks. The ceiling, too, was no longer constant, sometimes low and sometimes high. Drizzt could see the varied gradations of heat on the high walls ahead and knew that those walls were lined by ledges in many places.

A great cat could jump up there, watching its intended prey from above.

The thought was not a settling one, but Drizzt had to press on. To backtrack, he would have to go all the way to the chute and climb to a higher level, then wander about in the hopes that he would find another way down. Drizzt didn't have time to spare; neither did his friends.

He put his back against the wall as he continued, stalking in a crouch, one scimitar drawn and the other, Twinkle, ready in its sheath. Drizzt did not want the magical blade's glow to further reveal his position, though he knew that hunting cats in the Underdark needed no light.

He lightly stepped across the mouth of one wide and shallow alcove, then came to the edge of a second, narrower and deeper. When he was satisfied that this one, too, was unoccupied, he turned back for a general scan of the area.

Shining green eyes, cat eyes, stared back at him from the ledge on the opposite wall.

Out came Twinkle, flaring an angry blue, bathing the area in light. Drizzt, his eyes shifting back from the infrared spectrum, saw the great, dark silhouette as the monster leaped, and he deftly dove out of harm's way. The cat touched down lightly—with all six legs!—and it pivoted about, showing white teeth and sinister eyes.

It was pantherlike, its fur so black as to shimmer a deep blue, and it was nearly as large as Guenhwyvar. Drizzt didn't know what to think. If this had been a normal panther, he would have tried to calm it, tried to show it that he was no enemy and that he would go right past its lair. But this cat, this monster, had six legs! And from its shoulders protruded long, whiplike appendages, waving menacingly and tipped with bony ridges.

Snarling, the beast padded in, ears tight against its head, formidable fangs bared. Drizzt crouched low, scimitars straight out in front, feet perfectly balanced so that he could dodge aside.

The beast stopped its stalk. Drizzt watched carefully as its middle set of legs and its hind legs tamped down.

It came fast; Drizzt started left, but the beast skidded to a stop, and Drizzt did likewise, lurching ahead to cut with one blade in a straight thrust. Right between the panther's eyes went the scimitar, perfectly aligned.

It hit nothing but air, and Drizzt stumbled forward. He instinctively dove to the stone and rolled right as one tentacle whipped just above his head and the other scored a slight hit on his hip. Huge paws raked and swatted all about him, but he worked his scimitars wildly, somehow keeping them at bay. He came up running, quickly putting a few feet between himself and the dangerous cat.

The drow settled back into his defensive crouch, less confident now. The beast was smart—Drizzt would never have expected such a feint from an animal. Worse, the drow could not understand how he had missed. His blade's thrust had been true. Even the incredible agility of a cat could not have gotten the beast out of the way so quickly.

A tentacle came at him from the right, and he threw a scimitar out that way not just to parry, but hoping to sever the thing.

He missed, then barely managed, past his surprise, to twirl to the left, taking another hit on the hip, this one painful.

The beast rushed forward, one paw flying out in front to hook the spinning drow. Drizzt braced, Twinkle ready to block, but the paw caught him fully a foot below the scimitar's blocking angle.

Again Drizzt's ability to react saved him, for instead of fighting the angle of the in-turned paw (which would have ripped large lines in his body), he dove with it, down to the stone, scrambling and kicking his way past the panther's snapping maw. He felt like a mouse running back under a house cat, and, worse, this cat had two sets of legs left to cross!

Drizzt elbowed and batted, jabbed up, and scored a solid hit. He couldn't see in the sudden, wild flurry, and only when he came out the panther's back side did he realize that his blindness was his saving grace. He came up into a running step, then leaped into a headlong roll just ahead of twin snapping tentacles.

He hadn't been able to see, and he had scored his only hit.

The panther came around again, snarling in rage, its green eyes boring like lamplights into the drow.

Drizzt spat at those eyes, a calculated move, for though his aim seemed true and the beast made no move to dodge, the spittle hit only the stone floor. The cat was not where it appeared to be.

Drizzt tried to remember his training in Menzoberranzan's Academy. He had heard of such beasts once, but they were very rare and hadn't been a source of any major lessons.

In came the cat. Drizzt leaped forward, inside the snapping reach of those painful tentacles. He guessed, aiming his attack a couple of feet to the right of where he perceived the beast.

But the cat was left, and as his scimitar swished harmlessly through the air, Drizzt knew he was in trouble. He leaped straight up, felt a claw slash at his foot—the same foot that had been wounded in his fight with Artemis Entreri on the ledge outside Mithril Hall. Down sliced Twinkle, the magnificent blade gashing the front claw, forcing the cat to retreat. Drizzt landed half-entwined with the beast, felt the hot breath of its drooling maw about his forearm and punched out, twisting his wrist so that his weapon's crosspiece prevented the monster from tearing his hand off.

He closed his eyes—they would only confuse him—and bashed down with Twinkle's hilt, clubbing the monster's head. Then he jerked free and ran off. The bony end of a tentacle flew out behind him, caught up to his back, and he threw himself into a headlong roll, absorbing some of the sting.

Up again, Drizzt ran on in full flight. He came to the wide and shallow alcove and spun in, the monster right behind.

Drizzt reached within himself, into his innate magical abilities, and brought forth a globe of impenetrable darkness. Twinkle's light disappeared, as did the monster's shining eyes.

Drizzt circled two steps and came forward, not wanting the beast to escape the darkened area. He felt the swish of a tentacle, a near hit, then sensed it coming back again the other way. The drow smiled in satisfaction as his scimitar slashed out to meet it, cutting right through.

The beast's pained roar guided Drizzt back in. He couldn't get caught in too tight, he knew, but, with his scimitars, he had an advantage of reach. With Twinkle up to fend against the remaining tentacle, he jabbed the other blade repeatedly, scoring a few minor hits.

The enraged cat leaped, but Drizzt sensed it and fell flat to the floor, rolling to his back and thrusting both his blades straight up, scoring a serious double hit on the monster's belly.

The cat came down hard, skidding heavily into the wall, and, before it could recover, Drizzt was upon it. A scimitar bashed against its skull, creasing its head. The cat whipped about and sprang forward, paws extended, maw opened wide.

Twinkle was waiting. The scimitar's tip caught the beast on the chin and slid down under the maw to dig at its rushing neck. A paw batted the blade, nearly tearing it free from the drow's extended hand, but Drizzt knew that he had to hang on, for all his life. There came a savage flurry, but the drow, backpedaling, managed to keep the beast at bay.

Out of the darkness the two came, the beast pressing on. Drizzt closed his eyes. He sensed that the remaining tentacle would snap at him, and he reversed direction, suddenly throwing all his weight behind Twinkle. The tentacle wrapped his back; he got his opposite elbow up just in time to prevent its end from coming right around and slamming his face.

Twinkle was in the monster halfway to the hilt. A wheezing and gurgling sound came from the beast's throat, but heavy paws battered at Drizzt's sides, shredding pieces of his cloak and scratching the fine mithril armor. The cat tried to turn its impaled neck to the side to bite Drizzt's arm.

Drizzt free hand went to work, furiously pumping up and down, bashing his scimitar repeatedly against the cat's head.

He felt the claws grasp and hold him, biting maw just an inch from his belly. One claw slipped through a chain link in the metal coat, slightly puncturing the drow's side.

The scimitar bashed again and again.

Down they tumbled in a heap. Drizzt, on his side and staring into wicked eyes, thought he was doomed and tried to squirm free. But the cat's grip loosened, and Drizzt realized that the beast was dead. He finally wriggled from the hold and looked down at the slain creature, its green eyes shining even in death.

* * * * *

"Don't ye go in there," one of the two guards outside Bruenor's throne room said to Regis as he boldly approached the door. The halfling considered them carefully—he never remembered seeing a dwarf so pale!

The door banged open, and a contingent of dwarves, fully armed and armored, burst out, falling all over each other as they ran off down the stone corridor. Behind them came a verbal tirade, a stream of curses from their king.

One of the guards started to close the door, but Regis hopped up and pushed his way in.

Bruenor paced about his throne, punching the great chair whenever he passed close enough. General Dagna, Mithril Hall's military leader, sat in his appointed chair, looking rather glum, and Thibbledorf Pwent hopped about gleefully in Bruenor's shadow, cautiously dodging aside whenever Bruenor spun about.

"Stupid priests!" Bruenor growled.

"With Cobble dead, there are none powerful enough—" Dagna tried to intervene, but Bruenor wasn't listening.

"Stupid priests!" the dwarf king said more forcefully.

"Yeah!" Pwent readily agreed.

"Me king, ye've set two patrols off to Silverymoon, and another north o' the city," Dagna tried to reason. "And ye've got half me soldiers walking the tunnels below."

"And I'll be sending the other half if them that's there don't show me the way!" Bruenor roared.

Regis, still standing unnoticed by the door, was beginning to catch on, and he wasn't displeased by what he was seeing. Bruenor—and it seemed like the old Bruenor once more!—was moving heaven and earth to find Drizzt and Catti-brie. The old dwarf had stoked his inner fires!

"But there are a thousand separate tunnels down there," Dagna argued. "And some may take a week to explore before we learn that they're dead ends."

"Then send down a thousand dwarves!" Bruenor growled at him. He stalked past the chair again, then skidded to a stop—and Pwent bounced into his back—as he regarded the halfling.

"What're ye looking at?" Bruenor demanded when he noticed Regis's wide-eyed stare.

Regis would have liked to say, "At my oldest friend," but he merely shrugged instead. For an instant, he caught a flash of anger in the dwarf's one blue-gray eye, and he thought that Bruenor was leaning toward him, perhaps fighting an inner urge to rush over and throttle him. But the dwarf calmed and slid into his throne.

Regis cautiously approached, studying Bruenor and taking little heed of pragmatic Dagna's claims that there was no way to catch up with the two wayfaring friends. Regis heard enough to figure that Dagna wasn't too worried for Drizzt and Catti-brie, and that didn't surprise him much, since the crusty dwarf wasn't overly fond of anyone who wasn't a dwarf.

"If we had the damned cat," Bruenor began, and again came that flash of anger as he regarded the halfling. Regis put his hands behind his back and bowed his head.

"Or me damned locket!" Bruenor roared. "Where in the Nine Hells did I put me damned locket?"

Regis winced at every roaring outburst, but Bruenor's anger did not change his feelings that he had done the right thing in assisting Catti-brie, and in sending Guenhwyvar along with her.

And, though he half expected Bruenor to punch him in the face at any moment, it did not change the halfling's feelings that he was glad to see Bruenor full of life again.

Chapter 9

CAGED

lodding along a slow and rocky trail, they had to walk the horses more than ride them. Every passing inch tormented Catti-brie. She had seen the light of a campfire the previous night and knew in her heart that it had been Drizzt. She had gone straight to her horse, meaning to saddle up and head out, using the light as a beacon to the drow, but Fret had stopped her, explaining that the magical horseshoes that their mounts wore did not protect the beasts from exhaustion. He reminded her, too, of the dangers she would likely encounter in the mountains at night.

Catti-brie had gone back to her own fire then, thoroughly miserable. She considered calling for Guenhwyvar and sending the panther out for Drizzt, but shook the notion away. The campfire was just a dot somewhere on the higher trails, many miles away, and she had no way of knowing, rationally, that it was indeed Drizzt.

Now, though, crossing along the higher trails, making their steady but painfully slow way in that very same direction, Catti-brie feared that she had erred. She watched Fret, scratching his white beard, looking this way and that at the unremarkable landscape, and wished they had that campfire to guide them.

"We will get there!" the tidy dwarf often said to her, looking back into her disgusted expression.

Morning turned into afternoon; long shadows drifted across the landscape.

"We must make camp," Fret announced as twilight descended.

"We're going on," Catti-brie argued. "If that was Drizzt's fire, then he's a day up on us already, no matter for yer magical horseshoes!"

"I cannot hope to find the cave in the darkness!" the dwarf retorted. "We could find a giant, or a troll, perhaps, and I'm sure that many wolves will be about, but a cave?" Looking into Catti-brie's deepening scowl, Fret began to ponder the wisdom of his sarcasm.

"Oh, all right!" the tidy dwarf cried. "We will keep looking until the night is full."

They pressed on, until Catti-brie could hardly see her horse walking beside her and Fret's pony nearly stumbled over the edge of a ravine. Finally, even stubborn Catti-brie had to relent and agree to make camp.

After they had settled in, she went and found a tree, a tall pine, and climbed nearly to its top to keep her vigil. If the light of a campfire came up, the young woman determined, she would set out, or would at least send the panther.

There were no campfires that night.

As soon as the dawn's light permitted, the two set off again. Barely an hour out, Fret clapped his clean hands together excitedly, thinking that he had found a familiar trail. "We are not far," he promised.

Up and down went the trail, into rocky, tree-filled valleys, and up again across bare, windswept stone. Fret tethered his pony to a tree branch and led the way up the steep side of one mound, telling Catti-brie that they had found the place, only to discover, two hours of climbing later, that they had scaled the wrong mountain.

In midafternoon they discovered that Fret's earlier promise that they were "not far," was accurate. When he had made that statement, the cave the dwarf sought was no more than half a mile from their location. But finding a specific cave in mountain territory is no easy task, even for a dwarf, and Fret had been to the place only once—nearly twenty years before.

He found it, finally, as the shadows again grew long in the mountains. Catti-brie shook her head as she examined the entrance and the fire pit that had been used two nights before. The embers had been tended with great care, such as a ranger might do.

"He was here," the young woman said to the dwarf, "two nights ago." Catti-brie rose from the fire pit and brushed her thick auburn locks back from her face, eyeing the dwarf as though he was to blame. She looked out from the cave, back across the mountains, to where they had been, to the location from which they had seen this very fire.

"We could not have gotten here that night," the dwarf answered. "You could have run off, or ridden off, into the darkness with all speed, and—"

"The firelight would've shown us through," Catti-brie interrupted.

"For how long?" the dwarf demanded. "We found one vantage point, one hole through the towering peaks. As soon as we went into a ravine, or crossed close to the side of a mountain, the light would have been lost to us. Then where would we be, stubborn daughter of Bruenor?"

Again Catti-brie's scowl stopped the dwarf short. He sighed profoundly and threw up his hands.

He was right, Catti-brie knew. While they had gone no more than a few miles deeper into the mountains since that night, the trails had been treacherous, climbing and descending, winding snakelike around the many rocky peaks. She and the dwarf had walked a score of miles, at least, to get to this point, and even if she had summoned Guenhwyvar, there was no way the panther could have caught up to Drizzt.

That logic did little to quell the frustration boiling within Catti-brie. She had vowed to follow Drizzt, to find him and bring him home, but now, standing at the edge of a forlorn cave in a wild place, she faced the entrance to the Underdark.

"We will go back to Lady Alustriel," Fret said to her. "Perhaps she has some allies—she has so many of those!—who will be better able to locate the drow."

"What're ye saying?" Catti-brie wanted to know.

"It was a valiant chase," Fret replied. "Your father will be proud of your effort, but—"

Catti-brie rushed up to the dwarf, pushed him aside, and stumbled down toward the back of the cave, toward the blackness of a descending tunnel entrance. She stubbed her toe hard against a jag in the floor, but refused to cry out, even to grunt, not wanting Fret to think her ridiculous. In fumbling with her pack, though, trying to get to her tinderbox, lantern, and oil, Catti-brie thought herself so just the same.

"Do you know that she likes you?" Fret asked casually.

The question stopped the young woman. She looked back to regard the dwarf, who was just a short, dark silhouette before the lighter gray of the outside night.

"Alustriel, I mean," Fret clarified.

Catti-brie had no answer. She hadn't felt comfortable around the magnificent Lady of Silverymoon, far from it. Intentionally or not, Alustriel had made her feel little, perfectly insignificant.

"She does," Fret insisted. "She likes you and admires you."

"In an orc's thoughts," Catti-brie huffed. She thought she was being mocked.

"You remind her of her sister," Fret went on, without missing a beat, "Dove Falconhand, a spirited woman if ever there was one."

Catti-brie did not reply this time. She had heard many tales of Alustriel's sister, a legendary ranger, and had indeed fancied herself somewhat like Dove. Suddenly the dwarf's claims did not seem so outrageous.

"Alas for Alustriel," Fret remarked. "She wishes that she could be more like you."

"In an orc's thoughts!" Catti-brie blurted, unable to stop herself. The notion that Alustriel, the fabulous Lady of Silverymoon, could be the least bit jealous of Catti-brie seemed absurd.

"In a human's thoughts, I say!" Fret replied. "What is it about your race that none of you can seem to properly weigh your own value? Every human seems to think more of herself than she should, or less of herself than is sensible! Alustriel likes you, I say, even admires you. If she did not, if she thought you and your plans were silly, then why would she go to this trouble? Why would she send me, a valuable sage, along with you? And why, daughter of Bruenor Battlehammer, would she give you this?"

He lifted one hand, holding something delicate that Catti-brie could not make out. She paused a moment to digest what he had said, then walked back over to him.

The dwarf held a fine silver chain, a circlet headdress, with a gemstone set into it.

"It is beautiful," Catti-brie admitted, studying the pale green gem, a line of black running through its center.

"More than beautiful," Fret said, and he motioned for Catti-brie to put it on.

She clasped it in place, the gem set against the middle of her forehead, and then she nearly swooned, for the images around her —suddenly blurred and wavered. She could see the dwarf—not just his silhouette, but actually Fret's features! She glanced about in disbelief, focusing on the back of the cave. It seemed as if it was bathed in starlight, not brightly, but Catti-brie could make out the jags and the nooks clearly enough.

Catti-brie could not see it, of course, but the thin black line along the middle of the gemstone had widened like a pupil.

"Walking into the Underdark under a blazing torch is not the wisest move," Fret remarked. "A single candle would mark you as out of place and would leave you vulnerable. And how much oil could you carry, in any case? Your lantern would be useless to you before the first day had ended. The Cat's Eye eliminates the need, you see."

"Cat's eye?"

"Cat's Eye agate," Fret explained, pointing to the gemstone. "Alustriel did the enchanting herself. Normally a gem ensorcelled such would show you only shades of gray, but the lady does favor starlight. Few in the Realms could claim the honor of receiving such a gift."

Catti-brie nodded and didn't know how to reply. Pangs of guilt accompanied her scrutiny of her feelings for the Lady of Silverymoon, and she thought herself ridiculous for ever doubting—and for ever allowing jealousy to cloud her judgment.

"I was instructed to try to dissuade you from the dangerous course," the dwarf went on, "but Alustriel knew that I would fail. You are indeed so like Dove, headstrong and stubborn, and feeling positively immortal. She knew that you would go, even into the Underdark," Fret said. "And, although Alustriel fears for you, she knows that nothing could or should stop you."

The dwarf's tone was neither sarcastic nor demeaning, and again Catti-brie was caught off guard, unprepared for the words.

"Will you stay the night in the cave?" Fret asked. "I could start a fire."

Catti-brie shook her head. Drizzt was already too far ahead of her.

"Of course," the tidy dwarf muttered quietly.

Catti-brie didn't hear him; she was already walking toward the back of the cave, toward the tunnel. She paused and summoned Guenhwyvar, realizing that she would need the panther's support to get going. As the cat materialized, Catti-brie looked back to the cave entrance to tell the dwarf to relay her thanks to Alustriel, but Fret was already gone.

"Come along, Guen," the young woman said, a strained smile on her face. "We have to find Drizzt." The panther poked about the tunnel entrance for a bit, then started down, apparently on the trail.

Catti-brie paused a long moment, staring back to the cave entrance and the starry sky beyond. She wondered if she would ever see those stars again.

Chapter 10

OLD FRIENDS

e crossed through narrow tunnels and halls that spread beyond vision to either side and above. He trotted along muddy flats and bare stone, without splashes, without sound. Every step Drizzt Do'Urden took in the deeper tunnels of the Underdark jogged his memory a little bit more, brought him back to the days when he had survived the wilds, when he had been the hunter.

He had to find that inner being, that primal savage within him, that heard the call of his instincts so very well. There was no time for rational calculations in the wilds of the Underdark; there was only time to act.

Drizzt hated the prospect of giving in to that savage element, hated this whole journey, but he had to go on, knowing that if he failed, if he was killed in the wilds before he ever got to Menzoberranzan, his quest would prove detrimental to his friends. Then he would be gone, but the dark elves would not know it and would still go after Mithril Hall. For the sake of Bruenor, Regis, and dear Catti-brie, Drizzt had to go on, and had to become the primal hunter once more.

He climbed to the ceiling of a high corridor for his first break and slept lightly, hanging upside down, his legs wedged up to the knees in a narrow crack, his fingers hooked under his belt, near his scimitars.

An echo down a distant tunnel woke him after only an hour of dozing. It had been a slight sound, a step into sucking mud, perhaps, but Drizzt held perfectly still, sensing the disturbance in the still air, hearing minute residual echoes and correctly guessing the direction.

He pulled out his legs and rolled, dropping the fifteen feet to the ground, the toes of his soft boots touching first to absorb the impact and bring him down without a whisper. He ran on, taking care to keep far from those echoes, desiring no more conflicts before he got to the drow city.

He grew more confident with every step. His instincts were returning, along with his memories of that time he spent alone in the wilds of the Underdark. He came to another muddy area, where the air was warm, and the sound of hot, aerated water hissed and gurgled. Wet, gleaming stalagmite and stalactites, glowing warm to the drow's heat-seeing eyes, dotted the area, breaking this single tunnel into a virtual maze.

Drizzt knew this place, remembered it from the journey he had taken to the surface. That fact brought both relief and trepidation to the drow. He was glad that he was on course, but he could not deny his fear that he was on course. He let the water sound guide him along, knowing that he would find the proper tunnels just beyond the hot springs.

The air grew steadily warmer, soon uncomfortably so, but Drizzt kept his cloak on and drawn tight, not wanting to get caught up with anything more than a scimitar in his hands in this dangerous area.

And the drow knew that this was indeed a dangerous area. Any number of monsters might be crouched behind one of the ever-present mounds, and it took great effort for Drizzt to move silently through the thickening mud. If he kept his foot in one position for any length of time, the clinging stuff ran up around his boot, and subsequently lifting the gummed foot would inevitably result in a sucking sound. On one such occasion, Drizzt paused as he slowly hoisted his foot, trying to discern the echo patterns. It took only a moment for him to understand that the responding sounds he heard were made by more feet than his own.

Drizzt quickly surveyed the area and considered the air temperature and the intensity of the stalagmites' glow. The footsteps grew louder, and Drizzt realized that a band of more than a few approached. He scanned every side tunnel, quickly coming to the conclusion that this band carried no light source.

Drizzt moved under one narrow spike of a stalactite, its tip hanging no more than four feet from the floor. He tucked his legs under him and knelt beneath the thing. He positioned his cloak about his knees in a conical fashion, taking care so that there were no obvious jags, like a foot sticking out too far, along all his body. Then the drow looked up to the stalactite, studied its form. He lifted his hands to feel its tip, then ran them up and around the stalactite, joining with it smoothly, making sure that its tip remained the smallest taper.

He closed his eyes and tucked his head between his upper arms. He swayed a few times, feeling his balance, smoothing the outer edges of his form.

Drizzt became a stalagmite mound.

He soon heard sucking sounds, and squeaking, croaking voices that he knew to be goblins', all about him. He peeked out only once, and only for an instant, ensuring that they had no light sources. How obvious he would be if a torch passed near him!

But hiding in the lightless Underdark was very different from hiding in a forest, even on a dark night. The trick here was to blur the distinctive lines of body heat, and Drizzt felt confident that the air about him, and the stalagmites, was at least as warm as his outer cloak.

He heard goblin footsteps barely a few feet away, knew that the large troupe—it numbered at least twenty, Drizzt believed—was all about him. He considered the exact movements it would take for him to get his hands most quickly to his scimitars. If one of the goblins brushed against him, the game would be up and he would explode into motion, ripping at their ranks and trying to get beyond them before they even realized that he was there.

It never came to that. The goblin troupe continued on its way through the host of stalactites and stalagmites and the one drow that was not a mound of rock.

Drizzt opened his lavender eyes, which blazed with the inner fires of the hunter. He remained perfectly still for a few moments longer, to ensure that there were no stragglers, then he ran off, making not a sound.

*　*　*　*　*

Catti-brie knew immediately that Drizzt had killed this six-legged, tentacled, pantherlike beast. Kneeling over the carcass, she recognized the curving, slashing wounds and doubted that anyone else could have made so clean a kill.

"It was Drizzt," she muttered to Guenhwyvar, and the panther gave a low growl. "No more than two days old."

This dead monster reminded her of how vulnerable she might be. If Drizzt, with all his training in stealth and in the ways of the Underdark, had been forced into combat, then how could she hope to pass unscathed?

Catti-brie leaned against the black panther's muscled flank, needing the support. She couldn't keep Guenhwyvar with her for much longer, she knew. The magical cat was a creature of the Astral Plane and needed to return there often to rest. Catti-brie had meant to spend her first hour in the tunnel alone, had meant to leave the cave without the panther beside her, but her nerve had waned with the first few steps. She needed the tangible support of her feline ally in this foreign place. As the day had gone on, Catti-brie had become somewhat more comfortable with her surroundings and had planned to dismiss Guenhwyvar as soon as the trail became more obvious, as soon as they found a region with fewer side passages. It seemed that they had found that place, but they had found, too, the carcass.

Catti-brie started ahead quickly, instructing Guenhwyvar to keep close to her side. She knew that she should release the panther then, not tax Guenhwyvar's strength in case she should need the cat in an emergency, but she justified her delay by convincing herself that many carrion monsters, or other six-legged feline beasts, might be about.

Twenty minutes later, with the tunnels dark and quiet around them, the young woman stopped and searched for her strength. Dismissing Guenhwyvar then was among the most courageous things Catti-brie had ever done, and when the mist dissolved and Catti-brie replaced the statuette into her pouch, she was glad indeed for the gift Alustriel had given her.

She was alone in the Underdark, alone in deep tunnels filled with deadly foes. She could see, at least, and the starry illusion—beautiful even here against the gray stone—bolstered her spirits.

Catti-brie took a deep breath and steadied herself. She remembered Wulfgar and spoke again her vow that no other friends would be lost. Drizzt needed her; she could not let her fears defeat her.

She took up the heart-shaped locket, holding it tightly in her hand so that its magical warmth would keep her on the proper path. She set off again, forcing one foot in front of the other as she moved farther from the world of the sun.

* * * * *

Drizzt quickened his pace after the hot springs, for he now remembered the way, and remembered, too, many of the enemies he had to take care to avoid.

Days passed uneventfully, became a week, and then two for the running drow. It had taken Drizzt more than a month to get to the surface from Blingdenstone, the gnome city some forty to fifty miles west of Menzoberranzan, and now, with his belief that danger was pressing Mithril Hall, he was determined to shorten that time.

He came into tunnels winding and narrow, found a familiar fork in the trail, one corridor cutting north and one continuing to the west. Drizzt suspected that the northern route would get him more quickly to the drow city, but he stayed the course west, hoping that he might gain more information along that more familiar route, and secretly hoping that he might find some old friends along the way.

He was still running a couple of days later, but he now paused often and put his ear to the stone, listening for a rhythmic tap-tapping sound. Blingdenstone was not far away, Drizzt knew, and deep gnome miners might well be about. The halls remained silent, though, and Drizzt began to realize that he did not have much time. He thought of going straight into the gnome city, but decided against that course. He had spent too long on the road already; it was time to draw near to Menzoberranzan.

An hour later, cautiously rounding a bend in a low corridor that was lined with glowing lichen, Drizzt's keen ears caught a distant noise. At first the drow smiled, thinking that he had found the elusive miners, but as he continued to listen, catching the sounds of metal scraping metal, even a cry, his expression greatly changed.

A battle was raging, not so far away.

Drizzt sprinted off, using the increasingly loud echoes to guide his steps. He came into one dead end and had to backtrack, but soon was on the course again, scimitars drawn. He came to a fork in the corridor, both tunnels continuing on in a similar direction, though one rose sharply, and both resounding with the cries of battle.

Drizzt decided to go up, running, crouching. Around a bend he spotted an opening and knew that he had come upon the fight. He eased out of the tunnel, moving onto a ledge twenty feet above a wide chamber, its floor broken and dotted with stone mounds. Below, svirfnebli and drow forms scrambled all about.

Svirfnebli and drow! Drizzt fell back against the wall, his scimitars slipping down to his sides. He knew that the svirfnebli, the deep gnomes, were not evil, understood in his heart that the drow had been the ones to instigate this fight, probably laying an ambush for the gnome mining party. Drizzt's heart screamed at him to leap down to aid the sorely pressed gnomes, but he could not find the strength. He had fought drow, had killed drow, but never with a clear conscience. These were his kin, his blood. Might there be another Zak'nafein down there? Another Drizzt Do'Urden?

One dark elf, in hot pursuit of a wounded gnome, scrambled up the side of a rocky mound, only to find that it had become a living rock, an earth elemental, ally of the gnomes. Great stony arms wrapped about the dark elf and crushed him, the elemental taking no notice of the weapons that nicked harmlessly off its natural rocky armor.

Drizzt winced at the gruesome sight, but was somewhat relieved to see the gnomes holding their own. The elemental slowly turned about, smashing down a blocking stalagmite and tearing its great chunks of feet from the stone floor.

The gnomes rallied behind their giant ally, trying to reform some semblance of ranks amid the general chaos. They were making progress, many of them zigzagging through the rocky maze to link up with their mounting central force, and the dark elves inevitably fell back from the dangerous giant. One burly gnome, a burrow warden, Drizzt guessed, called for a straight march across the cavern.

Drizzt crouched low on the ledge. From his vantage point, he could see the skilled drow warriors fanning out about the gnomes, flanking and hiding behind mounds. Another group slipped toward the far exit, the gnomes' destination, and took up strategic positions there. If the elemental held out, though, the gnomes would likely punch their way through, and, once into the corridor, they could put their elemental behind them to block the way and run on to Blingdenstone.

Three drow females stepped out to confront the giant. Drizzt sighed, seeing that they wore the unmistakable spider-emblazoned robes of Lloth worshippers. He recognized that these were priestesses, possibly high priestesses, and knew then that the gnomes would not escape.

One after another, the females chanted and threw their hands out in front of them, sending forth a spray of fine mist. As the moisture hit the rocky elemental, the giant began to dissolve, streaks of mud replacing the solid stone.

The priestesses kept up their chants, their assaults. On came the rocky giant, growling with rage, its features distorted by the slipping mud.

A blast of mist hit it squarely, sending a thick line of mud running down the monster's chest, but the priestess who had made the assault was too concerned with her attack and did not get back fast enough. A rock arm shot out and punched her, breaking bones and hurling her through the air to crash against a stalagmite.

The remaining two drow hit the elemental again, dissolving its legs, and it crashed helplessly to the floor. It began to reform its appendages immediately, but the priestesses continued their deadly spray. Seeing that the ally was lost, the gnome leader called for a charge, and the svirfnebli rushed on, overwhelming one priestess before the flanking dark elves closed in like a biting maw. The fight was on in full again, this time right below Drizzt Do'Urden.

He gasped for breath as he witnessed the spectacle, saw a gnome slashed repeatedly by three drow, to fall, screaming, dying, to the floor.

Drizzt was out of excuses. He knew right from wrong, knew the significance of the appearance of Lloth's priestesses. Fires simmered in his lavender eyes; out came his scimitars, Twinkle flaring to blue-glowing life.

He spotted the remaining priestess down to the left. She stood beside a tall, narrow mound, one arm out touching a svirfneblin. The gnome made no moves against her, only stood and groaned, trembling from the priestess's magical assaults. Black energy crackled up the drow female's arm as she literally sucked the life force from her unfortunate victim.

Drizzt tucked Twinkle under his other arm and leaped out, hooking the top of that narrow mound and rotating about it as he quickly descended. He hit the floor right beside the priestess and snapped his weapons back to the ready.

The startled drow female uttered a series of sharp commands, apparently thinking Drizzt an ally. Twinkle dove into her heart.

The half-drained gnome eyed Drizzt curiously, then fainted away. Drizzt ran on, calling out warnings to the gnomes, in their own tongue, that dark elves were in position near the far exit. The ranger took care to keep out of the open, though, realizing that any gnome he encountered would likely attack him, and any drow he encountered might recognize him.

He tried not to think of what he had just done, tried not to think of the female's eyes, so similar to his sister Vierna's.

He rushed in hard and put his back against a mound, the cries of battle all about him. A gnome jumped out from behind another

118

stalagmite, waving a hammer dangerously, and before Drizzt could explain that he was no enemy, another drow came around the side, to stand shoulder to shoulder with Drizzt.

The suddenly hesitant gnome looked about, looked for an escape route, but the newest opponent leaped at him.

Purely on instinct, Drizzt slashed the drow's weapon arm, his scimitar drawing a deep gash. The ebon-skinned elf dropped his sword and half-turned to look back in horror at this drow who was not an ally. Stumbling, the surprised drow focused ahead, just in time to catch a gnomish hammer in the face.

The gnome didn't understand it, of course, and as the dark elf fell, all he thought about was readying his hammer for this second enemy. But Drizzt was long gone.

With the priestesses down, a gnome shaman ran over to the felled elemental. He placed a stone atop the pile of rubble and crushed it with his mattock, then began chanting. Soon the elemental reformed, as large as ever, and lumbered away like a moving avalanche in search of enemies. The shaman watched it go, but he should have been watching his own situation instead, for another dark elf crept out behind him, mace held high for a killing strike.

The shaman realized the danger only as the mace came crashing down . . . and was intercepted by a scimitar.

Drizzt shoved the shaman aside and stood to face the stunned drow.

Friend? the fingers of the drow's free hand quickly asked.

Drizzt shook his head, then sent Twinkle slamming against the drow's mace, batting it aside. The ranger's second scimitar quickly followed the same path, ringing loudly off the metal mace and knocking it far out to Drizzt's left.

Drizzt's advantage of surprise was not as great as he had supposed, though, for the drow's free left hand had already slipped to his belt and grabbed a slender dirk. Out of the folds of the drow's *piwafwi* cloak shot the new weapon, straight for Drizzt's heart, the evil drow snarling in apparent victory.

Drizzt spun to the right, backstepping out of harm's way. He brought his closest scimitar back across and down, hooking the dirk's hilt and pulling the drow's arm out straight. He completed his spin, putting his back tightly against his opponent's chest,

119

wrapping the outstretched arm right about him. The drow tried to work his mace into an angle so that he could strike at Drizzt, but Drizzt was in the better position and was the quicker. He stepped away, then came back in, elbow flying high to smash into his opponent's face, once, twice, and then again in rapid succession.

Drizzt flung the drow's dirk hand out wide, and wisely reversed his spin, getting Twinkle up just in time to catch the swinging mace. Drizzt's other arm shot forward, the hilt of his scimitar crushing the drow's face.

The evil drow tried to hold his balance, but he was clearly dazed. A quick twist and snap of Twinkle sent the mace flying into the air, and Drizzt punched out with his left hand, Twinkle's hilt catching the drow on the side of the jaw and dropping him to the floor.

Drizzt looked to the gnome shaman, who stood open-mouthed, clutching his hammer nervously. All around them, the fight had become a rout, with the revived elemental leading the svirfnebli to a decisive victory.

Two other gnomes joined the shaman and eyed Drizzt with suspicion and fear. Drizzt paused a moment to consider the Svirfneblin tongue, a language that used the melodic inflections similar to surface Elvish alongside the hard consonant sounds more typical of Dwarvish talk.

"I am no enemy," he said, and to prove his point he dropped his scimitars to the ground.

The drow on the floor groaned. A gnome sprang upon him and lined his pickaxe up with the back of the dark elf's skull.

"No!" Drizzt cried in protest, starting forward and bending low to intercept the strike.

Drizzt stood up straight suddenly, though, as a searing flash of pain erupted along his backbone. He saw the gnome finish the dazed drow, but couldn't begin to contemplate that brutal action as a series of minor explosions went off down his spine. The lip of some devious, flat-edged club ran down his vertebrae like a board snapping across a picket fence.

Then it was over and Drizzt stood motionlessly for what seemed like a very long time. He felt his legs tingle, as though they had gone to sleep, then felt nothing at all below his waist. He fought to hold his balance, but wobbled and fell, and lay scratching at the stone floor and trying to find his breath.

He knew that the darkness of unconsciousness—or a deeper darkness still—was fast approaching, for he could hardly remember where he was or why he had come.

He did hear the shaman, but that small flicker of consciousness that Drizzt had remaining was not comforted by the shaman's words.

"Kill him."

Chapter 11

FUTILITY

his the place?" the battlerager asked, shouting so that his gruff voice could be heard over the whipping wind. He had come out of Mithril Hall with Regis and Bruenor—had forced the halfling to take him out, actually—in search of the body of Artemis Entreri. "Ye find the clues where ye find them," Pwent had said in typically cryptic explanation.

Regis pulled the cowl of his oversized cloak low to ward off the wind's sting. They were in a narrow valley, a gully, the sides of which seemed to focus the considerable wind into a torrent. "It was around here," Regis said, shrugging his shoulders to indicate that he could not be sure. When he had come out to find the battered Entreri, he had taken a higher route, along the top of the ravine and other ledges. He was certain that he was in the general region, but things looked too different from this perspective to be sure.

"We'll find him, me king," Thibbledorf assured Bruenor.

"For what that's worth," the dejected Bruenor grumbled.

Regis winced at the dwarf's deflated tones. He recognized clearly that Bruenor was slipping back into despair. The dwarves had found no way through the maze of tunnels beneath Mithril Hall, though a thousand were searching, and word from the east was not promising—if Catti-brie and Drizzt had gone to Silverymoon, they were long past that place now. Bruenor was coming to realize the futility of it all. Weeks had passed and he had not found a way out of Mithril Hall that would take him anywhere near his friends. The dwarf was losing hope.

"But, me king!" Pwent roared. "He knows the way."

"He's dead," Bruenor reminded the battlerager.

"Not to worry!" bellowed Pwent. "Priests can talk to the dead— and he might have a map. Oh, we'll find our way to this drow city, I tell ye, and there I'll go, for me king! I'll kill every stinking drow— except that ranger fellow," he added, throwing a wink at Regis, "— and bring yer girl back home!"

Bruenor just sighed and motioned for Pwent to get on with the hunt. Despite all the complaining, though, the dwarf king privately hoped that he might find some satisfaction in seeing Entreri's broken body.

They moved on for a short while, Regis constantly peeking out from his cowl, trying to get his bearings. Finally, the halfling spotted a high outcropping, a branchlike jag of rock.

"There," he said, pointing the way. "That must be it."

Pwent looked up, then followed a direct line to the ravine's bottom. He began scrambling around on all fours, sniffing the ground as if trying to pick up the corpse's scent.

Regis watched him, amused, then turned to Bruenor, who stood against the gully's wall, his hand on the stone, shaking his head.

"What is it?" Regis asked, walking over. Hearing the question and noticing his king, Pwent scampered to join them.

When he got close, Regis noticed something along the stone

wall, something gray and matted. He peered closer as Bruenor pulled a bit of the substance from the stone and held it out.

"What is it?" Regis asked again, daring to touch it. A stringy filament came away with his retracting finger, and it took some effort to shake the gooey stuff free.

Bruenor had to swallow hard several times. Pwent ran off, sniffing at the wall, then across the ravine to consider the stone on the other side.

"It's what's left of a web," the dwarf king answered grimly.

Both Bruenor and Regis looked up to the jutting rock and silently considered the implications of a web strung below the falling assassin.

* * * * *

Fingers flashed too quickly for him to follow, conveying some instructions that the assassin did not understand. He shook his head furiously, and the flustered drow clapped his ebon-skinned hands together, uttered, "*Iblith*," and walked away.

Iblith, Artemis Entreri echoed silently in his thoughts. The drow word for offal, it was the word he had heard the most since Jarlaxle had taken him to this wretched place. What could that drow soldier have expected from him? He was only beginning to learn the intricate drow hand code, its finger movements so precise and detailed that Entreri doubted that one in twenty humans could even begin to manage it. And he was trying desperately to learn the drow spoken language as well. He knew a few words and had a basic understanding of drow sentence structure, so he could put simple ideas together.

And he knew the word *iblith* all too well.

The assassin leaned back against the wall of the small cave, this week's base of operations for Bregan D'aerthe. He felt smaller, more insignificant, than ever. When Jarlaxle had first revived him, in a cave in the ravine outside of Mithril Hall, he had thought the mercenary's offer (actually more of a command, Entreri now realized) to take him to Menzoberranzan a wonderful thing, a grand adventure.

This was no adventure; this was living hell. Entreri was *colnbluth*, non-drow, living in the midst of twenty thousand of the less-than-tolerant race. They didn't particularly hate humans, no more than they hated everybody else, but because he was *colnbluth*, non-drow, the once powerful assassin found himself beneath the lowest ranks of Bregan D'aerthe's drow force. No matter what he did, no matter who he killed, in Menzoberranzan, Artemis Entreri could never rank higher than twenty thousand and first.

And the spiders! Entreri hated spiders, and the crawly things were everywhere in the drow city. They were bred into larger, more poisonous varieties, and were kept as pets. And to kill a spider was a crime carrying the punishment of *jivvin quui'elghinn*, torture until death. In the great cavern's eastern end, the moss bed and mushroom grove near the lake of Donigarten, where Entreri was often put to work herding goblin slaves, spiders crawled about by the thousands. They crawled around him, crawled on him, hung down in strands, dangling inches from the tormented man's face.

The assassin drew his green-gleaming sword and held its wicked edge before his eyes. At least there was more light now in the city; for some reason that Entreri did not know, magical lights and flickering torches had become much more common in Menzoberranzan.

"It would not be wise to stain so marvelous a weapon with drow blood," came a familiar voice from the doorway, easily speaking the Common tongue. Entreri didn't take his gaze from the blade as Jarlaxle entered the small room.

"You presume that I would find the strength to harm one of the mighty drow," the assassin replied. "How could I, the *iblith*, . . ." he started to ask, but Jarlaxle's laughter mocked his self-pity. Entreri glanced over at the mercenary and saw the drow holding his wide-brimmed hat in his hand, fiddling with the *diatryma* feather.

"I have never underestimated your prowess, assassin," Jarlaxle said. "You have survived several fights against Drizzt Do'Urden, and few in Menzoberranzan will ever make that claim."

"I was his fighting equal," Entreri said through gritted teeth. Simply uttering the words stung him. He had battled Drizzt several times, but only twice had they fought without a premature interruption. On both those occasions, Entreri had lost. Entreri wanted desperately to even the score, to prove himself the better fighter. Still, he had to admit, to himself, at least, that in his heart he did not desire another fight with Drizzt. After the first time he had lost to Drizzt, in the muddy sewers and streets of Calimport, Entreri had lived every day plotting revenge, had shaped his life around one event, his rematch with Drizzt. But after his second loss, the one in which he had wound up hanging, broken and miserable, from a jag of rock in a windswept ravine . . .

But what? Entreri wondered. Why did he no longer wish to battle that renegade drow? Had the point been proven, the decision rendered? Or was he simply too afraid? The emotions were unsettling to Artemis Entreri, as out of place within him as he was in the city of drow.

"I was his fighting equal," he whispered again, with as much conviction as he could muster.

"I would not state that openly if I were you," the mercenary replied. "Dantrag Baenre and Uthegental Armgo would fight one another simply to determine which of them got to kill you first."

Entreri did not blink; his sword flared, as if reflecting his simmering pride and anger.

Jarlaxle laughed again. "To determine which would get to *fight* you first," the mercenary corrected, and he swept a low and apologetic bow.

Still the out-of-place assassin didn't blink. Might he regain a measure of pride by killing one of these legendary drow warriors? he wondered. Or would he lose again, and, worse than being killed, be forced to live with that fact?

Entreri snapped the sword down and slipped it into its scabbard. He had never been so hesitant, so unsure. Even as a young boy, surviving on the brutal streets of Calimshan's crowded cities, Entreri had brimmed with confidence, and had used that confidence to advantage. But not here, not in this place.

"Your soldiers taunt me," he snapped suddenly, transferring his frustration the mercenary's way.

Jarlaxle laughed and put his hat back on his bald head. "Kill a few," he offered, and Entreri couldn't tell if the cold, calculating drow was kidding or not. "The rest will then leave you alone."

Entreri spat on the floor. Leave him alone? The rest would wait until he was asleep, then cut him into little pieces to feed to the spiders of Donigarten. That thought broke the assassin's narrow-eyed concentration, forced him to wince. He had killed a female (which, in Menzoberranzan, was much worse than killing a male), and some house in the city might be starving their spiders right now in anticipation of a human feast.

"Ah, but you are so crude," the mercenary said, as though he pitied the man. Entreri sighed and looked away, bringing a hand up to rub his saliva-wetted lips. What was he becoming? In Calimport, in the guilds, even among the pashas and those others that called themselves his masters, he had been in control. He was a killer hired by the most treacherous, double-dealing thieves in all the Realms, and yet, not one had ever tried to cross Artemis Entreri. How he longed to see the pale sky of Calimport again!

"Fear not, my *abbil*," Jarlaxle said, using the drow word for trusted friend. "You will again see the sunrise." The mercenary smiled widely at Entreri's expression, apparently understanding that he had just read the assassin's very thoughts. "You and I will watch the dawn from the doorstep of Mithril Hall."

They were going back after Drizzt, Entreri realized. This time, judging from the lights in Menzoberranzan, which he now came to understand, Clan Battlehammer itself would be crushed!

"That is," Jarlaxle continued teasingly, "unless House Horlbar takes the time to discover that it was you who slew one of its matron mothers."

With a click of his boot and a tip of his hat, Jarlaxle spun out of the room.

Jarlaxle knew! And the female had been a matron mother! Feeling perfectly miserable, Entreri leaned heavily against the wall. How was he to know that the wicked beast in the alley was a damned matron mother?

The walls seemed to close in on the man, suffocating him. Cold sweat beaded on his normally cool brow, and he labored to draw breath. All his thoughts centered on possible escape, but they inevitably slammed against unyielding stone walls. He was caught by logistics as much as by drow blades.

He had tried to escape once, had run out of Menzoberranzan through the eastern exit, beyond Donigarten. But where could he go? The Underdark was a maze of dangerous tunnels and deep holes filled with monsters the assassin did not know how to fight.

127

Entreri was a creature of the very different surface world. He did not understand the wild Underdark, could not hope to survive there for long. Certainly he would never find his own way back to the surface. He was trapped, caged, stripped of his pride and his dignity, and, sooner or later, he was going to be horribly killed.

Chapter 12

RISING TO
THE OCCASION

 e can drop this whole section," General Dagna remarked as he poked a stubby finger against the map
spread on the table.

"Drop it?" bellowed the battlerager. "If ye drop it,
then how're we to kill the stinking drow?"

Regis, who had arranged this meeting, looked incredulously to
Dagna and the other three dwarven commanders huddled about the
table. Then he looked back to Pwent. "The ceiling *will* kill the stinking drow," he explained.

"Bah, sandstone!" huffed the battlerager. "What fun do ye call that? I got to grease up me armor with some drow blood, I do, but with yer stupid plan, I'll have to do a month's digging just to find a body to rub against."

"Lead the charge down here," Dagna offered, pointing to another section of open corridors on the map. "The rest of us'll give ye a hunnerd-foot head start."

Regis put a sour look on the general and moved it, in turn, to each of the other dwarves, who were all bobbing their heads in agreement. Dagna was only half-kidding, Regis knew. More than a few of Clan Battlehammer would not be teary-eyed if obnoxious Thibbledorf Pwent happened to be among the fallen in the potential fight against the dark elves.

"Drop the tunnel," Regis said to get them back on track. "We'll need strong defenses here and here," he added, pointing to two open areas in the otherwise tight lower tunnels. "I'm meeting later this day with Berkthgar of Settlestone."

"Ye're bringin' the smelly humans in?" Pwent asked.

Even the dwarves, who favored the strong smells of soot-covered, sweaty bodies, twisted their faces at the remark. In Mithril Hall, it was said that Pwent's armpit could curl a hardy flower at fifty yards.

"I don't know what I'm doing with the humans," Regis answered. "I haven't even told them my suspicions of a drow raid yet. If they agree to join our cause, and I have no reason to believe that they won't, I suspect that we would be wise to keep them out of the lower tunnels—even though we plan to light those tunnels."

Dagna nodded his agreement. "A wise choice indeed," he said. "The tall men are better suited to fighting along the mountainsides. Me own guess is that the drow'll come in around the mountain as well as through it."

"The men of Settlestone will meet them," added another dwarf.

* * * * *

From the shadows of a partly closed door at the side of the room, Bruenor Battlehammer looked on curiously. He was amazed at how quickly Regis had taken things into his control, especially given the fact that the halfling did not wear his hypnotic ruby

pendant. After scolding Bruenor for not acting quickly and deci-
sively, for falling back into a mire of self-pity with the trails to Catti-
brie and Drizzt apparently closed, the halfling, with Pwent in tow,
had gone straight to General Dagna and the other war commanders.

What amazed Bruenor now was not the fact that the dwarves
had gone eagerly into preparations for war, but the fact that Regis
seemed to be leading them. Of course, the halfling had concocted a
lie to assume that role. Using Bruenor's resumed indifference, the
halfling was faking meetings with the dwarf king, then going to
Dagna and the others pretending that he was bringing word straight
from Bruenor.

When he first discovered the ruse, Bruenor wanted to throttle
the halfling, but Regis had stood up to him, and had offered, more
than sincerely, to step aside if Bruenor wanted to take over.

Bruenor wished that he could, desperately wanted to find that
level of energy once more, but any thought of warfare inevitably led
him to memories of his recent past battles, most of them beside
Drizzt, Catti-brie, and Wulfgar. Paralyzed by those painful memories, Bruenor had simply dismissed Regis and allowed the halfling
to go on with his facade.

Dagna was as fine a strategist as any, but his experience was
rather limited regarding races other than dwarves or stupid goblins.
Regis was among Drizzt's best friends, had sat and listened to
Drizzt's tales of his homeland and his kin hundreds of times. Regis
had also been among Wulfgar's best friends, and so he understood
the barbarians, whom the dwarves would need as allies should the
war come to pass.

Still, Dagna had never been fond of anyone who wasn't a dwarf,
and the fact that he wholeheartedly accepted the advice of a halfling—and one not known for bravery!—surprised Bruenor more
than a little.

It stung the king as well. Bruenor knew of the dark elves and
the barbarians at least as well as Regis, and he understood dwarven
tactics better than anyone. He should be at that table, pointing out
the sections on the map; he should be the one, with Regis beside
him, to meet with Berkthgar the Bold.

Bruenor dropped his gaze to the floor, rubbed a hand over his
brow and down his grotesque scar. He felt an ache in the hollow

131

socket. Hollow, too, was his heart, empty with the loss of Wulfgar, and breaking apart at the thought that Drizzt and his precious Catti-brie had gone off into danger.

The events about him had gone beyond his responsibilities as king of Mithril Hall. Bruenor's first dedication was to his children, one lost, the other missing, and to his friends. Their fates were beyond him now; he could only hope that they would win out, would survive and come back to him, for Bruenor had no way to get to Catti-brie and Drizzt.

Bruenor could never get back to Wulfgar.

The dwarf king sighed and turned away, walking slowly back toward his empty room, not even noticing that the meeting had adjourned.

Regis watched Bruenor silently from the doorway, wishing that he had his ruby pendant, if for no other reason than to try to re-kindle the fires in the broken dwarf.

* * * * *

Catti-brie eyed the wide corridor ahead suspiciously, trying to make out distinct shapes among the many stalagmite mounds. She had come into a region where mud mixed with stone, and she had seen the tracks clearly enough—goblin tracks, she knew, and recent.

Ahead loomed the perfect place for an ambush. Catti-brie took an arrow from the quiver strapped behind her hip, then held Taul-maril the Heartseeker, her magical bow, ready in her hands. Tucked under one arm, ready to be dropped, was the panther figurine. She silently debated whether or not she should summon Guenhwyvar from the Astral Plane. She had no real proof that the goblins were about—all the mounds in the corridor seemed natural and benign—but she felt the hairs on the back of her neck tingle.

She decided to hold off calling the cat, her logic overruling her instincts. She fell against the left-hand wall and slowly started forward, wincing every time the mud sloshed around her lifting boot.

With a dozen stalagmite mounds behind her, the wall still tightly to her left, the young woman paused and listened once more. All seemed perfectly quiet, but she couldn't shake the feeling that her every step was being monitored, that some monster was poised not far away, waiting to spring out and throttle her. Would it be like this all the way through the Underdark? she wondered. Would she drive herself insane with imagined dangers? Or worse, would the false alarms of her misguided instincts take her off guard on that one occasion when danger really did rise against her?

Catti-brie shook her head to clear the thoughts and squinted her eyes to peer into the magically starlit gloom. Another benefit of Lady Alustriel's gift was that Catti-brie's eyes did not glow with the telltale red of infravision. The young woman, though, inexperienced in such matters, didn't know that; she knew only that the shapes ahead seemed ominous indeed. The ground and walls were not firmly set, as in other parts of the tunnels. Mud and open water flowed freely in different areas. Many of the stalagmites seemed to have appendages—goblin arms, perhaps, holding wicked weapons.

Again Catti-brie forced away the unwanted thoughts, and she started forward, but froze immediately. She had caught a sound, a slight scraping, like that of a weapon tip brushing against stone. She waited a long while but heard nothing more, so she again told herself not to let her imagination carry her away.

But had those goblin tracks been part of her imagination? she asked herself as she took another step forward.

Catti-brie dropped the figurine and swung about, her bow coming to bear. Around the nearest stalagmite charged a goblin, its ugly, flat face seeming broader for the wide grin it wore and its rusting and jagged sword held high above its head.

Catti-brie fired, point blank, and the silver-streaking arrow had barely cleared the bow when the monster's head exploded in a shower of multicolored sparks. The arrow blasted right through, sparking again as it sliced a chunk off the stalagmite mound.

"Guenhwyvar!" Catti-brie called, and she readied the bow. She knew she had to get moving, that this area had been clearly marked by the spark shower. She considered the gray mist that had begun to swirl about her, and, knowing the summoning was complete, scooped up the figurine and ran away from the wall. She hopped the dead goblin's body and cut around the nearest stalagmite, then slipped between two others. Out of the corner of her eye she saw another four-foot-tall huddled shape. An arrow streaked off in pursuit, its silvery trail stealing the darkness, and scored another hit.

Catti-brie did not smile, though, for the flash of light revealed a dozen more of the ugly humanoids, slinking and crawling about the mounds.

They screamed and hooted and began their charge.

Over by the wall, gray mist gave way to the powerful panther's tangible form. Guenhwyvar had recognized the urgency of the call and was on the alert immediately, ears flattened and shining green eyes peering about, taking full measure of the scene. Quieter than the night, the cat loped off.

Catti-brie circled farther out from the wall, taking a roundabout course to flank the approaching group. Every time she came past another blocking mound, she let fly an arrow, as often hitting stone as goblins. She knew that confusion was her ally here, that she had to keep the creatures from organizing, or they would surround her.

Another arrow streaked away, and in its illumination Catti-brie saw a closer target, a goblin crouched right behind the mound she would soon pass. She went behind the mound, skidded to a stop, and came back out the same way, desperately working to fit an arrow.

The goblin swung around the mound and rushed in, sword leading. Catti-brie batted with her bow, barely knocking the weapon aside. She heard a sucking sound behind her, then a hiss, and instinctively dropped to her knees.

A goblin pitched over her suddenly low form and crashed into its surprised ally. The two were up quickly, though, as quickly as Catti-brie. The woman worked her bow out in front to keep them at bay, tried to get her free hand down to grab at the jeweled dagger on her belt.

Sensing their advantage, the goblins charged—then went tumbling away along with six hundred pounds of flying panther.

"Guen," Catti-brie mouthed in silent appreciation, and she pivoted about, pulling an arrow from her quiver. As she expected, goblins were fast closing from behind.

Taulmaril twanged once, again, and then a third time, Catti-brie blasting holes in the ranks. She used the sudden and deadly explosions of streaking lines and sparks as cover and ran, not away, as she knew the goblins would expect, but straight ahead, backtracking along her original route.

She had them fooled as she ducked behind another mound, wide and thick, and nearly giggled when a goblin leaped out behind her, rubbing its light-stung eyes and looking back the other way.

Just five feet behind the stupid thing, Catti-brie let fly, the arrow blasting into the goblin's back, snaring on a bone, and sending the creature flying through the air.

Catti-brie spun and ran on, around the back side of the wide mound. She heard a roar from Guenhwyvar, followed by the profound screams of another group of goblins. Ahead, a huddled form was running away from her, and she lifted her bow, ready to clear the path.

Something jolted her on the hip. She released the bowstring, and the arrow zipped wide of the mark, scorching a hole in the wall.

Catti-brie stumbled off balance, startled and hurt. She banged her shin against a jutting stone and nearly pitched headlong, skidding to a stop down on one knee. As she reached down to get another arrow from her quiver, she felt the wet warmth of her lifeblood pouring generously from a deep gash in her hip. Only then did stunned Catti-brie realize the hot waves of agony.

She kept her wits about her and turned as she fitted the arrow.

The goblin was right above her, its breath coming hot and smelly through pointed yellow teeth. Its sword was high above its head.

Catti-brie let fly. The goblin jerked up into the air, but came back to its feet. Behind it, another goblin caught the arrow under the chin, the powerful bolt blowing the back of its skull off.

Catti-brie thought she was dead. How could she have missed? Did the arrow slip under the goblin's arm as it jumped in fright? It made no sense to her, but she could hardly stop to think it over. The moment of death was upon her, she was sure, for she could not maneuver her bow quickly enough to parry the goblin's next strike. She could not block the descending sword.

But the sword did not descend. The goblin simply stopped, held perfectly still for what seemed to Catti-brie an interminable time. Its sword then clanged to the stone; a wheeze issued from the center of its rib cage, followed by a thick line of blood. The monster toppled to the side, dead.

Catti-brie realized that her arrow had indeed hit the mark, had driven cleanly through the first goblin to kill the second.

Catti-brie forced herself to her feet. She tried to run on, but waves rolled over her, and before she understood what had happened, she was back to the floor, back to one knee. She felt a coldness up her side, a swirling nausea in her stomach, and, to her horror, saw yet another of the miserable goblins fast closing, waving a spiked club.

Summoning all of her strength, Catti-brie waited until the very last moment and whipped her bow across in front of her. The goblin shrieked and fell backward, avoiding the hit, but its sudden retreat gave Catti-brie the time to draw her short sword and the jeweled dagger.

She stood, forcing down the pain and the sick feeling.

The goblin uttered something in its annoying, high-pitched voice, something threatening, Catti-brie knew, though it sounded like a typical goblin whine. The wretched creature came at her all of a sudden, whipping the club to and fro, and Catti-brie leaped back.

A jolting flare of agony rushed up her side, nearly costing her her balance. On came the goblin, crouched and balanced, sensing victory.

It continued to talk to her, taunt her, though she could not understand its language. It chuckled and pointed to her wounded leg.

Catti-brie was confident that she could defeat the goblin, but she feared that it would be to no avail. Even if she and Guenhwyvar won out, killed all the goblins or sent them fleeing, what might come next? Her leg would barely support her—certainly she could not continue her quest—and she doubted that she could properly clean and dress the wound. The goblins might not kill her, but they had stopped her, and the waves of pain continued unabated.

Catti-brie's eyes rolled back and she started to sway.

Her eyes blinked open and she steadied herself as the goblin took the bait and charged. When it realized the ruse, it tried to stop, but skidded in the slippery mud.

The goblin whipped its club across frantically, but Catti-brie's short sword intercepted it, locking against one of the spikes. Knowing that she had not the strength to force the club aside, she pressed forward, into the goblin, tucking her sword arm in close as she went, forcing the goblin's arm to hook about her as she turned.

All the while, the jeweled dagger led the way, reaching for the creature's belly. The goblin got its free arm up to block, and only the dagger's tip slipped through its skin.

Catti-brie did not know how long she could hold the clinch. Her strength was draining; she wanted nothing more than to curl up in a little ball and faint away.

Then, to her surprise, the goblin cried out in agony. It whipped its head back and forth, shook its whole body wildly in an effort to get away. Catti-brie, barely holding the dangerous club at bay, had to keep pace with it.

A burst of energy pulsed through the dagger and coursed up her arm.

The young woman didn't know what to make of it, didn't know what was happening, as the goblin went into a series of violent convulsions, each one sending another pulse of energy flowing into its foe.

The creature fell back against a stone, its blocking arm limp, and Catti-brie's momentum carried her closer, the wicked dagger sinking in to the hilt. The next pulse of energy nearly knocked Catti-brie away, and her eyes widened in horror as she realized that Artemis Entreri's weapon was literally eating away at the goblin's life force and transferring it to her!

The goblin sprawled over the arcing edge of the stalagmite mound, its eyes open and unblinking, its body twitching in death spasms.

Catti-brie fell back, taking the bloodied dagger with her. She worked hard to draw breath, gasping in disbelief and eyeing the blade with sheer revulsion.

A roar from Guenhwyvar reminded her that the battle was not ended. She replaced the dagger on her belt and turned, thinking that she had to find her bow. She had gone two running steps before she even realized that her leg was easily supporting her now.

From somewhere in the shadows, a goblin heaved a spear, which skipped off the stone just behind the running woman and stole her train of thought. Catti-brie skidded down in the mud and scooped up her bow as she slid past. She looked down to her quiver, saw its powerful magic already at work replacing the spent arrows.

She saw, too, that no more blood was coming from her wound. Gingerly, the young woman ran a hand over it, felt a thick scab already in place. She shook her head in disbelief, took up her bow, and began firing.

Only one more goblin got close to Catti-brie. It sneaked around the back side of the thick mound. The young woman started to drop her bow and draw out her weapons for melee, but she stopped (and so did the goblin!) when a great panther's paw slapped down atop the creature's head and long claws dug into the goblin's sloping forehead.

Guenhwyvar snapped the creature backward with sudden, savage force such that one of the monster's shoddy boots remained where it had been standing. Catti-brie looked away, back to the area behind them, as Guenhwyvar's powerful maw closed over the stunned goblin's throat and began to squeeze.

Catti-brie saw no targets, but let fly another arrow to brighten the end of the corridor. Half a dozen goblins were in full flight, and Catti-brie sent a shower of arrows trailing them, chasing them, and cutting them down.

She was still firing a minute later—her enchanted quiver would never run short of arrows—when Guenhwyvar padded over to her and bumped against her, demanding a pat. Catti-brie sighed deeply and dropped a hand to the cat's muscled flank, her eyes falling to the jeweled dagger, sitting impassively on her belt.

She had seen Entreri wield that dagger, had once had its blade against her own throat. The young woman shuddered as she recalled that awful moment, more awful now that she understood the cruel weapon's properties.

Guenhwyvar growled and pushed against her, prodding her to motion. Catti-brie understood the panther's urgency; according to Drizzt's tales, goblins rarely traveled in the Underdark in secluded bands. If there were twenty here, there were likely two hundred somewhere nearby.

Catti-brie looked to the tunnel behind them, the tunnel from which she had come and down which the goblins had fled. She considered, briefly, going that way, fighting through the fleeing few and running back to the surface world, where she belonged.

It was a fleeting thought for her, an excusable instant of weakness. She knew that she must go on, but how? Catti-brie looked down to her belt once more and smiled as she untied the magical mask. She lifted it before her face, unsure of how it even worked.

With a shrug to Guenhwyvar, the young woman pressed the mask against her face.

Nothing happened.

Holding it tight, she thought of Drizzt, imagined herself with ebony skin and the fine chiseled features of a drow.

Biting tingles of magic nipped at her every pore. In a moment, she moved her hand away from her face, the mask holding fast of its own accord. Catti-brie blinked many times, for in the magical starlight afforded her by the Cat's Eye, she saw her receding hand shining perfectly black, her fingers more slender and delicate than she remembered them.

How easy it had been!

Catti-brie wished that she had a mirror so that she could check the disguise, though she felt in her heart that it was true. She considered how perfectly Entreri had mimicked Regis when he had come back to Mithril Hall, right down to the halfling's equipment. With that thought, the young woman looked to her own rather drab garb. She considered Drizzt's tales of his homeland, of the fabulous and evil high priestesses of Lloth.

Catti-brie's worn traveling cloak had become a rich robe, shimmering purple and black. Her boots had blackened, their tips curling up delicately. Her weapons remained the same, though, and it seemed to Catti-brie, in this attire, that Entreri's jeweled dagger was the most fitting.

Again the young woman focused her thoughts on that wicked blade. A part of her wanted to drop it in the mud, to bury it where no one could ever find it. She even went so far as to close her fingers over its hilt.

But she released the dagger immediately, strengthened her resolve, and smoothed her drowlike robes. The blade had helped her; without it she would be crippled and lost, if not dead. It was a weapon, like her bow, and, though its brutal tactics assaulted her sensibilities, Catti-brie came, in that moment, to accept them. She carried the dagger more easily as the days turned into a week, and then two.

This was the Underdark, where the savage survived.

Part 3

SHADOWS

here are no shadows in the Underdark.

Only after years on the surface have I come to understand the significance of that seemingly minute fact, the significance of the contrast between lightness and darkness. There are no shadows in the Underdark, no areas of mystery where only the imagination can go.

What a marvelous thing is a shadow! I have seen my own silhouette walk under me as the sun rode high; I have seen a gopher grow to the size of a large bear, the light low behind him, spreading his ominous silhouette far across the ground. I have walked through the woods at twilight, my gaze

143

alternating between the lighter areas catching the last rays of day, leafy green slipping to gray, and those darkening patches, those areas where only my mind's eye could go. Might a monster be there? An orc or a goblin? Or might a hidden treasure, as magnificent as a lost, enchanted sword or as simple as a fox's den, lay within the sheltering gloom?

When I walk the woods at twilight, my imagination walks beside me, heightens my senses, opens my mind to any possibilities. But there are no shadows in the Underdark, and there is no room for fanciful imagining. All, everywhere, is gripped in a brooding, continual, predatory hush and a very real, ever present danger.

To imagine a crouched enemy, or a hidden treasure, is an exercise in enjoyment, a conjured state of alertness, of aliveness. But when that enemy is too often real and not imagined, when every jag in the stone, every potential hiding place, becomes a source of tension, then the game is not so much fun.

One cannot walk the corridors of the Underdark with his imagination beside him. To imagine an enemy behind one stone might well blind a person to the very real enemy behind another. To slip into a daydream is to lose that edge of readiness, and in the Underdark, to be unwary is to die.

This proved the most difficult transition for me when I went back into those lightless corridors. I had to again become the primal hunter, had to survive, every moment, on that instinctual edge, a state of nervous energy that kept my muscles always taut, always ready to spring. Every step of the way, the present was all that mattered, the search for potential hiding places of potential enemies. I could not afford to imagine those enemies. I had to wait for them and watch for them, react to any movements.

There are no shadows in the Underdark. There is no room for imagination in the Underdark. It is a place for alertness, but not aliveness, a place with no room for hopes and dreams.

—Drizzt Do'Urden

Chapter 13

HUNGRY GODDESS

ouncilor Firble of Blingdenstone normally enjoyed his journeys out of the deep gnome city, but not this day. The little gnome stood in a small chamber, but its dimensions seemed huge to him, for he felt quite vulnerable. He kicked his hard boots about the rocks on the otherwise smooth floor, twiddled his stubby fingers behind his back, and every so often ran a hand over his almost-bald head, wiping away lines of sweat.

A dozen tunnels ran into this chamber, and Firble took some comfort in the knowledge that two score svirfnebli warriors stood ready to rush to his aid, including several shamans with enchanted stones that could summon elemental giants from the plane of earth. Firble understood the drow of Menzoberranzan, forty-five miles to the east of Blingdenstone, better than any of his kin, though, and even his armed escort's presence did not allow him to relax. The gnome councilor knew well that if the dark elves had set this up as an ambush, then all the gnomes and all the magic of Blingdenstone might not be enough.

A familiar clicking sounded from the tunnel directly across the small chamber and, a moment later, in swept Jarlaxle, the extraordinary drow mercenary, his wide-brimmed hat festooned with a giant *diatryma* feather, his vest cut high to reveal rolling lines of muscles across his abdomen. He strode before the gnome, glanced about a couple of times to take in the whole scene, then dipped into a low bow, brushing his hat across the floor with an outstretched hand.

"My greetings!" Jarlaxle said heartily as he came back upright, crooking his arm above him so that the hat tucked against his elbow. A snap of the arm sent the hat into a short spin, to land perfectly atop the swaggering mercenary's shaved head.

"High soar your spirits this day," Firble remarked.

"And why not?" the drow asked. "It's another glorious day in the Underdark! A day to be enjoyed."

Firble did not seem convinced, but he was amazed, as always, by the conniving drow's command of the Svirfneblin language. Jarlaxle spoke the tongue as easily and fluidly as any of Blingdenstone's deep gnome inhabitants, though the mercenary used the sentence structure more common to the drow language and not the inverted form favored by many of the gnomes.

"Many svirfneblin mining parties have been assaulted," Firble said, his tone verging on that of an accusation. "Svirfneblin parties working *west* of Blingdenstone."

Jarlaxle smiled coyly and held his hands out wide. "Ched Nasad?" he asked innocently, implicating the next nearest drow city.

"Menzoberranzan!" Firble asserted. Ched Nasad was many weeks away. "One dark elf wore the emblem of a Menzoberranzan house."

"Rogue parties," Jarlaxle reasoned. "Young fighters out for pleasure."

Firble's thin lips almost disappeared with his ensuing scowl. Both he and Jarlaxle knew better than to think that the raiding drow were simple young rowdies. The attacks had been coordinated and executed perfectly, and many svirfnebli had been slain.

"What am I to say?" Jarlaxle asked innocently. "I am but a pawn to the events about me."

Firble snorted.

"I thank you for your confidence in my position," the mercenary said without missing a beat. "But, really, dear Firble, we have been over this before. The events are quite out of my hands this time."

"What events?" Firble demanded. He and Jarlaxle had met twice before over the last two months, discussing this very issue, for the drow activity near the svirfneblin city had increased dramatically. At each meeting Jarlaxle had slyly eluded to some great events, but never had he come out and actually told Firble anything.

"Have we come to banter this same issue?" the mercenary asked wearily. "Really, dear Firble, I grow tired of your—"

"A drow we have captured," Firble interrupted, crossing his short but burly arms over his chest, as though that news should carry some weight.

Jarlaxle's expression turned incredulous and he held his hands out wide again, as if to ask, "So?"

"We believe this drow is a native of Menzoberranzan," Firble went on.

"A female?" Jarlaxle asked, thinking that the gnome, apparently viewing his information as vital, must be referring to a high priestess. The mercenary hadn't heard of any missing high priestesses (except, of course, Jerlys Horlbar, and she wasn't really missing).

"A male," Firble replied, and again the mercenary's expression turned dubious.

"Then execute him," the pragmatic Jarlaxle reasoned.

Firble tightened his arms across his chest and began tap-tapping his foot impatiently on the stone.

"Really, Firble, do you believe that a male drow prisoner gives your city some bargaining power?" the mercenary asked. "Do you expect me to run back to Menzoberranzan, pleading for this one male? Do you expect that the ruling matron mothers will demand that all activity in this area be ceased for his sake?"

"Then you admit sanctioned activity in this area!" the svirf-neblin retorted, pointing a stubby finger Jarlaxle's way and thinking he had caught the mercenary in a lie.

"I speak merely hypothetically," Jarlaxle corrected. "I was granting you your presumption so that I might correctly mirror your intentions."

"My intentions you do not know, Jarlaxle," Firble assured. It was clear to Jarlaxle, though, that the gnome was growing agitated by the mercenary's cool demeanor. It was always that way with Jarlaxle. Firble met with the drow only when the situation was critical to Blingdenstone, and often his meetings cost him dearly in precious gems or other treasures.

"Name your price, then," the gnome went on.

"My price?"

"Imperiled is my city," Firble said sharply. "And Jarlaxle knows why!"

The mercenary did not respond. He merely smiled and leaned back from the gnome.

"Jarlaxle knows, too, the name of this drow we have taken," Firble went on, in turn trying to be sly. For the first time, the merce-nary revealed, albeit briefly, his intrigue.

Firble really hadn't wanted to take the conversation this far. It was not his intent to reveal the "prisoner's" identity. Drizzt Do'Urden was, after all, a friend of Belwar Dissengulp, the Most Honored Bur-row Warden. Drizzt had never proven himself an enemy of Bling-denstone, had even aided the svirfnebli a score of years before, when he first had passed through the city. And by all accounts, the rogue drow had helped svirfnebli again on his return, out in the tunnels against his drow kin.

Still, Firble's first loyalty was to his own people and his city, and if giving Drizzt's name to Jarlaxle might aid the gnomes in their cur-rent predicament, might reveal the imposing events that Jarlaxle kept hinting at, then, to Firble, it would be worth the price.

Jarlaxle paused for a long while, trying to figure out where he should take this suddenly meaningful conversation. He figured that the drow was some rogue male, perhaps a former member of Bre-gan D'aerthe presumed lost in the outer tunnels. Or maybe the gnomes had bagged a noble from one of the higher-ranking houses, a fine prize indeed. Jarlaxle's ruby eyes gleamed at the thought of the profits such a noble might bring to Bregan D'aerthe.

"Has he a name?" the mercenary asked.

"A name that is known to you, and to us," Firble replied, feeling positively superior (a rare occurrence in his dealings with the crafty mercenary).

His cryptic answer, though, had given more information than intended to Jarlaxle. Few drow were known by name to the gnomes of Blingdenstone, and Jarlaxle could check on the whereabouts of most of those few quite easily. The mercenary's eyes widened suddenly, but he quickly regained his composure, his mind reeling down the path of a new possibility.

"Tell me of the events," Firble demanded. "Why are Menzoberranzan drow near Blingdenstone? Tell me, and to you I shall give the name!"

"Give the name if you choose," Jarlaxle scoffed. "The events? I have already told you to look to Ched Nasad, or to playful young males, students, perhaps, out of the Academy."

Firble hopped up and down, fists clenched in front of him as though he meant to jump over and punch the unpredictable mercenary. All feelings that he had gained the upper hand washed away in the blink of a drow eye.

"Dear Firble," Jarlaxle cooed. "Really, we should not be meeting unless we have more important matters to discuss. And, really, you and your escort should not be so far from home, not in these dark times."

The little svirfneblin let out an unintentional groan of frustration at the mercenary's continued hints that something dire was going on, that the increased drow activity was linked to some greater design.

But Jarlaxle, standing with one arm across his belly, his elbow in his hand and his other hand propping his chin, remained impassive, seeming positively amused by it all. Firble would get no pertinent information this day, he realized, so he gave a curt bow and spun about, kicking stones every step of the way out of the chamber.

The mercenary held his relaxed posture for some time after the gnome had left, then casually lifted one hand and signaled to the tunnel behind him. Out walked a human, though his eyes glowed red with the infravision common to Underdark races, a gift from a high priestess.

"Did you find that amusing?" Jarlaxle asked in the surface tongue.

"And informative," Entreri replied. "When we get back to the city, it should be a minor thing for you to discern the identity of the captured drow."

Jarlaxle regarded the assassin curiously. "Do you not already know it?" he asked.

"I know of no missing nobles," Entreri replied, taking time as he spoke to carefully study the mercenary. Had he missed something? "Certainly, their prisoner must be a noble, since his name was known not only to you, but to the gnomes. A noble or an adventurous drow merchant."

"Suppose I told you that the drow in Blingdenstone was no prisoner," Jarlaxle hinted, a wry smile on his ebon-skinned face.

Entreri stared at him blankly, apparently having no clue as to what the mercenary was talking about.

"Of course," Jarlaxle said a moment later. "You do not know of the past events, so you would have no way of putting the information together. There was once a drow who left Menzoberranzan and stopped, for a time, to live with the gnomes, though I hardly expected that he would return."

"You cannot be hinting that . . ." Entreri said, verily losing his breath.

"Precisely," Jarlaxle replied, turning his gaze to the tunnel through which Firble had disappeared. "It seems that the fly has come to the spiders."

Entreri did not know what to think. Drizzt Do'Urden, back in the Underdark! What did that mean for the planned raid on Mithril Hall? Would the plans be dropped? Would Entreri's last chance to see the surface world be taken from him?

"What are we to do?" he asked the mercenary, his tone hinting at desperation.

"Do?" Jarlaxle echoed. He leaned back and gave a hearty laugh.

"Do?" the drow asked again, as though the thought was absurd. "Why, we sit back and enjoy it, of course!"

His response was not totally unexpected to Entreri, not when the assassin took a moment to consider it. Jarlaxle was a lover of ironies—that was why he thrived in the world of the chaotic drow—and this unexpected turn certainly qualified. To Jarlaxle, life was a game, to be played and enjoyed without consideration for consequences or morality.

In other times, Entreri could empathize with that attitude, had even adopted it on occasion, but not now. Too much hung in the balance for Artemis Entreri, for the poor, miserable assassin. Drizzt's presence so near Menzoberranzan raised important questions for the assassin's future, a future that looked bleak indeed.

Jarlaxle laughed again, long and hard. Entreri stood solemnly, staring at the tunnel that led generally toward the gnome city, his mind staring into the face, the violet eyes, of his most hated enemy.

* * * * *

Drizzt took great comfort in the familiar surroundings about him. He almost felt that he must be dreaming, for the small stone dwelling was exactly as he remembered it, right down to the hammock in which he now found himself.

But Drizzt knew that this was no dream, knew it from the fact that he could feel nothing from his waist down, neither the hammock's cords nor even a tingle in his bare feet.

"Awake?" came a question from the dwelling's second, smaller, chamber. The word struck Drizzt profoundly, for it was spoken in the Svirfneblin tongue, that curious blend of elven melodies and crackling dwarven consonants. Svirfneblin words rushed back to Drizzt's thoughts, though he had neither heard nor spoken the language in more than twenty years. It took some effort for Drizzt to turn his head and see the approaching burrow warden.

The drow's heart skipped a few beats at the sight.

Belwar had aged a bit but still seemed sturdy. He banged his "hands" together when he realized that Drizzt, his long-ago friend, was indeed awake.

Drizzt was pleased to see those hands, works of metallic art, capping the gnome's arms. Drizzt's own brother had cut off Belwar's hands when Drizzt and Belwar had first met. There had been a battle between the deep gnomes and a party of drow, and, at first, Drizzt had been Belwar's prisoner. Dinin came fast to Drizzt's aid, though, and the positions were quickly reversed.

Dinin would have killed Belwar had it not been for Drizzt. But Drizzt wasn't sure how much his attempt to save the svirfneblin's life had been worth, for Dinin had ordered Belwar crippled. In the brutal Underdark, crippled creatures usually did not survive long.

When Drizzt had met Belwar again, when he had come into Blingdenstone as a refugee from Menzoberranzan, he had found that the svirfnebli, so unlike the drow, had come to their wounded friend's aid, crafting him apropos caps for his stubby arms. On the right arm, the Most Honored Burrow Warden (as the deep gnomes called Belwar) wore a mithril hammerhead etched with marvelous runes and sketchings of powerful creatures, including an earth elemental. The double-headed pickaxe Belwar wore on his left arm was no less spectacular. These were formidable tools for digging and fighting, and more formidable still, for the svirfneblin shamans had enchanted the "hands." Drizzt had seen Belwar burrow through solid stone as fast as a mole through soft dirt.

It was so good to see that Belwar had continued to thrive, that Drizzt's first non-drow friend, Drizzt's first true friend, other than Zak'nafein, was well.

"*Magga cammara*, elf," the svirfneblin remarked with a chuckle as he walked past the hammock. "I thought you would never wake up!"

Magga cammara, Drizzt's mind echoed, "by the stones." The curious phrase, one that Drizzt had not heard in twenty years, put the drow at ease, brought his thoughts cascading back to the peaceful time he had spent as Belwar's guest in Blingdenstone.

He came out of his personal thoughts and noticed that the svirfneblin was at his feet, studying his posture.

"How do they feel?" Belwar asked.

"They do not," Drizzt replied.

The gnome nodded his hairless head and brought his pickaxe up to scratch at his huge nose. "You got nookered," he remarked.

Drizzt did not reply, obviously not understanding.

"Nookered," Belwar said again, moving to a cabinet bolted to the wall. He hooked the door with his pickaxe and swung it open, then used both hands to tentatively grasp some item inside and take it out for Drizzt to see. "A newly designed weapon," Belwar explained. "Been around for only a few years."

Drizzt thought that the item resembled a beaver's tail, with a short handle for grasping on the narrow end and with the wide end curled over at a sharp angle. It was smooth all about, with the notable exception of one serrated edge.

"A nooker," Belwar said, holding it up high. It slipped from his tentative grasp and dropped to the floor.

Belwar shrugged and clapped his mithril hands together. "A good thing it is that I have my own weapons!" Belwar banged the hammer and pickaxe together a second time.

"Lucky you are, Drizzt Do'Urden," he went on, "that the svirfnebli in battle recognized you for a friend."

Drizzt snorted; he didn't, at that moment, feel very lucky.

"He could have hit you with the sharp edge," Belwar went on. "Cut your backbone in half, it would have!"

"My backbone feels as if it *has* been cut in half," Drizzt remarked.

"No, no," Belwar said, walking back to the bottom of the hammock, "just nookered." The gnome poked his pickaxe hard against the bottom of Drizzt's foot, and the drow winced and shifted. "See, coming back already is the feeling," Belwar declared, and, smiling mischievously, he prodded Drizzt again.

"I will walk again, Burrow Warden," the relieved drow promised, his tone threatening so that he could play along with the game.

Belwar poked him again. "A while will that be!" he laughed. "And soon you will feel a tickle as well!"

It seemed like old times to Drizzt; it seemed like the very pressing problems that had burdened his shoulders had been temporarily lifted. How good it was to see his old friend again, this gnome who had gone out with him, out of loyalty alone, into the wilds of the Underdark, who had been captured beside Drizzt by the dreaded mind flayers and had fought his way out beside Drizzt.

"It was a coincidence, fortunate for both me and your fellows in the tunnels, that I happened into the area when I did," Drizzt said.

"Not so much a chance of fate," Belwar replied, and a grim

153

demeanor clouded his cheerful expression. "The fights have become too common. One a week, at least, and many svirfnebli have died."

Drizzt closed his lavender eyes and tried to digest the unwelcome news.

"Lloth is hungry, so it is said," Belwar went on, "and life has not been good for the gnomes of Blingdenstone. The cause of it all we are trying to learn."

Drizzt took it all in stride, feeling then, more than ever before, that he had done right in returning. More was happening than a simple drow attempt to recapture him. Belwar's description, the assertion that Lloth was hungry, seemed on the mark.

Drizzt got prodded again, hard, and he popped open his eyes to see the smiling burrow warden staring down at him, the cloud of recent events apparently passed. "But enough of the darkness!" Belwar declared. "Twenty years we have to recall, you for me and me for you!" He reached down and hooked one of Drizzt's boots, lifting it up and sniffing at the sole. "You found the surface?" he asked, sincerely hopeful.

The two friends spent the rest of that day trading tales, with Drizzt, who had gone into so different a world, doing most of the talking. Many times Belwar gasped and laughed; once he shared tears with his drow friend, seeming sincerely hurt by the loss of Wulfgar.

Drizzt knew at that moment that he had rediscovered another of his dearest friends. Belwar listened intently, with caring, to Drizzt's every word, let him share the most personal moments of his last twenty years with the silent support of a true friend.

After they dined that night, Drizzt took his first tentative steps, and Belwar, who had seen the debilitating effects of a well-wielded nooker before, assured the drow that he would be running along rubble-filled walls again in a day or so.

That news came as a mixed blessing. Drizzt was glad that he would heal, of course, but a small part of him wished that the process would take longer, that he might extend his visit with Belwar. For Drizzt knew that, the moment his body was able, the time would be at hand for him to finish his journey, to return to Menzoberranzan and try to end the threat.

Chapter 14

DISGUISE

ait here, Guen," Catti-brie whispered to the panther, both of whom stared at the wider area, a chamber relatively clear of stalagmites, that loomed up ahead. Many goblin voices came from that chamber. Catti-brie guessed that this was the main host, probably growing nervous since their scouting party hadn't returned. Those few surviving goblins were likely coming fast behind her, the young woman knew. She and Guen had done a fine job in prodding them on their way, had sent them running in the opposite direction down the corridor, but they likely had already turned about. And that fight had occurred less than an hour's hike from this spot.

There was no other apparent way around the chamber, and Catti-brie understood without even seeing the goblin horde that there were simply too many of the wretches to fight or scare off. She looked down to her ebon-skinned hands one last time, took some comfort in their accurate drow appearance, then straightened her thick hair—showing stark white now instead of its normal auburn—and plush robes, and defiantly strode forward.

The closest goblin sentries fell back in terror as the drow priest-ess casually entered their lair. Numbers alone kept the group from running off altogether, for, as Catti-brie had guessed, more than a hundred goblins were camped here. A dozen spears came up, angled in her direction, but she continued to walk steadily toward the center of the cavern.

Goblins gathered all around the young woman, cutting off any retreat. Others crouched facing the tunnel from which Catti-brie had emerged, not knowing if other drow would come strolling through. Still, the sea of flesh parted before the unexpected visitor; Catti-brie's bravado and disguise had apparently put the creatures off their collective guard.

She reached the chamber's halfway point, could see the corridor continuing on across the way, but the sea closed around her, giving ground more slowly and forcing the woman-turned-drow to slow her pace as well.

Then she was stopped, goblin spears pointing her way from every direction, goblin whispers filling the room. "*Gund ha, moga moga*," she demanded. Her command of the Goblin tongue was rudimentary at best, and she wasn't quite sure if she had said, "move aside and let me pass," or "move my mother into the ditch."

She hoped it was the former.

"*Moga gund, geek-ik moon'ga'woon'ga!*" rasped one huge goblin, nearly as large as a man, and it shifted through the horde to stand right before Catti-brie. The young woman forced herself to remain calm, but a large part of her wanted to cry out for Guenhwyvar and run away, and a smaller part wanted to break out in laughter. This was obviously the goblin leader, or the tribe's shaman, at least.

But the creature needed a few fashion tips. It wore high black boots, like those of a nobleman, but with the sides cut out to allow for its wide, ducklike feet. A pair of women's pantaloons, ringed with wide frills, served as its breeches, and, though it was obviously male, the beast wore a woman's underpants and corset, as well, complete with cups for very ample breasts. Several mismatched necklaces, some gold, some silver, and one strand of pearls, circled its skinny neck, and a gaudy ring adorned every crooked finger. Catti-brie recognized the goblin's headdress as religious, though she wasn't quite certain of the sect. It resembled a sunburst trimmed with long gold ribbons, but Catti-brie was fairly sure that the goblin had it on backward, for it leaned forward over the ugly creature's sloping brow, one ribbon dangling annoyingly before the goblin's nose.

No doubt, the goblin thought itself the height of thieving fashion, dressed in the clothing of its tribe's unfortunate victims. It continued to ramble in its high-pitched voice, too fast for Catti-brie to make out more than a single word here or there. Then the creature stopped, abruptly, and pounded a fist against its chest.

"Do ye speak the surface tongue?" Catti-brie asked, trying to find some common ground. She fought hard to hold her nerve, but expected a spear to plunge into her back at any moment.

The goblin leader regarded her curiously, apparently not understanding a word she had said. It scanned the woman up and down, its red-glowing eyes finally coming to rest on the locket that hung about Catti-brie's neck. "*Nying so, wucka,*" it remarked, and it pointed to the locket, then to Catti-brie, then swept its hand about to indicate the far exit.

Had the locket been a normal piece of jewelry, Catti-brie willingly would have given it over in exchange for passage, but she needed the magic item if she was to have any chance of locating Drizzt. The goblin repeated its demand, its tone more urgent, and the young woman knew that she had to think fast.

On sudden inspiration, she smiled and stuck an upraised finger before her. "*Nying,*" she said, thinking that to be the goblin word for gift. She clapped her hands sharply twice before her and called out, "Guenhwyvar!" without looking back over her shoulder.

A startled cry from the goblins at the back end of the chamber told her that the panther was on its way.

"Come in with calm, Guen," Catti-brie called. "Walk to me side without a fight."

The panther stalked slowly and steadily, head down and ears flattened. Every so often, Guenhwyvar let out a low growl, just to keep the closest goblins on their heels. The crowd parted widely, giving the magnificent cat a large open path to the drow priestess.

Then Guenhwyvar was at Catti-brie's side, nuzzling the woman's hip.

"*Nying*," Catti-brie said again, pointing from the panther to the goblin. "Ye take the cat and I walk out the passage," she added, motioning as best she could with her hands to convey the message. The ugly goblin fashion king scratched its head, shifting the headpiece awkwardly to the side.

"Well, go over and make nice," Catti-brie whispered to Guenhwyvar. She pushed the cat away with her leg. The panther looked up to her, seemed more than a little annoyed by it all, then padded over to the goblin leader and plopped down at its feet (and the blood drained from the monster's face!).

"*Nying*," Catti-brie said again, motioning that the goblin should reach down and pet the cat. The creature eyed her incredulously, but gradually, with her coaxing, the goblin mustered the nerve to touch the cat's thick fur.

The goblin's pointy-toothed smile widened, and it dared to touch the cat again, more solidly. Again it dipped, and again, and each stroke went more firmly over the panther's back. Through it all, Guenhwyvar leveled a withering stare at Catti-brie.

"Now, ye're to stay here with this friendly goblin," Catti-brie instructed the cat, making sure that her tones did not give away her true meaning. She patted her belt pouch, the one holding the figurine, and added, "I'll be calling ye, don't ye doubt."

Then Catti-brie straightened and faced the goblin leader squarely. She slapped a hand against her chest, then snapped it straight out and pointed to the far exit, her expression a scowl. "I go!" she declared and took a step forward.

At first, the goblin leader seemed as though it would move to hinder her, but a quick glance to the powerful cat at its feet changed the creature's mind. Catti-brie had played the game perfectly; she had allowed the overly proud goblin leader to retain its dignity, had kept herself appearing as a potentially dangerous enemy, and had strategically placed six hundred pounds of fighting ally right at the goblin leader's feet.

"*Nying so, wucka,*" the goblin said again, pointing to Guenhwyvar, then to the far exit, and it gingerly stepped aside so that the drow could pass.

Catti-brie swept across the rest of the chamber, backhand slapping one goblin that didn't get far enough out of her path. The creature came right back at her, sword raised, but Catti-brie didn't flinch, and a cry from the goblin leader, still with the panther curled about its ankles, stopped the goblin's response.

Catti-brie laughed in its ugly face, showed it that she held her own dagger, a magnificent, jeweled thing, ready under the folds of her beautiful robes.

She made it to the narrower tunnel and continued walking slowly for many steps. Then she stopped, glanced back, and pulled out the panther figurine.

Back in the chamber, the goblin leader was showing off its new acquisition to the tribe, explaining how it had outsmarted a "stupid drow female thing," and had taken the cat as its own. It didn't matter that the other goblins had witnessed the whole affair; in goblin culture, history was recreated almost daily.

The leader's smug smile waned quickly when a gray mist rose up about the panther, and the cat's material form began to melt away.

The goblin wailed a stream of protests and curses and dropped to its knees to grab the fast-fading cat.

A huge paw shot out of the mist, hooked around the leader's head, and yanked the wretch in. Then there was only mist, the surprised and not-too-smart goblin leader going along with the panther on a ride to the Astral Plane.

The remaining goblins hooted and ran all about, bumping into and falling over each other. Some thought to take up the chase for the departing drow, but by the time they began to organize, Catti-brie was long gone, running with all speed along the corridor and thinking herself positively clever.

* * * * *

R. A. Salvatore

The tunnels were familiar to him—too familiar. How many times had young Drizzt Do'Urden traveled these ways, usually serving as the point in a drow patrol? Then he had Guenhwyvar with him; now he was alone.

He limped slightly, one of his knees still a bit weak from the svirfneblin nooker.

He couldn't use that as an excuse to remain in Blingdenstone any longer, though. He knew that his business was pressing, and Belwar, though the parting stung the burrow warden, had not argued with Drizzt's decision to be on his way, an indication to Drizzt that the other svirfnebli wished him gone.

That had been two days ago, two days and about fifty miles of winding caverns. Drizzt had crossed the trails of at least three drow patrols on his way, an unusually high number of warriors to be out so far from Menzoberranzan, and that led credence to Belwar's claim that something dangerous was brewing, that the Spider Queen was hungry. On all three of those occasions, Drizzt could have tracked down the drow group and attempted to link up. He thought of concocting some story that he was an emissary from a merchant of Ched Nasad. All three times, Drizzt had lost his nerve, had kept moving instead toward Menzoberranzan, putting off that fateful moment when he would make contact.

Now the tunnels were too familiar, and that moment was nearly upon him.

He measured every step, maintaining perfect silence, as he crossed into one wider way. He heard some noise up ahead, a shuffle of many feet. Not drow feet, he knew; dark elves made no noise.

The ranger scaled the uneven wall and moved along a ledge half a dozen feet up from the main floor. Sometimes he found himself grasping with fingertips and pulling himself forward, his feet dangling, but Drizzt was not hindered, and he did not make a sound.

He froze in place at the din of more movement ahead. Fortunately, the ledge widened once more, freeing his hands, and he gingerly slipped his scimitars free of their sheaths, concentrating to keep Twinkle from flaring with inner light.

Slurping sounds led him around a bend, where he viewed a

160

host of short, huddled humanoids, wearing ragged cloaks with cowls pulled over their faces. They spoke not at all, but milled about aimlessly, and only their floppy feet showed Drizzt that they were goblins.

Goblin slaves, he knew by their movements, by their slumped posture, for only slaves carried such a weight of broken resignation.

Drizzt continued to watch silently for a while, trying to spot the herding drow. There were at least four score goblins in this cavern, lining the edge of a small pond that the drow called Heldaeyn's Pool, scooping water up under their low-pulled cowls as though they had not drunk in many days.

They probably had not. Drizzt spotted a couple of rothe, small Underdark cattle, milling nearby, and he realized that this group probably was out of the city in search of the missing creatures. On such trips, slaves were given little or nothing to eat, though they carried quite a bit of supplies. The accompanying drow guards, though, ate handsomely, usually right in front of their starving slaves.

The crack of a whip brought the goblins back to their feet and shuffling back from the pool's edge. Two drow soldiers, one male, one female, came into Drizzt's view. They talked casually, the female every so often cracking her whip.

Another drow called out some commands from the other side of the cavern, and the goblins began to fall into a rough line, more of an elongated huddle than any organized formation.

Drizzt knew that the most opportune moment was upon him. Slavers were among the least organized and least regimented of Menzoberranzan's extracity bands. Any slaver contingent usually comprised dark elves from several different houses and a complement of young drow students from each of the Academy's three schools.

Drizzt quietly slipped down from the ledge and walked around the jutting wall, flashing the customary hand signal greetings (though his fingers felt awkward going through the intricate routine) to the drow in the cavern.

The female pushed her male escort forward and stepped to the side behind him. Immediately the male's hand came up, holding one of the typical drow hand-crossbows, its dart coated, most likely, with a powerful sleeping potion.

Who are you? the female's hand asked over the male's shoulder.

"All that is left of a patrol group that ventured near Blingden-stone," Drizzt answered.

"You should go in near Tier Breche, then," the female answered aloud. Hearing her voice, so typical of drow females, voices that could be incredibly melodic or incredibly shrill, sent Drizzt's thoughts cascading back to those long years past. He realized then, fully, that he was just a few hundred yards from Menzoberranzan.

"I do not wish to 'go in' at all," Drizzt answered. "At least, not announced." The reasoning made perfect sense, Drizzt knew. If he had indeed been the only survivor of a lost patrol, he would have been vigorously interrogated at the drow Academy, probably even tortured until the masters were certain that he played no treacherous role in the patrol's fate, or until he died, whichever came first.

"Who is the first house?" the female asked, her eyes locked on Drizzt's lavender-glowing orbs.

"Baenre," Drizzt answered immediately, expecting the test. Spying dark elves from rival cities were not unknown in Menzoberranzan.

"Their youngest son?" the female asked slyly. She curled her lips up in a lewd and hungry smile, Drizzt realized as she continued to stare deeply into his unusual eyes.

By fortunate coincidence, Drizzt had attended the Academy in the same class as House Baenre's youngest son—as long as ancient Matron Baenre had not reared another child in the three decades Drizzt had been gone.

"Berg'inyon," he answered confidently, dropping his hands in a cocky cross at his belt (and putting them near his scimitars).

"Who are you?" the female asked again, and she licked her lips, obviously intrigued.

"No one who matters," Drizzt replied, and he matched her smile and the intensity of her stare.

The female patted her blocking male on the shoulder and her fingers motioned for him to go.

Am I to be off this miserable duty? he responded silently with his hands, a hopeful expression on his face.

"The *bol* will take your place this day," the female purred, labeling Drizzt with the drow word that described something mysterious or intriguing.

The male smiled widely and moved to put his hand-crossbow away. Noticing that it was cocked and ready, and looking up to take note that a whole herd of goblins stood nearby, he widened his smile instead and lifted the weapon to fire.

Drizzt offered no reaction, though it pained him to see even goblins treated so miserably.

"No," the female said, putting her hand over the male's wrist. She reached up and removed the dart from the hand-crossbow, then replaced it with another. "Yours would put the creature to sleep," she explained, and she cackled in laughter.

The male considered her for just a moment, then apparently caught on. He took aim at a goblin loitering near the water's edge and fired. The goblin jerked as the small dart jabbed into its back. It started to turn about, but toppled instead, into the pool.

Drizzt gnawed at his lips, understanding, by the goblin's futile flopping, that the dart the female had supplied was coated with a paralyzing potion, one that left the doomed creature fully conscious. The goblin had little control of its limbs and would surely drown, and, worse, it would know its cruel fate. It managed to arch its back enough so that its face came above the water level, but Drizzt knew that it would tire long before the wicked potion expired.

The male laughed heartily, replaced the hand-crossbow in its small holster, which lay diagonally across his lower chest, and walked off down the tunnel to Drizzt's left. Before he had gone even a dozen steps, the female began cracking her whip and called for the few drow guards to get the caravan moving, down the tunnel to the right.

After a moment, she turned a cold glare on Drizzt. "Why are you standing there?" she demanded.

Drizzt pointed to the goblin in the pool, floundering badly now, barely able to keep its mouth out of the water. He managed a laugh, as if he was enjoying the macabre spectacle, but he seriously considered rushing over and cutting the evil female down at that moment.

All the way out of the small cavern, Drizzt looked for opportunities to get over to the goblin, to pull the creature out of the water so that it would have a chance to get away. The female drow never

163

stopped eyeing him, though, not for an instant, and Drizzt understood that she had more on her mind than simply including him in the slave caravan. After all, why hadn't *she* taken the break when the new slaver unexpectedly arrived?

The dying goblin's last splashes followed Drizzt out of that place. The renegade drow swallowed hard and fought away his revulsion. No matter how many times he witnessed it, he would never get used to the brutality of his kin.

And Drizzt was glad of that.

Chapter 15

MASKS

atti-brie had never seen such creatures. They somewhat resembled gnomes, at least in stature, being about three feet tall, but they had no hair on their lumpy, ruddy heads, and their skin, in the starlight afforded her by the magical circlet, showed grayish. They were quite stout, nearly as muscular as dwarves, and judging from the fine tools they carried and the well-fitting metal armor they wore, they were, like dwarves, adept at mining and crafting.

Drizzt had told Catti-brie of the svirfnebli, the deep gnomes, and that is what she presumed she was looking upon. She couldn't be sure, though, and was afraid that this might be some offshoot of the evil duergar, gray dwarves.

She crouched amid a cluster of tall, thin stalagmites in an area of many crisscrossing corridors. The deep gnomes, if that's what they were, had come down the opposite way, and were now milling about one wide, flat section of corridor, talking among themselves and paying little heed of the stalagmite cluster twenty feet away.

Catti-brie was not sure of how she should proceed. If these were svirfnebli, and she was fairly sure of that, they could prove to be valuable allies, but how might she approach them? They certainly did not speak the same language and probably were as unfamiliar with humans as she was with them.

She decided that her best course would be simply to sit tight and let the creatures pass. Catti-brie had never experienced the strangeness of infravision, though, and she did not fully appreciate that, sitting among the cool stalagmites, her body temperature fully thirty degrees warmer than the stone, she was practically glowing to the svirfnebli's heat-seeing eyes.

Even as the young woman crouched and waited, deep gnomes fanned out in the tunnels around her, trying to discern if this drow (for Catti-brie still wore the magical mask) was alone or part of a larger band. A few minutes slipped by; Catti-brie looked down to her hand, thinking that she felt something in the stone, a slight vibration, perhaps. The young woman continued to stare at her tingling hand curiously. She did not know that deep gnomes communicated in a method that was part telepathy and part psychokinesis, sending their thought patterns to each other through the stone, and that a sensitive hand could sense the vibrations.

She did not know that the minute tingling was the confirmation from the deep gnome scouts that this drow crouching in the stalagmite cluster was indeed alone.

One of the svirfnebli ahead suddenly burst into motion, chanting a few words that Catti-brie did not understand and hurling a rock her way. She dipped lower behind the stones for cover and tried to decide whether to call out a surrender or take out her bow and try to frighten the creatures away.

The stone bounced harmlessly short and shattered, its flecks spreading in a small area before the stalagmite cluster. Those flecks began to smoke and sizzle, and the ground began to tremble.

Before Catti-brie knew what was happening, the stones before her rose up like a gigantic bubble, then took on the shape of a giant fifteen-foot-tall humanoid, its girth practically filling the corridor. The creature had huge, rocky arms that could smash a building to pieces. Two of the front stalagmites had been caught up in the monstrous formation and now served as dangerous spikes protruding from the front of the monster's massive chest.

Down the passage, the deep gnomes let out battle cries—calls that echoed in corridors all about the frightened woman.

Catti-brie scrambled backward as a gigantic hand swooped in and took the top from one stalagmite. She dropped the onyx figuring and called frantically for Guenhwyvar, all the while fitting an arrow to her bowstring.

The earth elemental shifted forward, its bulky legs melding with, slipping right through, the stony stalagmites in its way. It moved again to grab the woman, but a silver-streaking arrow ripped through its rock face, blowing a clean crevice between the monster's eyes.

The elemental straightened and reeled, then used its hands to push its halved head back into one piece. It looked back to the cluster and saw not the female drow, but a huge cat, tamping down its hind legs.

Catti-brie came out the back of the cluster, thinking to flee, but found deep gnomes coming down every side passage. She ran along the main corridor, cutting from mound to mound for cover, not daring to glance back at Guenhwyvar and the elemental. Then something hard banged against her shin, tripping her, and she sprawled headlong. She squirmed about to see another of the svirfnebli rising from behind one mound, a pickaxe still angled out as it had been placed to trip her.

Catti-brie pulled her bow around and shifted into a sitting position, but the weapon was batted away. She instinctively rolled to the side, but heard shuffling feet as three gnomes kept pace with her, heavy mauls lifted high to squash her.

Guenhwyvar snarled and soared, thinking to fly right past the behemoth and turn it about. The elemental was faster than the panther suspected, though, and a great rocky hand shot out, catching the cat in midflight and pulling it to its massive chest. Guenhwyvar shrieked as a stalagmite spike dug into a shoulder, and the deep gnomes, running up beside their champion, shrieked as well, in glee that the drow and her unexpected ally were apparently soon to be finished.

A maul descended toward Catti-brie's head. She snapped out her short sword and caught it at the joint between handle and head, deflecting it enough so that it banged loudly off the floor. The young woman scampered and parried, trying to get far enough from the gnomes to regain her footing, but they paced her, every which way, banging their mauls with shortened, measured strokes so that this fast-tiring dark elf had no opportunities for clear counterstrikes.

The sight of the marvelous panther, soon to be fully impaled and crushed, brought victorious thrills to a handful of the trailing svirfnebli, but brought only confusion to two others. Those two, Seldig and Pumkato by name, had played with such a panther as fledglings, and since Drizzt Do'Urden, the drow renegade they had played beside almost thirty years before, had just passed through Blingdenstone, they felt the panther's appearance could not be coincidence.

"Guenhwyvar!" Seldig cried, and the panther roared in reply.

The name, so perfectly spoken, struck Catti-brie profoundly and made those three deep gnomes about her hesitate as well.

Pumkato, who had summoned the elemental in the first place, called for the monster to hold steady, and Seldig quickly used his pickaxe to scale partway up the behemoth. "Guenhwyvar?" he asked, just a few feet from the panther's face. The trapped cat's ears came up, and it put a plaintive look on the somewhat familiar gnome.

"Who is that?" Pumkato demanded, pointing to Catti-brie.

Although she did not understand any of the svirfneblin's words, Catti-brie realized that she would never find a better opportunity. She dropped her sword to the stone, reached up with her free hand and pulled off the magical mask, her features immediately reverting to those of a young human woman. The three deep gnomes near her cried out and fell back, regarding her with less-than-complimentary sour expressions, as though her new appearance was quite ugly by their standards.

168

Pumkato mustered the courage to shuffle over to her, and he stood right in front of her.

He had known one name, Catti-brie realized, and she hoped that he would recognize another. She pointed to herself, then held her arms out wide and pulled them in as if hugging someone. "Drizzt Do'Urden?" she asked.

Pumkato's gray eyes widened, then he nodded, as though he should not have been surprised. Hiding his disgust at the human's appearance, the gnome extended one hand and helped Catti-brie to her feet.

Catti-brie moved slowly, obviously, as she took out the figurine and dismissed Guenhwyvar. Pumkato, likewise, sent his elemental back into the stone.

* * * * *

"*Kolsen'shea orbb,*" Jarlaxle whispered, an arcane phrase rarely uttered in Menzoberranzan that roughly translated to "pull the legs off a spider."

The seemingly plain wall before the mercenary reacted to the passwords. It shifted and twisted into a spiderweb, then rotated outward, its strands tucked together, to leave a hole for the mercenary and his human escort to climb through.

Even Jarlaxle, usually one step ahead of other drow, was somewhat surprised—pleasantly surprised—to find Triel Baenre waiting for him in the small office beyond, the private chambers of Gromph Baenre at Sorcere, the school of magic in the drow Academy. Jarlaxle had hoped that Gromph would be about, to witness the return, but Triel was an even better witness.

Entreri came in behind the mercenary and wisely stayed behind at the sight of volatile Triel. The assassin eyed the intriguing room, perpetually bathed in soft-glowing bluish light, as was most of the wizards' tower. Parchments lay everywhere, on the desk, on the three chairs, and on the floor. The walls were lined with shelves that held dozens of large, capped bottles and smaller, hourglass-shaped containers, their tops off and with sealed packets lying next to them. A hundred other curious items, too strange for the surface dweller to even guess at what they might do, lay amid the jumble.

"You bring *colnbluth* to Sorcere?" Triel remarked, her thin eyebrows angling up in surprise.

Entreri took care to keep his gaze to the floor, though he managed a few peeks at the Baenre daughter. He hadn't viewed Triel in so strong a light before, and he thought now that she was not so beautiful by drow standards. She was too short and too stocky in the shoulders for her very angular facial features. It struck the assassin as odd that Triel had risen so high among the ranks of drow, a race that treasured physical beauty. Her station was testament to the Baenre daughter's power, he decided.

Entreri couldn't understand very much of the Drow tongue, though he realized that Triel probably had just insulted him. Normally, the assassin responded to insults with weapons, but not here, not so far from his element and not against this one. Jarlaxle had warned Entreri about Triel a hundred times. She was looking for a reason to kill him—the vicious Baenre daughter was always looking for a reason to kill any *colnbluth,* and quite a few drow as well.

"I bring him many places," Jarlaxle answered. "I did not think that your brother would be here to protest."

Triel looked about the room, to the fabulous desk of polished dwarf bones and the cushioned chair behind. There were no connecting rooms, no obvious hiding places, and no Gromph.

"Gromph must be here," Jarlaxle reasoned. "Else, why would the matron mistress of Arach-Tinilith be in this place? That is a violation of the rules, as I remember them, as serious a breach, at least, as my bringing a non-drow to Sorcere."

"Take care how you question the actions of Triel Baenre," the short priestess replied.

"*Asanque,*" Jarlaxle answered with a sweeping bow. It was a somewhat ambiguous word that could mean either "as you wish," or "likewise."

"Why are you here?" Triel demanded.

"You knew I was coming," Jarlaxle stated.

"Of course," Triel said slyly. "I know many things, but I wish to hear your explanation for entering Sorcere, through private doors reserved for headmasters, and into the private quarters of the city's archmage."

Jarlaxle reached into the folds of his black cloak and produced the strange spider mask, the magical item that had gotten him over House Baenre's enchanted web fence. Triel's ruby-red eyes widened.

"I was instructed by your mother to return this to Gromph," the mercenary said, somewhat sourly.

"Here?" Triel balked. "The mask belongs at House Baenre."

Jarlaxle couldn't hide a bit of a smile, and he looked to Entreri, secretly hoping that the assassin was getting some of this conversation.

"Gromph will retrieve it," Jarlaxle answered. He walked over to the dwarf bone desk, uttered a word under his breath, and quickly slipped the mask into a drawer, though Triel had begun to protest. She stalked over to the desk and eyed the closed drawer suspiciously. Obviously Gromph would have trapped and warded it with a secret password.

"Open it," she instructed Jarlaxle. "I will hold the mask for Gromph."

"I cannot," Jarlaxle lied. "The password changes with each use. I was given only one." Jarlaxle knew that he was playing a dangerous game here, but Triel and Gromph rarely spoke to each other, and Gromph, especially in these days, with all the preparations going on in House Baenre, rarely visited his office at Sorcere. What Jarlaxle needed now was to be rid of the mask—openly, so that it could not be tied to him in any way. That spider mask was the only item, spells included, in all of Menzoberranzan that could get someone past House Baenre's magical fence, and if events took the turns that Jarlaxle suspected, that mask might soon be an important piece of property—and evidence.

Triel chanted softly and continued to stare at the closed drawer. She recognized the intricate patterns of magical energy, glyphs and wards, on the drawer, but they were woven too tightly for her to easily unravel. Her magic was among the strongest in Menzoberranzan, but Triel feared to try her hand against her brother's wizardly prowess. Dropping a threatening gaze at the cunning mercenary, she walked back across the room and stood near Entreri.

"Look at me," she said in the Common tongue of the surface, which surprised the assassin, for very few drow in Menzoberranzan spoke the language.

Entreri lifted his gaze to peer into Triel's intense eyes. He tried

171

to keep his demeanor calm, tried to appear subjugated, broken in spirit, but Triel was too perceptive for such facades. She saw the strength in the assassin, smiled as though she approved of it.

"What do you know of all this?" she asked.

"I know only what Jarlaxle tells me," Entreri replied, and he dropped the facade and stared hard at Triel. If she wished a contest of wills, then the assassin, who had survived and thrived on the most dangerous streets of Faerun's surface, would not back down.

Triel matched the unblinking stare for a long while and became convinced that she would garner little of use from this skilled adversary. "Be gone from here," she said to Jarlaxle, still using the surface tongue.

Jarlaxle rushed past the Baenre daughter and scooped up Entreri in his wake. "Quickly," the mercenary remarked. "We should be long out of Sorcere before Triel tries that drawer!" With that, they were through the spidery door, which fast reverted to a plain wall behind them, blocking Triel's inevitable curses.

But the Baenre daughter was not as mad as she was intrigued. She recognized three courses coming together here, her own and her mother's, and now, apparently, Jarlaxle's. The mercenary was up to something, she knew, something that obviously included Artemis Entreri.

* * * * *

When they were safely away from Tier Breche and the Academy, Jarlaxle translated all that had transpired to Entreri.

"You did not tell her of Drizzt's impending arrival," the assassin remarked. He had thought that important bit of information to be the gist of Jarlaxle's brief conversation with Triel, but the mercenary said nothing about it now.

"Triel has her own ways of discerning information," Jarlaxle replied. "I do not wish to make her work easier—not without a clear and agreed upon profit!"

Entreri smiled, then bit his lower lip, digesting the mercenary's words. There was always so much going on in this infernal city, the assassin mused. It was no wonder that Jarlaxle enjoyed the place so! Entreri almost wished that he was a drow, that he could carve out a place such as Jarlaxle had done, playing on the edge of disaster. Almost.

"When did Matron Baenre instruct you to return the mask?" the assassin asked. He and Jarlaxle had been out of Menzoberranzan for some time, had gone into the outer caverns to meet with a svirfneblin informant. They had returned only a short time before their trip to Sorcere, and Jarlaxle, as far as Entreri knew, hadn't gone anywhere near House Baenre.

"Some time ago," Jarlaxle replied.

"To bring it to the Academy?" Entreri pressed. It seemed out of place to him. And why had Jarlaxle taken him along? He had never been invited to that high place before, had even been refused on one occasion, when he had asked to accompany Jarlaxle to Melee-Magthere, the school of fighters. The mercenary had explained that taking a *colnbluth*, a non-drow, there would be risky, but now, for some reason, Jarlaxle had thought it appropriate to take Entreri to Sorcere, by far the more dangerous school.

"She did not specify where the mask was to be returned," Jarlaxle admitted.

Entreri did not respond, though he realized the truth of that answer. The spider mask was a prized possession of the Baenre clan, a potential weak spot in its hardened defenses. It belonged in the secured quarters of House Baenre and nowhere else.

"Foolish Triel," Jarlaxle remarked offhandedly. "The same word, *asanque*, would get her into that drawer. She should know that her brother was arrogant enough to believe that none would ever try to steal from him, and so he would not spend too much time with password tricks."

The mercenary laughed, and Entreri followed suit, though he was more intrigued than amused. Jarlaxle rarely did or said anything without purpose, and the mercenary had told him all of this for a reason.

But why?

Chapter 16

MENZOBERRANZAN

he raft slid slowly across Donigarten, the small, dark lake on the eastern end of the great cavern that housed Menzoberranzan. Drizzt sat on the prow of the craft, looking west as the cavern opened wide before him, though, with his infravision, the image seemed strangely blurred. Drizzt initially attributed it to the lake's warm currents and gave it little thought. He was preoccupied, his mind looking as much in the past as in the present, reeling with stirring memories.

The rhythmic moaning of the orcan paddlers behind him allowed him to find a calmness, to flow his memories one at a time.

The drow ranger closed his eyes and willed the shift from heat-sensing infravision into the normal spectrum of light. He remembered the splendor of Menzoberranzan's stalagmite and stalactite structures, their intricate and crafted designs highlighted by glowing faerie fire of purple, blue, and red.

He wasn't prepared for what he found when he opened his eyes. The city was filled with light! Not just with faerie fires, but with sparkling dots of yellow and white, the light of torches and bright magical enchantments. For a very brief moment, Drizzt allowed himself to believe that the presence of light might be some remote indication of a changing of the dark elves' dark ways. He had always connected the perpetual gloom of the Underdark to the dark demeanor of drow, or, at least, had thought the darkness a fitting result of his kin's dark ways.

Why the lights? Drizzt was not arrogant enough to think that their presence might be somehow connected to the hunt for him. He did not think that he was that important to the drow, and had little more than the deep gnomes' supposition that things were awry. (He had no idea that plans were being laid for an all-out surface raid.) He wanted to question one of the other drow on the matter—the female, in particular, would likely have some information—but how could he broach the subject without giving away his identity as an outsider?

As if on cue, the female was at his side, sitting uncomfortably close.

"The days are long on the Isle of Rothe," she said coyly, obvious attraction reflected in her red-glowing eyes.

"I will never get used to the light," Drizzt replied, changing the subject and looking back toward the city. He kept his eyes operating in the normal spectrum and hoped that his leading statements might prompt some conversation on the matter. "It stings my eyes."

"Of course it does," the female purred, moving closer, even putting a hand inside Drizzt's elbow. "But you will get used to it in time."

In time? In time for what? Drizzt wanted to ask, for he suspected from her tone that she was referring to some specific event. He had no idea of how to begin the question, though, and, as the female moved ever closer, he found that he had more pressing problems.

In drow culture, males were subservient, and to refuse the advances of a female could invite serious trouble. "I am Khareesa," she whispered in his ear. "Tell me that you wish to be my slave."

Drizzt jumped up suddenly and snapped his scimitars from their sheaths. He turned away from Khareesa, focused his attention on the lake to make sure that she understood he meant no threat against her.

"What is it?" the surprised female demanded.

"A movement in the water," Drizzt lied. "A subtle undercurrent, as though something large just passed under our craft." Khareesa scowled but stood and peered into the gloomy lake. It was common knowledge in Menzoberranzan that dark things resided under the usually still waters of Donigarten. One of the games the slavers played was to make the goblins and orcs swim from the isle to the shore, to see if any of them would be pulled down to terrible deaths.

A few moments passed quietly, the only sound the continual moaning chants of the orcs lining the sides of the raft.

A third drow joined Drizzt and Khareesa on the prow, eyeing Drizzt's blue-flaring scimitar. *You mark us for every enemy in the area*, his hands flashed in the silent code.

Drizzt slid the scimitars away and let his eyes drift back into infravision. *If our enemies are beneath the waters, then the motion of our craft marks us more than any light*, his hands answered.

"There are no enemies," Khareesa added, motioning for the third drow to go back to his station. When he left, she turned a lewd look upon Drizzt. "A warrior?" she asked, carefully regarding the purple-eyed male. "A patrol leader, perhaps?"

Drizzt nodded and it was no lie; he had indeed been a patrol leader.

"Good," Khareesa remarked. "I like males who are worth the trouble." She looked up then, took note that they were fast approaching the Isle of Rothe. "We will speak later, perhaps." Then she turned and swept away, brushing her hands behind her so that her robes rode high on her shapely legs.

Drizzt winced as though slapped. The last thing Khareesa had on her mind was speaking. He couldn't deny that she was beautiful, with sculpted features, a thick mane of well-groomed hair, and a finely toned body. But in his years among the drow, Drizzt Do'Urden had learned to look beyond physical beauty and physical attraction. Drizzt did not separate the physical from the emotional. He was a superb fighter because he fought with his heart and would no sooner battle merely for the sake of battle than he would mate for the sake of the physical act.

"Later," Khareesa said once more, glancing back over her delicate, perfectly squared shoulder.

"When worms eat your bones," Drizzt whispered through a phony smile. For some reason, he thought of Catti-brie then, and the warmth of that image pushed away the chill of this hungry drow female.

* * * * *

Blingdenstone charmed Catti-brie, despite her obvious predicament and the fact that the svirfnebli did not treat her as a long-lost friend. Stripped of her weapons, armor, jewelry, and even her boots, she was taken into the city in just her basic clothes. The gnome escorts did not abuse her, but neither were they gentle. They tightly clasped her arms at the elbows and hoisted her and pulled her around the narrow, rocky ways of the city's defensible anterooms.

When they had taken the circlet from the woman's head, the gnomes had easily come to guess its function, and as soon as the anterooms were past, they gave the precious item back to Catti-brie. Drizzt had told her of this place, of the deep gnomes' natural blending with their environment, but she had never pictured that the drow's words would ring so true. Dwarves were miners, the best in all the world, but the deep gnomes went beyond that description. They were part of the rock, it seemed, burrowing creatures wholly at one with the stone. Their houses could have been the randomly tumbled boulders of a long-past volcanic eruption, their corridors, the winding ways of an ancient river.

A hundred sets of eyes followed Catti-brie's every step as she was led across the city proper. She realized that she was probably the first human the svirfnebli had ever seen, and she did not mind the attention, for she was no less enchanted by the svirfnebli. Their features, seeming so gray and dour out in the wild tunnels, appeared softer now, gentler. She wondered what a smile would look like on the face of a svirfneblin, and she wanted to see it. These were Drizzt's friends, she kept reminding herself, and she took comfort in the drow ranger's judgment.

She was brought into a small, round room. A guard motioned for her to sit in one of three stone chairs. Catti-brie did so hesitantly, for she recalled a tale that Drizzt had told her, of a svirfneblin chair that had magically shackled him and held him fast.

No such thing happened now, though, and a moment later, a very unusual deep gnome entered the room, dangling the magical locket with Drizzt's picture from the end of a hand that was crafted into a mithril pickaxe.

"Belwar," Catti-brie stated, for there could not be two gnomes who so perfectly fit Drizzt's description of his dear svirfneblin friend.

The Most Honored Burrow Warden stopped in his tracks and eyed the woman suspiciously, obviously caught off guard by her recognition.

"Drizzt . . . Belwar," Catti-brie said, again wrapping her arms about her, as though hugging someone. She pointed to herself and said, "Catti-brie . . . Drizzt," and repeated the motion.

They could not speak two words of each other's language, but, in a short time, using hand and body language, Catti-brie had won over the burrow warden, had even explained to him that she was searching for Drizzt.

She did not like the grave face Belwar wore at that remark, and his explanation, a single common name, the name of a drow city, was not reassuring; Drizzt had gone into Menzoberranzan.

She was given a meal of cooked mushrooms and other plantlike growths that she did not recognize, then she was given back her items, including the locket and the onyx panther, but not the magical mask.

She then was left alone, for hours it seemed, sitting in the starlit darkness, silently blessing Alustriel for her precious gift and thinking how perfectly miserable the trek would have been without the Cat's Eye. She would not even have seen Belwar to recognize him!

Her thoughts were still on Belwar when he at last returned, along with two other gnomes wearing long, soft robes, very unlike the rough, leatherlike, metal-plated outfits typical of the race. Catti-brie figured that these two must be important, perhaps councilors.

"Firble," Belwar explained, pointing to one of the svirfnebli, one that did not look happy.

Catti-brie figured out why a moment later, when Belwar pointed to her, then to Firble, then to the door and spoke a long sentence, the only word of which Catti-brie caught was, "Menzoberranzan."

Firble motioned for her to follow him, apparently anxious to be on their way, and Catti-brie, though she would have loved to stay in Blingdenstone and learn more about the intriguing svirfnebli, thoroughly agreed. Drizzt was too far ahead of her already. She rose from the chair and started out, but was caught at the arm by Belwar's pickaxe hand and turned about to face the burrow warden.

He pulled the magical mask from his belt and lifted it to her. "Drizzt," he said, pointing his hammer hand at her face. "Drizzt."

Catti-brie nodded, understanding that the burrow warden thought it would be wise of her to walk as a drow. She turned to leave, but, on a sudden impulse, turned back and gave Belwar a peck on the cheek. Smiling appreciatively, the young woman walked from the house, and, with Firble leading the way, strode from Blingdenstone.

"How did you get Firble to agree to take her into the drow city?" the remaining gnome councilor asked the burrow warden when they were alone.

"Bivrip!" Belwar bellowed. He clapped his mithril hands together and immediately sparks and arcing lines of energy ran along his crafted hands. He put a wry look on the councilor, who merely laughed in a squeaky svirfneblin way. Poor Firble.

* * * * *

Drizzt was glad to escort a group of orcs from the isle back to the mainland, if only so that he could avoid the eager Khareesa. She watched him go from the shore, her expression caught somewhere between a pout and anticipation, as if to say that Drizzt might have escaped, but only for now.

With the isle behind him, Drizzt put all thoughts of Khareesa from his mind. His task, and dangers, lay ahead, in the city proper,

179

and he honestly did not know where he would begin looking for answers. He feared that it would all come down to his surrender, that he would have to give himself over to protect the friends that he had left behind.

He thought of Zak'nafein, his father and friend, who had been sacrificed to the evil Spider Queen in his stead. He thought of Wulfgar, his lost friend, and memories of the young barbarian strengthened Drizzt's resolve.

He offered no explanation to the surprised slavers awaiting the craft on the beach. His expression alone told them not to question him as he walked past their encampment, away from Donigarten.

Soon he moved easily, warily, along the winding ways of Menzoberranzan. He passed close by several dark elves, under the more-than-curious eyes of dozens of house guards, standing watch from their parapets along the sides of hollowed stalactites. Drizzt carried with him an irrational notion that he might be recognized, and had to tell himself many times that he had been out of Menzoberranzan for more than thirty years, that Drizzt Do'Urden, even House Do'Urden, was now part of Menzoberranzan's history.

But, if that were true, why was he here, in this place where he did not want to be?

Drizzt wished that he had a *piwafwi*, the black cloak typical of drow outerwear. His forest-green cloak, thick and warm, was more suited to the environs of the surface world and might connect him, in the eyes of onlookers, to that rarely seen place. He kept the hood up, the cowl low, and pushed on. This would be one of many excursions into the city proper, he believed, as he familiarized himself once more with the winding avenues and the dark ways.

The flicker of light around a bend surprised him, stung his heat-seeing eyes, and he moved tightly against the wall of a stalagmite, one hand under his cloak, grasping Twinkle's hilt.

A group of four drow males came around the bend, talking easily, paying Drizzt no heed. They wore the symbol of House Baenre, Drizzt noted as his vision shifted back to the normal spectrum, and one of them carried a torch!

Little that Drizzt had witnessed in all his life seemed so out of place to him. Why? he asked himself repeatedly, and he felt that this all was somehow related to him. Were the drow preparing an offensive against some surface location?

The notion rocked Drizzt to his core. House Baenre soldiers carrying torches, getting their Underdark eyes desensitized to the light. Drizzt did not know what to think. He would have to go back to the Isle of Rothe, he decided, and he figured that that out-of-the-way place was as good a base as any he could secure in the city. Perhaps he could get Khareesa to tell him the meaning of the lights, so that the next excursion into the city proper might prove fruitful.

He stalked back through the city, cowl low, thoughts inward, and did not notice the movements shadowing his own; few in Menzoberranzan ever noticed the movements of Bregan D'aerthe.

* * * * *

Catti-brie had never viewed anything so mysterious and wonderful and, in the starlight of her vision, the glow of the stalagmite towers and hanging stalactites seemed more wonderful still. The faerie fires of Menzoberranzan highlighted ten thousand wondrous carvings, some of definite shape (mostly spiders), and others freeflowing forms, surrealistic and beautiful. She would like to come here under different circumstances, Catti-brie decided. She would like to be an explorer that discovered an empty Menzoberranzan, that she might study and absorb the incredible drow workmanship and relics in safety.

For, as overwhelmed as Catti-brie was by the magnificence of the drow city, she was truly terrified. Twenty thousand drow, twenty thousand deadly enemies, were all about her.

As proof against the fear, the young woman tightly clasped Alustriel's magic locket and thought of the picture therein, of Drizzt Do'Urden. He was here, somewhere close, she believed, and her suspicions were confirmed when the locket flared suddenly with warmth.

Then it cooled. Catti-brie moved methodically, turning back to the north, to the secret tunnels Firble had taken her through to get to this place. The locket remained cool. She shifted to her right and faced west, across the chasm near her—the Clawrift, it was called— and past the great, sweeping steppes that led to a higher level. Then she faced south, toward the highest and grandest section of all, judging from the elaborate, glowing designs. Still the locket remained cool, then began to warm as the young woman continued to turn, looking past the nearest stalagmite mounds to the relatively clear section in the east.

Drizzt was there, in the east. Catti-brie took a deep breath then another, to steady her nerves and muster the courage to come fully out of the protected tunnel. She looked to her hands again, and her flowing robes, and took comfort in the apparently perfect drow disguise. She wished that she had Guenhwyvar beside her—remembered the moment in Silverymoon when the panther had loped down the streets beside her—but wasn't sure how the cat would be received in Menzoberranzan. The last thing she wanted to do was call attention to herself.

She moved quickly and quietly, throwing the hood of her robes low over her head. She hunched as she walked, and kept her grasp on the locket to guide her way and bolster her strength. She worked hard to avoid the stares of the many house sentries, and pointedly looked away whenever she saw a drow coming down the avenue toward her from the other direction.

She was almost past the area of stalagmites, could see the moss bed, the mushroom grove, even the lake beyond, when two drow came out of the shadows suddenly, blocking the way, though their weapons remained sheathed.

One of them asked her a question, which she, of course, did not understand. She subconsciously winced and noticed that they were looking at her eyes. Her eyes! Of course, they were not glowing with infravision, as the deep gnomes had informed her. The male asked his question again, somewhat more forcefully, then looked over his shoulder, toward the moss bed and the lake.

Catti-brie suspected that these two were part of a patrol, and that they wanted to know what business she might have on this side of the city. She noted the courteous way they addressed her, and remembered those things that Drizzt had taught her about drow culture.

She was a female; they, only males.

The undecipherable question came again, and Catti-brie responded with an open snarl. One of the males dropped his hands to the hilts of his twin swords, but Catti-brie pointed at them and snarled again, viciously.

The two males looked to each other in obvious confusion. By their estimation, this female was blind, or at least was not using infravision, and the lights in the city were not that bright. She should not have been able to see the movement clearly, and yet, by her pointing finger, she obviously had.

Catti-brie growled at them and waved them away, and to her surprise (and profound relief), the males backed off, eyeing her suspiciously but making no moves against her.

She started to hunch over, thinking to hide again under her cowl, but changed her mind instead. This was Menzoberranzan, full of brash dark elves, full of intrigue, a place where knowing—even *pretending* to know—something your rival did not know could keep you alive.

Catti-brie threw off the hood and stood straight, shaking her head as her thick hair freed itself of the folds. She stared at the two males wickedly and began to laugh.

They ran off.

The young woman nearly toppled with relief. She took another deep breath, clasped the locket in a clenched fist, and headed toward the lake.

Chapter 17

EPITOME OF ENEMIES

o you know who he is? the drow soldier's fingers asked imperatively in the intricate hand code.

Khareesa rocked back on her heels, not quite understanding any of this. A contingent of well-armed drow had come to the Isle of Rothe, demanding answers, interrogating both the orc and goblin slaves and the few drow slavers on the island. They wore no house emblems and, as far as Khareesa could tell, were exclusively males.

That did not stop them from treating her roughly, though, without the proper protocol typically afforded her gender.

"Do you?" the drow asked aloud. The unexpected noise brought two of the male's comrades rushing to his sides.

"He is gone," the male explained to calm his companions, "into the city."

But he is on his way back, a fourth drow replied in the silent hand code as he rushed to join the others. *We just received the code flashes from the shore.*

The heightening intrigue was more than curious Khareesa could take. "I am Khareesa H'kar," she proclaimed, naming herself a noble of one of the city's lesser houses, but a noble nonetheless. "Who is this male you speak of? And why is he so important?"

The four males looked to each other slyly, and the newcomer turned an evil glare on Khareesa.

"You have heard of Daermon N'a'shezbaernon?" he asked softly.

Khareesa nodded. Of course she had heard of the powerful house, House Do'Urden by its more common name. It had once been the eighth-ranked house in all the city, but had met a disastrous end.

"Of their secondboy?" the male went on.

Khareesa pursed her lips, unsure. She tried to remember the tragic story of House Do'Urden, something about a renegade, when another of the males jogged her memory.

"Drizzt Do'Urden," he said.

Khareesa started to nod—she had heard the name before, in passing—then her eyes went wide as she realized the significance of the handsome, purple-eyed drow that had left the Isle of Rothe.

She is a witness, one of the males reasoned.

She was not, argued another, *until we told her the renegade's name.*

"But now she is," said the first, and they looked in unison at the female.

Khareesa had long caught on to their wicked game and was steadily backing away from them, sword and whip in hand. She stopped as she felt the tip of yet another sword gently prod her fine armor from behind, and she held her hands out wide.

"House H'kar—" she began, but abruptly ended as the drow behind her plunged his fabulous drow-made sword through the fine armor and through a kidney. Khareesa jerked as the male yanked the weapon back out. She slumped to one knee, trying to hold her concentration against the sudden assault of agony, trying to hold fast to her weapons.

The four soldiers fell over her. There could be no witnesses.

* * * * *

Drizzt's gaze remained toward the strangely lighted city as the raft slipped slowly across Donigarten's dark waters.

Torches? The thought hung heavily in his mind, for he had pretty much convinced himself that the drow were preparing a huge excursion to the surface. Why else would they be stinging their sensitive eyes so?

As the raft floated across the weedy bay of the Isle of Rothe, Drizzt noticed that no other craft were docked at the island. He gave it little thought as he climbed over the prow and sprang lightly to the mossy beach. The orcs had barely put up their oars when another drow whisked past Drizzt and sprang into the boat, ordering the slave crew to put back out for the mainland.

Orc rothe herders congregated by the shore, each squatting in the mossy muck, ragged cloaks pulled tight. This was not unusual, for there was really little for them to do. The isle was not large, barely a hundred yards long and less than that in width, but it was incredibly thick with low vegetation, mainly mosses and fungi. The landscape was broken, filled with valleys and steep-sloping hillocks, and the biggest job facing the orcs, aside from taking rothe from the isle to the mainland and chasing down strays, was simply to make sure that none of the herd fell into any ravines.

So the slaves sat down by the shore, silent and brooding. They seemed somewhat edgy to Drizzt, but, consumed by his fears over what was happening in the city, he again gave it little thought. He did glance about to the drow slaver posts, and took comfort in the fact that all the dark elves were apparently in place, standing quietly and calmly. The Isle of Rothe was not an eventful place.

Drizzt headed straight inland, away from the small bay and toward the highest point on the island. Here stood the isle's lone structure, a small, two-chambered house constructed of gigantic mushroom stalks. He considered his strategy as he moved, thought of how he might get the necessary information from Khareesa without open confrontation. Events seemed to be moving quickly about him, though, and he resolved that if he had to use his scimitars to "convince" her, he would.

Barely ten feet from the structure's door, Drizzt stopped and watched as the portal gently swung in. A drow soldier stepped to the threshold and casually tossed Khareesa's severed head at Drizzt's feet.

"There is no way off the island, Drizzt Do'Urden," the drow remarked.

Drizzt didn't turn his head, but shifted his eyes, trying to get a clear measure of his surroundings. He inconspicuously worked one toe under the soft moss, burying his foot to the ankle.

"I'll accept your surrender," the drow went on. "You cannot—"

The drow stopped abruptly as a wad of moss flew at his face. He snapped out his sword and instinctively threw his hands up before him in defense.

Drizzt's charge followed the moss divot. The ranger sprang across the ten feet to his enemy, then dropped in a deceptive spin, pivoting on one planted knee. Using his momentum, Drizzt sent Twinkle in a wicked, low cut that caught the surprised drow on the side of the knee. The drow turned a complete somersault over that stinging hit, striking the soft ground with a thud and a cry of pain as he clutched at his ripped leg.

Drizzt sensed that other dark elves were in the house behind this one, so he was up and running quickly, around the structure and out of sight of the door, then down the hillock's steep back slope. He dove, skidded, and rolled to build momentum, his thoughts a jumble, his desperation mounting.

Several dozen rothe milled about the mossy bank, and they bleated and grunted as Drizzt scrambled among them. Drizzt heard several clicks behind him, heard a hand-crossbow quarrel slap into one rothe. The creature tumbled, asleep before it hit the ground.

Drizzt kept low, scrambling, trying to figure where he could run. He had been on the island only a short time, had never been here in his earlier years in the city, and wasn't familiar with its landscape. He knew that this hillock dropped into a steep ravine, though, and thought that was his best chance.

More shots came from behind; a javelin joined the quarrels.

187

Muck and divots flew wildly as the rothe, frightened by the rushing dark elf and missiles, kicked about, threatening to stampede. They were not large creatures, only three feet high at the shoulder, but were solidly built. If caught on his hands and knees in the midst of a rothe stampede, Drizzt knew he would be crushed.

His problems compounded as he neared the back of the rothe herd, for between the legs of one creature he spotted boots. Hardly thinking, Drizzt lifted his shoulder and barreled sidelong into the rothe, pushing it down the slope, into his enemy. One scimitar went up high and sang as it struck a descending sword; another scimitar jabbed low, under the rothe's belly, but the enemy drow hopped back, out of range.

Drizzt coiled his legs under him and heaved with all his strength, using the ground's fairly steep angle to his advantage. The rothe lifted off the ground and skipped sidelong, slamming the drow. He was agile enough to lift a leg over the creature's low back and come cleanly over it, spinning about in an attempt to face Drizzt squarely. But Drizzt was nowhere to be seen.

A bleat to the side was the only warning the drow got as the fierce ranger rushed in, scimitars flashing. The surprised drow threw both his swords out in front as he spun about, barely deflecting the scimitar cuts. One foot skidded out from under him, but he came back up quickly, fire in his eyes and his swords thrusting wildly, holding Drizzt at bay.

Drizzt moved quickly to the right, gained the higher ground again, though he knew that that move would put his back to the archers at the top of the hillock. He kept his scimitars moving, his eyes focused ahead, but listened to sounds from the back.

A sword darted in low, was caught by Twinkle and held down. A second thrust came in parallel to the first but a bit higher, and Drizzt's second scimitar responded, coming unexpectedly straight across, angling the drow's sword right for Drizzt's low arm.

Drizzt heard a slight whistle behind him.

The enemy drow flashed a wicked grin, thinking he was about to score a hit as the blades flashed across, but Drizzt sent Twinkle in motion as well, equally fast, taking the drow's sword arm with him in the wide-flying move. Drizzt swept the scimitars under and up, using their curving blades to keep the swords moving in line. He turned a complete circuit, moving the blades high above his head and moving himself one step to the side of the enemy drow.

His trust in the unseen archer's skill was not misplaced, and his melee opponent jerked his hips to the side in a frantic effort to dodge the javelin. He took a stinging hit and grimaced in pain.

Drizzt heaved him away, sent him skidding down the slope. The drow caught his balance as the ranger descended over him in a wild rush.

Scimitar batted sword again and again and again. Drizzt's second scimitar worked a more direct and devious pattern, thrusting and angling for the drow's belly.

The wounded drow's parries were impressive against the onslaught, but with one leg numb from pain, he was backing up and inevitably building momentum. He managed to glance back and noticed one spur of stone rising above the ledge of the twenty-foot sheer drop. He thought to make for that spur and put his back against it for support. His allies were rushing down the slope; they would be beside him in a matter of seconds.

Seconds he didn't have.

Both scimitars came in rapid succession, beating against the steel of the drow's swords, forcing him down the hill. Near the drop, Drizzt launched his weapons simultaneously, side-by-side, in crossing cuts, turning the tips of his enemy's swords. Then Drizzt launched himself, slamming against the drow's chest, knocking him off balance to crash against the rocky spur. Explosions went off in the dazed drow's head. He slumped to the moss, knowing that this renegade, Drizzt Do'Urden, and his wicked scimitars would be right behind.

Drizzt hadn't the time or the desire to complete the kill. Before the drow finished collapsing, Drizzt had leaped over the ledge, hoping to find moss and not sharp rocks, below.

What he found was mud, and he hit with a splash, turning an ankle, then turning a somersault. He finally hauled himself out and ran off as fast as he could, zigzagging around stalagmite pillars, keeping low to the cover of the mounds, for he expected that the archers would soon be at the ledge.

Enemies were all about him, and very close, he realized, seeing a form paralleling him along a stalagmite row to his right. Drizzt went behind one mound and, instead of coming out the other side, veered to meet his enemy head-on. He dropped to his knees as he came behind the second mound, slashing across low in the expectation that his enemy would be back there.

Twinkle hit a low-riding sword this time. Drizzt had not gained surprise, not with his maneuver, at least, but the drow was certainly off guard, his second sword high for a strike, when Drizzt snapped his second scimitar straight up, quicker than his enemy could anticipate. The pointed tip punctured the drow's diaphragm, and though Drizzt, as he continued his slide, could not extend his arm enough to complete the move, the drow fell back against the stalagmite, out of the fight.

An ally was right behind him, though, and this soldier fell upon the kneeling Drizzt with abandon, swords hacking fiercely.

Pure instinct kept the darting blades from Drizzt as the ranger worked his scimitars over his head, feeling more than seeing his opponent's moves. Understanding his sudden disadvantage, Drizzt called upon his innate magic and summoned a globe of darkness over himself and his enemy.

Ringing steel continued to sound, weapons meeting and sliding, with both combatants taking nicks. Drizzt growled and increased his intensity, parrying and countering, still slashing up over his head. Gradually, the skilled ranger shifted his weight to get one foot under him.

The enemy drow came with a sudden and fierce double chop—and nearly fell over when his blades caught nothing but air. He spun immediately, whipping his swords across—and nearly lost both blades as they slammed the side of the stony stalagmite mound.

In the heat of battle, he had forgotten the layout of the immediate area, forgotten the mound not so far away. The drow had heard the reputation of Drizzt Do'Urden and suddenly understood the magnitude of his mistake.

Drizzt, perched high on a rounded shoulder of the mound, winced as he heard the swords connect with stone below him, taking little satisfaction in this action. He couldn't see Twinkle's flaring blue light as the scimitar descended through the darkness globe.

He ran free a moment later, his ankle still sore but supporting him. He came out the back side of the ravine and moved up on the ledge opposite the high hillock. The ledge ran toward the more remote eastern end of the isle. There lay a lagoon, Drizzt believed, not so far away, and if he could reach it, he intended to dive right in. Damn the legends of monsters in the water; the enemies about him were all too real!

* * * * *

Catti-brie heard the continuing scuffles from the isle. The sounds drifted clearly across the still, dark waters of Donigarten. From behind the stalk of one mushroom, she called up Guenhwyvar and ran off as the mist took its solid form.

By the lake, the young woman, still not confident of her drow disguise, avoided the few dark elves that were about and motioned to a nearby orc instead. Then she motioned to a boat, trying to indicate that the creature should take her out to the isle. The orc seemed nervous, or at least confused. It turned away and started to walk off.

Catti-brie punched it in the back of the head.

Cowering, obviously terrified, it turned about to face her. Catti-brie shoved it toward the small boat, and this time the creature got in and took up a paddle.

Before she could join the orc, Catti-brie was intercepted by a male drow, his strong hand closing tightly over her elbow.

She eyed him dangerously and growled, trying to bluff once again, but this determined dark elf was not taking the bait. In his free hand he held a dagger, poised below Catti-brie's elbow, just inches from her ribs.

"Be gone!" he said. "Bregan D'aerthe tells you to be gone!"

Catti-brie didn't understand a word of it, but her enemy's confusion was at least equal to hers as six hundred pounds of black fur flew past, taking the surprised male on a splashing ride many feet from the boat.

Catti-brie turned fiercely on the orc, who pretended not to see a thing and began paddling frantically. The young woman looked back to the shore a moment later, fearful that Guenhwyvar would be left behind and would have to swim the entire distance.

A huge splash beside the boat (nearly overturning it) told her

191

differently, and the panther was now the one leading.

It was simply too much for the terrified orc to take. The pitiful creature shrieked and leaped for the water, swimming desperately for the shore. Catti-brie took up the paddle and never looked back.

* * * * *

The ledge was open to both sides at first, and Drizzt heard the hiss of crossbow quarrels cutting the air over his head and just behind him. Fortunately for Drizzt, the firing drow were back across the ravine, at the base of the tall hillock, and hand-crossbows were not very accurate at long range.

Drizzt wasn't surprised when his running form began to glow in purplish hues, tiny faerie fires igniting along his arms and legs, not burning, but marking him clearly to his enemies.

He felt a sting in his left shoulder and quickly reached over and popped out the small quarrel. The wound was only superficial, the dart's momentum mostly stalled by the dwarf-crafted mithril chain mail that Drizzt wore. He ran on, and could only hope that not enough poison had entered his blood to tire him.

The ledge veered to the right, putting Drizzt's back to his enemies. He felt even more vulnerable then, for just a moment, but soon realized that the turn might be a good thing, putting more distance between him and the stinging crossbows. Soon after, as the quarrels bounced harmlessly behind him, the ledge veered again, back to the left, going around the base of another hillock.

This put the lapping waters of Donigarten at Drizzt's right, a dozen feet below him. He thought of sheathing his blades and jumping in right there, but too many jagged mounds protruded from the water for him to chance it.

The ledge remained mostly open on his right as he sped along, the drop sporadically blocked by only a few anchoring stalagmites. The hillock loomed on Drizzt's left, fully protecting him from the distant archers . . . but not from nearer enemies, he realized. As he came around a slight bend, he discovered at the last instant that beyond the bend lay a hollow, and in the hollow waited an enemy.

The soldier leaped out into Drizzt's path, sword and dirk waving. A scimitar turned the sword aside, and Drizzt thrust straight ahead, knowing his second weapon would be intercepted by the dirk. When the weapons predictably locked, Drizzt used his momentum to push the dirk out wide and lifted one knee to collide heavily with the drow's belly.

Drizzt clapped his wide-spread hands together, simultaneously snapping his scimitar hilts against his enemy's face. He snapped his weapons back out immediately, fearing that either the sword or dagger would dive at him, but his opponent was past retaliation. The evil drow fell straight to the ground, unconscious, and Drizzt plowed over him and kept on going.

The ranger had hit his stride, literally. Savage instincts churned within Drizzt, and he believed that no single drow could stand against him. He was fast reverting to the hunter again, the embodiment of primal, passionate rage.

A dark elf leaped out from behind the next stalagmite; Drizzt skidded down to one knee and spun, a similar maneuver to the one he had used against the drow at the mushroom house's door.

This time, though, his enemy had more time to react, had his sword down to the stone to block.

The hunter knew that he would.

Drizzt's lead foot caught hold, and he spun up from his slide, his trailing foot flying wide in a circle kick that caught the surprised drow under the chin and dropped him over the side of the ledge. He caught a handhold just a few feet down, groggy from the blow and thinking that this purple-eyed fiend would surely kill him.

The hunter was already gone, though, running on, running for freedom.

Drizzt saw another drow on the path in front of him, this one's arm held up before him, probably aiming a hand-crossbow.

The hunter was quicker than the quarrel. His instincts told him that, repeatedly, and they were proven correct when a flashing scimitar intercepted the dart.

Then Drizzt was upon the drow, and the drow's ally, who came out from behind the nearest mound. The two enemies worked furiously with their weapons, thinking their numerical advantage more than sufficient.

They didn't understand the hunter—but the red-glowing eyes of Artemis Entreri, watching from a nearby hollow, did.

Part 4

IN THE WEB

ne of the sects of Faerun names the sins of humanity as seven, and foremost among them is pride. My interpretation of this had always been to think of the arrogance of kings, who proclaimed themselves gods, or at least convinced their subjects that they spoke with some divine beings, thus conveying the image that their power was god-given.

That is only one manifestation of this most deadly of sins. One does not have to be a king to be taken down by false pride. Montolio DeBrouchee, my ranger mentor, warned me about this, but his lessons concerned a personal aspect of pride. "A ranger often walks alone, but never walks without *friends nearby," the wise man explained. "A ranger knows his surround-ings and knows where allies might be found."*

To Montolio's way of thinking, pride was blindness, a blurring of insight and wisdom, and the defeat of trust. A too-proud man walked alone and cared not where allies might be found.

When I discovered the web of Menzoberranzan growing thick about me, I understood my error, my arrogance. Had I come to think so much of myself and my abilities that I forgot those allies who had, to this point, allowed me to survive? In my anger over the death of Wulfgar and my fears for Catti-brie, Bruenor, and Regis, I never considered that those living friends could help to take care of themselves. The problem that had befallen us all was my own fault, I had decided, and, thus, was my duty to correct, however impossible that might be for a single person.

I would go to Menzoberranzan, discover the truth, and end the con-flict, even if that end meant the sacrifice of my own life.

What a fool I had been.

Pride told me that I was the cause of Wulfgar's death; pride told me that I could be the one to right the wrong. Sheer arrogance prevented me from dealing openly with my friend, the dwarven king, who could muster the forces necessary to combat any forthcoming drow attacks.

On that ledge on the Isle of Rothe, I realized that I would pay for my arrogance; later, I would learn that others dear to me might pay as well.

It is a defeat of the spirit to learn that one's arrogance causes such loss and pain. Pride invites you to soar to heights of personal triumph, but the wind is stronger at those heights and the footing, tentative. Farther, then, is the fall.

—Drizzt Do'Urden

Chapter 18

VALIANT FAILURE

She noticed a dark elf on the isle's dock, waving his arms and motioning for her to go back. He seemed to be alone.

Catti-brie lifted Taulmaril and let fly. The arrow cut the darkness as would a bolt of lightning, slamming into the surprised drow's chest and hurling him back a dozen feet. Catti-brie and Guenhwyvar stepped onto the beach a minute later. The young woman felt the locket and started to tell Guenhwyvar to run around to the right, but the panther had already sensed the nearness of its master, was already in full flight across the broken landscape, veering in from the beach as it ran.

The woman followed as quickly as she could, but lost sight of the speeding cat almost immediately as Guenhwyvar cut a sharp turn around the base of the nearest hillock, claws throwing up moist turf.

Catti-brie heard a startled cry and, when she came around the base of that mound, she saw a dark elf soldier, looking away from her, his gaze apparently following the run of the panther. One of his arms was upraised, steadying a hand-crossbow.

Catti-brie fired on the run, her arrow going high and scorching a hole in the side of the mound, just inches above the drow's head. He spun about immediately and retaliated, the dart clipping the turf near the diving and rolling woman.

Quick to fit another arrow, Catti-brie fired next, driving a hole in the drow soldier's trailing *piwafwi* as he scrambled to the side. He skidded to one knee, fitted a quarrel as he went, and raised his arm again.

Catti-brie fired also, the arrow blasting through the hand-crossbow and the drow's hand, slicing out his wrist and burying deep in his upper chest.

She had won the duel, but had lost precious time. Disoriented, the young woman needed the locket again to direct her, and off she ran.

* * * * *

His skilled opponents' fierce attacks soon became measured strikes as Drizzt parried every move and often managed an effective counter. One of the drow held just one weapon now, with his dirk arm tucked in close to his side to stem the flow of blood from a curving scimitar gash.

Drizzt's confidence continued to soar. How many enemies were here on the isle? he wondered, and he dared to believe that he might win.

His blood froze when he heard a roar behind him, thinking that some monstrous ally had come to his enemies' aid. The wounded drow soldier widened his eyes in terror and began to backpedal, but Drizzt took little comfort in that. Most drow allies were tentative at best, chaotic creatures of incredible and unpredictable power. If this were indeed some summoned monster, some demonic ally, stalking from behind him, then Drizzt was surely its primary target.

The backpedaling drow broke into a dead run, fleeing along the ledge, and Drizzt used his departure to work around to the side, to try to get a look at what he would face next.

A black feline form whipped past him, pursuing his fleeing enemy. For an instant, he thought that some drow must have a figurine similar to his own, must have summoned a cat similar to Guenhwyvar. But this *was* Guenhwyvar! Drizzt knew instinctively. This was his Guenhwyvar!

Excitement fast turned to confusion. Drizzt thought that Regis must have called the panther, back in Mithril Hall, and that the cat must have come running out after him. It made no sense, though, for Guenhwyvar could not remain on the Material Plane long enough to make the journey all the way from the dwarven stronghold. The figurine had to have been carried to Menzoberranzan.

A cunning sword thrust slipped through Drizzt's defenses momentarily, the weapon tip nicking into his fine armor and stinging his breast. It brought the distracted ranger from his reverie, reminding Drizzt that he had to take one enemy and one problem at a time.

He came forward in a blinding burst, scimitars waving and rolling, cutting in at the opposing dark elf from many different angles. The drow soldier was up to the test, though, his swords banging away the deadly blades, even smacking the side of Drizzt's boot as the ranger tried to kick out at the drow's knee.

"Patience," Drizzt reminded himself, but with Guenhwyvar's appearance and so many unanswered questions, patience was hard to come by.

* * * * *

The fleeing drow rounded a bend. Then, with the panther quickly gaining, he hooked his good arm around a narrow stalagmite and spun to the right, leaping over the ledge to splash into the muck. He got his feet back under him and was bent over, trying to recover his dropped sword, when Guenhwyvar crashed down, driving him into the water.

He spun and kicked briefly, and when the jumble sorted out, the panther's maw was clamped about the pinned drow's neck, squeezing. He had his face above the water, but could not draw breath, would never again draw breath.

Guenhwyvar came up from the kill, turned to spring back the dozen feet to the ledge, but dropped low and turned its head, snarling suspiciously as a rainbow-hued bubble floated over it. Before Guenhwyvar could react, the strange thing burst, and Guenhwyvar was showered by flecks of tingling material.

Guenhwyvar leaped for the ledge, but felt as though the intended target was getting farther and farther away. The panther roared again, in protest, understanding then the nature of those flecks, understanding that they were sending it back to its own plane of existence.

The roar was soon lost to the gentle lapping of the stirred ripples and the clang of steel from up on the ledge.

Jarlaxle leaned against the stone wall, considering this new development. He put away his valuable metal whistle, the item that had dismissed the dangerous panther, and lifted one of his boots so that he could wipe the muck from it. Casually, the cocky mercenary looked up to the continuing sounds of battle, confident that Drizzt Do'Urden would soon be taken.

* * * * *

Catti-brie was pinned down in the ravine; two dark elves stood sheltered behind twin mounds directly ahead of her, and a third plucked away with his hand-crossbow from the base of the hillock to her left. She squeezed in close to her own stalagmite cover as best she could, but still felt vulnerable as darts ricocheted all about her. Every now and then she managed a shot, but her enemies were well under cover and the streaking arrows skipped and sparked harmlessly off the many stones.

A quarrel nicked the young woman's knee; another forced her to duck deeper into the cubby, forced her to angle her body so that she probably wouldn't be able to fire her bow again. Catti-brie grew scared then, thinking that defeat had caught up with her. There was no way she could win against three well-trained and well-armed drow soldiers.

A quarrel stuck into the heel of her boot, but did not penetrate. The young woman took a long, deep breath. She told herself stubbornly that she had to try to retaliate, that crouching here would prove worthless and would ensure her—and Drizzt's—death.

The thought of her friend gave her courage, and she wriggled about for a shot. She cursed aloud as she fired, for her enemies, again, were well hidden.

Or were they? Catti-brie scrambled suddenly to the back side of the stalagmite cluster, putting as much interference between herself and the drow on the hillock as possible. She was an open target now to the two soldiers ahead of her, but she was only a target if they managed to get off any shots.

Taulmaril hummed repeatedly, continuously, as the woman loosed a mighty barrage. She saw no dark elf forms to shoot at, but went after their cover instead, each enchanted arrow pounding away at the twin stalagmites. Sparks flew all about the target area. Chips of flying stone sizzled as they arced into the air.

Unable to come out long enough to retaliate, the two drow lost their nerve and fled down the ravine. Catti-brie got one in the back, then lifted an arrow for the second.

She felt a sting in her side and turned about to see another enemy barely ten feet away, smiling confidently with his hand-crossbow out in front of him.

Catti-brie whipped about, her deadly bow falling in line. The drow's mouth opened wide in a suddenly terrified scream, and Catti-brie put the arrow right into his face, hurling him head over heels through the air.

The young woman looked to her bleeding side. She grimaced and yanked out the stinging quarrel, then pulled herself up to her feet and looked all about. She couldn't be certain that this last drow had been the one from the hillock, but she felt the insidious poison creeping into her limbs and knew that she couldn't wait around to make sure that no other enemies were creeping behind her. Determinedly, the young woman began to scale the ravine's broken wall and soon she was up on the ledge, trotting along, trying to keep her focus and her balance.

R. A. Salvatore

* * * * *

Twinkle hooked inside the drow's sword, and Drizzt sent it rotating, the two weapons cutting great circles in the air between the combatants. His opponent sneaked a thrust in behind the fast-flying blades, but Drizzt's other scimitar was in line, knocking the second sword harmlessly aside.

Drizzt kept the momentum up, even increased the pressure of the spin. Around went the blades, low and high, and now it was Drizzt who kept his free weapon slipping in through their wake, with cunning strikes that kept his opponent dancing back and off balance. With his superior agility, Drizzt was in control of the circling blades, and both opponents knew that the ranger was gaining the advantage.

The enemy drow tightened his muscles to apply counterpressure against Twinkle—exactly what cunning Drizzt had been waiting for. The instant he felt the pressure on his blade, sword and scimitar coming up again before his eyes, he ended his roundabout cut, reversed direction, and snapped Twinkle in a short loop, striking the drow's sword on the other side. Overbalanced by the sudden release, the drow soldier stumbled and could not reverse his pressure on the sword.

His blade dove low and flew out wide across his body, twisting him to the side. He tried to get his other sword around for a block, but Drizzt's second scimitar was too quick, jabbing hard into the side of his abdomen.

He fell back, reeling, one sword dropping to the stone.

Drizzt heard a call; someone rammed him hard in the shoulder, slamming him against the stone wall. He bounced off and spun, scimitars up.

Entreri! Drizzt's jaw dropped with his guard.

* * * * *

Catti-brie spotted Drizzt on the ledge, saw the other drow fall away, clutching his side, and she cried out as another dark form rushed from a cranny and barreled into Drizzt. She put her bow up, but realized that if the enemy's body did not stop her arrow, it would drive through to strike Drizzt. Besides, a wave of dizziness assaulted the young woman as the effects of the sleeping poison began to course through her veins.

She kept Taulmaril ready and staggered on, but the fifty-or-so feet to Drizzt seemed like a hundred miles.

* * * * *

Entreri's sword flared a green light, further revealing the assassin. But how could it be? Drizzt wondered. He had defeated this one, had left Entreri for dead in a windy ravine outside Mithril Hall.

Apparently, not everyone had left Entreri for dead.

The sword came in a devilish two-stroke routine, thrusting low at Drizzt's hip, then slashing high, nearly connecting across the drow's eyes.

Drizzt tried to recover his balance, and his sensibilities, but Entreri was all over him, hacking wildly, growling all the while. A snap kick caught the ranger in the knee, and he had to throw himself away from the wall as the green-glowing sword sliced down, igniting a line of sparks.

The snarling assassin spun with Drizzt, sending his dirk in a wide-flying hook. Drizzt's scimitar banged against the shorter weapon and it flew away, but Entreri's hand came on, balling into a fist, now inside the blocking angle of Drizzt's weapon.

A split second before the assassin's fist smacked into his nose, Drizzt realized that Entreri had been one step ahead of him, had expected, even desired, that exact parry.

The stunned ranger tumbled backward. Only a narrow stalagmite mound prevented Drizzt from flying over the ledge. Entreri was on him instantly. Sparks, green and blue, erupted as a brutal swipe of the assassin's sword took Twinkle from Drizzt's hands.

Drizzt's remaining blade parried the ensuing backhand, but before he could begin to bend to retrieve his dropped weapon, Entreri crouched and kicked Twinkle from the ledge.

Still off balance, Drizzt tried a downward chop that was easily foiled, and the assassin countered with another heavy punch, connecting solidly with Drizzt's belly.

Up swooped Entreri, his sword running an outward-circling

arc, taking Drizzt's scimitar with it. It was a game of chess, and Entreri was playing white, advantage gained, and not relinquishing the offensive. Sword and scimitar out wide, the enraged assassin hurled himself into the ranger, forearm leading, smashing Drizzt in the face and snapping the drow's head back brutally against the stone. Entreri's sword hit the scimitar again, knocking it straight out, then again, straight up, and Drizzt, with his sword arm high and Entreri's poised to come in at him, recognized his doom. He rolled away to his right as the sword sliced across, slashing through his fine cloak, banging hard against his dwarf-forged armor and cutting a line across his armpit, aiding the momentum of his dive.

Then Drizzt was flying free over the ledge, diving face first into the muck.

Entreri instinctively leaped and rolled as he noticed a flash out of the corner of his eye. A silver-streaking arrow sliced across the jumble of man and cloak, then continued on along the ledge, leaving Entreri prone on the stone, groaning. He managed to slip a hand out from under him, fingers inching to his dropped dirk.

"Drizzt!" Catti-brie called, her grogginess temporarily defeated by the sight of her fallen friend. Drawing her sword, the woozy woman increased her pace, not sure of whether to finish the assassin first or look for the downed drow.

Nearing the spot, she veered for the stalagmite, but the choice was moot, for the assassin sprang to his feet, apparently unhurt. The arrow had missed, cutting only a clean hole in Entreri's flapping cloak.

Catti-brie fought through teary eyes and gritted teeth, smacked aside Entreri's first sword thrust and reached for the jeweled dagger on her belt. Her movements were sluggish, though, for the insidious sleeping poison was fast overwhelming the adrenaline rush, and, as her fingers closed on the dagger, she suddenly found her sword slapped away and a dirk pressing the back of her hand, pinning it in place against the dagger hilt.

Entreri's sword tip was up, dangerously high and dangerously free.

The end was upon her, Catti-brie knew, and all her world had flown away. She felt only the cold steel of Entreri's sword slipping through the tender skin of her neck.

Chapter 19

FALSE PRIDE

e is alive, the soldier signaled to Jarlaxle as he inspected the downed ranger.

The mercenary leader motioned for the soldier to turn the fallen Drizzt so that his head was out of the water. Jarlaxle looked across the still lake, understanding that the sound of battle had echoed clearly across its waters. The mercenary saw the distinctive, pale blue glow of driftdisks, flying disks of energy typically used to carry matron mothers across the city, floating out from the banks. They held House Baenre soldiers, Jarlaxle knew.

R. A. Salvatore

Leave him, the mercenary leader signaled to his soldier, *and his equipment.* Almost as an afterthought, Jarlaxle pulled his whistle out once more, put it to his lips, and faced Drizzt, then blew a high note. The whistle's dweomer showed him that the ranger wore magical armor, at least as fine as drow make, and Jarlaxle sighed when he saw the intensity of Twinkle's enchantment. He would have loved to add that scimitar to his armory, but it was well known in Menzoberranzan that Drizzt Do'Urden fought with two scimitars, and if one was missing, the mercenary would only be inviting trouble from Matron Baenre.

Drizzt carried little else that was enchanted, except for one item that caught and held the mercenary's attention. Its magic was strong indeed, shining in the hues common to charm enchantments, exactly the type of item that cagey Jarlaxle used to best effect.

His soldier, having shifted the unconscious ranger so that Drizzt's face was above the murky water, started toward Jarlaxle, but the mercenary leader stopped him. *Take the pendant,* Jarlaxle's fingers instructed.

The soldier turned about and seemed to notice the approaching driftdisks for the first time. "Baenre?" he asked quietly as he turned back to his leader.

They will find their quarry, Jarlaxle signaled confidently. *And Matron Baenre will know who delivered Drizzt Do'Urden to her.*

* * * * *

Entreri wasn't about to ask what drow female he was killing this time. He was working in concert with Bregan D'aerthe, and this drow, like the one in the mushroom house, had interfered, and was a witness.

A timely glance showed him something that gave him pause, though, showed him a familiar jeweled dagger hanging on this drow's belt.

Entreri studied the female closely, kept his sword tip at her neck, drawing small droplets of blood. He shifted the weapon deftly, and a subtle ridge showed along the female's smooth skin.

"Why are you here?" Entreri asked breathlessly, honestly surprised. He knew that this one had not come to Menzoberranzan beside Drizzt—Councilor Firble of Blingdenstone certainly would have mentioned her. Jarlaxle certainly would have known about her!

Yet, here she was, surprisingly resourceful.

Entreri shifted his sword again from her neck, then delicately tipped it up under the crease beneath her chin and used it to remove the magical mask.

Catti-brie fought hard to sublimate her mounting terror. This was too much like the first time she had been in Artemis Entreri's clutches; the assassin evoked an almost irrational horror in her, a deep fear that no other monster, neither a dragon nor a fiend of Tarterus, could bring.

Here he was again, amazingly alive, with his sword to her vulnerable throat.

"An unexpected bonus," Entreri mused. He chuckled evilly, as though he was trying to sort out the best way to make his prisoner profitable.

Catti-brie thought of leaping over the ledge—if she had been near a cliff a thousand feet in the air, she would have considered it! She felt the hairs on the back of her neck tingle, felt sweat beading on her brow.

"No," she uttered, and Entreri's features twisted with confusion.

"No?" he echoed, not understanding that her remark had been aimed inward.

Catti-brie steeled her gaze at him. "So ye've survived," she remarked matter-of-factly. "To go and live among those who're most akin to ye."

She saw by the assassin's slight grimace that Entreri did not like that description. He confirmed that fact by punching her with his sword hilt, raising a welt on the woman's cheek and bringing a trickle of blood from her nose.

Catti-brie fell back, but straightened immediately, and stared at the assassin with unblinking eyes. She would not give Entreri the satisfaction of terror, not this time.

"I should kill you," Entreri whispered. "Slowly."

Catti-brie laughed at him. "Then do," she replied. "Ye've no hold over me, not since I've seen the proof that Drizzt is yer better."

Entreri, in sudden rage, almost ran her through. "Was," he corrected, then he looked wickedly to the ledge.

"I've seen ye both fall more than once," Catti-brie asserted with as much conviction as she could muster in that dark moment. "I'll not call either of ye dead until I've felt the cold body!"

"Drizzt is alive," came a whisper from behind, spoken in perfect surface Common, as Jarlaxle and two Bregan D'aerthe soldiers moved to join the assassin. One of them stopped to finish off the squirming drow with the wounded side.

His rage taking control, Entreri instinctively swung again at Catti-brie, but this time the woman lifted a stiffened hand and turned her wrist, subtly diverting the blow.

Then Jarlaxle was between them, eyeing Catti-brie with more than a passing interest. "By the luck of a Lloth-blessed spider," the mercenary leader remarked, and he lifted a hand to stroke Catti-brie's bruised cheek.

"Baenre approaches," the soldier behind the mercenary leader reminded, using the Drow tongue.

"Indeed," Jarlaxle replied absently, again in the surface language. He seemed wholly absorbed by this exotic woman standing before him. "We must be on our way."

Catti-brie straightened, as though she expected the killing blow to fall. Jarlaxle reached up instead and removed the circlet from her head, in effect, blinding her. She offered no resistance as Taulmaril and her quiver were taken from her, and knew that it was Entreri's rough grasp that snapped the jeweled dagger from her belt sheath.

A strong but surprisingly gentle hand hooked her upper arm and led her away—away from the fallen Drizzt.

* * * * *

Caught again, Drizzt thought, and this time he knew that the reception would not be as pleasant as his stay in Blingdenstone. He had walked into the spider's web, had delivered the prized catch to the dinner table.

He was shackled to a wall, standing on his tiptoes to keep from hanging by his sore wrists. He did not remember coming to this place, did not know how long he had hung here, in the dark and dirty room, but both his wrists ached and showed hot welts to his infravision, as though most of the skin had been worn away. Drizzt's left shoulder also hurt, and he felt an uncomfortable stretch along his upper chest and armpit, where Entreri's sword had hit him.

He realized, though, that one of the priestesses must have cleaned the gash and healed him, for the wound had been worse when he had gone off the ledge. That supposition did little to bolster Drizzt's spirits, though, for drow sacrifices were usually in the very best of health before they were given to the Spider Queen.

But, through it all, the pain and the helplessness, the ranger fought hard to find some measure of comfort. In his heart Drizzt had known all along that it would end this way, that he would be taken and killed so that his friends in Mithril Hall might live in peace. Drizzt had long ago accepted death, and had resigned himself to that probability when he had last ventured from Mithril Hall. But why, then, was he so uncomfortable?

The unremarkable room was just a cave with shackles built into the stone along three walls and a cage hanging from the ceiling. Drizzt's survey of the place was cut short as the iron-bound door creaked open and two uniformed drow female soldiers rushed in, going to rigid attention at either side of the portal.

Drizzt firmed his jaw and set his gaze, determined to face his death with dignity.

An illithid walked through the door.

Drizzt's mouth dropped open, but he quickly regained his composure. A mind flayer? He balked, but when he took the moment to consider the creature, he came to realize that he must be in House Baenre's dungeon. That was not a comforting thought, for either him or his friends.

Two drow priestesses, one small and vicious-looking, her face angular and her mouth tight in a perpetual pout, the other taller, more dignified, but no less imposing, came in behind the illithid. Then came the legendary, withered matron mother, sitting easily on a floating driftdisk, flanked by another female, a younger, more beautiful version of Matron Baenre. At the end of the train came two males, fighters, judging from their attire and weapons.

The glow from Matron Baenre's disk allowed Drizzt to shift his gaze to the normal spectrum—and he noticed a pile of bones under one of the other pairs of shackles.

Drizzt looked back to the entourage, to the drow males, his gaze settling on the younger of the two for a long moment. It was Berg'inyon, he believed, a classmate of his at the drow Academy, the second-ranking fighter of Drizzt's class—second behind Drizzt.

The three younger females fanned out in a line behind Matron Baenre's driftdisk; the two males stood beside the female soldiers at the door. The illithid, to Drizzt's amazement, and supreme discomfort, paced about the captured drow, its tentacles waving near Drizzt's face, brushing his skin, teasing him. Drizzt had seen such tentacles suck the brains out of a dark elf, and it was all he could do to hold his nerve with the wretched creature so near.

"Drizzt Do'Urden," Matron Baenre remarked.

She knew his name. Drizzt realized that to be a bad sign. That sickly, uncomfortable feeling welled within him again, and he was beginning to understand why.

"Noble fool!" Matron Baenre snapped suddenly. "To come to Menzoberranzan, knowing the price upon your pitiful head!" She came forward, off the driftdisk, in a sudden rush and slapped Drizzt across the face. "Noble, arrogant fool! Did you dare to believe that you could win? Did you think that five thousand years of what has been could be disrupted by pitiful you?"

The outburst surprised Drizzt, but he kept his visage solid, his eyes straight ahead.

Matron Baenre's scowl disappeared, replaced suddenly by a wry smile. Drizzt always hated that typical trait of his people. So volatile and unpredictable, dark elves kept enemies and friends alike off guard, never letting a prisoner or a guest know exactly where they stood.

"Let your pride be appeased, Drizzt Do'Urden," Matron Baenre said with a chuckle. "I introduce my daughter Bladen'Kerst Baenre, second eldest to Triel." She indicated the female in the middle. "And Vendes Baenre," she continued, indicating the smallest of the three. "And Quenthel. Behind stand my sons, Dantrag and Berg'inyon, who is known to you."

"Well met," Drizzt said cheerily to Berg'inyon. He managed a smile with his salutation and received another vicious slap from the matron mother.

"Six Baenres have come to see you, Drizzt Do'Urden," Matron Baenre went on, and Drizzt wished that she would quit repeating his name with every sentence! "You should feel honored, Drizzt Do'Urden."

"I would clasp wrists," Drizzt replied, "but . . ." He looked helplessly up to his chained hands and barely flinched as another stinging slap predictably came against his face.

"You know that you will be given to Lloth," Baenre said.

Drizzt looked her straight in the eye. "In body, but never in soul."

"Good," purred the matron mother. "You will not die quickly, I promise. You will prove a wellspring of information, Drizzt Do'Urden."

For the first time in the conversation, a dark cloud crossed Drizzt's features.

"I will torture him, Mother," Vendes offered eagerly.

"Duk-Tak!" Matron Baenre scolded, turning sharply on her daughter.

"Duk-Tak," Drizzt mouthed under his breath, then he recognized the name. In the Drow tongue, *duk-tak* meant, literally, unholy executioner. It was also the nickname of one of the Baenre daughters—this one apparently—whose handiwork, in the form of dark elves turned into ebony statues, was often on display at the drow Academy.

"Wonderful," Drizzt muttered.

"You have heard of my precious daughter?" Matron Baenre asked, spinning back to the prisoner. "She will have her time with you, I promise, Drizzt Do'Urden, but not before you provide me with valuable information."

Drizzt cast a doubting look the withered drow's way.

"You can withstand any torture," Matron Baenre remarked. "That I do not doubt, noble fool." She lifted a wrinkled hand to stroke the illithid who had moved to her side. "But can you withstand the intrusions of a mind flayer?"

Drizzt felt the blood drain from his face. He had once been a prisoner of the cruel illithids, a helpless, hapless fool, his mind nearly broken by their overpowering wills. Could he fend such intrusions?

213

"You thought this would end, O noble fool!" Matron Baenre screeched. "You delivered the prize, stupid, arrogant, noble fool!"

Drizzt felt that sick feeling return tenfold. He couldn't hide his cringe as the matron mother went on, her logic following an inescapable course that tore into Drizzt Do'Urden's heart.

"You are but one prize," she said. "And you will aid us in the conquest of another. Mithril Hall will be ours more easily now that King Bruenor Battlehammer's strongest ally is out of the way. And that very ally will show us the dwarven weaknesses."

"Methil!" she commanded, and the illithid walked directly in front of Drizzt. The ranger closed his eyes, but felt the four octopus-like tentacles of the creature's grotesque head squirm across his face, as if looking for specific spots.

Drizzt cried out in horror, snapped his head about wildly, and even managed to bite one of the tentacles.

The illithid fell back.

"Duk-Tak!" Matron Baenre commanded, and eager Vendes rushed forward, slamming a brass-covered fist into Drizzt's cheek. She hit him again, and a third time, gaining momentum, feeding off the torture.

"Must he be conscious?" she asked, her voice pleading.

"Enough!" Drizzt heard Matron Baenre reply, though her voice seemed far away. Vendes smacked him once more, then he felt the tentacles squirm over his face again. He tried to protest, to move his head about, but he hadn't the strength.

The tentacles found a hold; Drizzt felt little pulses of energy run through his face.

His screams over the next ten minutes were purely instinctive, primal, as the mind flayer probed his mind, sent horrid images careening through his thoughts and devoured every mental counter Drizzt had to offer. He felt naked, vulnerable, stripped of his very emotions.

Through it all, Drizzt, though he did not know it, fought valiantly, and when Methil moved back from him, the illithid turned to Matron Baenre and shrugged.

"What have you learned?" the matron mother demanded.

This one is strong, Methil replied telepathically. *It will take more sessions.*

"Continue!" snapped Baenre.

"*He will die*," Methil somehow said in a gurgling, watery-sounding voice. "*Tomorrow.*"

Matron Baenre thought for a moment, then nodded her accord. She looked to Vendes, her vicious Duk-Tak, and snapped her fingers, sending the wild drow into a fierce rush.

Drizzt's world fell away into blackness.

Chapter 20

PERSONAL AGENDA

he female?" Triel asked impatiently, pacing Jarlaxle's private quarters in a secret cave along one wall of the Clawrift, a great chasm in the northeastern section of Menzoberranzan.

"Beheaded," the mercenary answered easily. He knew that Triel was employing some sort of lie detection magic, but was confident that he could dance around any such spells. "She was a youngest daughter, an unimpressive noble, of a lower house."

Triel stopped and focused her glare on the evasive mercenary. Jarlaxle knew well that the angry Baenre was not asking about that

216

female, that Khareesa H'kar creature. Khareesa, like all the slavers on the Isle of Rothe, had been killed, as ordered, but reports filtering back to Triel had suggested another female, and a mysterious great cat as well.

Jarlaxle played the staring game better than any. He sat comfortably behind his great desk, even relaxed in his chair. He leaned back and dropped his booted feet atop the desk.

Triel swept across the room in a rush and slapped his feet away. She leaned over the desk to put her scowl close to the cocky mercenary. The priestess heard a slight shuffle to one side, then another from the floor, and suspected that Jarlaxle had many allies here, concealed behind secret doors, ready to spring out and protect the leader of Bregan D'aerthe.

"Not that female," she breathed, trying to keep things somewhat calm. Triel was the leader of the highest school in the drow Academy, the eldest daughter of the first house of Menzoberranzan, and a mighty high priestess in full favor (as far as she knew) of the Spider Queen. She did not fear Jarlaxle or his allies, but she did fear her mother's wrath if she was forced to kill the often helpful mercenary, if she precipitated a covert war, or even an atmosphere of uncooperation, between valuable Bregan D'aerthe and House Baenre.

And she knew that Jarlaxle understood her paralysis against him, knew that Jarlaxle grasped it better than anyone and would exploit it every step of the way.

Pointedly throwing off his smile, pretending to be serious, the mercenary lifted his gaudy hat and ran a hand slowly over the side of his bald head. "Dear Triel," he replied calmly. "I tell you in all honesty that there was no other drow female on the Isle of Rothe, or near the isle, unless she was a soldier of House Baenre."

Triel backed off from the desk, gnawed at her lips, and wondered where to turn next. As far as she could tell, the mercenary was not lying, and either Jarlaxle had found some way to counter her magic, or he was speaking the truth.

"If there was, I certainly would have reported it to you," Jarlaxle added, and the obvious lie twanged discordantly in Triel's mind.

Jarlaxle hid his smile well. He had thrown out that last lie just to let Triel know that her spell was in place. By her incredulous expression, Jarlaxle knew that he had won that round.

"I heard of a great panther," Triel prompted.

"Magnificent cat," Jarlaxle agreed, "the property of one Drizzt Do'Urden, if I have read the history of the renegade correctly. Guenhwyvar, by name, taken from the corpse of Masoj Hun'ett after Drizzt slew Masoj in battle."

"I heard that the panther, this Guenhwyvar, was on the Isle of Rothe," Triel clarified impatiently.

"Indeed," replied the mercenary. He slid a metallic whistle out from under his cloak and held it before his eyes. "On the isle, then dissolved into an insubstantial mist."

"And the summoning device?"

"You have Drizzt, my dear Triel," Jarlaxle replied calmly. "Neither I nor any of my band got anywhere near the renegade except in battle. And, in case you've never witnessed Drizzt Do'Urden in battle, let me assure you that my soldiers had more on their minds than picking that one's pockets!"

Triel's expression grew suspicious.

"Oh, one lesser soldier did go to the fallen renegade," Jarlaxle clarified, as though he had forgotten that one minor detail. "But he took no figurine, no summoning device at all, from Drizzt, I assure you."

"And neither you nor any of your soldiers happened to find the onyx figurine?"

"No."

Again, the crafty mercenary had spoken nothing but the truth, for Artemis Entreri was not, technically, a soldier of Bregan D'aerthe.

Triel's spell told her that Jarlaxle's words had been correct, but all reports claimed that the panther had been about on the isle and House Baenre's soldiers had not been able to locate the valuable figurine. Some thought it might have flown from Drizzt when he had gone over the ledge, landing somewhere in the murky water. Magical detection spells hadn't located it, but that could be readily explained by the nature of Donigarten. Calm on the surface, the dark lake was well known for strong undercurrents, and for darker things lurking in the deep.

Still, the Baenre daughter was not convinced about either the female or the panther. Jarlaxle had beaten her this time, she knew, but she trusted in her reports as much as she didn't trust in the mercenary.

Her ensuing expression, a pout so uncommon to the proud Baenre daughter, actually caught Jarlaxle off guard.

"The plans proceed," Triel said suddenly. "Matron Baenre has brought together a high ritual, a ceremony that will be heightened now that she has secured a most worthy sacrifice."

Jarlaxle considered the words carefully, and the weight with which Triel had spoken them. Drizzt, the initial link to Mithril Hall, had been delivered, but Matron Baenre still planned to proceed, with all speed, to the conquest of Mithril Hall. What would Lloth think of all this? the mercenary had to wonder.

"Surely your matron will take the time to consider all options," Jarlaxle replied calmly.

"She nears her death," Triel snapped in reply. "She is hungry for the conquest and will not allow herself to die until it has been achieved."

Jarlaxle nearly laughed at that phrase, "will not allow herself to die," then he considered the withered matron mother. Baenre should have died centuries ago, and yet she somehow lived on. Perhaps Triel was right, the mercenary mused. Perhaps Matron Baenre understood that the decades were finally catching up with her, so she would push on to the conquest without regard for consequences. Jarlaxle loved chaos, loved war, but this was a matter that required careful thinking. The mercenary truly enjoyed his life in Menzoberranzan. Might Matron Baenre be jeopardizing that existence?

"She thinks Drizzt's capture a good thing," Triel went on, "and it is—indeed it is! That renegade is a sacrifice long overdue the Spider Queen."

"But . . ." Jarlaxle prompted.

"But how will the alliance hold together when the other matron mothers learn that Drizzt is already taken?" Triel pointed out. "It is a tentative thing, at best, and more tentative still if some come to believe that Lloth's sanction of the raid is no more, that the main goal in going to the surface has already been achieved."

Jarlaxle folded his fingers in front of him and paused for a long while. She was wise, this Baenre daughter, wise and as experienced in the ways of the drow as any in the city—except for her mother and, perhaps, Jarlaxle. But now she, with so much more to lose, had shown the mercenary something he had not thought of on his own, a potentially serious problem.

Trying vainly to hide her frustration, Triel spun away from the desk and marched across the small room, hardly slowing as she plunged straight into the unconventional portal, almost an inter-planar goo that made her walk along a watery corridor for many steps (though the door seemed to be only several inches thick) before exiting between two smirking Bregan D'aerthe guardsmen in a corridor.

A moment later, Jarlaxle saw the heated outline of a drow hand against his almost translucent door, the signal that Triel was gone from the complex. A lever under the top of the mercenary's desk opened seven different secret doors—from the floor and the walls—and out stepped or climbed several dark elves and one human, Artemis Entreri.

"Triel heard reports of the female on the isle," Jarlaxle said to the drow soldiers, his most trusted advisors. "Go among the ranks and learn who, if any, betrayed us to the Baenre daughter."

"And kill him?" asked one eager drow, a vicious specimen whose skills Jarlaxle valued when conducting interrogations.

The mercenary leader put a condescending look over the impetuous drow, and the other Bregan D'aerthe soldiers followed suit. Tradition in the underground band did not call for the execution of spies, but rather the subtle manipulation. Jarlaxle had proven many times that he could get as much done, plant as much disinformation, with an enemy informant as with his own spies and, to disciplined Bregan D'aerthe, any plant that Triel had in place among the ranks would be a benefit.

Without needing to speak another word to his well-trained and well-practiced advisors, Jarlaxle waved them away.

"This adventure grows more fun by the hour," the mercenary remarked to Entreri when they were gone. He looked the assassin right in the eye. "Despite the disappointments."

The remark caught Entreri off guard. He tried to decipher what Jarlaxle might be talking about.

"You knew that Drizzt was in the Underdark, knew even that he was close to Menzoberranzan and soon to arrive," the mercenary began, though that statement told Entreri nothing enlightening.

"The trap was perfectly set and perfectly executed," the assassin argued, and Jarlaxle couldn't really disagree, though several soldiers were wounded and four had died. Such losses had to be expected when dealing with one as fiery as Drizzt. "I was the one who brought Drizzt down and captured Catti-brie," Entreri pointedly reminded him.

"Therein lies your error," Jarlaxle said with an accusing snicker.

Entreri eyed him with sincere confusion.

"The human woman called Catti-brie followed Drizzt down here, using Guenhwyvar and this," he said, holding up the magical, heart-shaped locket. "She followed blindly, by all reasoning, through twisting caverns and terrible mazes. She could never hope to retrace her steps."

"She will not likely be leaving," Entreri added dryly.

"Therein lies your error," Jarlaxle repeated. His smile was wide, and now Entreri was beginning to catch on.

"Drizzt Do'Urden alone could have guided you from the depths of the Underdark," Jarlaxle told him plainly. The mercenary tossed the locket to Entreri. "Feel its warmth," he explained, "the warmth of the warrior's blood coursing through the veins of Drizzt Do'Urden. When it cools, then know that Drizzt is no more, and know that your sunlight world is lost to you forever.

"Except for an occasional glance, perhaps, when Mithril Hall is taken," Jarlaxle added with a sly wink.

Entreri resisted the impulse to leap over the desk and murder the mercenary—mostly because he suspected that another lever under that desktop would open seven other trap doors and bring Jarlaxle's closest, closest advisors storming upon him. But truly, after that initial moment, the assassin was more intrigued than angered, both by Jarlaxle's sudden proclamation that he would never see the surface world, and by the thought that Drizzt Do'Urden could have led him out of the Underdark. Thinking, still holding the locket, the assassin started for the door.

"Did I mention that House Horlbar has begun its inquiry into the death of Jerlys?" Jarlaxle queried at his back, stopping the assassin in midstride. "They have even approached Bregan D'aerthe, willing to pay dearly for information. How ironic, wouldn't you agree?"

Entreri did not turn about. He simply walked to the door and pushed out of the room. It was more food for thought.

Jarlaxle, too, was thinking—thinking that this entire episode might become more delicious yet. He thought that Triel had pointed out some snares that Matron Baenre, blinded by her lust for power, would never notice. He thought most of all that the Spider Queen, in her love of chaos, had placed him in a position to turn the world of Menzoberranzan upon its head.

Matron Baenre had her own agenda, and Triel certainly had hers, and now Jarlaxle was solidifying one of his own, for no better reason than the onslaught of furious chaos, from which the cunning mercenary always seemed to emerge better off than before.

* * * * *

The semiconscious Drizzt did not know how long the punishment had gone on. Vendes was brilliant at her cruel craft, finding every sensitive area on the hapless prisoner and beating it, gouging, it, raking it with wickedly tipped instruments. She kept Drizzt on the verge of unconsciousness, never allowing him to black out completely, kept him feeling the excruciating pain.

Then she left, and Drizzt slumped low on his shackles, unable to comprehend the damage the hard-edged rings were doing to his wrists. All the ranger wanted at the terrible time was to fall away from the world, from his pained body. He could not think of the surface, of his friends. He remembered that Guenhwyvar had been on the island, but could not concentrate enough to remember the significance of that.

He was defeated; for the first time in his life, Drizzt wondered if death would be preferable to life.

He felt someone grab roughly at his hair and yank his head back. He tried to see through his blurry and swollen eyes, for he feared that wicked Vendes had returned. The voices he heard, though, were male.

A flask came up against his lips, and his head was yanked hard to the side, angled so that the liquid would pour down his throat. Instinctively, thinking this some poison, or some potion that would steal his free will, Drizzt resisted. He spat out some of the liquid, but got his head slammed hard against the wall for the effort, and more of the sour-tasting stuff rolled down his throat.

Drizzt felt burning throughout his body, as though his insides were on fire. In what he believed were his last gasps of life, he struggled fiercely against the unyielding chains, then fell limp, exhausted, expecting to die.

The burn became a tingling, sweet sensation; Drizzt felt stronger suddenly, and his vision returned as the swelling began to subside from his eyes.

The Baenre brothers stood before him.

"Drizzt Do'Urden," Dantrag said evenly. "I have waited many years to meet you."

Drizzt had no reply.

"Do you know me? Of me?" Dantrag asked.

Again Drizzt did not speak, and this time his silence cost him a slap across the face.

"Do you know of me?" Dantrag asked more forcefully.

Drizzt tried hard to remember the name Matron Baenre had tagged on this one. He knew Berg'inyon from their years together at the Academy and on patrol, but not this one; he couldn't remember the name. He did understand that this one's ego was involved, and that it would be wise to appease that false pride. He studied the male's outfit for just a moment, drawing what he hoped to be the correct conclusion.

"Weapon master of House Baenre," he slurred, blood following every word from his battered mouth. He found that the sting of those wounds was not so great now, as though they were quickly healing, and he began to understand the nature of that potion that had been forced down his throat.

"Zak'nafein told you, then, of Dantrag," the male reasoned, puffing out his chest like a barnyard rooster.

"Of course," Drizzt lied.

"Then you know why I am here."

"No," Drizzt answered honestly, more than a little confused.

Dantrag looked over his own shoulder, drawing Drizzt's gaze

across the room to a pile of equipment—Drizzt's equipment!—stacked neatly in a far corner.

"For many years I desired a fight with Zak'nafein," Dantrag explained, "to prove that I was the better. He was afraid of me and would not come out of his hiding hole."

Drizzt resisted the urge to scoff openly; Zak'nafein had been afraid of no one.

"Now I have you," Dantrag went on.

"To prove yourself?" Drizzt asked.

Dantrag lifted a hand, as if to strike, but held his temper in check.

"We fight, and you kill me, and what does Matron Baenre say?" Drizzt asked, understanding Dantrag's dilemma. He had been captured for greater reasons than to appease the pride of an upstart Baenre child. It all seemed like such a game suddenly—a game that Drizzt had played before. When his sister had come to Mithril Hall and captured him, part of her deal with her associate was to let the man, Artemis Entreri, have his personal fight with Drizzt, for no better reason than to prove himself.

"The glory of my victory will forestall any punishments," Dantrag replied casually, as though he honestly believed the claim. "And perhaps I will not kill you. Perhaps I will maim you and drag you back to your chains so that Vendes can continue her play. That is why we gave you the potion. You will be healed, brought to the brink of death, and healed again. It will go on for a hundred years, if that is Matron Baenre's will."

Drizzt remembered the ways of his dark people and did not doubt the claim for a minute. He had heard whispers of captured nobles, taken in some of the many interhouse wars, who were kept for centuries as tortured slaves of the victorious houses.

"Do not doubt that our fight will come, Drizzt Do'Urden," Dantrag said. He put his face right up to Drizzt's. "When you are healed and able to defend yourself." Faster than Drizzt's eyes could follow, Dantrag's hands came up and slapped him alternately on both cheeks. Drizzt had never seen such speed before and he marked it well, suspecting that he would one day witness it again under more dangerous circumstances.

Dantrag spun on his heels and walked past Berg'inyon, toward the door. The younger Baenre merely laughed at the hanging prisoner and spat in Drizzt's face before following his brother.

* * * * *

"So beautiful," the bald mercenary remarked, running his slender fingers through Catti-brie's thick tangle of auburn hair.

Catti-brie did not blink; she just stared hard at the dimly lit, undeniably handsome figure. There was something different about this drow, the perceptive young woman realized. She did not think that he would force himself on her. Buried within Jarlaxle's swashbuckling facade was a warped sense of honor, but a definite code nonetheless, somewhat like that of Artemis Entreri. Entreri had once held Catti-brie as a prisoner for many days, and he had not placed a hand on her except to prod her along the necessary course.

So it was with Jarlaxle, Catti-brie believed, hoped. If the mercenary truly found her attractive, he would probably try to woo her, court her attention, at least for a while.

"And your courage cannot be questioned," Jarlaxle continued in his uncomfortably perfect surface dialect. "To come alone to Menzoberranzan!" The mercenary shook his head in disbelief and looked to Entreri, the only other person in the small, square room. "Even Artemis Entreri had to be coaxed here, and would leave, no doubt, if he could find the way.

"This is not a place for surface-dwellers," Jarlaxle remarked. To accentuate his point, the mercenary jerked his hand suddenly, again taking the Cat's Eye circlet from Catti-brie's head. Blackness, deeper than even the nights in the lowest of Bruenor's mines, enveloped her, and she had to fight hard to keep a wave of panic from overwhelming her.

Jarlaxle was right in front of her. She could feel him, feel his breath, but all she saw was his red-glowing eyes, sizing her up in the infrared spectrum. Across the room, Entreri's eyes likewise glowed, and Catti-brie did not understand how he, a human, had gained such vision.

She dearly wished that she possessed it as well. The darkness continued to overwhelm her, to swallow her. Her skin felt extra sensitive; all her senses were on their very edge.

225

She wanted to scream, but would not give her captors the satisfaction.

Jarlaxle uttered a word that Catti-brie did not understand, and the room was suddenly bathed in soft blue light.

"In here, you will see," Jarlaxle said to her. "Out there, beyond your door, there is only darkness." He teasingly held the circlet before Catti-brie's longing gaze, then dropped it into a pocket of his breeches.

"Forgive me," he said softly to Catti-brie, taking her off her guard. "I do not wish to torment you, but I must maintain my security. Matron Baenre desires you—quite badly I would guess, since she keeps Drizzt as a prisoner—and knows that you would be a fine way to gnaw at his powerful will."

Catti-brie did not hide her excitement, fleeting hope, at the news that Drizzt was alive.

"Of course they have not killed him," the mercenary went on, speaking as much to Entreri, the assassin realized, as to Catti-brie. "He is a valuable prisoner, a wellspring of information, as they say on the surface."

"They will kill him," Entreri remarked—somewhat angrily, Catti-brie had the presence of mind to note.

"Eventually," Jarlaxle replied, and he chuckled. "But both of you will probably be long dead of old age by then, and your children as well. Unless they are half-drow," he added slyly, tossing a wink at Catti-brie.

She resisted the urge to punch him in the eye.

"It's a pity, really, that events followed such a course," Jarlaxle continued. "I did so wish to speak with the legendary Drizzt Do'Urden before Baenre got him. If I had that spider mask in my possession, I would go to the Baenre compound this very night, when the priestesses are at the high ritual, and sneak in for a talk with him. Early in the ceremony, of course, in case Matron Baenre decides to sacrifice him this very night. Ah, well." He ended with a sigh and a shrug and ran his gentle fingers through Catti-brie's thick hair one final time before he turned for the door.

"I could not go anyway," he said to Entreri. "I must meet with Matron Ker Horlbar to discuss the cost of an investigation."

Entreri only smiled in response to the pointedly cruel remark.

He rose as the mercenary passed, fell in behind Jarlaxle, then stopped suddenly and looked back to Catti-brie.

"I think I will stay and speak with her," the assassin said.

"As you will," the mercenary replied, "but do not harm her. Or, if you do," he corrected with another chuckle, "at least do not scar her beautiful features."

Jarlaxle walked out of the room and closed the door behind, then let his magical boots continue to click loudly as he walked along the stone corridor, to let Entreri be confident that he had gone. He felt in his pocket as he went, and smiled widely when he discovered, to no surprise, that the circlet had just been taken.

Jarlaxle had sown the seeds of chaos; now he could sit back and watch the fruit of his labors grow.

Chapter 21

THE LAYERS
STRIPPED AWAY

atti-brie and Entreri spent a long moment staring at each other, alone for the first time since her capture, in the small room at Bregan D'aerthe's secret complex. By the expression on Entreri's face, Catti-brie knew that he was up to something.

He held his hand up before him and shifted his fingers, and the Cat's Eye agate dropped to the end of its silver chain.

Catti-brie stared at it curiously, unsure of the assassin's motives. He had stolen it from Jarlaxle's pocket, of course, but why would he risk a theft from so dangerous a dark elf?

"Ye're as much a prisoner as I am," Catti-brie finally reasoned. "He's got ye caught here to do his bidding."

"I do not like that word," Entreri replied, "prisoner. It implies a helpless state, and I assure you, I am never helpless."

He was nine parts bravado, one part hope, Catti-brie knew, but she kept the thought to herself.

"And what are ye to do when Jarlaxle finds it missing?" she asked.

"I shall be dancing on the surface by that time," the assassin replied coolly.

Catti-brie studied him. There it was, spoken plainly and clearly, beyond intrigue. But why the circlet? she continued to wonder, and then she grew suddenly afraid. Entreri may have decided that its starlight was preferable to, or complementary to, his infravision. But he would not have told her that he meant to go if he meant to leave her behind—alive.

"Ye do not need the thing," Catti-brie reasoned, trying to keep her voice steady. "Ye've been given the infravision and can see yer way well enough."

"But you need it," Entreri said, tossing the circlet to the young woman. Catti-brie caught it and held it in her hands, trying to weigh the consequences of putting it on.

"I cannot lead ye to the surface," she said, thinking that the assassin had miscalculated. "I found me way down only because I had the panther and the locket showing me the way to follow Drizzt."

The assassin didn't blink.

"I said I cannot lead ye out o' here," Catti-brie reiterated.

"Drizzt can," Entreri said. "I offer you a deal, one that you are in no position to refuse. I will get both you and Drizzt out of Menzo-berranzan, and you two will escort me back to the surface. Once there, we go our separate ways, and may they stay separate through all eternity."

Catti-brie took a long moment to digest the startling proposi-tion. "Ye're thinking that I'm to trust ye?" she asked, but Entreri didn't answer, didn't have to answer. Catti-brie sat imprisoned in a room surrounded by fierce drow enemies, and Drizzt's predicament was likely even worse. Whatever the evil Entreri might offer her, it could be no worse than the alternatives.

"What about Guenhwyvar?" Catti-brie asked. "And me bow?"

"I've the bow and quiver," Entreri answered. "Jarlaxle has the panther."

"I'll not leave without Guenhwyvar," Catti-brie said.

Entreri looked at her incredulously, as if he thought she were bluffing.

Catti-brie threw the circlet to his feet. She hopped up on the edge of a small table and crossed her arms defiantly over her chest.

Entreri looked down to the item, then to Catti-brie. "I could make you leave," he promised.

"If ye think ye could, then ye're thinking wrong," Catti-brie answered. "I'm guessing that ye'll need me help and cooperation to get through this place, and I'm not to give it to ye, not for meself and not for Drizzt, without the cat.

"And know ye that Drizzt will agree with me choice," Catti-brie went on, hammering home the point. "Guenhwyvar's a friend to us both, and we're not for leaving friends behind!"

Entreri hooked his toe under a loop in the circlet and casually flipped it across the room to Catti-brie, who caught it once more and, this time, put it on her head. Without another word, the assassin motioned for the woman to sit tight, and he abruptly left the room.

The single guard outside Jarlaxle's private room showed little interest in the approaching human; Entreri practically had to prod the drow to get his attention. Then the assassin pointed to the strange, flowing door and asked, "Jarlaxle?"

The soldier shook his head.

Entreri pointed again to the watery door, his eyes suddenly popping wide with surprise. When the soldier leaned over to see what was wrong, the assassin grabbed him across the shoulders and heaved him through the portal, both of them slipping through, into the watery corridor. Entreri tugged and twisted in a slow-motion wrestling match with the surprised drow. He was bigger than this one, and equally agile, and gradually made progress in moving the guard along.

They plunged out the other side, falling into Jarlaxle's room. The drow went for his sword, but Entreri's left hook staggered him.

A quick combination of punches followed, and when the drow went down to one knee, the assassin's foot slammed hard against his cheek.

Entreri half-dragged, half-carried the drow to the side of the room, where he slammed him against the wall. He slugged him several times to make sure that he would offer no further resistance. Soon he had the dark elf helpless, down on his knees, barely conscious, with his hands tied behind his back and his mouth tightly gagged. He pinned the drow against the wall and felt about for a releasing mechanism. The door to a secret cubby slid open, and Entreri forced the drow inside.

Entreri considered whether or not to kill this one. On the one hand, if he killed the drow, there would be no witnesses and Jarlaxle would have to spend some time figuring out who had committed the crime. Something held Entreri's dagger hand in check, though, some instinct that told him to proceed with this operation cleanly, with no losses to Bregan D'aerthe.

It was all too easy, Entreri realized when he found not only the figurine of Guenhwyvar, but Catti-brie's magical mask as well, waiting for him—yes, waiting for him!—on Jarlaxle's desk. Entreri picked them up gingerly, looking for some devious traps nearby and checking to make sure that these were the genuine items.

Something strange was going on.

Entreri considered the not-so-subtle hints that Jarlaxle had been dropping, the fact that the mercenary had taken him to Sorcere and conveniently showed him the way to the spider mask. He reached into a pocket and took out the magical locket of Alustriel, the homing beacon to Drizzt Do'Urden that Jarlaxle had casually tossed to him. Jarlaxle had even managed to slip in the proper time for the attempt, the early hours of the high ritual being celebrated at House Baenre this very night.

What was it all about? Entreri wondered. Jarlaxle had some private agenda, one that apparently went against House Baenre's designs on Mithril Hall. Standing there in the mercenary's office, it seemed obvious to Entreri that Jarlaxle had set him up as a pawn.

Entreri clutched the locket tightly, then thrust it back into his pocket. Very well, he decided. He would be an effective pawn indeed.

R. A. Salvatore

Twenty minutes later, Entreri, using the magical mask to appear as a drow soldier, and Catti-brie moved quietly and swiftly along the winding ways of Menzoberranzan, cutting a northeastern path along the stalagmite mounds, toward the higher level of Tier Breche and the drow Academy.

* * * * *

He saw again the tiered steps of the great dwarven Undercity, the heart of Mithril Hall. He imagined the entryway from the western gate, through Keeper's Dale, and pictured again the great chasm known as Garumn's Gorge.

Drizzt fought hard to warp those images, to distort the truth about Mithril Hall, but the details were so clear to him! It was as if he were there again, walking freely beside Bruenor and the others. In the throes of the mind flayer's hypnosis, Drizzt found himself overwhelmed. He had no more barriers to stack against the mental intrusion of Matron Baenre's pet, no more willpower against the mental giant.

As the images came to Drizzt, he felt them stripped away, mentally scraped from his brain, like so much food for the wretched illithid. Each intrusion burned painfully, shot electrical shocks along the synaptical connections of the drow ranger's mind.

Finally Drizzt felt the creature's insidious tentacles loosening their grip on the skin of his forehead, and he slumped, his mind a jumble of confusing images and his head throbbing with agony.

"We have gained some information this day," he heard the distant, watery voice say.

Gained some information . . .

The words rang over and over ominously in Drizzt's mind. The illithid and Matron Baenre were still talking, but he was not listening, concentrating on those three words, remembering the implications of those three terrible words.

Drizzt's lavender orbs slipped open, but he kept his head bowed, covertly peeking at Methil. The creature had its back to him, was only a couple of feet away.

The illithid now knew part of the layout of Mithril Hall, and its continuous intrusions into Drizzt's mind would soon show it the

232

entire complex.

Drizzt could not let that happen; slowly the drow's hands clenched more tightly on the chains.

Drizzt's bare foot came up, his heel slamming the wretched creature's spongy head. Before Methil could move away, the ranger wrapped his legs about Methil's neck in a choke hold and began thrashing back and forth, trying to snap the thing's neck.

Drizzt felt the tentacles probing for his skin, felt them boring into his legs, but he fought away his revulsion and thrashed wildly. He saw wicked Vendes coming around the side and knew what would come, but he concentrated on his task. For the sake of his friends, Methil had to be killed!

The illithid threw its weight straight back, trying to confuse Drizzt and break the hold, but the skilled drow ranger turned with the move and Methil fell to the ground, half slumped against the wall and half held aloft by Drizzt's strong hold. Drizzt heaved him up and slammed him back, releasing the ineffective choke. Illithids were not physically imposing creatures, and Methil raised his three-fingered hands pitifully, trying to fend the sudden barrage of stomping feet.

Something hard slammed Drizzt at the base of his ribs, stealing his breath. He stubbornly continued to stomp, but was slammed again, then a third time and a fourth.

Hanging limply from the chains, the ranger tried to curl up to protect the area as Vendes hammered away. Drizzt thought that he was surely dead when he looked into the furious eyes of wicked Duk-Tak, which were filled with a mixture of venom and hatred and ecstacy, as she was allowed to vent that perpetual fury.

She stopped, sooner than Drizzt dared to hope, and calmly walked away, leaving Drizzt hanging from the shackles, trying to curl but unable to find the strength.

Methil had joined Matron Baenre, who sat comfortably on her driftdisk, and was looking back at Drizzt with his pupilless, milky white eyes.

Drizzt knew that the next time the illithid encroached on his mind, Methil would go out of his way to make the pain even more intense.

"No potion for him," Matron Baenre instructed Dantrag, standing impassively by the door. Dantrag followed his mother's gaze to several flasks along the wall to Drizzt's left and nodded.

"*Dobluth*," she said to Drizzt, using the derisive drow word for outcast. "The high ritual will be better served with our knowledge that you are here in agony." She nodded to Vendes, who wheeled about, hurling a small dart as she turned.

It caught Drizzt in the stomach, and he felt a small but stinging pinch. Then his entire belly felt as if it had ignited into roaring fires. He gagged, tried to scream, then sheer agony gave him the strength to curl up. The change in posture didn't help. The magical little dart continued to pump its droplets of poison into him, continued to burn at his insides.

Through tear-filled eyes, Drizzt saw the driftdisk slide from his cell, Vendes and Methil obediently following Matron Baenre. Dantrag, expressionless, remained leaning against the doorjamb for some time, then walked over near Drizzt.

Drizzt forced himself to stop screaming, and merely groaned and grunted through gritted teeth with the weapon master standing so close to him.

"You are a fool," Dantrag said. "If your attempts force my mother to kill you before I get the chance, I promise you that I will personally torture and slaughter every living creature that calls itself a friend of Drizzt Do'Urden!"

Again with speed that defied Drizzt's vision, Dantrag smacked Drizzt across the face. The ranger hung limp for just a second, then was forced to curl up again as the fiery explosions of the poisoned dart erupted across his stomach.

* * * * *

Out of sight, around the corner at the base of the wide stairs leading to Tier Breche, Artemis Entreri tried hard to recall an image of Gromph Baenre, the archmage of the city. He had seen Gromph only a few times, mostly while spying for Jarlaxle. (Jarlaxle had thought that the archmage was shortening the nights in Menzoberranzan by lighting the lingering heat fires in the time clock of Narbondel a few instants too soon, and was interested in what the dangerous wizard might be up to, and so he had sent Entreri to spy on the drow.)

Entreri's cloak changed to the flowing robes of the wizard; his hair became thicker and longer, a great white mane, and subtle, barely visible wrinkles appeared about his eyes.

"I cannot believe ye're trying this," Catti-brie said to him when he moved out of the shadows.

"The spider mask is in Gromph's desk," the assassin answered coldly, not thrilled with the prospects either. "There is no other way into House Baenre."

"And if this Gromph is sitting at his desk?"

"Then you and I will be scattered all over the cavern," Entreri answered gruffly, and he swept by the young woman, grabbed her hand, and pulled her up the wide stairway.

Entreri was counting as much on luck as on skill. He knew that Sorcere, the school of wizards, was full of reclusive masters who generally stayed out of each other's way, and he could only hope that Gromph, though only a male, had been invited to House Baenre's high ritual. The walls of the secretive place were protected against scrying and against teleportation, and if his disguise worked against whatever magical barriers might be in place, he should be able to get in and out of Gromph's room without too much interference. The city's archmage was known as a surly one, with a violent temper; no one got in Gromph's way.

At the top of the stairway, on the level of Tier Breche, the companions saw the three structures of the drow Academy. To their right was the plain, pyramidal structure of Melee-Magthere, the school of fighters. Directly ahead loomed the most impressive structure, the great spider-shaped building of Arach-Tinilith, the school of Lloth. Entreri was glad that he did not have to try to enter either of those buildings. Melee-Magthere was a place of swarming guardsmen and tight control, and Arach-Tinilith was protected by the high priestesses of Lloth, working in concert for the good of their Spider Queen. Only the gracefully spired structure to the left, Sorcere, was secretive enough to penetrate.

Catti-brie pulled her arm away and nearly bolted in sheer terror. She had no disguise and felt totally vulnerable up here. The young woman found her courage, though, and did not resist when Entreri roughly grabbed her arm once more and tugged her along at a great pace.

They walked into Sorcere's open front doorway, where two guards promptly blocked their way. One started to ask Entreri a question, but the assassin slapped him across the face and pushed past, hoping that Gromph's cruel reputation would get them through.

The bluff worked, and the guards went back to their posts, not even daring to mutter to themselves until the archmage was far away.

Entreri remembered the twisting ways perfectly and soon came to the plain wall flanking Gromph's private chambers. He took a deep breath and looked to his companion, silently reiterating his feelings that if Gromph was behind this door, they were both surely dead.

"*Kolsen'shea orbb,*" the assassin whispered. To Entreri's relief, the wall began to stretch and twist, becoming a spiderweb. The strands rotated, leaving the hole and revealing the soft blue glow, and Entreri quickly (before he lost his nerve) rushed through and pulled Catti-brie in behind him.

Gromph was not inside.

Entreri made for the dwarf bone desk, rubbing his hands together and blowing in them before reaching for the appropriate drawer. Catti-brie, meanwhile, intrigued by the obviously magical paraphernalia, walked about, eyeing parchments (from a distance), even going over to one ceramic bottle and daring to pop off its cork.

Entreri's heart leaped into his throat when he heard the archmage's voice, but he relaxed when he realized that it came from the bottle.

Catti-brie looked at the bottle and the cork curiously, then popped the cork back on, eliminating the voice. "What was that?" she asked, not understanding a word of the Drow language.

"I know not," Entreri replied harshly. "Do not touch anything!"

Catti-brie shrugged as the assassin went back to his work on the desk, trying to make sure that he uttered the password for the drawer perfectly. He recalled his conversation with Jarlaxle, when the mercenary had given him the word. Had Jarlaxle been honest, or was this whole thing part of some elaborate game? Had Jarlaxle baited him to this place, so that he might speak some false word, open the drawer, and destroy himself and half of Sorcere? It occurred to Entreri that Jarlaxle might have put a phony replica of the spider mask in the drawer, then tricked Entreri into coming here and setting off Gromph's powerful wards, thus destroying the evidence.

Entreri shook the disturbing thoughts away. He had committed himself to this course, had convinced himself that his attempt to free Drizzt was somehow part of the framework of Jarlaxle's grand plans, whatever they might be, and he could not surrender to his fears now. He uttered the phrase and pulled open the drawer.

The spider mask was waiting for him.

Entreri scooped it up and turned to Catti-brie, who had filled the top of a small hourglass with fine white sand and was watching it slip away with the moments. Entreri leaped from the dwarf bone desk and scrambled across the room, tipping the item to the side.

Catti-brie eyed him curiously.

"I was keeping the time," she said calmly.

"This is no timepiece!" the assassin roughly explained. He tipped the hourglass upside down and carefully removed the sand, replacing it in its packet and gently resealing it. "It is an explosive, and when the sand runs out, all the area bursts into flame. You must not touch anything!" he scolded harshly. "Gromph will not even know that we have been here if all is in proper order." Entreri looked around at the jumbled room as he spoke. "Or, at least, in proper disorder. He was not here when Jarlaxle returned the spider mask."

Catti-brie nodded and appeared genuinely ashamed, but it was only a facade. The young woman had suspected the general, if not the exact, nature of the hourglass all along, and would not have let the sand run out. She had only started it running to get some confirmation from the worldly Entreri.

The two quickly departed the wizard's room and Sorcere. Catti-brie did not let on that she had several more of those dangerous hourglasses, and their corresponding packets of detonating sand, tucked into a belt pouch.

Chapter 22

BREAK-IN

u'ellarz'orl, the plateau occupied by some of the proudest noble houses, was strangely quiet. Entreri, appearing as a common drow soldier again, and Catti-brie made their silent and inconspicuous way along the great mushroom grove, toward the twenty-foot-high spiderweb fence surrounding the Baenre compound.

Panic welled in both the companions and neither said a thing, forced themselves to concentrate on the stakes in this game: ultimate victory or ultimate loss.

Crouched in the shadows behind a stalagmite, the two watched as a grand procession, led by several priestesses sitting atop blue-glowing driftdisks, made its way through the open compound and toward the great doors of the huge central chapel. Entreri recognized Matron Baenre and knew that some of the others near her were probably her daughters. He watched the many disks curiously, coming to understand that matron mothers of other houses were in the procession.

It was a high ritual, as Jarlaxle had said, and Entreri snickered at how completely the sly mercenary had arranged all of this.

"What is it?" Catti-brie asked, not understanding the private joke.

Entreri shook his head and scowled, indicating that the troublesome young woman should shut her mouth. Catti-brie bit her bottom lip and did not spew the many venomous replies she had in mind. She needed Entreri now, and he needed her; their personal hatred would have to wait.

And wait is exactly what Catti-brie and Entreri did. They squatted behind the mound for many minutes as the long procession gradually disappeared into the domed chapel. Entreri figured that many more than a thousand drow, maybe even two thousand, had gone into the structure, and few soldiers, or lizard-riders, could now be seen from his position.

Another benefit of their timing soon showed itself as songs to Lloth filtered out of the chapel's doors, filling the air about the compound.

"The cat?" Entreri whispered to Catti-brie.

Catti-brie felt the statuette in her pouch and considered the question, then looked doubtfully at the Baenre web fence. "When we get over," she explained, though she had no idea of how Entreri meant to pass that seemingly impenetrable barrier. The strands of the fence were as thick as Catti-brie's forearm.

Entreri nodded his agreement and took out the black velvet spider mask and slipped it over his head. Catti-brie couldn't contain a shudder as she regarded the assassin, his head now resembling some grotesque caricature of a huge spider.

"I will warn you only once," the assassin whispered. "You are a merciful one, foolishly so, but there is no place for mercy in the realm of the drow. Do not think to wound or knock unconscious any opponents we cross. Go for the kill."

Catti-brie didn't bother to reply, and if Entreri could see into the fires raging inside the young woman, he would not have bothered to utter the remark.

He motioned for her to follow, then picked his careful way from shadow to shadow to the base of the fence.

Entreri touched the strands tentatively, making certain that his fingers would not stick, then he took a firm hold and bade Catti-brie to climb on his back.

"Take care that you do not touch the fence!" he warned. "Else I will have to remove whatever limb you have stuck."

Catti-brie gingerly took hold of the evil man, wrapping her arms about his chest, one over one shoulder, the other under Entreri's arm. She clasped her hands tightly and squeezed with all her strength.

Entreri was not a big man, not forty pounds heavier than Catti-brie herself, but he was strong, his muscles honed for fighting, and he easily began his ascent, keeping his body as far from the dangerous fence as possible so that the young woman's hands did not get entangled. The trickiest part came at the top of the barrier, particularly when Entreri spotted a couple of lizard-riding soldiers approaching.

"Do not even breathe," he warned Catti-brie, and he inched along the top rim of the fence to take as much cover as possible in the shadows of an anchoring stalagmite post.

If there had been no lights in the Baenre compound, the two surely would been caught, their warm forms showing distinctively against the cooler stone of the mound. But lights were on, including many burning torches, and the Baenre soldiers were not using their infravision as they walked their posts. They passed by the fence no more than a dozen feet from the two intruders, but so adept at hiding in the shadows was Artemis Entreri that they never noticed the strange jut in the previously smooth stalagmite.

When they were gone, Entreri pulled himself to a standing position atop the fence and twisted to the side, so that Catti-brie could brace herself against the mound. He had only intended to take a short rest, but the young woman, desperate to be on with things, unexpectedly shifted off his back, onto the mound, and half slid, half climbed down its back side, coming to a roll in the Baenre compound.

Entreri hustled down the fence to join her, snapped off the mask, and glared at her, thinking her actions rash and stupid.

Catti-brie did not retreat from that look, just eyed the hated assassin dangerously and mouthed, "Where?"

Entreri slipped a hand into one pocket and felt for the magical locket, then turned about, facing different directions until the item seemed most warm. He had guessed Drizzt's location before the locket had even confirmed it: the great mound, the best guarded position in the entire compound.

They could only hope that most of Baenre's elite soldiers were attending the high ritual.

Crossing the compound to the elaborate structure was not difficult, for few guards were apparent, the shadows were many, and the singing emanating from the chapel amply covered any noise. No house would expect an attack, or dare to invoke the Spider Queen's anger by launching an attack, during a high ritual, and since the only possible threat to House Baenre was from another drow house, security in the compound was not at its highest point.

"In there," Entreri whispered as he and Catti-brie came flat against the walls flanking the doorway to the huge, hollowed stalagmite. Gently, Entreri touched the stone door to try to discern any traps (though he figured that any traps would be magical in nature and he would find them when they blew up in his face). To his surprise, the portal suddenly rose, disappearing into a crack in the top of the jamb and revealing a narrow, dimly lit corridor.

He and Catti-brie exchanged doubtful looks, and after a long, silent pause, both stepped in together—and both nearly fell over with relief when they realized that they were still alive in the corridor.

Their relief was not long-lived, however, for it was stolen by a guttural call, a question, perhaps. Before the pair could decipher any of the words, the form of a huge, muscular humanoid, easily seven feet tall and as wide as the five-foot corridor, stepped into the other end, almost completely stealing the diminutive light. The creature's sheer bulk, and its distinctive, bull-like head, revealed its identity.

Catti-brie nearly jumped out of her boots when the door slid closed behind her.

The minotaur grunted the question again, in the Drow tongue.

"He's asking for a password," Entreri whispered to Catti-brie. "I think."

"So give it to him."

Easier said than done, Entreri knew well, for Jarlaxle had never mentioned any password to the inner Baenre structures. Entreri would have to take issue with the mercenary over that small slip, he decided—if he ever got the chance.

The monstrous minotaur advanced a threatening step, waving a spiked adamantite rod out in front of it.

"As if minotaurs aren't formidable enough without giving them drow-made weapons," Entreri whispered to Catti-brie.

Another step put the minotaur barely ten feet from the companions.

"*Usstan belbol . . . usstan belbau ulu . . . dos*," Entreri stuttered, and he jingled a pouch on his belt. "*Dosst?*"

The minotaur stopped its advance and screwed up its bullish features.

"What did you say?" Catti-brie whispered.

"I have no idea," Entreri admitted, though he thought he had mentioned something about a gift.

A low snarl emitted from the increasingly impatient minotaur guard's mouth.

"*Dosst?*" Catti-brie asked boldly, holding out her bow in one hand and trying to appear cheerful. She smiled widely and bobbed her head stupidly, as though offering the bow, all the while slipping her other hand inside the folds of her traveling cloak, feeling for an arrow in the quiver at her hip.

"*Dosst?*" she asked again, and the minotaur poked itself in the chest with a huge, stubby finger.

"Yeah, yerself!" Catti-brie growled, and out snapped the arrow, fitted to the string and fired before the stupid minotaur even got its back down. The arrow slammed into the monster's chest and sent it staggering backward.

"Use yer finger to fill the hole!" Catti-brie roared, fitting another arrow. "And how many fingers ye got?"

She glanced quickly to Entreri, who was staring at her dumb-foundedly. Catti-brie laughed at him and put another arrow into the monster's chest, driving it back several more steps, where it toppled into the wider room beyond the corridor. When it fell, more than half a dozen other minotaurs were ready to take its place.

"You are crazy!" Entreri shouted at the woman.

Not bothering to answer, Catti-brie slammed an arrow into the closest minotaur's belly. It doubled over in pain and was plowed under by its charging comrades.

Entreri drew out his blades and met the charge, realizing that he had to keep the giants away from Catti-brie so that she might utilize her bow. He met the first minotaur two steps in from the end of the corridor, throwing his sword up to deflect a blow from the creature's spiked rod (and the assassin's whole side tingled with numbness from the sheer weight of the blow).

Much quicker than the lumbering giant, Entreri countered with three rapid dagger strikes to the monster's midsection. Down swooped the spiked rod, and, though his sword intercepted the blow, Entreri had to spin a complete circuit to absorb the shock and get out of harm's way.

He came around with his sword leading, its green-glowing point cutting a neat line under the minotaur's jaw, slicing through bone and the creature's cowlike tongue.

Blood spewed from the beast's mouth, but it swung again, forcing Entreri back.

A silver streak stole the sight from both combatants as Catti-brie's arrow flew over the engaged minotaur's shoulder to drive into the thick skull of the next creature in line.

Entreri could only hope that the minotaur was similarly blinded as he made his desperate rush, jabbing viciously with his dagger, cutting his sword in a brutal downward slash. He scored lightning-fast hit after hit on the stunned and wounded beast, and his sight returned as the minotaur slumped down in front of him.

Entreri didn't hesitate. He sprang right atop the thing's back, then leaped farther along to the back of the next dead beast, using its bulk to bring him up even with the next monster in line. His sword beat the minotaur to the attack, scoring a solid hit on the creature's shoulder. Entreri thought this one an easy kill as its weapon arm inevitably slumped useless at its side, but he had never fought the likes of a bull-headed minotaur before, and his surprise was complete when the creature snapped a head butt that caught him in the chest.

The minotaur jerked to the side and began a charge across the room, still carrying the assassin between its horns.

"Oh, damn," Catti-brie muttered as she saw the line between her and the remaining monsters suddenly open. She dropped to one knee and began frantically tearing out her arrows and launching them down the corridor.

The blinding barrage dropped one, then two minotaurs, but the third in line grabbed the falling second and hoisted it up as a shield. Catti-brie managed to skip an arrow off that one's thick head, but it did no real damage and the minotaur rapidly closed.

The young woman fired off one more shot, as much to blind the monsters as in any hope of stopping the charge, then she dove to the floor and boldly scrambled ahead, sliding aside the trampling legs.

The minotaur crashed hard into the outer door. Holding its dead comrade in front of it, it could not tell that Catti-brie had slipped away, and it heaved the huge corpse back from the wall and slammed it in again repeatedly.

Still on the floor, Catti-brie had to pick her way past three sets of treelike legs. All three minotaurs were roaring, offering some cover, for they thought that the one in front was squashing the puny woman.

She almost made it.

The last minotaur in line felt a brush against its leg and looked down, then bellowed and grabbed its spiked rod in both hands.

Catti-brie rolled to her back, her bow coming out in front. Somehow she got off a shot, knocking the creature back for just an instant. The woman instinctively threw her feet straight up and over her, launching herself into a backward roll.

The blinded minotaur's rod took a fair-sized chunk out of the stone floor an inch below Catti-brie's angled back.

Catti-brie came right to her feet, facing the beast. She whipped her bow across in front of her and spun away, stumbling out of the corridor.

* * * * *

The breath was taken from his body with the impact. The minotaur wrapped its good arm about Entreri's waist, holding him steady, and hopped back, obviously meaning to slam the assassin into the wall once more. Just a few feet away, another minotaur cheered its winning comrade on.

Entreri's dagger arm pumped wildly, futilely trying to penetrate the beast's thick skull.

The assassin felt as though his backbone had shattered when they hit the wall a second time. He forced himself to see through the pain and the fear, forced himself to take a quick survey of his situation. A cool head was the fighter's best advantage, Entreri knew, and his tactics quickly changed. Instead of just smashing the dagger down against solid bone, he placed its tip on the flesh between the creature's bull horns, then ran it down the side of the minotaur's face, applying equal pressure to slide it and push it in.

They hit the wall again.

Entreri held his hand steady, confident that the dagger would do its work. At first, the blade slipped evenly, not able to penetrate, but then it found a fleshy spot and Entreri immediately changed its angle and plunged it home.

Into the minotaur's eye.

The assassin felt the hungry dagger grab at the creature's life force, felt it pulse, sending waves of strength up his arm.

The minotaur shuddered for a long while, holding steady against the wall. Its watching comrade continued to cheer, thinking that it was making mush of the human.

Then it fell dead, and Entreri, light-footed, hit the ground running, coming up into the other's chest before it could react. He launched a one-two-three combination, sword-dagger-sword, in the blink of an eye.

The surprised minotaur fell back, but Entreri paced it, keeping his dagger firmly embedded, drawing out, feeding on this one's energy as well. The dying creature tried a lame swing with its club, but Entreri's sword easily parried.

And his dagger feasted.

* * * * *

She came into the small room running, spun a half-circle as she fell to one knee. There was no need to aim, Catti-brie knew, for the bulk of the pursuing minotaurs fully filled the corridor.

The closest one was not at full speed, fortunately, having an arrow driven halfway through its inner thigh. The wounded minotaur was a stubborn one, though, taking brutal hit after hit and still coming on.

Behind the beast, the next minotaur screamed frantically for the third, the one pressing a corpse against the wall, to go the other way. But minotaurs were never known for intelligence, and the last in line insisted that it had the human pinned and squashed.

The last arrow was point blank, its tip, as it left Taulmaril, only half a foot from the charging creature's nose. It split the nostrils and the skull, nearly halving the stubborn minotaur's head. The creature was dead instantly, but its momentum carried it on, bowling over Catti-brie.

She wasn't badly injured, but there was no way that she could extract her body and bow in time to stop the second charging minotaur, just coming out of the corridor.

A sliding figure cut across the monster's path, slashing and jabbing, and when the blur had passed, the minotaur stood in a crouch and grabbed at its torn knees. It lumbered to the side in pursuit of this newest foe, but Entreri spun up to his feet and easily danced away.

He ran to the center of the room, behind a black marble pillar, and the minotaur followed, leaning forward. Entreri went around, and the minotaur, thinking quickly (for a minotaur), allowed itself to fall into a staggered run, hooked one arm about the pillar, and used its momentum to whip around.

Entreri had thought quicker. As soon as he knew that he was out of the minotaur's line of sight, he stopped his rush about the pillar and took a couple of steps back. The spinning minotaur rolled right in between the assassin and the pillar, affording Entreri a dozen clean jabs at its side and back.

Artemis Entreri never needed that many.

* * * * *

The minotaur hoisted its dead companion and jumped back three steps, then roared ahead, slamming the thing against the outer stone door.

An enchanted arrow sizzled into its back.

"Huh?" it asked and tried to turn.

A second arrow blew into its side, collapsing a lung.

"Huh?" it asked breathlessly, stupidly, finally turning enough to see Catti-brie, standing at the end of the corridor, grim-faced and with that wicked bow out in front of her.

The third arrow blew into the side of the minotaur's face. The beast took a step forward, but the fourth arrow slammed it in the chest, knocking it back against its dead comrade.

"Huh?"

It got hit five more times—and didn't feel any of them—before Entreri could get to Catti-brie and tell her that the fight was over.

"We are fortunate that there were no drow about," the assassin explained, looking nervously to the twelve doors and alcoves lining this circular room. He felt for the locket in his pouch, then turned to the floor-to-ceiling central pillar.

Without a word of explanation, the assassin ran to the pillar. Sensitive fingers rubbed against its smooth surface.

"What do ye know?" Catti-brie asked when Entreri's hands stopped moving and he turned and smiled her way. She asked again and, in response, the assassin pushed on the stone, and a portion of the marble slid away, revealing that this pillar was hollow. Entreri went in, pulling Catti-brie along with him, and the door closed of its own accord behind them.

"What is it?" Catti-brie demanded, thinking that they had just gone into a closet. She looked to the hole in the ceiling to her left, and the one in the floor to her right.

Entreri didn't answer. Following the locket's pull, he inched over to the hole in the floor, then crouched to one knee and peered down it.

Catti-brie slid down beside him, looking to him curiously when she saw no ladder. Then she looked around the unremarkable marble room, searching for some place to set a rope.

247

"Perhaps there is a foothold," Entreri remarked, and he slid over the edge, easing himself down the shaft. His expression became incredulous as he felt the weight lifted from his body, felt himself floating in midair.

"What is it?" Catti-brie asked impatiently, seeing the amazed look.

Entreri lifted his hands from the floor, held them wide, and smiled smugly as he gently descended. Catti-brie was into the hole right behind him, floating freely, gently descending through the darkness. Catti-brie noticed Entreri below her, replacing the magical mask of disguise now, and concentrating.

"You are my prisoner," the assassin said coldly, and for an instant, Catti-brie did not understand, thought that Entreri had double-crossed her. As she came down to the floor beside him, the assassin motioned for Taulmaril, and she recognized his intentions.

"The bow," Entreri said impatiently.

Catti-brie stubbornly shook her head, and the assassin knew her better than to argue the point. He moved to the closest wall and began feeling about, and soon had the door to this level open. Two drow males were waiting for them, hand-crossbows up and ready, and Catti-brie wondered if she had been wise in holding fast to her bow.

How quickly those crossbows (and two drow jaws) dropped when the guards saw Triel Baenre standing before them!

Entreri roughly grabbed Catti-brie and pulled her forward.

"Drizzt Do'Urden!" he cried in Triel's voice.

The guards wanted no argument with the eldest Baenre daughter. Their orders said nothing about escorting Triel, or anyone other than Matron Baenre, to the valuable Drizzt, but their orders had mentioned nothing about any human female prisoners. One scrambled ahead, while the other rushed to grab Catti-brie.

The young woman slumped, dropping her bow, and forcing one of the dark elves and Entreri to support her, one under each arm. The other drow quickly retrieved Taulmaril, and Catti-brie couldn't help a slight wince in seeing the magnificent weapon in the hands of an evil creature.

They walked along a dark corridor, past several iron-bound doors. The drow in front stopped before one of these and took out a tiny rod. He rubbed it down a metal plate beside the door handle, then tapped the plate twice. The door popped open.

The leading drow started to turn, smiling as though he was grateful to please Triel. Entreri's hand slapped across his mouth, jerking his head back and to the side, and the assassin's dagger hand followed swiftly, the blade plunging through the stunned drow's throat.

Catti-brie's assault was not as skilled, but even more brutal. She pivoted on one foot, her other leg flying high to slam the drow in the belly as they crashed against the wall. Catti-brie hopped back half a step and snapped her head forward, her forehead splattering the drow's delicate nose.

A flurry of punches followed, another knee to the belly, and Catti-brie wrestled her opponent into the room. She came up behind the drow, lifting him from the floor, with her arms wrapped under the drow's armpits and her fingers clenched tightly behind his neck.

The drow thrashed wildly but could not break the hold. Entreri was in by then, and had dropped the corpse to the side.

"No mercy!" Catti-brie growled through clenched teeth.

Entreri calmly walked over. The drow kicked out, banging his foot off Entreri's blocking forearm.

"Triel!" the confused soldier cried.

Entreri stepped back, smiled, and took off the mask, and as an expression of horror widened over the helpless drow's face, Entreri whipped a dagger into his heart.

Catti-brie felt the dark elf jerk, then go limp. A sick feeling washed over her, but it did not take hold as she glanced to the side and saw Drizzt, beaten and chained. He hung from the wall, groaning and trying futilely to curl up into a ball. Catti-brie dropped the dead drow to the floor and ran to her dear friend, immediately noticing the small but obviously wicked dart protruding from his stomach.

"I've got to take it!" she said to Drizzt, hoping that he would agree. He was beyond reason, though; she didn't think he even realized that she was in the room.

Entreri came up beside her. He gave only a slight glance at the dart, more concerned with the bindings holding Drizzt.

With a quick puff of steadying breath, Catti-brie took hold of the nasty dart and tugged it free.

Drizzt curled and gave a sharp cry of pain, then fell limp, unconscious.

"There are no locks to pick!" Entreri snarled, seeing that the shackles were solid rings.

"Move away," came Catti-brie's instructions as she ran out from the wall. When Entreri turned to regard her, he saw the woman lifting her deadly bow and promptly skittered to the side.

Two shots took out the chains, and Drizzt fell, to be caught by Entreri. The wounded ranger somehow managed to open one swollen eye. He could hardly comprehend what was happening, didn't know if these were friends or foes.

"The flasks," he begged.

Catti-brie looked about and spotted the rows of bottles resting against the wall. She rushed over, found a full one, and brought it to Drizzt.

"He should not be alive," Entreri reasoned when she came up with the foul-smelling liquid. "His scars are too many. Something has sustained him."

Catti-brie looked doubtfully at the flask.

The assassin followed her gaze and nodded. "Do it!" he commanded, knowing that they would never get Drizzt out of the Baenre compound in this condition.

Catti-brie shoved the flask against Drizzt's lips and forced his head back, compelled him to take a huge swallow. He sputtered and spat, and for a moment, the young woman feared that she had poisoned or drowned her dearest friend.

"How are you here?" Drizzt asked, both eyes suddenly wide, as the strength began to flow through his body. Still, the drow could not support himself and his breath was dangerously shallow.

Catti-brie ran over to the wall and came back with several more flasks, sniffing them first to make sure that they smelled the same, then pouring them down Drizzt's throat. In just a few minutes, the ranger was standing solidly, looking more than a little amazed to see his dearest friend and his worst enemy standing before him side by side.

"Your equipment," Entreri remarked, roughly turning Drizzt about to see the pile.

Drizzt looked more to Entreri than to the pile, wondering what macabre game the evil assassin was playing. When Entreri noticed the expression, the two enemies locked unblinking stares.

"We've not the time!" Catti-brie called harshly.

"I thought you dead," Drizzt said.

"You thought wrong," Entreri answered evenly. Never blinking, he stepped past Drizzt and lifted the suit of chain, holding it out for the following drow.

"Watch the corridor," Entreri said to Catti-brie. The young woman turned that way just as the iron-bound door swung in.

Turned that way to look down the length of Vendes Baenre's wand.

Part 5

EYE OF A WARRIOR

ourage.

In any language, the word has a special ring to it, as much, I suspect, from the reverent way in which it is spoken as from the actual sounds of the letters. Courage. The word evokes images of great deeds and great character: the grim set of the faces of men defending their town's walls from raiding goblins; the resilience of a mother caring for young children when all the world has seemingly turned hostile. In many of the larger cities of the Realms, young waifs stalk the streets, without parents, without homes. Theirs is a unique courage, a braving of hardships both physical and emotional.

255

R. A. Salvatore

I suspect that Artemis Entreri fought such a battle in the mud-filled lanes of Calimport. On one level, he certainly won, certainly overcame any physical obstacles and rose to a rank of incredible power and respect.

On another level, Artemis Entreri surely lost. What might he have been, I often wonder, if his heart had not been so tainted? But I do not mistake my curiosity for pity. Entreri's odds were no greater than my own. He could have won out over his struggles, in body and in heart.

I thought myself courageous, altruistic, when I left Mithril Hall determined to end the threat to my friends. I thought I was offering the supreme sacrifice for the good of those dear to me.

When Catti-brie entered my cell in House Baenre, when, through half-closed eyes, I glimpsed her fair and deceivingly delicate features, I learned the truth. I did not understand my own motivations when I walked from Mithril Hall. I was too full of unknown grief to recognize my own resignation. I was not courageous when I walked into the Underdark, because, in the deepest corner of my heart, I felt as if I had nothing to lose. I had not allowed myself to grieve for Wulfgar, and that emptiness stole my will and my trust that things could be put aright.

Courageous people do not surrender hope.

Similarly, Artemis Entreri was not courageous when he came with Catti-brie to rescue me. His actions were wrought of sheer desperation, for if he remained in Menzoberranzan, he was surely doomed. Entreri's goals, as always, were purely selfish. By his rescue attempt he made a conscious choice that coming after me was his best chance for survival. The rescue was an act of calculation, not of courage.

By the time Catti-brie had run out of Mithril Hall in pursuit of her foolish drow friend, she had honestly overcome her grief for Wulfgar. The grieving process had come full circle for Catti-brie, and her actions were motivated only by loyalty. She had everything to lose, yet had gone alone into the savage Underdark for the sake of a friend.

I came to understand this when first I looked into her eyes in the dungeons of House Baenre. I came to understand fully the meaning of the word courage.

And I came, for the first time since Wulfgar fell, to know inspiration. I had fought as the hunter, savagely, mercilessly, but it wasn't until I looked again upon my loyal friend that I regained the eyes of the warrior. Gone was my resignation and acceptance of fate; gone was my belief that all would be right if House Baenre got its sacrifice—gave my heart to Lloth.

In that dungeon, the healing potions returned strength to my battered limbs; the sight of grim, determined Catti-brie returned strength to my heart. I vowed then that I would resist, that I would fight the overwhelming events, and would fight to win.

When I saw Catti-brie, I remembered all that I had to lose.

—Drizzt Do'Urden

Chapter 23

DUK-TAK

S he reached for an arrow, then shifted her bow out in front of her in defense as a glob of greenish goo erupted from the wand and flew at her.

Catti-brie's bow was suddenly tight against her chest, and she was flying, to smack hard against the wall. One arm was pinned tightly against her chest, the other tightly to her hip, and she could not move her legs. She could not even fall from the wall!

She tried to call out, but her jaw would not work, and one eye would not open. She could see, barely, with the other eye, and she

258

somehow managed to continue to draw breath.

Entreri spun about, sword and dagger coming to the ready. He dove to the side, to the middle of the room, in front of Catti-brie, when he saw the three drow females enter, two of them aiming loaded hand-crossbows his way.

The agile assassin rolled back to his feet and started forward, rising up as if he would leap into his attackers. Then he dove low, sword leading.

The skilled drow females held their shots through the assassin's feint, then brought their hands in line. The first dart hit Entreri's shoulder and jolted him more than he would have expected. Suddenly, his momentum was stolen and he was standing straighter. Black arcs of electricity, writhing like sparking tentacles, shot out from the dart, burning him, jolting him back a few steps.

The second dart got him in the belly and, though the initial hit did not pain the assassin too greatly, a huge electrical blast followed, hurling him backward to the floor. His sword went flying, narrowly missing the trapped Catti-brie.

Entreri came to a stop at the young woman's feet. He still clutched his jeweled dagger, and thought immediately that he might have to throw the thing. But he could only watch in astonishment as the fingers of that hand twitched involuntarily, his grasp on the dagger weakening. He willed his arm to heave the blade, but his muscles would not respond, and the dagger soon toppled out of his trembling hand.

He lay on the stone at Catti-brie's feet, confused and scared. For the first time in his life, those finely honed warrior muscles would not answer his call.

It was the third female, in the middle of the trio, that held Drizzt's attention: Vendes Baenre, Duk-Tak, his merciless torturer for all these long days. Drizzt stood very still, holding the coat of chain mail in front of him, not even daring to blink. The females flanking the cruel Baenre daughter put away their hand-crossbows and drew two shining swords each.

Drizzt expected to be blown away, or held by some magical intrusion, as Vendes quickly chanted under her breath.

"Valiant friends," the wicked noble remarked sarcastically, using perfect surface Common.

R. A. Salvatore

Drizzt understood the nature of her spell then, a dweomer that allowed her to communicate with Entreri and Catti-brie.

Entreri's mouth moved weirdly, and the expression on his face revealed what he was trying to say more than any decipherable words. "High ritual?"

"Indeed," Vendes replied. "My mother and sisters, and many visiting matron mothers, are gathered in the chapel. I was excused from the initial ceremonies and was instructed to bring Drizzt Do'Urden in to them later." She eyed Drizzt and seemed perfectly content. "I see that your friends have saved me the trouble of forcing the healing potions down your throat.

"Did you really expect to so easily walk into House Baenre, steal our most valuable prisoner, and walk out?" Vendes asked Entreri. "You were seen before you ever crossed the web fence—and there will be inquiries as to how you got your unclean hands on my brother's mask! Gromph, or perhaps that dangerous Jarlaxle, will have many questions to answer.

"I am surprised at you, too, assassin," she went on. "Your reputation precedes you—I would have expected a better performance. Did you not understand the significance of mere males guarding our prized catch?"

She looked to Drizzt and shook her head. "Those pretend guards I put in place were expendable, of course," she said. Drizzt made no move, showed no reply in his features. He felt the strength returning to him as the healing potions did their work, but that strength would make little difference, he realized, facing the likes of Vendes and two supremely armed and trained females. The ranger looked to his coat of armor disdainfully—it would do him little good held in his hands.

Entreri's mind was working more clearly now, but his body was not. The electrical impulses continued, defeating any coordinated attempt at movement. He did manage to drop one hand into his pouch, though, in response to something Vendes had said, some hint at fleeting hope.

"We suspected that the human woman was alive," Vendes explained, "in the clutches of Jarlaxle, most likely—and we hardly hoped that she would be so easily delivered to us."

Entreri had to wonder if Jarlaxle had double-crossed him. Had

260

the mercenary concocted this elaborate plan for no better reason than to deliver Catti-brie to House Baenre? It made no sense to Entreri—but little about Jarlaxle's actions these last hours made sense to him.

The mention of Catti-brie brought a measure of fire to Drizzt's eyes. He couldn't believe that the young woman was here, in Menzoberranzan, that she had risked so much to come after him. Where was Guenhwyvar? he wondered. And had Bruenor or Regis come along beside Catti-brie?

He winced as he eyed the young woman, wrapped in greenish goo. How vulnerable she seemed, how utterly helpless.

The fires burned brighter in Drizzt's lavender eyes when he returned his gaze to Vendes. Gone was his fear of his torturer; gone was his resignation about how things had to end.

In one swift motion, Drizzt dropped the suit of armor and snapped out his scimitars.

On a nod from Vendes, the two females were on Drizzt, one circling to each side. One tapped her sword against Twinkle's curving blade, indicating that Drizzt should drop the weapon. He looked down to Twinkle, and all logic told him to comply.

He spun the scimitar in a wild arc instead, swishing the female's sword aside. His second blade came up suddenly, defeating a thrust from the other side before it ever began.

"O fool!" Vendes cried at him in obvious glee. "I do so wish to see you fight, Drizzt Do'Urden—since Dantrag is so intent on slaughtering you!"

The way she said it made Drizzt wonder who Vendes would want to win that potential fight. He had no time to ponder the continuing intrigue of the chaotic world, though, not with two drow females pressing him so.

Vendes reverted to the Drow language then, commanding her soldiers to beat Drizzt fiercely, but not to kill him.

Drizzt turned a sudden spin, like a screw, his blades weaving a dangerous pattern on all sides. He came out of it suddenly, viciously, snapping a thrust at the female on his left. He scored a minor hit, doing no real damage against the fabulous drow armor—armor that Drizzt was not wearing.

That point was driven home by the tip of a sword that then

nicked Drizzt from the right. He grimaced and pivoted back, his backhanded cut taking the sword away before it could do any real damage.

* * * * *

Entreri prayed that Vendes was as intent on the fight as her soldiers, for every movement he made seemed so very clumsy and obvious. Somehow, he managed to get the spider mask out of his pouch and over his trembling hand, and then he reached up and grabbed Catti-brie's belt.

His trembling fingers could not support the hold, though, and he fell back to the floor.

Vendes glanced casually his way, snickered—apparently not noticing the mask—and turned back to the fight.

Entreri sat half-propped by the wall, trying to find some inner control to ward off the nasty drow enchantment, but all his efforts proved useless; his muscles continued their involuntary twitching.

* * * * *

Swords cut in at Drizzt from every angle. One drew a line on his cheek, stinging him painfully. The skilled females, working perfectly in concert, kept him pinned near the corner, gave him no room to maneuver. Still, Drizzt's parrying work was excellent, and Vendes applauded his outstanding, if futile, efforts.

Drizzt knew that he was in serious trouble. Unarmored and still weak (though the magical potions continued to flow through his veins), he had few tricks that could get him past so powerful a tandem.

A sword cut low; Drizzt hopped the blade. Another chopped down, from the other side, but Drizzt, crouching as he leaped, got Twinkle up to deflect it. His other scimitar snapped back and forth in front of him, defeating the two middle-height attacks, one from each female, and completing the four-parry.

But Drizzt could not counter with any offensive routines as the relentless barrage continued, forcing him back on his heels, forcing him to react in awkward angles.

He hopped and ducked, spun his blades this way and that, and somehow managed to keep those stinging swords from cutting any deep holes in his vulnerable body, though the minor hits were beginning to add up.

The ranger glanced forlornly at Catti-brie, terrified at the prospects of what she would soon face.

* * * * *

Entreri continued to wage his futile war, then finally slumped low, defeated, thinking that he could not possibly fight his way past the powerful enchantment.

But the assassin had not survived the streets of dangerous Calimport, had not risen to a position of leadership in the evil underworld of the southern city, by accepting defeat. He changed his thinking, decided that he had to work within the parameters offered to him.

Entreri's arm shot up above him. His fingers did not grasp—he did not try to grasp—but rather, he slapped his arm hard against the binding goo.

That was all the grip he would need.

With tremendous effort, Entreri coiled his stuck arm and pulled himself halfway up beside the trapped woman.

Catti-brie was watching him, helpless and hopeless, having no idea what he meant to do. She even winced and tried to duck (though of course her head would not move an inch) as the assassin's free arm swung about, as though she feared that he meant to strike her.

It was not the jeweled dagger perched in that free hand, though, but the spider mask, and Catti-brie began to understand as it came over the very top of her head. It wouldn't slip down very far at first, blocked by the binding goo, but that greenish sludge instantly began to give way to the item's mighty magic.

Catti-brie was fully blinded as a wave of goo, then the bottom lip of the spider mask, covered her one free eye.

A moment later, her other eye blinked open.

* * * * *

R. A. Salvatore

Sparks flew as the battle intensified, the females pressing more fiercely against the stubborn defenses of the renegade male.

"Be done with it!" impatient Vendes growled. "Take him down, that we might drag him to the chapel, that he might bear witness as we sacrifice the foolish woman to Lloth!"

Of all the things that Vendes could have said, of all the threats that she could have then laid upon Drizzt Do'Urden, none would have been so foolish. The notion of Catti-brie, dear and innocent Catti-brie, being given to the horrid, wretched Spider Queen was too much for Drizzt's sensibilities to bear.

No longer was he Drizzt Do'Urden, for his rational identity was replaced by the welling urges of the primal hunter, the savage.

The female on his left came with another measured counter, but the one on his right struck more daringly, one of her swords thrusting far beyond the tip of Drizzt's blocking scimitar.

It was a cunning move, but in the heightened sensibilities of the hunter, that thrusting sword seemed to move almost in slow motion. Drizzt let the tip get within a few inches of his vulnerable abdomen before the blade in his left hand slashed across, deflecting the sword out wide, crossing under his upraised arm as his other scimitar worked against the female's second sword.

His scimitars then crossed in a powerful diagonal parry, alternating their targets, his left arm shooting across and up, his right across and down.

He dove to his knees, straight ahead, using his closest enemy's body to prevent the other female from hitting him. In came his right hand, deftly turning the blade so that it slashed against the outside of his opponent's knee, buckling the leg. Drizzt punched out with his left, connecting on the female's belly and throwing her back over that collapsing leg.

Still on his knees, the ranger spun desperately, hacking across with his left as the other female rushed in on him.

She was too high. The scimitar took one sword out wide, but the other sword poked lower.

The hunter's second scimitar intercepted it and turned it aside, though it slashed Drizzt's skin and nicked a rib.

Back and forth went the parries and thrusts, the hunter feeling no pain from this newest and most serious wound. It seemed impossible to Vendes, but Drizzt managed to get a foot under him and was soon standing even with her skilled soldier.

The other female writhed on the ground, clutching her blasted leg and tucking her arm tightly over her slashed belly.

"Enough!" Vendes cried, holding her wand Drizzt's way. She had enjoyed the spectacular battle, but had no intention of losing any females.

"Guenhwyvar!" came a shrill cry.

Vendes looked to the side, to the human woman—wearing the spider mask!—crouching low, away from the binding goo. Catti-brie charged out from the wall, dropping the magical figurine and scooping up a certain dagger as she went.

Instinctively, Vendes loosed another gob of goo, but it seemed to pass right through the charging woman to splat harmlessly against the wall.

Somewhat disoriented and certainly off balance, Catti-brie simply dove forward, dagger out. She managed to nick Vendes' hand, but the parrying wand rushed across and turned the deadly blade before it could dig in.

Catti-brie crashed heavily into the drow's thighs, and both females went sprawling, the woman trying to hold on, and Vendes kicking and scrambling fiercely to get away.

* * * * *

Drizzt's scimitars banged against the remaining female's swords so rapidly that it sounded like one long, scraping ring. She kept up with his fury for a few moments, to her credit, but gradually her parries came later and later against the barrage of thrusts and cuts.

A sword snapped up to her right, defeating Twinkle. Her second sword turned up and out to take the second thrusting scimitar to the side.

But the second scimitar was not really thrusting, and it was the female's sword that went out. She recognized the feint and halted her own weapon's progress, bringing it right back in.

She was too late. Drizzt's scimitar plunged through the fine mesh armor. He was open to any counter, but the female had no strength, no life, left as the wicked scimitar jabbed at her heart. She shuddered as Drizzt withdrew the blade.

* * * * *

A flurry of punches battered Catti-brie's head as she hugged tightly to the vicious drow's legs. The spider mask had turned about, and Catti-brie could not see, but she realized that if Vendes had a weapon handy, she would be in trouble.

Blindly, Catti-brie reached up with one hand, trying to grab at a drow wrist. Vendes was too quick for the move, though, and not only got her arm out of the way, but wriggled one leg free as well. She coiled and kicked, and Catti-brie nearly swooned.

Vendes pushed powerfully against her, slipping free, then Catti-brie was scrambling, trying to catch up to the suddenly receding legs. The young woman hesitated for just an instant, to pull the troublesome mask from her face, then cried out in denial as she saw Vendes's feet slipping too far from her grasp. The Baenre daughter quickly regained her footing and ran from the room.

Catti-brie could easily fathom the consequences of letting this one get away. Stubbornly, she put her arms under her and started to rise, but was pushed back to the floor by a gentle hand as someone came over her. She saw the bare feet of Drizzt Do'Urden hit the stone floor in front of her, in full pursuit.

Drizzt twisted weirdly as he came into the corridor. He threw himself backward and to the floor so fiercely that Catti-brie feared he had been clotheslined. She understood the move as Drizzt's own doing, though, as a gob of greenish goo flew harmlessly above him.

A twisting roll realigned Drizzt and put his feet back under him, and he shot off like a springing cat.

And a springing cat, Guenhwyvar, followed, leaping over Catti-brie and into the corridor, turning so perfect an angle, the instant the paws touched the stone, that Catti-brie had to blink to make sure she was not seeing things.

"*Nau!*" came the doomed drow's cry of protest from out in the corridor. The warrior whom Vendes had tortured, had beaten without mercy, was upon her, his eyes raging with fires of vengeance.

Guenhwyvar came right behind, desperate to help Drizzt, but in the instant it took the cat to reach the fighting, a scimitar had already plunged deep into Vendes's stomach.

* * * * *

A groan from the side refocused Catti-brie's attention. She spotted the wounded female crawling for her dropped weapons.

Catti-brie scrambled immediately, staying on the floor, and wrapped her legs about the drow's neck, squeezing with all her strength. Both ebon-skinned hands came up to tear at her, to punch at her. But then the female calmed, and Catti-brie thought she had surrendered—until she noticed the drow's lips moving.

She was casting a spell!

Purely on instinct, Catti-brie poked her finger repeatedly into the drow's eyes. The chant became cries of pain and protest, and they became no more than a wheeze as Catti-brie clamped her legs down tighter.

Catti-brie hated this with all her generous heart. The killing revolted her, especially a fight such as this, where she would have to watch for agonizing seconds, minutes perhaps, while she suffocated her opponent.

She spied Entreri's dagger not far away and grabbed it. Tears of rage and innocence lost filled her blue eyes as she brought the deadly blade to bear.

* * * * *

Guenhwyvar skidded to a stop, and Drizzt roughly retracted the embedded blade and took a step back.

"Nau?" stunned Vendes repeated, the drow word for "no." Vicious Duk-Tak seemed little to Drizzt then, almost pitiful. She was doubled over in pain, trembling violently.

She fell over at Drizzt's feet. Her mouth moved, forming the denying word one last time, but no sound came from her breathless lips and the red glow left her eyes forever.

Chapter 24

HEAD FIRST

rizzt came back into his cell to see Catti-brie still lying on the stone floor, holding the spider mask and gasping heavily as she tried to steady her breathing. Behind her, Entreri hung awkwardly by one arm, twisted and stuck to the gooey wall.

"This'll get him down," Catti-brie explained, tossing the mask to Drizzt.

Drizzt caught the mask but made no move, having much more on his mind than freeing the assassin.

"Regis told me," Catti-brie explained, though that point

seemed obvious enough. "I made him tell me."

"You came alone?"

Catti-brie shook her head, and for a moment Drizzt nearly swooned, thinking that another of his friends might be in peril, or might be dead. But Catti-brie motioned to Guenhwyvar, and the ranger breathed a sigh of relief.

"You are a fool," Drizzt replied, his words wrought of sheer incredulity and frustration. He scowled fiercely at Catti-brie, wanting her to know that he was not pleased.

"No more than yerself," the young woman answered with a wistful smile, a smile that stole the scowl from Drizzt's face. The dark elf couldn't deny his joy at seeing Catti-brie again, even in this dangerous circumstance.

"Are ye wanting to talk about it now?" Catti-brie asked, smiling still. "Or are ye wanting to wait until we're back in Mithril Hall?"

Drizzt had no answer, just shook his head and ran a hand through his thick mane. He looked to the spider mask then, and to Entreri, and his scowl returned.

"We've a deal," Catti-brie quickly put in. "He got me to ye, and said he'd get us both out, and we're to guide him back to the surface."

"And once there?" Drizzt had to ask.

"Let him go his way, and we're to go our own," Catti-brie answered firmly, as though she needed to hear the strength of her voice for the sake of her own resolve.

Again Drizzt looked doubtfully from the mask to the assassin. The prospects of setting Artemis Entreri free on the surface did not sit well in the noble ranger's gut. How many would suffer for Drizzt's actions now? How many would again be terrorized by the darkness that was Artemis Entreri?

"I gived me word," Catti-brie offered in the face of her friend's obvious doubts.

Drizzt continued to ponder the consequences. He couldn't deny Entreri's potential value on the ensuing journey, particularly the fight they would likely face in getting out of the Baenre complex. Drizzt had fought beside the assassin before on similar occasions, and together they had been nothing short of brilliant.

Still . . .

"I came in good faith," Entreri stuttered through chattering, barely controlled teeth. "I saved . . . I . . . saved that one." His free arm twitched out as though to indicate Catti-brie, but it jerked suddenly, violently, and banged against the wall instead.

"I'll have your word then," Drizzt offered, moving toward the man. He meant to go on and exact a promise from Entreri that his evil deeds would be at an end, even that once on the surface he would willingly stand trial for his dark past. Entreri saw it coming clearly, though, and cut Drizzt short, his rising anger giving him temporary control over his uncooperative muscles.

"Nothing!" he snarled. "You have what I offered to her!"

Drizzt immediately looked back to Catti-brie, who was up and moving for her bow.

"I gived me word," she replied, more emphatically, matching his doubtful stare.

"And we are running . . . short . . . of time," Entreri added.

The ranger moved the last two steps swiftly and plopped the mask over Entreri's head. The man's arm slid out of the goo and he dropped to the floor, unable to gain enough control to even stand. Drizzt went for the remaining potion bottles, hoping that they might restore the assassin's muscle control. He still wasn't wholly convinced that showing Entreri back to the surface was the right choice, but he decided that he couldn't wait around and debate the issue. He would free Entreri, and together the three and Guenhwyvar would try to escape the compound and the city. Other problems would have to be dealt with later.

It would all be moot, after all, if the potion's healing magic did not help the assassin, for Drizzt and Catti-brie surely could not carry the man out of there.

But Entreri was standing again before he had even finished his first draw on the ceramic flask. The effects of the dart were temporary and fast fading, and the revitalizing potion spurred the recovery even more quickly.

Drizzt and Catti-brie shared another flask, and Drizzt, after strapping on his armor, belted on two of the six remaining and gave two each to his companions.

"We have to go back out of Baenre's great mound," Entreri said, readying himself for the journey. "The high ritual is still in progress, no doubt, but if the slain minotaurs on the higher level have been discovered, then we'll likely find a host of soldiers waiting for us."

"Unless Vendes, in her arrogance, came down here alone," Drizzt replied. His tone, and the assassin's responding stare revealed that neither of them thought that possibility likely.

"Head first," Catti-brie offered. Both her companions looked to her, not understanding.

"The dwarven way," the young woman explained. "When ye've a back to yer wall, ye put yer head down low and let it lead."

Drizzt looked to Guenhwyvar, to Catti-brie and her bow, to Entreri and his deadly blades, and to his own scimitars—how convenient for cocky Dantrag, in anticipation of his fight with the captured ranger, to have placed all of Drizzt's items so near at hand! "They may have us cornered," Drizzt admitted, "but I doubt that they understand what it is they have cornered!"

* * * * *

Matron Baenre, Matron Mez'Barris Armgo, and K'yorl Odran stood in a tight triangle atop the central altar of House Baenre's immense chapel. Five other matron mothers, rulers of the fourth- to eighth-ranking houses of the city, formed a ring about the trio. This elite group, Menzoberranzan's ruling council, met often in the small, secret room used as council chambers, but not in centuries had they come together in prayer.

Matron Baenre felt truly at the pinnacle of her power. She had brought them together, one and all, had banded the eight ruling houses in an alliance that would force all of Menzoberranzan to follow Matron Baenre's lead to Mithril Hall. Even vicious K'yorl, so resistant to the expedition and the alliance, now seemed honestly caught up in the budding frenzy. Earlier in the ceremony, K'yorl, with no prompting, had offered to go along personally on the attack, and Mez'Barris Armgo—not wanting the ruler of the house ranked behind her own to shine darker in Matron Baenre's eyes—had immediately offered likewise.

Lloth was with her, Matron Baenre believed with all of her evil heart. The others believed that Lloth was with the withered matron mother, too, and, thus, the alliance had been firmly joined.

Matron Baenre did well to hide her smile through the next portions of the ceremony. She tried hard to be patient with Vendes. She had sent her daughter to get Drizzt, after all, and Vendes was experienced enough in the ways of drow rituals to understand that the renegade might not survive the ceremony. If Vendes took a few torturing liberties with the prisoner now, Matron Baenre could not fault her. Baenre did not plan to sacrifice Drizzt at the ceremony. She had many games left to play with that one, and dearly wanted to give Dantrag his chance to outshine all other weapon masters in Menzoberranzan. But these religious frenzies had a way of deciding their own events, Baenre knew, and if the situation demanded that Drizzt be given over to Lloth, then she would eagerly wield the sacrificial dagger.

The thought was not an unpleasant one.

* * * * *

At the front of the circular structure, beside the great doors, Dantrag and Berg'inyon found themselves faced with equally difficult choices. A guard sneaked in, whispering word that some commotion had occurred at the great mound, that several minotaurs were rumored killed, and that Vendes and her escort had gone to the lower levels.

Dantrag looked down the rows of seated dark elves, to the raised central dais. All of his other sisters were down there, and his elder brother, Gromph, as well (though he didn't doubt that Gromph would have eagerly accepted the excuse to be out of that female-dominated scene). The high ritual was a ceremony of emotional peaks and valleys, and the ruling matron mothers, turning faster and faster circles on the dais, slapping their hands together and chanting wildly, were surely heading for a peak.

Dantrag looked into the waiting gaze of Berg'inyon, the younger Baenre obviously at a loss as to how they should proceed.

The weapon master moved out of the main hall, taking the guard and Berg'inyon with him. Behind them there came a succession of crescendos as the frenzied cheers mounted.

Go to the perimeter, Dantrag's hands flashed to Berg'inyon, for he would have had to shout to be heard. *See that it is secure.*

Berg'inyon nodded and moved off down the bending corridor, to one of the secret side doors, where he had left his lizard mount.

Dantrag took a quick moment to check his own gear. Likely, Vendes had the situation—if there even was a situation—well under control, but deep inside, Dantrag almost hoped that she did not, hoped that his fight with Drizzt would be thrust upon him. He felt his sentient sword's agreement with that thought, felt a wave of vicious hunger emanate from the weapon.

Dantrag let his thoughts continue down that path. He would carry the slain renegade's body in to his mother at the high ritual, would let her and the other matron mothers (and Uthegental Armgo, who sat in the audience) witness the result of his prowess.

The thought was not an unpleasant one.

* * * * *

"Head first," Catti-brie mouthed silently as the companions came up into the main level within the marble cylinder. Guenhwyvar crouched in front of her, ready to spring; Drizzt and Entreri stood to either side of the cat, weapons drawn. Catti-brie bent back Taulmaril.

A high-ranking drow soldier, a female, stood right before the opening as the marble door slid aside. Wide went her red eyes, and she threw her hands up before her.

Catti-brie's arrow blew right through the meager defense, blew right through the female, and took down the drow behind her as well. Guenhwyvar leaped in the arrow's wake, easily clearing the two falling dark elves and barreling into a host of others, scattering them all across the circular room.

Out went Drizzt and Entreri, one on either side of the opening, their flashing weapons leading. They came back into Catti-brie's line of sight almost immediately, both of them bearing suddenly blood-stained blades.

Catti-brie fired again, right between them, pounding a hole in the fleshy drow wall blocking the entrance to the exit corridor. Then she leaped out, between her companions, with Drizzt and Entreri doing equally brilliant sword work on either side of her. She fired again, nailing a drow to one of the side doors in the circular room.

Entreri's dagger bit hard into a drow heart; Drizzt's scimitars crossed up an opponent's attack routine, then countered, one over the other in opposing, diagonal, downward swipes, drawing a neat X on the drow's throat.

But this was Guenhwyvar's show. Inside the crowded room, nothing in all the world could have created more general havoc and panic than six hundred pounds of snarling, clawing fury. Guenhwyvar dashed this way and that, swiping one drow on the backside, tripping up another with a bite to the ankle. The cat actually killed no dark elves in that wild rush through the room and into the corridor, but left many wounded, and many more fleeing, terrified, in its wake.

Catti-brie was first into the corridor.

"Shoot the damned door!" Entreri cried to her, but she needed no prodding and put the first and second arrows away before the assassin even finished the command. Soon she could hardly even see the door for the blazing shower of sparks igniting all about it—but what she could make out continued to appear solid.

"Open, oh, open!" the young woman shouted, thinking that they were going to be trapped in the corridor. Once the chaos in the room behind them subsided, their enemies would overwhelm them. Just to accentuate Catti-brie's fears, the corridor suddenly went black.

Good fortune alone saved them, for the woman's next shot struck one of the opening mechanisms within the door, and up it slid. Still running blindly, Catti-brie stumbled out into the Baenre compound, Drizzt and Entreri, and then Guenhwyvar, coming fast behind.

They saw the streaks of glowing house emblems, leaving a residual trail of light as several lizard-riders swarmed to the area of the commotion. The companions had to make their choice immediately, as crossbow quarrels clicked off the stone around them. Entreri took up the lead. His first thought was to go for the fence, but he realized that the three of them, with only one spider mask, could not get past that barrier in time. He ran to the right, around the side of the great mound. It was an uneven wall, for the structure was really a tight cluster of several huge stalagmites. Catti-brie and Drizzt came right behind, but Guenhwyvar pivoted completely about just outside the doorway, and rushed back in, scattering the closest pursuing dark elves.

Entreri's mind worked furiously, trying to remember the general layout of the huge compound, trying to discern how many guards were likely on duty, and where they were all normally located. The immense house grounds covered nearly half a mile in one direction and a quarter of a mile in the other, and many of the guards, if Entreri chose correctly, would never get near the fighting.

It seemed as if all the drow of the house were about them now, though, a mounting frenzy on all sides of the escaping prisoners.

"There's nowhere to go!" Catti-brie cried. A javelin slammed the stone just above her head, and she swung about, Taulmaril ready. The enemy dark elf was already moving, diving out of sight behind a mound near the fence, but Catti-brie let fly anyway. The magical arrow skipped off the stone and slammed the fence, disintegrating into a tremendous shower of silver and purple sparks. For a moment, the woman dared to hope that luck had shown her a way to blow through the barrier, but when the sparks cleared, she realized that the strand of the mighty fence wasn't even scratched.

Catti-brie hesitated for a moment to consider the shot, but Drizzt slammed roughly against her back, forcing her to run on.

Around another bend went the assassin, only to find that many drow were coming at them from the other direction. With enemies so close, to run out into the open compound would have been suicide, and they could go neither forward nor back the way they had come. Entreri rushed forward anyway, then cut a sharp right, leaping up onto the mound, onto a narrow, ascending walkway used mostly by the goblin slaves the Baenre family had put to work sculpting the outside of the gorgeous palace.

The ledge was not difficult for the assassin, who was used to running along the high, narrow gutters of the great houses of southern cities. Neither was it difficult for Drizzt, so agile and balanced. If Catti-brie had found the time to pause a moment and consider her course, though, she likely would not have been able to go on. They were running up a path a foot and a half wide, open on one side (to an increasingly deep drop) and with an uneven wall on the other. But the dark elves were not far behind, and none of the fugitives had time to consider his or her course. Catti-brie not only paced

Entreri step for step, but she managed to fire off a couple of shots into the compound below, just to keep her enemies scrambling for cover.

Entreri thought that they had met an obstacle when he rounded a bend to find two stupidly staring goblin workers. The terrified slaves wanted no part of any fight, though, and they dove over the edge of the walkway, sliding the bumpy ride down the side of the mound.

Around the next bend the assassin spotted a wide and decorated balcony, five feet to the side of the continuing walkway. Entreri leaped onto it, seeing a better carved stairway ascending from that point.

As soon as he landed, two dark elves burst out of doors set in the back of the balcony, against the mound. A silver-streaking arrow greeted the first, blowing her back into the carved room, and Entreri made short work of the other, finishing her before Drizzt and Catti-brie had even leaped across to join him.

Then came Guenhwyvar, the panther flying past the three surprised companions to take up the lead along the stairway.

Higher and higher went the companions, fifty feet, a hundred feet, two hundred feet, off the ground. Huffing and puffing, the tired group ran on, having no choice. Finally, after they had put a thousand feet below them, the huge stalagmite became a stalactite, and the stair gave way to horizontal walkways, connecting many of the larger hanging stones over the Baenre compound.

A group of drow charged along the walkway from the other direction, cutting off the companions. The dark elves fired their hand-crossbows as they came, into the great panther as Guenhwyvar flattened its ears and charged. Darts stung the cat, pumping their poison, but Guenhwyvar would not be stopped. Realizing this, the trailing members of the group turned and fled, and some of those caught too close to the cat simply leaped over the side of the railed walkway, using their innate powers of levitation to keep them aloft.

Catti-brie immediately hit one of them with an arrow, the force of the impact spinning the dying drow over and over in midair, to hang grotesquely at a diagonal, upside-down angle, lines of his blood running freely from the wound to scatter like rain on the stone floor many hundreds of feet below. The other levitating dark elves, realizing how vulnerable they were, quickly dropped from sight.

Guenhwyvar buried the remaining elves on the walkway. Entreri came right behind and finished off those wounded drow left broken in the fierce panther's wake. Entreri looked back to his companions and gave a determined shout, seeing running room ahead of them.

Catti-brie responded in kind, but Drizzt kept silent. He knew better than the others how much trouble he and his friends were really in. Many of the Baenre drow could likely levitate, an ability that Drizzt had for some reason lost after he had spent some time on the surface. The Baenre soldiers would be up all along the walkways before long, hiding among the stalactites with their hand-crossbows ready.

The walkway came to another stalactite and split both ways around the structure. Guenhwyvar went left, Entreri right.

Suspecting an ambush, the assassin rushed around the bend in a slide on his knees. A single drow was waiting for him, arm extended. The dark elf snapped the hand-crossbow down as soon as she saw the assassin coming in low. She fired but missed, and Entreri's sword punctured her side. Up came the assassin in a flourish. Having no time for any extended battles, Entreri used his prodding sword as leverage and heaved the female over the railing.

Drizzt and Catti-brie heard a roar and saw a dark elf, swatted by the panther, go tumbling away on the left as well. Catti-brie started that way to follow, but heard a whistle from behind and looked over her shoulder just as Drizzt's tattered green cloak waved in the air. The woman reflexively ducked, then stood staring at a crossbow dart that had tangled up in the thick cloth, a crossbow dart that had been aimed at the back of her head.

Drizzt dropped the cloak and skipped to Catti-brie's side, affording her a fine view of the walkway behind them and the group of drow fast approaching.

On the narrow walkway, there was no better weapon in all the world than Taulmaril.

Streak after streak flashed down the length, killing and wounding several drow. Catti-brie thought she could keep up the attack indefinitely, until all the pursuing enemies were slain, but suddenly Drizzt grabbed her by the shoulders and heaved her to the side, falling flat with her under him halfway around the round stalactite.

A lightning bolt slammed the stone, right where they had been standing, showering them both with multicolored sparks.

"Damn wizard!" the fiery woman shouted. She came up on one knee and fired again, thinking she had located the mage. Her arrow dove for the approaching group, but hit some magical barrier and exploded into nothingness.

"Damn wizard!" Catti-brie cried again, then she was running, pulled on by Drizzt.

The walkway beyond the stalactite was clear, and the companions far outdistanced those pursuing, as the dark elves had to be wary of any ambush near the pillar.

Many intersecting walkways, a virtual maze above the great compound, presented themselves, and very few Baenre soldiers were anywhere to be seen. Again it seemed as though the friends had some running room, but where could they go? The entire cavern of Menzoberranzan was opened wide before them, below them, but the walkways ended far short of the perimeter of the Baenre compound in every direction, and few stalactites hung low enough to join with the great stalagmite mounds that might have offered them a way to get back to the ground.

Guenhwyvar, apparently sharing those confused thoughts, fell back into the group, and Entreri again took up the lead. He soon came to a fork in the walkway and looked back to Drizzt for guidance, but the drow only shrugged. Both of the seasoned warriors realized that the defenses were fast organizing around them.

They came to another stalactite pillar and followed a ringing walkway ascending its curving side. They found a door, for this one pillar was hollowed, but there was only a single, empty room inside—no place to hide. At the top of the ascending ring, the bridging walkways continued on in two directions. Entreri started left, then stopped abruptly and fell flat to his back.

A javelin soared just over him, hitting and sinking into the stone stalactite right in front of Catti-brie's face. The young woman stared at it as writhing black tentacles arched along its quivering length, crackling and biting at the rock. Catti-brie could only imagine what pains that evil-looking enchantment might cause.

"Lizard-riders," Drizzt whispered into her ear, pulling her along once more. Catti-brie looked all about for a shot and heard the scuttling feet of subterranean lizards as they ran along the cavern's ceiling. But in the dimly lit view afforded her by her magical circlet, she made out no clear targets.

"Drizzt Do'Urden!" came a cry from a lower, parallel walkway. Drizzt stopped and looked that way, to see Berg'inyon Baenre on his lizard, hanging under the closest edge of the stone walkway and readying a javelin. The young Baenre's throw was remarkable, given the distance and his curious angle, but still the weapon fell short.

Catti-brie responded with a shot as the rider darted back under the stone bridge, her arrow skimming the stone and flying freely to the ground so very far below.

"That was a Baenre," Drizzt explained to her, "a dangerous one indeed!"

"Was," Catti-brie replied evenly, and she took up her bow and fired again, this time aiming for the center of the lower bridge. The magical arrow burrowed through the stone, and there came a shriek.

Berg'inyon fell free from below the bridge, and his dead lizard tumbled after. Out of the companions' sight, the young noble enacted his levitational powers and turned about in the air, slowly descending to the cavern floor.

Drizzt kissed Catti-brie on the cheek in admiration of the remarkable shot. Then they ran on, after Entreri and Guenhwyvar. Around the next stalactite, the two saw Entreri and the cat bury another dark elf.

It all seemed so hopeless, though, to no avail. They could keep scoring minor victories for hours on end and not deplete the resources of House Baenre. Even worse, sooner or later the compound's defense would organize fully, and the matron mother and high priestesses, and probably more than a few powerful wizards as well, would come out of the domed chapel to join in the chase.

They climbed a walkway ringing another stalactite, going to the highest worked levels of the cavern. Still there were drow above them, they knew, hiding in the shadows, on their lizard mounts, carefully picking their shots.

Guenhwyvar stopped suddenly and sprang straight up, disappearing into a cluster of hanging stones fully twenty-five feet above the walkway. Back down came the mighty panther, raking and gouging the lizard it brought along. The two crashed to the stone walkway, rolling and biting, and for a moment, Drizzt thought that Guenhwyvar would surely go over the side.

Entreri skidded to a stop a safe distance from the battling beasts, but the ranger sprang beyond him, putting his scimitars to deadly work on the entangled lizard.

Catti-brie had wisely kept her stare upward, and when a drow drifted slowly out of the stalactite cluster, Taulmaril was waiting. The dark elf fired his hand-crossbow and missed, the quarrel skipping off the bridge behind her; Catti-brie responded and blew the tip off a stalactite just to the side of the drow.

The drow realized immediately that he could not win against the woman and that deadly bow. He scrambled along the stalactites, kicking off them and flying along the cavern's ceiling. Another arrow cracked into the stone, not so far behind, and then another blew out the hanging stone right in front of him, just as he went to grab at it.

The levitating drow was stuck with no handholds, hanging in midair twenty feet up and now a few dozen feet to the side of the walkway. He should have released his levitation spell and dropped for the ground, recalling the magical energies when he was far below Catti-brie's level. He went up instead, seeking the safety of the nooks in the uneven ceiling.

Catti-brie took deadly aim and let fly. The streaking arrow drove right through the doomed drow and thundered up into the ceiling above, disappearing into the stone. A split second later, there came another explosion from above, from somewhere above the cavern roof.

Catti-brie stared curiously, trying to decipher the meaning of that second blast.

Chapter 25

THE DESPERATE RUN

 atron Baenre swelled with pride as the ritual continued, undisturbed by the events in the compound. She did not know that Dantrag and Berg'inyon had gone out from the chapel, did not know that her vicious Duk-Tak was dead, slain by the very renegade Matron Baenre hoped to soon present before the other ruling matron mothers.

All that Matron Baenre knew was the sweet taste of power. She had brought together the most powerful alliance in recent drow history, with herself at its head. She had outmaneuvered K'yorl Odran, always a clever one, and had virtually cowed Mez'Barris Armgo, the second most influential drow in all the city. Lloth was smiling brightly on the matron mother of House Baenre, she believed.

All she heard was the singing, and not the sounds of battle, and all she saw, looking up, was the magnificent illusion of the Spider Queen, going through its perpetual shift from arachnid to drow and back to arachnid. How could she, or any of the others, watching that specter with similar awe, know of the raging fight nearly a thousand feet above the roof of that domed chapel, along the bridged stalactites of House Baenre?

* * * * *

"A tunnel!" Catti-brie cried to Drizzt. She grabbed him by the shoulder and turning him toward the still-levitating dead drow.

Drizzt looked at her as though he did not understand.

"Up above!" she cried. Catti-brie brought her bow up and fired again into the general area. The arrow slammed into the base of a stalactite, but did not go through.

"It's up there, I tell ye!" the young woman exclaimed. "Another tunnel, above the cavern!"

Drizzt looked doubtfully to the area. He did not question Catti-brie's claim, but he had no idea of how they might get to this supposed tunnel. The closest walkway was fully a dozen feet from the area, and to get to that walkway, though it was barely thirty feet away from and a few feet higher than their current position, the companions would have to take a roundabout route, many hundreds of yards of running.

"What is it?" cried Entreri, rushing back to join his hesitating companions. Looking past them, back down the walkway, the assassin saw the forms of many gathering drow.

"There may be a tunnel above us," Drizzt quickly explained.

Entreri's scowl showed that he hardly believed the information valuable, but his doubts only spurred Catti-brie on. Up came her bow and off flew the arrows, one after another, all aimed for the base of that stubborn stalactite.

A fireball exploded on their walkway, not far behind them, and the whole bridge shuddered as the metal and stone in the area of the blast melted and shifted, threatening to break apart.

Catti-brie spun about and let fly two quick shots, killing one drow and driving the others back behind the protection of the closest supporting stalactite. From somewhere in the darkness ahead, Guenhwyvar growled and crossbows clicked.

"We must be off!" Entreri prodded them, grabbing Drizzt and trying to tug him on. The ranger held his ground, though, and watched with faith as Catti-brie turned again to the side and fired another of her arrows. It smacked solidly into the weakened stone.

The targeted stalactite groaned in protest and slipped down on one side to hang at an awkward angle. A moment later, it fell free into the far drop below. For a moment, Drizzt thought that it might hit the purple-glowing chapel dome, but it smashed to the stone floor a short distance away, shattering into a thousand pieces.

Drizzt, his ears keen, widened his eyes as he focused on the hole, a flicker of hope evident in his expression. "Wind," he explained breathlessly. "Wind from the tunnel!"

It was true. An unmistakable sound of rushing wind emanated from the hole in the ceiling as the air pressure in the caves above adjusted to match the air pressure in the great cavern.

"But how are we to get there?" Catti-brie asked.

Entreri, convinced now, was already fumbling with his pack. He took out a length of rope and a grappling hook and soon had the thing twirling above him. With one shot, he hooked it over the bridge nearest the tunnel. Entreri rushed to the nearest railing of his own walkway and tied off the rope, and Drizzt, without the slightest hesitation, hopped atop the cord and gingerly began to walk out. The agile drow picked up speed as he went, gaining confidence.

That confidence was shattered when an evil dark elf suddenly appeared. Coming out of an invisibility enchantment, he slashed at the rope with his fine-edged sword.

Drizzt dropped flat to the rope and held on desperately. Two cuts sliced it free of the grappling hook, and Drizzt swung down like a pendulum, rocking back and forth ten feet below his companions on the walkway.

The enemy drow's smug smile was quickly wiped away by a silver-streaking arrow.

Drizzt started to climb, then stopped and flinched as a dart whistled past. Another followed suit, and the drow looked down to see a handful of soldiers approaching, levitating up and firing as they came.

Entreri tugged fiercely at the rope, trying to help the ranger back to the walkway. As soon as Drizzt grabbed the lip, the assassin pulled him over, then took the rope from him. He looked at it doubtfully, wondering how in the Nine Hells he was supposed to hook it again over the distant walkway without the grappling hook. Entreri growled determinedly and made the cord into a lasso, then turned to search for a target.

Drizzt threw one knee over the bridge and tried to get his feet under him, just as a thunderous blast struck the walkway right below them. Both the ranger and Catti-brie were knocked from their feet. Drizzt fell again, to hang by his fingertips, and the stone under Catti-brie showed an unmistakable crack.

A crossbow quarrel hit the stone right in front of the drow's face; another popped against the bottom of his boot but did not get through. Then Drizzt was glowing, outlined by distinctive faerie fire, making him an even easier target.

The ranger looked down to the approaching dark elves and called upon his own innate abilities, casting a globe of darkness in front of them. Then he pulled himself up over the lip of the bridge, to find Catti-brie exchanging volleys with the dark elves behind them on the walkway, and Entreri pulling in the thrown lasso, cursing all the while.

"I've no way to hook it," the assassin growled, and he didn't have to spell out the implications. Drow were behind them and below them, inevitably working their way toward the band. The walkway, weakened by the magical assaults, seemed not so secure anymore, and, just to seal their doom, the companions saw Guenhwyvar rushing back to them, apparently in full retreat.

"We're not to surrender," Catti-brie whispered, her eyes filled with determination. She put another arrow back down the walkway, then fell to her belly and hooked her arms over the lip. The ascending drow wizard was just coming through Drizzt's darkness globe, a wand pointed for the walkway.

Catti-brie's arrow hit that wand squarely, split it apart, then gashed the drow's shoulder as it whistled past him. His scream was more of terror than of pain as he regarded his shattered wand, as he considered the release of magical energy that would follow. With typical drow loyalty, the wizard threw the wand below him, into the darkness and into the midst of his rising comrades. He urged his levitation on at full speed to get away from the unseen, crackling lightning balls, and heard the horrified calls of his dying companions.

He should have looked up instead, for he never knew what hit him as Catti-brie's next arrow shattered his backbone. That threat eliminated, or at least slowed, the young woman went back up to her knees and opened up another barrage on the stubborn dark elves behind her on the walkway. Their hand-crossbows couldn't reach Catti-brie, and they couldn't hope to hurl their javelins that far, but the woman knew that they were up to something, plotting some way to cause havoc.

Guenhwyvar was no ordinary panther; it possessed an intelligence far beyond the norm of its feline kind. Coming fast toward the cornered companions, Guenhwyvar quickly discerned their troubles and their hopes. The panther was sorely wounded, carrying a dozen poisoned crossbow darts in its hide as it ran, but its fierce loyalty was fully with Drizzt.

Entreri fell back and cried aloud as the cat suddenly rushed up and bit the rope from his hand. The assassin went immediately for his weapons, thinking that the cat meant to attack him, but Guenhwyvar skidded to a stop—knocking both Entreri and Drizzt several feet back—turned a right angle, and leaped away, flying through the air.

Guenhwyvar tried to stop, claws raking over the top of the target walkway's smooth stone. The cat's momentum was too great, though, and Guenhwyvar, still clamping tightly to the rope, pitched over the far side, coming to a jerking stop at the rope's end, some twenty feet below the bridge.

More concerned for the cat than for himself, Drizzt instinctively sprang onto the taut rope and ran across, without regard for the fact that Guenhwyvar's hold was tentative at best.

Entreri grabbed Catti-brie and pulled her over, motioning for her to follow the drow.

"I cannot walk a tightrope!" the desperate woman explained, eyes wide with horror.

285

"Then learn!" the assassin roughly replied, and he pushed Catti-brie so hard that she nearly fell right over the side of the walkway. Catti-brie put one foot up on the rope and started to shift her weight to it, but she fell back immediately, shaking her head.

Entreri leaped past her, onto the rope. "Work your bow well!" he explained. "And be ready to untie this end!"

Catti-brie did not understand, but had no time to question as Entreri sped off, walking as surefootedly along the hemp bridge as had Drizzt. Catti-brie fired down the walkway behind her, then had to spin about and fire the other way, ahead, at those drow who had been pursuing Guenhwyvar.

She had no time to aim either way as she continued to turn back and forth, and few of her arrows hit any enemies at all.

Catti-brie took a deep breath. She sincerely lamented the future she would never know. But she followed the sigh with a resigned but determined smile. If she was going down, then Catti-brie had every intention of taking her enemies down with her, had every intention of offering Drizzt his freedom.

* * * * *

Some of those inside the great Baenre chapel had heard and felt the stalactite crash on the compound's floor, but only slightly, since the chapel's walls were of thick stone and two thousand drow voices within the place were lifted in frantic song to Lloth.

Matron Baenre was notified of the crash several moments later, when Sos'Umptu, her daughter in charge of chapel affairs, found the opportunity to whisper to her that something might be amiss out in the compound.

It pained Matron Baenre to interrupt the ceremony. She looked around at the faces of the other matron mothers, her only possible rivals, and remained convinced that they were now wholly committed to her and her plan. Still, she gave Sos'Umptu permission to send out—discreetly—a few members of the chapel elite guard.

Then the first matron mother went back to the ceremony, smiling as though nothing out of the ordinary—except, of course, this extraordinary gathering—was going on. So secure was Matron Baenre in the power of her house that her only fears at that time were that something might disturb the sanctity of the ceremony, something might lessen her in the eyes of Lloth.

She could not imagine the antics of the three fugitives and the panther far, far above.

* * * * *

Hanging low over the bridge, coaxing his dear, wounded companion, Drizzt did not hear Entreri touch down on the stone behind him.

"There is nothing we can do for the cat!" the assassin said roughly, and Drizzt spun about, noticing immediately that Catti-brie was in dire straits across the way.

"You left her!" the ranger cried.

"She could not cross!" Entreri spat back in his face. "Not yet!" Drizzt, consumed by rage, went for his blades, but Entreri ignored him and focused back on Catti-brie, who was kneeling on the stone, fumbling with something that the assassin could not discern.

"Untie the rope!" Entreri called. "But hold fast as you do and swing out!"

Drizzt, thinking himself incredibly stupid for not understanding Entreri's designs, released his grip on his weapon hilts and dove down to help Entreri brace the hemp. As soon as Catti-brie untied the other end, six hundred pounds of pressure—from the falling panther—would yank the rope. Drizzt held no illusions that he and Entreri could hold the panther aloft for more than a short while, but they had to make the tug on the other end of the rope less violent, so that Catti-brie would be able to hold on.

The young woman made no immediate move for the rope, despite Entreri's screams and the dark elves approaching from both sides. Finally she went for it, but came up immediately and cried out, "Suren it's too tight!"

"Damn, she has no blade," Entreri groaned, realizing his mistake.

Drizzt drew out Twinkle and skipped back atop the rope, determined to die beside his dear Catti-brie. But the young woman hooked Taulmaril over her shoulder and leaped out onto the tentative bridge, wearing an expression of sheer terror. She came across hanging under the hemp, hands and knees locked tight. Ten feet out, then fifteen, halfway to her friends.

The dark elves closed quickly, seeing that no more of those wicked arrows would be coming at them. The lead drow were nearly up to the rope, hand-crossbows coming up, and Catti-brie would be an easy target indeed!

But then the dark elves in front skidded to a sudden stop and began scrambling to get away, some leaping off the bridge.

Drizzt did not understand what he was seeing, and had no time to sort it out as a ball of fire exploded on the other walkway, right between the converging groups of dark elves. Walls of flame rolled out at Drizzt, and he fell back, throwing his hands up in front of him.

A split second later, Entreri cried out and the rope, burned through on the other walkway, began to whip past them, with Guenhwyvar more than balancing Catti-brie's weight.

Entreri and Drizzt were quick enough to dive and grab at the rope when it stopped flying past, when valiant Guenhwyvar, understanding that Catti-brie would be knocked from her tentative grasp as she collided with the side of the walkway, let go and plummeted into the darkness.

The bridge across the way creaked apart and fell, crashing against one levitating drow who had survived the wand explosion, and dropping those dark elves remaining on the platform. Most of those still alive could levitate, and would not fall to their deaths, but the explosion had certainly bought the companions precious time.

Catti-brie, her face red from the heat and small flames dancing along her cloak, kept the presence of mind to reach up and grab Drizzt's offered hand.

"Let Guen go!" she pleaded breathlessly, her lungs pained by the heat, and Drizzt understood immediately. Still holding fast to the woman's hand, the ranger fished the figurine out of Catti-brie's pouch and called for Guenhwyvar to be gone. He could only hope that the magic took hold before the panther hit the floor.

Then the ranger heaved Catti-brie up to the walkway and wrapped her in a tight hug. Entreri, meanwhile, had retrieved the grappling hook and was tying it off. A deft shot put the thing through the hole Catti-brie had created by blasting away the stalactite.

"Go!" the assassin said to Drizzt, and the drow was off, climbing hand over hand as Entreri anchored the rope around the metal railing. Catti-brie went next, not nearly as fast as Drizzt, and Entreri shouted curses at her, thinking that her slowness would allow their enemies to catch up with them.

Drizzt could already see dark elves levitating up from the cavern floor beneath his newest position, though it would take them many minutes to get that high.

"It is secured!" Drizzt called from the tunnel above—and all were indeed relieved to learn that there truly was a tunnel up above, and not just a small cubby!

Entreri let go of his hold, then sprang onto the rope as it swung directly under the hole.

Drizzt pulled Catti-brie in and considered the climbing man. He could cut the rope and drop Entreri to his death, and surely the world would have been a better place without the assassin. But honor held Drizzt to his word, to Catti-brie's word. He could not dispute the assassin's daring efforts to get them all this far, and he would not now resort to treachery.

He grabbed Entreri when the man got close and hauled him in. Holding Taulmaril, Catti-brie went back to the hole, looking for any dark elves that might be on their way. Then she noticed something else: the purple faerie fire of the great, domed chapel, almost directly below her position. She thought of the expression on the faces of those drow at the high ritual inside if Guenhwyvar had crashed through that roof—and that notion led her mind to other ideas. She smiled wickedly as she looked again to the dome, and to the ceiling above it.

The tunnel was natural and uneven, but wide enough for the three to walk abreast. A flash stole the darkness up ahead, telling the companions that they were not alone.

Drizzt ran ahead, scimitars in hand, thinking to clear the way. Entreri moved to follow, but hesitated, seeing that Catti-brie was inexplicably going back the other way.

"What are you about?" the assassin demanded, but the woman didn't answer. She merely fitted an arrow to her bow as she measured her steps.

She fell back and cried out as she crossed a side passage and a drow soldier leaped out at her, but before he got his sword in line, a hurled dagger sank into his rib cage. Entreri rushed in, meeting the next drow in line, calling for Catti-brie to run back the other way, to join Drizzt.

"Hold them!" was all the explanation the young woman offered, and she continued on in the opposite direction.

"Hold them?" Entreri echoed. He cut down the second drow in line and engaged the third as two others ran off the way they had come.

* * * * *

Drizzt careened around a bend, even leaped onto the curving wall to keep his desperate speed.

"Valiant!" came a greeting call, spoken in the Drow tongue, and the ranger slowed and stopped when he saw Dantrag and Berg'inyon Baenre sitting casually atop their lizard mounts in the middle of the passage.

"Valiant attempt!" Dantrag reiterated, but his smile mocked the whole escape, made Drizzt feel that all their efforts had done no more good than offer amusement to the cocky weapon master and his unbeatable charge.

Chapter 26

CATTI-BRIE'S SURPRISE

 thought that your lizard was shot out from under you," Drizzt remarked, trying to sound confident in the face of his disappointment.

Berg'inyon steeled his red-glowing gaze upon the impetuous renegade and did not respond.

"A fine shot," Dantrag agreed, "but it was only a lizard, after all, and well worth the entertainment you and your pitiful friends have provided." Dantrag casually reached over and took the long death lance from his brother's hand. "Are you ready to die, Drizzt Do'Urden?" he asked as he lowered the deadly tip.

Drizzt crouched low, feeling his balance, and crossed his scimitars in front of him. Where were Catti-brie and Entreri? he wondered, and he feared that they had met resistance—Dantrag's soldiers?—back in the corridor.

Despair washed over him suddenly with the thought that Catti-brie might already be dead, but the ranger pushed it away, reminded himself to trust her, to trust that she could take care of herself.

Dantrag's lizard leaped ahead, then skittered sideways along a wall. Drizzt had no idea of which way the creature would veer when it came near him. Back to the floor? Higher on the wall? Or might it turn right up onto the ceiling and carry its hanging rider right above the target?

Dantrag knew that Drizzt had been on the surface, where there were no ceilings, for many years—did he think the last choice the most devious?

Drizzt started toward the opposite wall, but fell to his knees instead at the same instant that Dantrag coaxed his fast-running, sticky-footed mount up to the ceiling. The tip of the long lance just missed the ducking ranger's head, and Drizzt leaped up as the rider passed, grabbing at the weapon's shaft.

He felt a sting in his lower back, and turned to see Berg'inyon sitting calmly atop his mount, reloading his hand-crossbow.

"It does not have to be a fair fight, Drizzt Do'Urden!" Dantrag explained with a laugh. He swung his well-trained mount about, brought it back to the floor, and lowered the lance once more.

* * * * *

Sword and dagger flashed wildly as Entreri tried to finish the stubborn dark elf. This one was a skilled fighter, though, and his parries were fast and on target. Behind the drow, the other dark elves were steadily inching toward Entreri, gaining confidence as they watched their companion hold the assassin's devilish attacks at bay.

"What are you doing?" Entreri demanded of Catti-brie, seeing her kneeling beside a large mound of rock. The woman stood up and fired an arrow into the stone, then a second, then dropped back to her knees.

"What are you doing?" Entreri demanded more emphatically.

"Stop yer whining and be done with the drow," Catti-brie snarled back, and Entreri regarded her incredulously, suddenly not so sure of what to make of this surprising creature. Almost as an afterthought, Catti-brie tossed the onyx panther figurine to the floor. "Come back, Guenhwyvar," she said too calmly. "Me heroic companion's needing yer help."

Entreri growled and went at his opponent with renewed fury—just the effect conniving Catti-brie had hoped for. His sword went into a circular movement, and his jeweled dagger poked in behind it at every opportunity.

The dark elf called out something, and one of those nearest him mustered some courage and came forward to join the combatants. Entreri growled and reluctantly fell back a step, across the corridor.

A streaking arrow cut in front of the assassin, stealing his sight, and when his vision returned, he faced only one drow again, and those others watching from behind, in the side passage, were long gone.

Entreri put a sarcastic glance at Catti-brie, but she was firing into the stone again (and talking to the returned panther) and did not hear.

* * * * *

Drizzt felt the burn of drow poison in his back, but felt, too, the tingling of the recently quaffed healing potions. He started to swoon—purposely—and heard Dantrag laughing at him, mocking him. The predictable click of Berg'inyon's crossbow sounded, and Drizzt fell right to the stone, the dart arcing over him and stealing the mirth from the smug weapon master as it skipped off the stone not so far from Dantrag's head.

Dantrag's charge was on before Drizzt was fully back to his feet, the weapon master coming straight at him this time. Drizzt fell to one knee, shot back up, and spun away, frantically batting at the dangerous and enchanted lance as it passed just under his high-flying arm. Dantrag, incredibly fast, snapped off a backhanded slap into Drizzt's face as he passed. Drizzt, both his blades intent on keeping the lance at bay, could not respond.

293

Back came the weapon master, impossibly quick, and Drizzt had to dive to the side as the mighty lance scratched a deep line into the stone. Drizzt reversed his direction immediately, hoping to score a hit as the lance went past, but again Dantrag was too quick, snapping out his own sword and not only deflecting Drizzt's lunge, but countering with a slapping strike against the side of Drizzt's outstretched hand. And then the sword went back into its sheath, too fast for Drizzt to follow the move.

Around wheeled the lizard, going up on a wall for this pass and sending Drizzt into a frantic roll back the other way.

"How long, Drizzt Do'Urden?" the cocky weapon master asked, knowing that Drizzt, with all his frantic dodging had to be tiring.

Drizzt growled and could not disagree, but as he rose from the floor, turning to follow the lizard's progress, the ranger saw a glimmer of hope from the corner of his eye: the welcome face of a certain black panther as it bounded around the corridor's bend.

Dantrag was just turning his mount about for a fifth pass when Guenhwyvar barreled in. Over went the lizard, with Dantrag strapped in for the ride. The weapon master managed to somehow get loose of his bindings as the beasts continued to roll, and he came up, quite shaken, facing the ranger.

"Now the fight is fair," Drizzt declared.

A crossbow quarrel whistled past Dantrag, and past Drizzt's blocking scimitar, to score a hit on the ranger's shoulder.

"Hardly," Dantrag corrected, his smile returning. Faster than Drizzt's eye could follow, he snapped his two swords from their sheaths and began his measured advance. In his head his sentient sword, hungering for this fight perhaps more than the weapon master himself, telepathically agreed.

Hardly.

* * * * *

"What are you about?" Entreri screamed when Guenhwyvar bounded past him, giving no apparent regard to his opponent. The flustered assassin took out his frustration on the lone drow facing him, hitting the unfortunate soldier with a three-cut combination that left him off balance and with one of his arms severely bleeding.

Entreri probably could have finished the fight right then, except that his attention was still somewhat focused on Catti-brie.

"I'm just digging holes," the young woman said, as though that should explain everything. Several more bow shots followed in rapid succession, chipping away at the hard stone of an enormous stalactite. One arrow went through then, back into the cavern below.

"There is fighting ahead," Entreri called. "And dark elves will soon be floating through that hole in the ceiling."

"Then be done with yer work!" Catti-brie shouted at him. "And be leaving me to me own!"

Entreri bit back his next retort, gnawed on his lips instead, and determined that if he was alive when this was all over, Catti-brie would wish that she was not.

The drow facing the assassin came on suddenly, thinking that his opponent was distracted and thinking to score a quick victory. But Entreri's sword snapped left, right, and straight ahead, batting aside both weapons and scoring a minor hit, again on the bleeding arm.

* * * * *

They were no more than a tumbling ball of fur and scales, Guenhwyvar and the subterranean lizard locked in a raking, biting jumble. With its longer neck, the lizard had its head far to the side, biting at Guenhwyvar's flank, but Guenhwyvar stubbornly kept a firm hold on the base of the lizard's neck. More deadly still, the panther's claws were inside the lizard's reach, affording Guenhwyvar a distinct advantage as they rolled. The panther's front claws kept a tight and steady hold, while Guenhwyvar's rear legs tucked in close and began a vicious kicking rake, tearing at the reptilian beast.

Victory was at hand for the beleaguered panther, but then Guenhwyvar felt a wicked sting in the back, the sting of a sword.

The panther whipped its maw about in a frenzy, tearing out a chunk of the lizard's shoulder, but the pain brought blackness, and Guenhwyvar, already battered from the run along the walkways, had to give in, had to melt away into an insubstantial mist and follow the tunnel back to the Astral Plane.

The torn lizard rolled about on the stone, bleeding from its neck and sides, its belly hanging free of its skin. It crept away as swiftly as it could, seeking a hole in which to crawl.

Berg'inyon paid it no heed. He simply sat back on his own mount and watched the impending battle with more than a passing interest. He started to load his hand-crossbow, but changed his mind and just sat back.

It occurred to Berg'inyon then that he stood only to gain, no matter who won this contest.

Hands out, his sword blades resting across his shoulders, the weapon master casually walked up to stand before Drizzt. He started to say something, so Drizzt thought, when a sword abruptly whipped out. Drizzt heaved his own weapon up to block, heard the ring of steel on steel, then Dantrag sliced out with his second blade, and punched ahead with the hilt of his first.

Drizzt could hardly register the moves. He got Twinkle up in time to block the second blade, and got punched solidly in the face. Then he was struck in the face a second time as Dantrag's other hand flew up, too quick for Drizzt to catch.

What magic did this drow possess? Drizzt wondered, for he did not believe that anyone could move so quickly.

The razorlike edge of one of Dantrag's swords began to glow a distinct line of red, though it seemed no more than a dull blur to Drizzt as the weapon master continued his lightning-fast routines. Drizzt could only react to each move, snap his blades this way and that and take some relief in hearing the ring of steel. All thoughts of countering the moves were gone; Drizzt could hope only that Dantrag would quickly tire.

But Dantrag smiled, realizing that Drizzt, like any other drow, could not move fast enough to effectively counter.

Twinkle caught a slice coming in at Drizzt's left; Dantrag's other sword, the glowing one, arced out wide to the right, and Drizzt was somewhat off balance as his second scimitar rushed, tip straight up, to block. The sword connected on the scimitar near its tip, and Drizzt knew that he hadn't the strength to fully stop that blow with that difficult angle. He dove straight down as his blade inevitably tipped in, and the sword swished above his head, went right across as Drizzt spun away, to slash against—and cut deeply into!—the stone wall.

Drizzt nearly screamed aloud at the incredible edge that weapon displayed, to cut stone as easily as if it had been a wall of

Bruenor Battlehammer's favorite smelly cheese!

"How long can you continue?" Dantrag asked him, mocked him. "Already your moves are slowing, Drizzt Do'Urden. I will have your head soon." In stalked the confident weapon master, even more confident now that he had seen the legendary renegade in battle.

Drizzt had been caught by surprise, back on his heels and fearful of the consequences of his loss. He forced himself to realize that now, forced himself to fall into a meditative trance, purely focused on his enemy. He could not continue to react to Dantrag's flashing movements; he had to look deeper, to understand the methods of his cunning and skilled adversary, as he had when Dantrag had first charged on the lizard. Drizzt had known the charging Dantrag would go to the ceiling, because he had managed to understand the situation through the weapon master's eyes.

And so it went now. Dantrag came with a left, right, left, left, thrust combination, but Drizzt's blades were in line for the parry every time, Drizzt actually beginning the blocks before Dantrag had begun the attacks. The weapon master's attacks were not so different from Zak'nafein's during all those years of training. While Dantrag moved faster than any drow Drizzt had ever encountered, the ranger began to suspect that Dantrag could not improvise in the middle of any moves.

He caught a high-riding sword, spun a complete circuit to whip Twinkle across and knock away the predictable thrust of the second. It was true, Drizzt then knew; Dantrag was as much a prisoner of his own speed as were his opponents.

In came a vicious thrust, but Drizzt was already down on his knees, one scimitar snapping up above his head to keep Dantrag's weapon riding high. The weapon master's second strike was on the way, but it fell a split second after Twinkle had reached out and cut a fine line on the side of Dantrag's shin, forcing the Baenre into a hopping retreat instead.

With a growl of rage, the weapon master bore right back in, slapping at Drizzt's blades, slowly working them up high. Drizzt countered every move, falling in line with the attack patterns. At first, the ranger's mind worked ahead to find an effective counterstrike, but then Drizzt understood Dantrag's aim in this routine, a scenario that Drizzt had played out before with his father.

Dantrag could not know—only Drizzt and Zak'nafein knew—that Drizzt had found the solution to this usually unbeatable offense.

Up higher went the scimitars, Dantrag moving under them and in. The attack was called double-thrust-low, wherein the aim was to get your opponent's weapons up high, then step back suddenly and come straight in with both your own blades.

Drizzt hopped back and snapped his crossed scimitars down atop the flying blades, the only parry against the cunning move, the cross-down. But Drizzt was countering even as he blocked, shifting his weight to his lead foot as his back foot kicked out, between his scimitar hilts, between Dantrag's surprised eyes.

He connected squarely on the weapon master's face, staggering Dantrag back several steps. Drizzt sprang right ahead, all over the stunned drow in a wild flurry. Now he was forcing the moves, striking repeatedly so that his opponent could not again gain the offensive, could not use that unbelievable speed to its fullest advantage.

Now it was Dantrag who was reacting to Drizzt's blinding attacks, scimitars snapping in at him from every conceivable angle. Drizzt didn't know how long he could keep up the wild flurry, but he understood that he could not allow Dantrag to regain the offensive, could not allow Dantrag to again put him back on his heels.

To Dantrag's credit, he managed to keep his balance well enough to defeat the attacks, and the weapon master dodged aside whenever a scimitar slipped through. Drizzt noticed that only Dantrag's hands seemed possessed of that impossible speed; the rest of the drow's body moved well, perfectly balanced, as would be expected of a Baenre weapon master. But, ultimately, except for the hands, Dantrag moved no faster than Drizzt could move.

Twinkle went straight in. Dantrag's sword banged against its side. Sly Drizzt twisted the scimitar, used its curving blade to roll it over the weapon master's sword and bite at his arm.

Dantrag leaped back, trying to break the clinch, but Drizzt paced him, scimitars waving. Again, then a third time, Drizzt turned Dantrag's perfect parries into minor hits, the fluid motions of his curving blades trapping the straight blocks of the swords.

Could Dantrag anticipate Drizzt's moves as well as Drizzt had anticipated the weapon master's? Drizzt wondered with more than a little sarcasm, and he sublimated his wicked smile. Straight ahead went Twinkle, and out snapped the blocking sword, the only possible defense. Drizzt started to twist the blade, and Dantrag started to retract the arm.

But Drizzt stopped suddenly and reversed the flow, Twinkle shooting across faster than Dantrag could react. The deadly scimitar gashed deeply into the weapon master's other forearm, poking it out wide, then came back across, Drizzt stepping into the move so that his extended blade slashed a tight line across Dantrag's belly.

Wincing in pain, the weapon master managed to leap back from his deadly adversary. "You are good," he admitted, and though he tried to keep his confident facade, Drizzt could tell by the quiver in his voice that the last hit had been serious.

Dantrag smiled unexpectedly. "Berg'inyon!" he called, looking to the side. His eyes widened indeed when he saw that his brother was no longer there.

"He wishes to be the weapon master," Drizzt reasoned calmly.

Dantrag roared in outrage and leaped ahead, his attacks coming in rapid fire, suddenly stealing the offensive.

* * * * *

Up flashed the sword and in stepped the furious assassin, his jeweled dagger drinking eagerly of his opponent's lifeblood. Entreri jerked the weapon once, then again, then stepped back and let the dead drow fall to the stone.

The assassin kept the presence of mind to immediately jump to the side of the passage, and shook his head helplessly as several darts knocked against the corridor wall opposite the opening.

Entreri turned to the still-kneeling Catti-brie and demanded again to know what she was up to.

The auburn-haired woman, so deceptively innocent-looking, smiled widely and held up the last of the loaded hourglasses, then put it into one of her arrow-blasted holes.

The blood drained from the assassin's face as he realized how Catti-brie had blown up the walkway back in the cavern, as he realized what she was doing now.

"We should be running," Catti-brie remarked, coming up from her crouch, Taulmaril in hand.

Entreri was already moving, not even looking down the side corridor as he passed it.

Catti-brie came right behind, actually laughing. She paused long enough at the hole in the floor, leading back into the main cavern, to shout out to those levitating dark elves drifting up toward her that they weren't likely to enjoy the reception.

* * * * *

Thrust left, thrust right, down-cut left, down-cut right. Dantrag's attack came brutally swift and hard, but Drizzt's scimitars were in place for the parries and blocks, and again the cunning ranger used a third weapon—his boot—to counter. He snapped his foot up to slam the weapon master's already wounded belly.

Dantrag couldn't stop from lurching over, and then he was back on the defensive again, reacting desperately as Drizzt relentlessly waded in.

Around the bend came Entreri. "Run on!" he cried, and though the assassin needed Drizzt for his ultimate escape, he did not dare to stop and pull the ranger along.

Catti-brie came next, just in time to see Drizzt's scimitars flash straight ahead, to be taken out wide and held by Dantrag's blocking swords. Up came Drizzt's knee, quicker than Dantrag's, as the two inevitably moved together, and in a sudden explosion of agony, the wounded weapon master understood that he could not hold Drizzt back.

Drizzt turned Twinkle over the blocking sword and put it in line for Dantrag's ribs, then the two seemed to pause for an instant, eye to eye.

"Zak'nafein would have defeated you," the ranger promised grimly, and he plunged Twinkle deep into Dantrag's heart.

Drizzt turned to Catti-brie, trying to fathom the level of terror apparent in her wide eyes.

Then she was coming at him, weirdly, and it took the ranger a moment to even realize that she was off her feet, propelled by the shock wave of an explosion.

Chapter 27

SORTING IT OUT

t creaked and groaned in protest, shock waves and searing flames melting its hold on the cavern ceiling. Then it fell, like a great spear, whistling along its thousand-foot descent.

Helpless and horrified, those dark elves levitating nearby watched it fly past.

Inside the domed chapel, the ceremony continued undisturbed.

A female soldier, an elite guard of House Baenre but certainly no noble, rushed up to the central dais, screaming wildly. At first, Matron Baenre and the others thought her caught up in the outrageous frenzy, an all-too-common sight in the out-of-control drow rituals. Gradually they came to understand that this soldier was screaming cries of warning.

Seven matron mothers turned suddenly suspicious gazes on Matron Baenre, and even her own daughters did not know what she was about.

Then the stalactite hit.

* * * * *

Drizzt caught Catti-brie in midair, then he, too, was flying. He rolled over as the two touched down, burying the young woman under him protectively.

They were both screaming, but neither heard anything beyond the thunderous roar of the widening fireball. Drizzt's back warmed, and his cloak ignited in several places as the very edge of the firestorm rolled over him.

Then it was done as quickly as it had begun. Drizzt rolled off Catti-brie, scrambled to get out of his burning cloak, and rushed to get to his still-down companion, fearing that she had been knocked unconscious, or worse, in the explosion.

Catti-brie opened a blue eye and flashed a wistful, mischievous smile.

"I'm betting that the way is clear behind us," she smirked and Drizzt nearly laughed aloud. He scooped her up in his arms and hugged her tightly, feeling in that instant as though they might actually be free once more. He thought of the times to come in Mithril Hall, times that would be spent beside Bruenor and Regis and Guenhwyvar, and, of course, Catti-brie.

Drizzt could not believe all that he had almost thrown away.

He let Catti-brie go for a moment and rushed back around the bend, just to confirm that all those drow pursuing them were gone.

"Hello," Catti-brie whispered under her breath, looking down to a magnificent sword lying next to the fallen weapon master. Catti-brie gingerly picked the weapon up, confused as to why an evil drow noble would wield a sword whose hilt was sculpted in the shape of a unicorn, the symbol of the goodly goddess Mielikki.

"What have you found?" Drizzt asked, returning calmly.

"I think that this one'd suit yerself," Catti-brie remarked, holding up the weapon to display the unusual pommel.

Drizzt stared at the sword curiously. He had not noticed that hilt in his fight with Dantrag, though he certainly remembered that blade as the one that had so easily cut through the stone wall. "You keep it," he offered with a shrug. "I favor the scimitar, and if that is truly a weapon of Mielikki, then she would be pleased to have it on the hip of Catti-brie."

Catti-brie saluted Drizzt, smiled widely, and slipped the sword into her belt. She turned about, hearing Entreri's return, as Drizzt bent over Dantrag's body and quietly slipped the bracers off the dead drow's wrists.

"We cannot delay!" the obviously flustered assassin snapped. "All of Menzoberranzan knows of us now, and a thousand miles will not be enough ground between me and that wretched city."

For perhaps the first time, Drizzt found that he completely agreed with the assassin.

Belted as it was on the hip of the human woman was not exactly what the sentient Khazid'hea had in mind. The sword had heard much talk of Drizzt Do'Urden and, upon Dantrag's defeat, had altered the appearance of its magical pommel so that it might rest in the grasp of the legendary warrior.

Drizzt hadn't taken the bait, but the sword that had rightfully earned the name Cutter could wait.

* * * * *

The going was smooth, with no pursuit evident for the rest of that day and long into the night. Finally the group had no choice but to stop and rest, but it was a fitful and nervous time indeed.

So it went for three days of running, putting the miles behind them. Drizzt kept the lead, and kept the companions far from Blingdenstone, fearful of involving the svirfnebli in any of this incredible and dangerous web. He could not understand why lizard-riding drow patrols had not overtaken them, could hardly believe that scores of dark elves were not crouched in corridors behind them, or on their flanks, waiting to spring an ambush.

Thus, Drizzt was not surprised to see a familiar, outrageous dark elf standing in the middle of the corridor, wide-brimmed hat in hand, waiting to greet him and his fleeing companions.

Catti-brie, still seething, still on her warrior's edge, brought Taulmaril up immediately. "Ye're not for running free this time," she muttered under her breath, remembering how the crafty Jarlaxle had eluded them after the fight in Mithril Hall.

Entreri grabbed the arrow before Catti-brie had bent the bow, and the young woman, seeing that Drizzt was making no move to go for his weapons, did not continue.

"Please, dear and beautiful woman," the mercenary said to her. "I have only come out to say farewell."

His words grated on Catti-brie's nerves, but at the same time, she could not deny that Jarlaxle had treated her with dignity, had not abused her when she had been his helpless prisoner.

"From my perspective, that would seem a strange thing," Drizzt remarked, taking care to keep his voice calm. He felt in the pouch for the onyx figurine, but took little comfort in its presence, knowing that if he found the need to summon Guenhwyvar, they would all likely die. Both Drizzt and Entreri, understanding the methods of Bregan D'aerthe and the precautions of its elusive leader, knew that they were surrounded by skilled warriors in overwhelming numbers.

"Perhaps I was not so opposed to your escape, Drizzt Do'Urden, as you seem to think," Jarlaxle replied, and there was no doubt in anyone's mind that he had aimed that remark directly at Artemis Entreri.

Entreri did not seem surprised by the claim. Everything had fallen neatly into place for the assassin—Catti-brie's circlet and the locket that helped to locate Drizzt; the spider mask; Jarlaxle's references to the vulnerability of House Baenre during the high ritual; even the panther figurine, waiting for him to take it, on Jarlaxle's desk. He did not know how purposeful and involved Jarlaxle had been in arranging things, but he certainly understood that the mercenary had anticipated what might come to pass.

"You betrayed your own people," the assassin said.

"My own people?" Jarlaxle balked. "Define that term, people." Jarlaxle paused a few moments, then laughed, hearing no answer to his request. "I did not cooperate with the plans of one matron mother," he corrected.

"The first matron mother," Entreri put in.

"For now," the mercenary added with a wistful smile. "Not all the drow of Menzoberranzan were so pleased by the alliance Baenre had formed—not even all of Matron Baenre's own family."

"Triel," Entreri said, more to Drizzt than to the mercenary.

"Among others," said Jarlaxle.

"What're the two talking about?" Catti-brie whispered to Drizzt, who only shrugged, not understanding the larger picture.

"We are discussing the fate of Mithril Hall," Jarlaxle explained to her. "I commend your aim, dear and beautiful lady." He swept into a graceful bow that, for some reason, made Catti-brie more than a little uncomfortable.

Jarlaxle looked to Drizzt. "I would pay dearly for a glimpse of the expressions worn by those matron mothers inside the Baenre chapel when your lovely companion's stalactite spear plunged through the roof!"

Both Drizzt and Entreri turned to stare at Catti-brie, who just shrugged and smiled innocently.

"You didn't kill many drow," Jarlaxle quickly added. "Only a handful in the chapel, and no more than two dozen throughout your entire escape. House Baenre will recover, though it may take a while to figure out how to extract your handiwork from their no-longer-perfectly-domed ceiling! House Baenre will recover."

"But the alliance," Drizzt remarked, beginning to understand why no drow other than Bregan D'aerthe had come into the tunnels in pursuit.

"Yes, the alliance," Jarlaxle replied, offering no explanation. "In truth, the alliance to go after Mithril Hall was dead the minute that Drizzt Do'Urden was taken captive.

"But the questions!" Jarlaxle continued. "So many to be answered. That is why I have come out, of course."

The three companions looked to each other, not understanding what the mercenary might be hinting at.

"You have something that I must return," Jarlaxle explained, looking directly at Entreri. He held out his empty hand. "You will turn it over."

"And if we don't?" Catti-brie demanded fiercely.

Jarlaxle laughed.

The assassin immediately produced the spider mask. Of course Jarlaxle would need to put it back in Sorcere, else he would be implicated in the escape.

Jarlaxle's eyes gleamed when he saw the item, the one piece left to put into his completed puzzle. He suspected that Triel Baenre had watched Entreri and Catti-brie's every step when they had gone into Sorcere to pilfer the thing. Jarlaxle's actions in guiding the assassin to the mask, though, in precipitating the escape of Drizzt Do'Urden, were perfectly in line with the eldest Baenre daughter's desires. He took faith that she would not betray him to her mother.

If he could just get that mask back into Sorcere—no difficult feat—before Gromph Baenre realized that it was missing . . .

Entreri looked to Drizzt, who had no answers, then tossed the mask to Jarlaxle. Almost as an afterthought, the mercenary reached up and took a ruby pendant off his neck.

"It is not so effective against drow nobles," he explained dryly, and threw it unexpectedly to Drizzt.

Drizzt's hand snapped out, too soon, and the pendant, Regis's pendant, slapped against the ranger's forearm. Quick as could be, Drizzt snapped his hand back in, catching the thing before it had fallen half an inch.

"Dantrag's bracers," Jarlaxle said with a laugh as he noticed the ranger's covered wrist. "I had suspected as much of them. Fear not, for you will get used to them, Drizzt Do'Urden, and then how much more formidable you will be!"

Drizzt said nothing, but didn't doubt the mercenary's words.

Entreri, not yet free of his rivalry with Drizzt, eyed the ranger dangerously, not the least bit pleased.

"And so you have defeated Matron Baenre's plans," Jarlaxle went on grandly, sweeping into another bow. "And you, assassin, have earned your freedom. But look ever over your shoulders, daring friends, for the memories of dark elves are long and the methods of dark elves are devious."

There came an explosion, a blast of orange smoke, and when it cleared, Jarlaxle was gone.

"And good riddance to ye," Catti-brie muttered.

"As I will say to you when we part company on the surface," Entreri promised grimly.

"Only because Catti-brie gave you her word," Drizzt replied, his tone equally grave. He and Entreri locked uncompromising stares, looks of pure hatred, and Catti-brie, standing between them, felt uncomfortable indeed.

With the immediate threat of Menzoberranzan apparently behind them, it seemed as though the old enemies had become enemies again.

EPILOGUE

he companions did not go back to the cave beyond Dead Orc Pass. With Guenhwyvar's guidance, they came into the tunnels far beneath Mithril Hall, and Entreri knew the way well enough from there to guide them back to the tunnels connecting to the lower mines. The assassin and the ranger parted company on the same ledge where they had once battled, under the same starry sky they had seen the night of their duel.

Entreri walked off along the ledge, pausing a short distance away to turn and regard his hated rival.

"Long, too, is my own memory," he remarked, referring to Jar-laxle's parting words. "And are my methods less devious than those of the drow?"

Drizzt did not bother to respond.

"Suren I'm cursing me own words," Catti-brie whispered to Drizzt. "I'd be liking nothing better than to put an arrow through that one's back!"

Drizzt hooked his arm over the young woman's shoulder and led her back into the tunnels. He would not disagree that Catti-brie's shot, if taken, would have made the world a better place, but he was not afraid of Artemis Entreri anymore.

Entreri had a lot on his mind, Drizzt knew. The assassin hadn't liked what he had seen in Menzoberranzan, such a clear mirror to his own dark soul, and he would be long in recovering from his emotional trials, long in turning his thoughts back to a drow ranger so very far away.

Less than an hour later, the two friends came upon the site of Wulfgar's death. They paused and stood before it for a long while, silently, arm in arm.

By the time they turned to leave, a score of armed and armored dwarves had appeared, blocking every exit with engines of war.

"Surrender or be squished!" came the cry, followed by howls of surprise when the two intruders were recognized. In rushed the dwarven soldiers, surrounding, mobbing the pair.

"Take them to the watch commander!" came a call, and Drizzt and Catti-brie were shuffled off at breakneck speed, along the winding ways and through the formal entrance to the tunnels of Mithril Hall. A short distance from there, they found the aforementioned commander, and the two friends were as startled to see him in that position as Regis was to see them.

"The commander?" was Catti-brie's first words as she looked again at her little friend. Regis bounded over and leaped into her arms, at the same time throwing an arm about Drizzt's neck.

"You're back!" he cried repeatedly, his cherubic features beaming brightly.

"Commander?" Catti-brie asked again, no less incredulously.

Regis gave a little shrug. "Somebody had to do it," he explained.

"And he's been doing it fine by me own eyes," said one dwarf.

The other bearded folk in the room promptly agreed, putting a blush on the halfling's deceivingly dimpled face.

Regis gave a little shrug, then kissed Catti-brie so hard that he bruised her cheek.

* * * * *

Bruenor sat as if turned to stone, and the other dwarves in his audience hall, after giving their hearty welcomes to Catti-brie, wisely departed.

"I bringed him back," the young woman began matter-of-factly when she and her father were alone, trying to sound as if nothing spectacular had occurred. "And suren yer eyes should feast on the sights of Menzoberranzan!"

Bruenor winced; tears welled in his blue-gray eye. "Damned fool girl," he uttered loudly, stealing Catti-brie's cavalier attitude. She had known Bruenor since her earliest recollections, but she wasn't sure if the dwarf was about to hug her or throttle her.

"Damned fool yerself," she responded with characteristic stubbornness.

Bruenor leaped forward and lifted his hand. He had never before hit his adopted daughter, but only managed to stop himself at the last moment now.

"Damned fool yerself!" Catti-brie said again, as if daring Bruenor to strike her. "Sitting here wallowing in something that ye cannot change, when them things that are needing changing go merrily along their way!"

Bruenor turned away.

"Do ye think I'm missing Wulfgar any less than yerself?" Catti-brie went on, grabbing his shoulder (though she could not begin to turn the solid dwarf). "Do ye think Drizzt's missing him less?"

"And he's a fool, too!" Bruenor roared, spinning about to eye her squarely. For just a fleeting instant, Catti-brie saw that old spark, that old fire, burning in the dwarf's moist eye.

"And he'd be the first to agree with ye," Catti-brie replied, and a smile widened on her fair face. "And so are we all at times. But it's a friend's duty to help when we're being fools."

Bruenor gave in, offered the hug that his dear daughter

310

desperately needed. "And Drizzt could never be asking for a better friend than Catti-brie," he admitted, burying his words in the young woman's neck, wet with an old dwarf's tears.

* * * * *

Outside Mithril Hall, Drizzt Do'Urden sat upon a stone, heedless of the stinging wind heralding the onslaught of winter, basking in the dawn he thought he would never see.